WHEN
WE WHIR

Lodeco Books LLC

Paperback ISBN: 979-8-218-56908-2
Ebook ISBN: 979-8-218-56909-9

Cover and book design by Jess LaGreca, Mayfly book design

Library of Congress Catalog Number: 2024925841
First Printing: 2025

WHEN WE WHIR

A NOVEL

ENNIS BEGLEY

LODECO

ONE

He didn't want to do it.

But he was expected to. His teammates' eyes tracked him as they ran by. They circled him like hungry hyenas, snarling and panting, desperate for a laugh. He wanted to give them a laugh. He wanted to remind himself of their approval. That he was part of the gang and no longer the outsider from the city. He was one of them, maybe even the best. The funny one, the brave one, the sharpshooter, the risk-taker. He wanted to feel their approving whacks on his back, to hear them cheer his name.

He didn't want to do it.

But everything had lined up so perfectly. He had the ball. Mr. Ray had his back to the field as he timed the freshmen sprint sets. Head Coach Fritz was distracted, yelling at the groundskeeper over a muddy patch at centerfield, as if the moisture and evaporation would bend to his will by the sheer volume of his voice. And even though Mr. Ray was all the way at the other end of the field, that didn't matter. Cole could easily make the shot. It would be a piece of cake because Clara was around—he didn't know where, but he knew she was somewhere nearby. He could feel it. Asa, his best friend, was next to him, egging him on: "Do it, Cole. Do it."

He didn't want to do it.

But he did it anyway. Taking a few steps back from the ball, he focused on the feeling, that curious vibration that pulsed and flickered inside him whenever Clara was nearby. Emanating from the base of his neck, it hummed in his ears, it buzzed in his teeth, it fluttered his heart with nervous energy. He focused on it. He tuned out the world and brought the feeling to the surface— revving it up. As he ran toward the ball, he pushed the feeling down, down through his chest, down through his stomach, through his right hip, right knee, shin, ankle and out through his toes into the soccer ball.

As the ball left the ground, the collective gasp of his teammates seemed to suck all the air from the valley. Everything froze in a vacuum of anticipation—everything except the ball, which flew at top speed, spinning in its arch toward the unexpecting target.

On impact, the loud thwack against the back of Mr. Ray's head released the breath of Cole's teammates in the form of praiseful woops and cheers. Asa tackled Cole to the ground, Asa laughing all the way down. But Cole wasn't hearing any of that. All he could hear was the sound of the ball striking Mr. Ray, echoing in Cole's ears and rolling over onto itself like thunder rumbling off the surrounding hills. His body lying on the ground. Cole's heart sank down through the grass and the mud and the rock below the ribbons of coal that had long ago put their town on the map. *Why do I do things like that? Mr. Ray is my friend.*

Cole, lifting himself up, scanned the school grounds for his sister and spotted her through the crisscrossing poles holding up the bleachers. Walking alone along the path leading from the high school's main building, Clara was hunched under her oversized backpack, her eyes fixed on the ground, as usual. He watched her, wondering what she was sulking about this time.

An odd gasping sound, like a drowning bird, pulled his attention back to the far end of the field.

Mr. Ray was bent over with his hands on his knees and his back to the field. His shoulders strained in desperate bursts. When he suddenly whipped himself around to face the team, his eyes were wide and terrified. Mouth open, his gasps were loud and frantic, wheezing and whistling.

By the time Cole crossed the field, one of the other assistant coaches—a local community college student named Chuck or Chad—Cole was never sure—was already giving Mr. Ray the Heimlich maneuver, but without success. The whistling, wheezing sounds stopped and was quickly replaced with Head Coach Fritz's panicked yells and the deep silence of worried onlookers.

"What's happening? What's going on?" asked Cole.

"His whistle. He's choking on it. Somebody do something," said a voice from the crowd.

Mr. Ray's eyes closed. His head hung loosely, swaying slightly to the side with each pump of the Heimlich, which Coach Fritz had taken over after Chuck-or-Chad's efforts failed. Mr. Ray's skin was grey.

Someone was about to die, all because of something he'd done, something he'd done on purpose. It was just supposed to be funny. He had to act, and act quickly. He looked back for Clara, but she was gone—and so was the feeling. Across the field, the schoolground's east gate still swung on its hinges, but she was already out of sight down the hill toward their house.

"Clara!" Cole yelled in the direction of the gate. He caught the puzzled expressions of his teammates. There wasn't time to care. "Clara! Come back!"

He looked back at Mr. Ray, by then laid out on the grass. Coach Fritz was digging a hand into his mouth as another coach leaned over his chest. Cole turned and sprinted to the gate, still yelling for his sister. Across the field, he pushed through the gate with such violent force that it swung around and crashed against the chain-link fence. He saw the top of Clara's backpack over the crest of the hill. The feeling returned.

"Clara! Stop! Please!"

"Jesus. Chill out." From half a block down the hill, she turned to look up at him. "What is your problem?"

"It's Mr. Ray—he's choking."

"What do you want *me* to do about it?"

"Just stop walking for a second." Cole craned his neck, trying to see the field.

"What on earth are you doing? I can't just stand here. I have a ton of homework." She took a step down the hill.

"Clara! Please! Just stay there. I need to try it. He'll die."

"What are you talking about?"

"This is not the time for that. Just stay where you are. I'm begging you."

Inching his way back up the hill, Cole found a spot on the sidewalk where he felt the feeling and could see the field. The nervous crowd was hovering over Mr. Ray's body. Someone was bent over performing chest compressions, the back of a royal blue t-shirt beating up and down.

"Fine." Clara swung her large backpack off her shoulder and set it down on the sidewalk.

Cole focused on the feeling while looking back at the field. He imagined the whistle being forced out of Mr. Ray's throat, picturing a wet, pink, fleshy tube contracting around the whistle until it popped out like a champagne cork. He concentrated as hard as he could, squeezing his eyes shut and clenching his teeth. He heard himself mumbling, "C'mon, c'mon, c'mon, c'mon." As the seconds ticked by, as he directed all of his energy and focus on the feeling and Mr. Ray, Cole's body wanted to stop, to open his eyes, to breathe—if only for an instant? To stop and look around? To feel and think other feeling and thoughts? But Cole fought against his exhausted body and mind. He couldn't take the risk, not until he was sure. "C'mon, c'mon, c'mon."

Diving deeper into the sensation, giving into the vibration of it, the hum of it, he felt himself rolling forward into it, like a frightened pill bug balling itself up. In the darkness of his clenched eyes, the vibration intensified, nearing unbearable. The sound of it hammered at his ears. Cole wanted to scream and cover his ears, but suddenly all sound stopped and his body seemed to unfurl into the silence. And then he heard it.

Relieved cheers and clapping rose from the field. Cole opened his eyes to see someone helping Mr. Ray onto his side and then into a kneeling position.

Cole slumped forward, propping his hands against his knees. "Everything is fine. You did it. You saved him," he whispered to himself. Calmer, he stood facing the field. Two of his teammates were lifting Mr. Ray to his feet, an arm over each set of shoulders.

"Thank you." Cole turned to Clara.

But there was no answer. She was already a block away, crossing Miners Street. *Maybe she really doesn't feel it*, he thought.

After practice, Cole skipped the showers and went to check on Mr. Ray, whom Coach Fritz had sent to the nurse's office. After over two years of playing three varsity-level contact sports, Cole was no stranger to Nurse Campbell's office, tucked at the end of a row of classrooms on the school's windowless lower level. His cleats clicked along the hallway's linoleum floor, leaving a trail of bits of grass and compacted mud behind. He usually tried to be more considerate—other than the occasional kick of a soccer ball at an assistant coach—but his shoes were the farthest thing from his mind at the moment. All thoughts were centered on Mr. Ray. *Will he still be there? Is he okay? Is he mad?*

As Cole neared the end of the hall, a light shone from the nurse's office. Muffled conversation seeped through the wall. Mr. Ray was still there. Cole's cheeks burned in anticipation of facing the man he had almost killed. The office door was propped open and Mr. Ray was lying down on the examination table with his eyes closed and a washcloth on his forehead.

"Um, hi, Mr. Ray."

"Cole? Is that you? Practice is over already?" Mr. Ray held the washcloth in place as he turned his head to face Cole.

"Yeah, it's me. Practice just ended." Cole was acutely aware of each step he took into the room. Walking felt unnatural, like he was on stilts but confined to a normal-sized gait. He approached the examination table like an open casket. "Are . . . are you okay?"

"Hi, Cole. He's fine. Don't look so worried," said a voice from the darkness of an open closet.

"Oh, right. Hi, Ms. Campbell."

"Mr. Ray just got a little faint when he coughed up—"

"I'm fine, I'm fine," the patient interrupted.

"—some blood. But it looks like the whistle caused only minor lesions in his esophagus—either on the way in or the way out," Ms. Campbell said in her soft voice. "And his ribs are a little sore from the Heimlich, but I don't think they're broken." She was still fumbling with something in the closet.

"I feel fine, hon. Can I just go, please? I need to see Fritz before he leaves." It was clearly not Mr. Ray's first request to be discharged.

"Not until you rest a little and some color returns to your face. Have another sip of juice." She handed him a Dixie cup half full of orange liquid. "My ice machine is broken. I need to run upstairs to get some for those ribs. *Do not* leave while I'm gone. Cole, you make sure he stays put, okay?" She shot Cole a little grin and ran out before he could respond.

Mr. Ray chuckled quietly, but the effort clearly hurt. He groaned, grabbing at his ribs on both sides. Cole pulled a small plastic step stool forward and sat down. His perch was so low to the ground that his knees almost came up to his chin. It was uncomfortable, but not uncomfortable enough to not sit there—his legs still ached from practice.

"I'm really sorry, Mr. Ray."

"Don't worry about it. I know it was an accident. Well," he added under his breath, "at least the whistle part was."

Cole lowered his head and stared intensely at a red square of the linoleum floor. He wondered if his face was a similar color.

"Hey, I'm serious. Don't worry about it. I know how it goes. I was on a team once, too." Mr. Ray let out a light groan as he shifted position. The table creaked and the paper under him crinkled loudly.

"Really? A soccer team?"

"There weren't soccer teams where I went to school. At least not when I was there. I played basketball."

"Me, too!" Cole sounded more excited than he'd intended.

"Yeah, I know. I'm one of your coaches." Mr. Ray rolled his eyes.

"Right, duh. What was it like back then?"

"Pretty much the same. We also picked on one of the coaches. It's just something that happens. I don't mind playing that role as long as you guys listen to me and learn something every once in a while."

"Was that in . . ." Cole paused to consider whether to continue. "Was that in Philadelphia?"

"Yes, I'm from Philly, and no, I was not in a gang. Why do you kids always ask me that? Year after year, the same question. You know that's kind of racist, right?"

"Yeah, I mean, I didn't think you were. It's just what people say. I'm from Philly, too."

"Yeah, and I bet no one asks if you were in a gang."

"Why did you move way out here?"

"My wife grew up across the river in Weissport and we moved back to be near her parents."

"Does she stay home with the kids?"

"No. She's a nurse at a local high school—very local." Mr. Ray gave a sly grin as if he expected Cole to say something. Cole wasn't sure what he was supposed to say, so he remained silent. Mr. Ray's expectant look turned to disappointment.

"Are your kids in school?"

"We don't have kids."

"Why not?"

"Cole, that's private."

"Okay, but if you want kids, you should talk to my uncle. He's a big shot baby doctor in New York. He can give anyone kids."

"Thanks, but again—private matter. You know, you don't have to stick around. I feel fine."

"It's okay."

"No, really. I appreciate you stopping by, but you probably have some homework to get to. My—I mean, Ms. Campbell will be back soon."

Cole looked up at the clock. It was a quarter to six. "Yeah, I better get going. I'm really sorry. It won't happen again."

"Don't worry about it. But, you know, Cole, you're a junior now. You should be setting a better example for the younger players. You've got talent—freakish talent, at times—so they look up to you. Even some of the seniors do. If you don't take practice seriously, they won't either."

"I'll work on it. I promise."

"And I'm sure Coach Fritz is already thinking about who would make a good captain next year, so it might be in your interest to start showing some leadership potential."

"Oh, wow. I hadn't thought about that. Thanks."

"Do you have a ride home?"

"No, I walk. We live right on the square."

Rising from the step stool, Cole strained to straighten his stiff legs.

"Have a nice night, Mr. Ray. Sorry again."

"Don't worry about it, kid. See you tomorrow."

On the way back down the hall, Cole passed Ms. Campbell carrying a large clear bag full of little ice-maker ice. The swish of the ice echoed in the empty hall.

"Heading home? How's my favorite patient doing?"

"He seems okay. See ya, Ms. Campbell."

"Bye, Cole. And try to be more careful where you kick the ball."

"I will." Cole looked down at the floor again. His cleats had made quite a mess on his way in.

Cole went out into the crisp early autumn air. He walked to where Mr. Ray had choked and, after scanning the grass for a few minutes, caught sight of the glint of the whistle reflecting the setting sun. He examined it, mainly looking for little bits of blood or skin. Turning it around in his hands, he thought about what had happened. He'd almost killed a man just for some laughs. Now, with the feeling, or power, or whatever it was, he needed to be more careful. Otherwise, he could do some real damage.

Actions have consequences—today's lesson learned. Thanks, Mr. Ray, but there was probably a safer way to teach that one.

But he could also do good things with the feeling—great things, like save a life. If Clara had walked a little faster, who knows what would have happened to Mr. Ray? By the looks of him at the time, he probably would've been a goner.

There was some spit and grass clippings on the whistle. Cole wiped it off with the front of his jersey. He held it in both hands and raised it up above his head like priests do with chalices in movies. He positioned it so its shiny surface caught the pinkish orange light of the sun behind him and he imagined rays of smoky, mystical brilliance beaming off it in all directions—a beacon, calling him and all mankind from the darkness.

"I pledge to you, oh whistle—my new lucky whistle—that I shall, from this day forth, only use the feeling—or power, or whatever it is—for good, not evil. And I will keep you with me always as a reminder of this solemn vow." He could almost hear the dramatic music crescendo from the surrounding hilltops. He could definitely picture the expression Clara would have made: eyes squinting with judgment, upper lip tightened to repress a smile at his utter hokeyness. *That girl needs to lighten up.*

Cole reflected on his pledge for a moment and considered that perhaps his occasional use of the power to be a better soccer player was basically cheating and not necessarily "good." He revised: "I shall only use the power for good *and for sports.*" He kissed the whistle—regretting that immediately upon remembering it had last been in Mr. Ray's throat—and then put it in his pocket.

The sun had set behind him, but the cloudless sky was still pale blue. As he neared the gate to leave the school grounds, the valley and the rooftops of the town came into view, darkened by the vast shadow cast by the mountains to his back. A few fleeting rays of sunlight still shone on the mountaintops across the river, tingeing their green, tree-covered slopes with a golden glow. Cole thought back to last autumn, trying to remember when the leaves would turn and encircle the valley in a mesmerizing jumble of colors. "Cole, stop staring at the goddamn hills," he recalled Coach Fritz yelling at him one practice last year.

He stopped at the bench near the east gate to take out his colored contacts. After wearing them for most of his life, he still wasn't used to it. They felt scratchy and dried out his eyes. He wished he could just take them out and flick the little eye-scrapers into the trash once and for all. But he and Clara had long ago promised Uncle Ted that they would always wear the contacts whenever the sun was out. It was probably for the best anyway. He couldn't imagine the abuse he would get from the football players if they ever found out about his eyes. Poor Kevin Derrig still avoided the cafeteria, even two years after they publicly humiliated him to the point of tears. And for what? Having red hair, a perfectly normal thing to have, unlike Cole's eyes.

There was a slight chill in the air and it was starting to get dark. Not so many people were out on their porches during Cole's walk home. About halfway to the center of town, he saw moving shadows on the sidewalk in front of him. The figures scrambled up the porch stairs of a house about three down from where Cole was walking. He pretended not to notice, walking casually down the street. He ducked down behind a bush, just out of sight. Creeping forward quietly, he heard whispers. Just as he got to the steps of the house, Cole leapt forward and yelled "Boooo!" The children on the porch shrieked and squealed and giggled as they scattered in all directions.

"Hi, Cole," said one of the smaller ones. She patted Cole's leg and then ran down the sidewalk at full speed.

Cole walked by the Lehighton Square Pizzeria, which everyone called "Sal's" after its owner. Sal had been one of the first people Cole met when his family first moved out there. They had moved in June, right after the end of eighth grade, and his parents had decided to spend the summer settling into their new hometown, rather than going up to Maine, as usual. Cole thought a summer job would be a good way for him to meet some friends before starting high school in the fall. He put in a job application to almost every place in town, but only Sal had been willing to hire a city kid with absolutely no work experience. She put him to work on the register a few days a week.

Before long, he knew all the locals who liked pizza—which was almost everyone—including many kids his age who would be starting high school at the same time. He was grateful to Sal for taking a chance on him back then and he still helped her out on shifts here and there when the usual staff were out sick or slacking off.

"Hey, dummy," a familiar voice called from the narrow alleyway between the shop and the house next door.

It was dark now, particularly in the alley. Just as Cole turned, Sal took a drag of her cigarette which cast an orange glow on her unmistakable face. She had a puffy red scar running vertically down the right side of her forehead to her right eyebrow, picking up again at her cheekbone and running down her right cheek. The scar glistened in the cigarette's dim light.

"Hey, Sal. How's it going?"

"Have fun playing with your balls today?" Sal laughed and wheezed at her own joke.

"Eh, not my best practice today. But oh well."

"Poor baby. Wanna pick up a shift this weekend? Crystal's grandmother is sick again, which seems to keep happening whenever her boyfriend is back from duty."

"Let me see what our plans are this weekend. I'll let you know tomorrow, okay?"

"Oh, right, of course. You probably spend October weekends in Vail or something." Sal barely got the sentence out before being overcome by a deep, phlegmy belly laugh, followed by a fit of coughing.

"Har har. I'll let you know. See ya."

"Okay, fancy pants. Have a good night."

Cole continued down the street until it ended at the top of the square where the whole town slanted down toward the river in the east. There were people laughing and sharing a smoke in the square's gazebo. Someone spotted him and a chorus of "Cohhhl!" echoed off the houses surrounding the square. Cole waved to the smoky shadows and headed up the stairs to his family's porch. Fumbling for his keys, he thought, *I love this town. I don't know what Clara's problem is.*

TWO

other? Mother, are you there? It's me, Adler. I need you mother. It hasn't gone away. And no one believes me. The doctors, the frauds, they think it's in my head. Hypochondria, they say. Even father. All hail the great doctor. He doesn't believe me. He pretends to. But I can tell he has doubts. But I know it's real. I feel it. Always. It's not in my head. It's real. And I'm not crazy, Mother. I'm not. You know I'm not. And that's all that matters.

THREE

Clara heard the familiar metallic scraping sound of the front door unlocking. Sitting at the dining room table, she didn't need to see that it was Cole. She could feel it the moment the door opened. He snuck up behind her and pounced, giving her a big, dramatic smooch on the top of her head.

"Why are you so annoying?" Clara flailed her arms and swatted at him.

"Me? What? You don't love your favorite identical twin brother?"

"We are not identical, you moron. Is Mr. Ray okay?"

"Yeah, he's fine now. Thanks for waiting."

"What was all that about?"

"I think you know."

"Um, if you say so."

Clara didn't want to talk about it. It wasn't real. It couldn't be. And if it were real, it was just temporary. It would go away. It was just a phase, a blip, a glitch in the matrix.

Cole narrowed his eyes and opened his mouth to speak, but then shut it and shrugged. He sat down in the chair next to her and scooted it over to be well within Clara's personal space. "Whatcha up to?"

"Ew, get away from me." Clara pinched her nose with one hand and tried to push him away with the other. "You smell like a dead racoon."

"Or do I smell like someone who just played soccer for two hours?"

"Can't it be both?"

"Yeah, yeah. Whatever." Cole moved himself and the chair a few inches away, but not enough to make any difference. "Hey, you know what? *You* should join a team. That would help you meet people and get out of your funk."

"I'm not in a funk."

"True. Over two years of moping is more than a funk. But seriously, what about swimming? You were good at that in middle school."

"Our school doesn't have a swim team. It doesn't even have a pool."

"Oh, right."

"Unless you think I should go swim around in circles in one of the trailer parks' above-ground pools?"

"I mean, that's not a terrible idea. Some exercise will help clear your mind."

"Then you must get a lot of exercise." Clara let out a laugh.

"Good one. But seriously, think about it. You need to get out there—make some friends. I worry about you."

Clara wondered when exactly it was that he worried about her. Was it during all the times he was goofing around with his jock friends instead of spending any time with her? "There's nothing to worry about. I'm fine and all of this is just temporary. Anyway, it's too late for me to make friends here."

"Why too late?"

"Well, for one, half the girls here hated me even before our first day of school."

"No they didn't. Did they? Why?"

Clara turned from the laptop to watch him as the gears slowly turned in his brain.

"Oh, right. Asa."

"And, second, I don't have anything in common with the girls here. I'm not about to spend all day talking about what tattoos I want or which fat football player is hot."

"What about guy friends? Come sit at my table during lunch. You'll like my friends, they're super funny."

"We tried that already and it was extremely awkward. Look, don't worry about me. I'm fine. I just need to keep my head down, do well in school and get into a good college. Then I can get the hell out of here and start my real life with people like me."

"That's just sad. High school is supposed to be the best time of our lives."

"Is it? Maybe for you with all your pizza place friends and your all-star jock status. For most people, high school just sucks, so I'm not going to waste my energy on it. I'll just power through to college. Only two more years to go—halfway there."

"Will you at least think about joining a team?"

"If it makes you happy, I will consider thinking about it—but that's the most I can promise."

"I'll take whatever I can get." Cole put his face in front of Clara's laptop. "What's that?"

"It's homework. You should try it."

"Ouch. I do homework." He raised his hand to his chest in mock offense. "Anyway, you're coming to my game tomorrow, right?" Cole had a huge grin on his face. Clara noticed white streaks of dried sweat on his temple.

"Can't. Midterms are coming up."

"Pleeeease! I'll do all your weekend chores."

Clara considered for a moment. "Home or away?"

"Away but just in Jim Thorpe. School is providing a bus for spectators."

"Oh yay. A bus ride with Lehighton High soccer fans. Sounds fun!" Clara pretended to go back to working on her paper.

"So is that a yes?" Cole asked.

"Yes, now buzz off."

"Sweet!" Cole pumped his fist in the air. "I knew you loved me!" Cole hopped up from his seat and headed toward the stairwell in the front hall.

"Speaking of love, where's your boyfriend?" Clara smirked as she typed away on her laptop.

"Dunno. Maybe having fun in the square. Remember fun? You should try it." He ran up the stairs before Clara could have the last word. The feeling faded away as he climbed the stairs.

She was asking about Asa, Cole's best friend and a common presence at the Lund house. Asa was dirt poor and lived in a trailer park with his camo-wearing father, who seemed to always have a can of beer in his hand and a lit Marlboro Red dangling below his mustache. They literally lived in a trailer—the two of them, grown men, together, in one trailer. Before moving to Lehighton, Clara didn't even know what a trailer looked like, other than the mangled ones shown in news coverage of Midwest tornadoes.

Asa would often come home with Cole and eat meals with the family and hang out late into the night, or sleep over in the attic guest room. When he wasn't around for meals, their mom would set out a plate of food for him, carefully covering it in aluminum foil for when he eventually showed up. Even Clara had to admit that it was sweet of her parents to take care of him like that. Asa was like their very own alley cat.

In Clara's opinion, however, Asa was a troublemaker and a bad influence on Cole. Of course, some of her hard feelings toward him could stem from their short-lived fling and subsequent awkward parting. Clara had met Asa a little over two years ago, during the summer when she and her family first moved to Lehighton, just before the start of freshman year. Cole took a job at the pizza shop, while Clara mostly wandered around in wide-eyed disbelief, trying to accept that that town, that shithole, was her new reality.

In a particularly downtrodden mood, she made her first and only visit to the ice cream shop on First Street. Asa was working behind the counter. She still remembered the tan line on his bicep as he scooped her order of one scoop of vanilla on a sugar cone. He had tried in vain to convince her to get a topping: sprinkles, chocolate sauce, wet nuts, which he said with a goofy smile. Anything to make it less boring. In retrospect, his aversion to "boring" was a clue to how things would play out between them. He asked for her number, but she didn't have a cellphone—and *still* didn't—and hadn't yet memorized the home phone number. She told him she had just moved into the green house on the north side of the square. That evening, he rang the doorbell and their summer fling followed. They tried to keep it up when school started, but she was the quiet new girl and he was the popular jock, which apparently didn't sit well with the more territorial girls of Lehighton. Without much in common, they started running out of things to talk about and Asa wanted to do things she wasn't quite ready for—it was her first relationship after all—if two fifteen-year-olds making out in a public gazebo could be called a relationship. Come to think of it, it would probably be her only relationship until college. *Power through.*

Eventually, they just faded apart without any official ending or fight. It wasn't long before Cole and Asa became besties through their shared interest in kicking, throwing and hitting spheres of various sizes in particular directions. Clara figured it was a good thing that she had ended it with Asa before that had happened, but she still secretly had a little thing for him—he was cute and had the whole "bad boy" thing going on. She also thought it was endearing how he was always appreciative of her parents taking care of him. He was constantly thanking "Mrs. L" and helping out around the house however he could, but it did seem like maybe he was doing that more often when Clara was in the room. She didn't mind at all. That aside, things were over between them and he was mostly annoying to have around all the time. He was the epitome of what she didn't like about this trashy town that she had been plopped into. His favorite thing in the world was turkey hunting, for God's sake!

———

Clara, her freshly-showered brother and their parents ate dinner around the kitchen table because her papers were still spread out in the dining room. Asa didn't show up, but his aluminum-foiled plate sat in its usual spot on the stove so it could stay warm.

After dinner, Clara grabbed her laptop and followed her parents to the room on the second floor that they had converted into a library. The room's floor-to-ceiling bookshelves were jam-packed with countless books, mostly of history and art, shoved in vertically, horizontally, diagonally, anywhere and any way they fit. Not a single square inch of wall was visible. It might as well have been that the books were holding up the room—pull out the wrong one and the whole shebang could come tumbling down. An overflow of books had settled into haphazard piles of varying heights, rising from the floor at the base of the shelves and slowly growing like stalagmites. The library's long windows were covered by flowing white curtains that blocked the next-door neighbors' house and their ugly unfinished wooden decks.

In the center of the room there were two couches with dark red velvet upholstery, Victorian curves and squat legs of dark carved wood. Little tables and Tiffany lamps and comfy reading chairs were scattered around the edges of the room. Clara loved the library because it didn't feel like it was in Lehighton; it felt like it could be anywhere else, somewhere of consequence, like Paris or Milan, or even Gran's apartment in New York.

Clara wanted to finish up her homework. It wasn't long before her parents, both U.S. history professors at nearby colleges, started one of their history debates. Mr. Lund taught at Penn State's Hazleton campus about a forty-minute drive to the northwest and Mrs. Lund taught at Lehigh University, about fifty minutes to the southeast. Lehighton was the lucky town smack dab in the middle. For the past several months, they had been eagerly planning a summer trip to follow the Lewis and Clark expedition up the Missouri River and down the Columbia to the Pacific. It was a life-long dream of theirs and it willingly consumed all of their free time. That evening's debate was a familiar one. Her father mentioned a scholarly work praising Sacagawea's contributions to the expedition. That was a trigger for her mother, which her dad knew full well. Her mother took the bait.

"That baloney drives me crazy." She snapped her book closed and took off her reading glasses. "Why is the country's narrative that she was some lone, benevolent Indian who volunteered to help the mission? I mean, I know why, but why are people still buying that hogwash?"

"Well, she *did* help the mission and should be honored for it." Mr. Lund had a twinkle in his eye as he settled into his favorite pastime.

"That's not the point. She was kidnapped by the Hidatsa when she was only twelve years old and sold to a white man to be his wife." Mrs. Lund accentuated "wife" with distinctive air quotes. "Then her husband—more like master—agreed, for a fee, to drag her and her newborn across the continent because she spoke Shoshone."

"Yes, and she should be honored for that struggle."

"Ugh! You are impossible. She had no choice. She was being used by white men back then and her memory is being used by them now to make themselves feel better. Has anything really changed for women? Am I right, Clara?" Clara looked up and just shrugged. She knew not to get involved, much less take sides.

"I'll remind you that it was the suffragettes who first wanted to raise her profile," said Mr. Lund.

"Look, we don't see anyone trying to put York's face on a coin, do we? What's the difference between him and Sacagawea?" Mrs. Lund asked. Clara knew from prior debates that York was William Clark's slave who also took part in the expedition.

"He has a statue in Louisville."

"Enough! I need some tea." Mrs. Lund rose from her usual spot on one of the red couches, placing her book and glasses on the coffee table. "Want some?" she asked her husband.

"I'm okay, thanks. Love you, honey." Mr. Lund had the good grace to look a little sheepish as he went back to reading the article.

"Uh-huh." Mrs. Lund poured herself a cup of tea from the teapot sitting on a table in the corner.

Clara closed her laptop and stood up. "Goodnight, nerds."

Walking up the stairs to her bedroom, she heard hushed voices and the crinkling of aluminum foil rising up the stairwell. Asa was there. It would have been nice to see him, but she was too tired to do their play-fighting routine. She took out her contacts and thought about how lucky she was that the contacts worked. She felt different enough as it was. She brushed her teeth and went to bed.

The next morning, Clara woke up late and had to rush through getting ready for school. There was a note on the kitchen counter from her parents saying that they were planning to go to Cole's game and to let them know if she wanted a ride. The note ended with two boxes labeled "Yes" and "No" and a postscript: "No, you cannot have a cellphone." Her latest strategy in the quest for a cellphone was to take every possible opportunity to point out when having one would have been useful to her and her parents—and arranging a ride to Cole's game was certainly one such instance. But every time, without fail, Clara's mother would say something like, "we are out here to have a nice, simple, suburban life and to spend quality time together, not to stare at little screens like zombies." Clara thought they were in Lehighton because it was convenient for her parents' jobs, but she guessed that was beside the point.

She checked the "Yes" box and wolfed down a vanilla yogurt. Cole had already left for his morning game-day team meeting, so she had to walk to school alone and quickly.

After cutting across the square, she walked by the pizza place. Clara's neck and shoulders tensed at the sight of the owner. Her face had a sickening scar and her fat, pink body was scattered with tattoos that had turned a dark, runny green with age. Clara kept her head down, hoping not to be noticed.

"Hey, where's numbnuts?"

"Uh, Cole?" Clara's voice was barely audible.

"Yeah, dumb dumb. Why else would I talk to *you*?" The pizza lady cackled.

"He's already at school."

"Ask him to let me know about his shift this weekend."

"Okay." Clara lowered her head and continued walking. She tried to let it slide. *I guess if I were that ugly, I'd be a bitch too.*

Clara couldn't help noticing the horrible aluminum siding and the rickety, unfinished wooden decks and stairs that had been added to many of the houses. As she walked past the narrow spaces between the houses, she saw backyards littered with tires and rusted out car frames that looked like they had been sitting in the same spot for decades. Tied up to a fence in one yard there was a large stuffed animal, deformed and matted from years of rain and snowstorms. From its faded, dirty pink color and what appeared to be a long ear hanging to the side, she thought it might have once been a large bunny, maybe from some lame boardwalk at the Jersey Shore or the even lamer Carbon

County Fair. *That's what this town does over time. It turns a pretty pink prize into an ugly, mildewed heap of garbage.*

Up ahead, she saw a few girls walking to school. At least one was smoking, based on the cloud hovering above them. Clara didn't recognize them from behind, but she knew she wanted to avoid them. They probably didn't want to talk to her either. She crossed the street, successfully avoiding any interaction. When she was almost at school, a group of little kids ran right in front of her like she didn't exist. She didn't blame them; she wasn't sure living in that town qualified as existence.

Just outside the east gate of the school grounds, she turned back to look down at the rooftops of the town below. *What a dump,* she thought. *I don't know what Cole sees in this shit town.*

I

There was a man named Beine who had a wife whose name was Thora. Beine was wise and prosperous. He was not the largest landowner on Stóra Dímun, but he owned that arrowhead-shaped island's northern tip, which had some of the best fowling cliffs in all of the Faroe Islands.

Beine and Thora had two daughters, Gudrid and Estrid. Gudrid, the elder, was well-nigh the fairest of all women to look on. She was so beautiful that tales of her beauty were told across the land and sea. She was known as Gudrid the Fire-Eyed. Like all people of Stóra Dímun, and Dímun Lítla before it was abandoned, Gudrid's eyes glowed in direct sunlight, like the eyes of wild beasts in the moonlight. Because of this trait of glinting eyes, the people of Stóra Dímun were known by foreigners as Glints, though they called themselves the Dímuners.

Unlike the other people of the Faroes, the Dímuners were not descendants of early Viking settlers. As far back as anyone knew, the Dímuners had always lived on the two islands and the story of their first settlement and the origin of their ancestors had long been lost to time. It was said that they once had their own language and culture, but that too was lost, overcome by the great influences of the Norse.

Beine's younger daughter, Estrid, was also beautiful but not as so as her sister. Estrid was wise like her father and well-respected on the island.

FOUR

Clara wasn't on the spectator bus provided by the school. Cole carefully watched the fans step off while he stretched on the field with his teammates. The rivalry with Jim Thorpe often drew big crowds from Lehighton, even for soccer. No Clara. Maybe there wasn't room or she was getting a ride. It's not like she had any friends, though. Maybe their parents were driving her, thought Cole. She had to come—she just had to. She knew how important it was to him and the team to beat Jim Thorpe. He needed her there to make sure that happened.

Asa was finishing up a story that Cole had already heard. It was one of his many that ended with him running from the cops. When he was done—and the high fives had finally ended—Asa sat down on the grass next to Cole.

"What's the matter, bro?"

"What? Oh, nothing. Just stressed about the game." Cole stopped looking at the parking lot and switched the leg he was stretching.

"Why, man? We got this. These Thorpers are pussies."

"I know, I know. I just think too much."

"Ha! Compared to me, maybe. Anyway, snap out of it." Asa whacked Cole on the back of his head and got up to do laps.

Jim Thorpe was built up during the coal and railroad boom, like the rest of the valley, except it was where all the rich people had lived. The founder of the main coal company and connecting railroad was named Asa Packer. He and his rich friends settled in the town and developed it to Asa's specifications: rows of beautiful Victorian townhomes, gothic-inspired churches, ornate municipal buildings, a postcard-worthy train station and town square marked by a huge boulder of coal in the center. Asa Packer's imposing mansion still stood on a hill overlooking—looking down on—the town. Usually, the best part about away games was hearing the announcers pronounce Asa's name like "ass-ah" instead of "ace-ah," but that wasn't going to happen at a Jim Thorpe game. There were probably four or five Asas on their team.

Catering more to tourists from Philadelphia and New York, very few people actually lived in the center of Jim Thorpe. The place had more of a museum vibe than the feeling of a living, breathing town. The real citizens lived farther out from the center or across the river in East Jim Thorpe. The high school was on the outskirts where the town looked just like any other town in the valley and not like the imaginary Victorian village of a model train set. The kids at Jim Thorpe High were just like the Lehighton High kids, except, of course, that Thorpers were pussies.

There were two minutes left in the first half, but still no Clara. Asa had scored a goal in the first few minutes of the game, but by then they were down, three to one. Mr. Ray called Cole over to the sideline.

"Is everything okay?"

"Yeah. I'm fine, Mr. Ray. Just a little distracted."

"I can tell. Try to get your head back in the game. There's plenty of time to make a comeback. Just focus on the ball and stop looking at the bleachers." Mr. Ray patted Cole on the shoulder.

"Sorry. I will, I will."

Cole ran over to the Lehighton bench, gave his lucky whistle—formerly Mr. Ray's choking whistle—a good squeeze, and tossed it back into his bag. He ran onto the field and got into position.

He needed to focus. "Head in the game. Head in the game. Head in the game," he said to himself as he sprinted up the field. Then, suddenly, he felt it: Clara was there. He scanned the bleachers and saw her and his parents taking seats in the top row. They waved, his dad adding two thumbs up.

Cole focused on the feeling—or was it a sound? It was hard to describe. It was like someone turning on an old ceiling fan in the room next door, a sound you more felt than heard. It was a low rumbling or hum that seemed to be emanating from above his heart, rattling his teeth and eardrums with nervous energy. Sometimes it was louder—if louder was the right word—than other times and he only felt it when Clara was nearby.

He concentrated on it, the hum, and chased after the ball. Wrangling it from a Thorper, he dribbled toward their goal at top speed. He focused on the hum and the ball and the hum and the ball and then took a deep breath and kicked as hard as he could at the Jim Thorpe goal. The ball left his foot with an intense spin, curved dramatically around two defenders and barely clipped the inside right corner of the goal, hitting the net to the great cheers and heavy groans from the spectators. The whole team rushed at him as he ran around in celebration. He looked up at the Lehighton section of the bleachers and saw a mass of happy fans, smiling and jumping in place, except for Clara. She just sat there, staring at the field with a concerned look. *She can feel it too*, Cole thought. She broke her worried daze and gave Cole a smile as she stood up to cheer with the others. The hum had faded a little.

"Awesome shot, man. That spin was crazy!" Asa called.

"Thanks." He was still catching his breath.

"Two more to go. Let's do this." Asa sprinted ahead toward the Thorper with the ball. The first half ended shortly after with Jim Thorpe's lead narrowed, three to two.

In the second half, Asa scored another goal and then Lehighton took the lead with a goal by Paul Beiler. Paul's family had some sort of Mennonite thing going on—or was it Amish?—but Cole liked him anyway. Cole easily scored the last goal of the game in a penalty kick, again thanks to the hum. After the game-winning shot, the Lehighton crowd cheered and Cole raised up both arms in celebration and started jogging backward away from the goal. He hadn't noticed that just behind him a player from Jim Thorpe was crouched down adjusting a cleat. Cole fell backward over the other player and hit the turf with a thud. The few spectators who noticed gasped but quickly saw that it was an accident and that Cole was fine. On impact with the ground or in his efforts to catch himself, Cole's right contact somehow dislodged from his eye. The Jim Thorpe player offered a hand to help, which Cole gladly accepted. As the Thorper raised Cole up, the setting sun shone on Cole's face and his eyes.

The Jim Thorpe player was clearly taken aback. "What's wrong with your eye? Freak!" He quickly let go of Cole's hand and ran back to his team.

FIVE

other? Are you there? I can barely see you. This mirror is so filthy. Sylvia is forgetting to dust again. Ah. There you are. I went to our spot today. The tunnel. I sat there on the dirty asphalt, trash scattered, drips rippling the stagnant puddles. I thought about it. Yes, the feeling is still there. I thought about it and how alone I am. I went there to be close to you. I sat there and started to cry into my knees. A nurse on her way to work stopped and put her hand on my shoulder. I told her I was fine without looking up and watched her teal scrub pants and white sneakers walk away toward the hospital. Nurses always think they know best. Always thinking they can fix things with their kindness. Acting all superior. They use kindness to get their way. To manipulate. The one thing I like about nurses though is that they believe me. They know it's real. Just by looking at me, they know. They have seen things. Things not in the med school books. They've seen things. They know it's real. But they don't say anything to the doctors. Why would they? I sat there crying until I heard more nurses coming. Gaggling away. So, I got up and left our spot. The place where my life began and yours ended. Don't worry, Mother. I'll get them for what they did to us. I will get them. All of them. You'll see, Mother. You'll see.

SIX

During the drive home, Mr. Lund gushed on and on about Cole's first goal, how perfect the spin was, and how it had landed at just the right spot. Mrs. Lund's only observation was that Coach Fritz yelled a lot.

Clara sat quietly in the back seat and looked out the window. The valley was cast in shadow except for the very tops of the hills across the river, which glowed in the setting sun's last few rays. The leaves were beginning to change, which she knew would be exciting for her soccer hero brother. He loved that sort of thing, for some reason that she that didn't quite grasp.

Cole wouldn't be home for dinner. After Friday night games, the team would eat at the pizza place and go out, usually drinking at a friend's house or some predesignated place in the woods. Clara thought of Asa. He loved drinking in the woods. He had asked her to go with him a few times when they were together, but she had always declined. No one from school had asked her to do anything social since. That had been over two years ago.

Over dinner, Clara half listened as her parents debated what hiking route to take on their way back from the Pacific. On the return trip of the actual Lewis and Clark, the expedition split into five subunits, each of which took a different path for a portion of the journey. Lewis and his unit headed north to find the source of the Marias River. Mr. Lund wanted to take that route, but Mrs. Lund opposed that out of principle. Lewis's decision to split up the party had put the whole expedition at risk and was highly criticized. Mrs. Lund was fine with any of the other subunit routes, just not Lewis's "route of utter irresponsibility," as her mother put it. Clara's parents would occasionally ask for Clara's opinion, but her answers were never what they wanted. She would suggest "the prettiest route" or "the safest route," but they wanted answers grounded in history. Clara's real answer was *I don't give a crap and I can't believe this is my life*, but she kept that to herself.

A little past eleven o'clock, Clara heard a car horn blare, followed by the screech of tires down their street. She was enjoying some alone time in the library, her parents having gone to bed hours ago. Soon she heard faint singing and then the jingling clunk of keys dropping. The keys dropped again, then a third time. She closed her book, rolled her eyes and went downstairs to help. When she opened the front door, Cole was sitting on the porch floor, his legs spread and the contents of his backpack scattered in front of him.

"Clara!" Cole gave her a huge smile.

"Shhh. They're in bed. It's late."

"Oh, right. Sorry." He tried again, this time in an exaggerated stage whisper. "Clara!"

"Ugh, you're drunk. Get up." Clara leaned over and directed his arm around her shoulder. He smelled of cheap beer and garlic knots.

"We won! Did you see my kick? I'm, I'm so good at balling, I mean . . . soccerballing."

"Uh-huh. You're the best."

"Asa too. Asa is the best and I am the best. We are both the best at it." Cole slurred his words and then burped.

Clara helped him into the house and, with some effort, managed to shut the door behind them while propping him up.

"Home!"

"Shhhh!"

"Right, right. Okay."

She guided him up the two flights of stairs to his room. When he saw his bed, he flopped face first into the pillows. She took off his shoes and went to the bathroom to get him some water. By the time she got back, he had managed to roll himself up under the covers.

"Did you see my kick?" He was finally whispering.

"Yeah."

"When are we going to talk about it?"

"What's to talk about? It was a good kick."

"Not the kick. The hum."

"The what? I don't hear anything."

"You know what I mean. The buzz, the rumble." He struggled to pronounce the words.

"I said I don't hear anything." She didn't want to talk about it. If they don't talk about it or think about it, it might go away. It wasn't real. It's too scary—too different—to be real. And it's not part of the plan.

"Fine. *Feel*, whatever. You know what I'm talking about."

"No, I don't. You're drunk. Just go to sleep," she said and placed the cup of water on his nightstand.

"What do you want?" he asked.

"I want you to go to sleep."

"No, I mean, why are you always so sad? What's missing?" Cole tried to prop his head up with his hand but failed and his head fell back to the pillow.

"I want to go home."

"We are home."

"No, *home*—Philadelphia."

"Why?"

"We were happy there. Our lives were interesting. We had potential." Clara's eyes fixed on a framed photo on Cole's desk. It was of the two of them at their middle school graduation, their arms over each other's shoulders and their mangled, pre-braces smiles dominating the scene.

"Weren't you bored there?"

"No. How could we be bored? We had museums and shows and art and restaurants and a good school."

"But it was lonely. There were no other kids in our neighborhood. It was just the two of us all the time." Cole eyes were shut and he was becoming increasingly difficult to understand. He seemed to be dozing in and out of sleep.

"We had each other . . . and I guess that was enough for me. At least back then I had someone to talk to." From his steady breathing, Clara could tell that he had fallen fully asleep. She pulled the blanket up over his shoulder, which momentarily roused him.

"I love you, sis. It doesn't matter where we are."

"I love you too, Cole. And yes, it does," she added under her breath.

Looking back at the photo on the desk, she tried to remember what it felt like to be that happy. She couldn't remember and wasn't entirely convinced it was really her. Had she really been that person? That fluffy, prized pink bunny? Had they really been so happy, and so close, sharing their bucktooth smiles with the world? Could she ever be that person again? It was hard to believe. She turned off the light and shut the door.

The next morning, Clara hitched a ride with her parents to Jim Thorpe. They were headed to the gym at her mom's college to train for their Lewis and Clark trek on the treadmills. Clara was mortified by the image of them next to each other on treadmills in their hiking gear with weighted down backpacks and walking sticks, surrounded by college students working out. She reminded her parents that there were hundreds of miles of actual hiking trails in the vicinity of their house, but, once again, Clara was off the mark. The point of the treadmills, as her father explained, was so that they could program the treadmills with the exact elevation of the specific trails they would be taking. Clara thought it might be better to train on actual trails, with rocks and all, rather than just on a rubber belt, but she didn't feel like fighting over it. At least this way she could get a ride to Jim Thorpe, which was on the way.

Clara didn't have any specific plans in Jim Thorpe. She just wanted to sit in the coffee shop and be around normal people for a change, to read the paper and to overhear conversations about anything other than hunting. She didn't want to be home when Cole woke up and didn't want to think about the feeling. All she wanted was some civilization for a change—and a goddamn latte.

In the afternoon, her parents picked her up on their way home from the college gym. She didn't ask them how the treadmilling went. She was cringing just thinking about it.

Cole brought a couple pizzas home from his shift, so they ate that for dinner. They sat around the kitchen table and, for once, Mr. and Mrs. Lund took a break from Lewis and Clark talk—they had walked on the treadmills for five hours and probably talked the whole time—and actually asked Cole and Clara about their lives and how school was going. As Cole spoke, Clara realized that she hadn't known any of what he was saying, another reminder of how far apart they had drifted. They used to tell each other everything, but now she didn't even know what classes he was taking, except for Spanish, their only class together. After Cole complained about their Spanish teacher's pop quizzes, Clara asked him if he wanted to work on Spanish homework after dinner or if he was going out. He laughed and said he was never going out again. He still looked a little greenish. Their parents didn't pick up on that, or at least chose to ignore it. Since the move to Lehighton, their parental style had departed from their usual helicoptering. Now it could be more accurately described as loving submarines, occasionally raising their periscopes to take a look around.

After dinner, Cole and Clara set up across from each other at the dining room table. Watching Cole fumble in his backpack and pull out various crinkled pieces of paper, Clara smiled. She wondered why they didn't always do their Spanish homework together. Were they just not making an effort to spend time to-gether? Was Cole too busy with sports? Was she avoiding him—avoiding the feeling?

Spanish was Clara's worst subject. She hated it and just couldn't seem to get any better, year after year. It was Cole's best subject, which was why they were in Spanish class together. Clara was otherwise in more advanced classes. That night's homework was a combination of different annoying tasks, such as matching the Spanish words to the English words, writing explanations of pictures in Spanish, translating from English to Spanish, translating from Spanish to English, etc. They worked on the assignments mostly in silence, but would occasionally ask each other questions.

After completing a matching assignment—the easiest type, in Clara's opinion—she moved to a translation-from-Spanish as-signment—the second easiest. She did the first few sentences without any issue, but then got stuck on one word. *Ugh, I hate this,* she thought. She considered whether she should just ask Cole. No, she knew this word. She had seen it countless times. Why was Spanish such a pain in the ass for her? *What is that word?*

Abierto.

Think.

You know this.

Abierto. Focus. *Abierto. Abierto.* Her mind seemed to wander to the feeling—the hum, as Cole described it. She forced it away.

Just focus on the word, Clara.

Abierto.

But again, her mind went to the hum, and again she fought it.

Abierto. Abierto.

Thoughts of the hum came rushing back. She couldn't fight it anymore.

Why am I fighting it anyway?

She let go and let it wash over her and the word.

Abierto.

The hum.

Abierto.

The hum.

Abierto.

The letters suddenly rose slightly above the page. The *o* slowly moved to the beginning. The *b* flipped upside down. The *a* and *i* vanished into the paper. The *r* and *t* fused together to make an *n*. *Open. Open. Open.* Cole looked up suddenly with his brows furrowed. Clara gasped, grabbed the page in both hands and crinkled it into a ball and bolted from her chair. She ran out into the crisp autumn night air and across the street into the square. Stopping short, she caught her breath.

"You okay?" A familiar voice called from the darkness.

Looking up, she could make out Asa sitting alone in the gazebo. Taking a deep breath and steadying herself, she walked over to him.

"Yeah, I'm fine. Just needed some air."

"You sure? You seemed upset."

"Uh-huh. Just stressed about schoolwork. I hate Spanish. What are you doing out here? Cole is home."

"I know. I can't bother you guys all the time. Anyway, I'm meeting some friends here." Asa took a drag of his cigarette.

"Big night of drinking in the woods?"

"I hope so. You want my coat?" Asa unzipped his windbreaker.

"No, thanks, but I'll take a drag of that, if you don't mind."

Asa looked surprised but handed Clara his cigarette. She took a long drag and closed her eyes as she exhaled. Scooting over slightly, Asa put his arm on the gazebo railing behind her. She leaned back and rested her head on his arm, keeping her eyes shut. For a few minutes they quietly sat there together in the darkness.

"Thanks, I needed that," said Clara, breaking the silence as she lifted her head and opened her eyes. "I better get back to homework. Sure you don't want to come in?"

"Nah, they'll be here in a few minutes." Asa looked down at his phone, which lit up the gazebo. "Thanks, though."

"Okay, see you tomorrow, probably. Have fun running from the cops later." Clara walked back toward the house. Even poor-ass Asa had a cellphone.

Cole was still at the dining room table when Clara got back. He looked up at her with a concerned expression that she didn't want to see. She was exhausted and just wanted the night to be over.

"Are you okay? Why can't we just talk about it?"

"I'm fine. There's nothing to talk about."

"Oh, c'mon. I know you feel it. Just talk to me."

"Feel it? I don't know what you're talking about. Look, I'm really tired. I can't do any more homework tonight. See you tomorrow." She ran up the stairs before he could reply. The feeling faded.

Clara went straight to her room and got into bed. Her mind was racing. She thought about the letters moving around on the page, Cole's soccer kick, the warmth of Asa's arm on the back of her head, the look Cole had given her, how annoying it was that they were not allowed to have cellphones and whether Asa was still sitting all alone in the gazebo. Her thoughts jumped from topic to topic for what seemed like hours. Eventually, she heard

Cole come up and open the door to his room, which was adjacent to hers. It was getting late so she resolved to put all the nagging thoughts aside and attempt to fall asleep.

In the middle of trying to empty her mind, the hum started up. It usually didn't happen when they were separated by the thick, old walls of their house. Cole must have been standing close to their shared wall. Then it went away. Then it came back. Away again. Back again. He was pacing his room, purposely making her feel the hum go on and off. On. Off. On. Off. Over and over again. She couldn't relax. She couldn't escape it. On. Off. On. Off.

It was real. It was time to accept that.

She got out of bed and walked over to the wall that separated their rooms. She cupped her hands, placed them on the wall and shouted into her hands. "Knock it off!" Seconds later, she heard Cole's door open and then a soft knocking on her door.

"I'm in bed. We'll talk about it tomorrow," she said.

She heard a faint "okay" as Cole closed his door.

II

There was a man named Brestir. Thurid was the name of his wife. Brestir was prosperous and powerful. He owned the largest parcel of land on Stóra Dímun and he was a skilled farmer. Brestir and Thurid had one son named Sigmundr. Sigmundr was intelligent and independent from a young age, but showed little interest in farming. He preferred to spend his days with the merchants in the village, learning new trades and taking on apprenticeships. He was a quick learner and a hard worker, and soon ran his own trading operation from a shed by the harbor.

His principal trade was importing lumber from Norway, Ireland or farther afield, and then exporting it to the other Faroe Islands. Stóra Dímun was a favorable base for such trade, it being halfway between the northern Faroes and the southern Faroes, close enough that on clear days the bright green hills of both sets of islands could be seen on opposite horizons. Sigmundr also imported other goods to Stóra Dímun from his associates in the northern island town of Tórshavn, the Faroe Islands' largest settlement. Sigmundr Brestirson and Estrid Beinedottir were close companions and were expected by all to be married when she came of age and had her Freya ceremony, as was the practice in those heathen times.

SEVEN

When Cole woke up, his first thought was that he would finally get to talk about the feeling. His second thought was waffles, a Sunday morning tradition in their house. The smell of the warm, battery goodness crept through the crevasses of his room. He wasn't even out of bed yet and there were already two things to be pumped about. It was going to be a good day.

He was curious about what had happened with Clara during Spanish homework. At least she was finally coming to her senses and agreed to talk. Their first order of business should be to come up with a cool name for it, like the "funbration," he thought. He threw on sweatpants and grabbed his lucky whistle to put in his pocket.

Breakfast was in full swing. Cole's dad was making the waffles, carefully pouring the batter on the checkered iron, his mom was cutting bananas. Clara was just sitting there pretending to read one of her snobby magazines.

"Ah, Cole. Good morning. Let me get your take on this." Mrs. Lund gave him a kiss on the cheek. "Your father has come up with the brilliant idea of us getting a dog to bring on our expedition."

"A Newfoundland, like Meriwether Lewis's dog," said Mr. Lund.

"A *huge* Newfoundland." Mrs. Lund raised up her arms like she was hugging an invisible sumo wrestler. "I will remind everyone that we've never owned a dog, but now we're going to take on the responsibility of training and feeding a dog, and then bring it along on a trek of hundreds of miles."

"*Thousands* of miles," said Mr. Lund. "It will be perfect. We'll name him Seaman, like Lewis's Newfie. And, hey, he might come in handy in the wilderness—like to scare off bears."

"And what about the kayaks? Is he going to sit on your lap?" asked Mrs. Lund. "Although, I would like to talk about the bear thing another time."

"That sounds awesome," said Cole. "It would be so funny."

"And how exactly would it be funny?" Clara deigned to look up from her *New Yorker*.

"Because Newfies are black. The name . . . it's ironic."

"I'm not following," said Clara.

"Newfies are black and semen is white. It's hysterical."

"Ew, you're disgusting," said Clara. "And you have no idea what ironic means."

"Cole, honey, it's Sea-*MAN*, like a sailor." Mrs. Lund put her hand on Cole's shoulder. "And get your mind out of the gutter."

Cole smiled and shrugged. Mr. Lund went into action with the waffle maker and they took their seats around the kitchen table. During breakfast, the conversation focused on Mr. Lund's dog idea. Besides the expedition, Cole thought it would be cool to have a big fluffy dog around the house, assuming it survived the trip, which seemed questionable.

Clara made some good points about slobber and shedding, but those weren't speaking their parents' language. Their father's argument was that the dog would be an authentic addition to the trip and the real Seaman had proved very useful during the actual expedition. Mrs. Lund agreed and suggested they also bring a slave, thirty armed militia men, some Indians and a huge boat full of supplies and gifts and gadgets, which were also "authentic" and quite useful. In the end, Mrs. Lund won with, "If you get a dog, I'm not coming."

⁓

After Cole ate the last waffle, he followed Clara into the living room.

"Sooo . . . ?"

"So what?" Clara answered.

"When are we going to talk about it?"

"Whenever. Now is good, but we should probably get out of here." Clara was apparently trying her best to be nonchalant about the whole thing.

"Okay, we can take a walk. I need to stop at the drugstore anyway and then we can walk along the river trail. That work?"

"Fine. We'll need coats."

It was a beautiful, crisp autumn day. The temperature had dropped noticeably overnight and the leaves on the hills surrounding the town were now unquestionably showing hints of yellow, red and orange. There were no clouds in the sky and a faint crescent moon was still visible. They walked in silence toward the drugstore. Cole wasn't really sure how to get the conversation started. Maybe he should just let her kick it off. Maybe they should wait until they got to the river, but he didn't think he could hold out that long.

They still hadn't started talking by the time they reached the drugstore. Cole quickly found what he needed and went to the checkout. The cashier was one of the soccer team moms, so they chatted about the game. Cole tried to keep it short. They left and headed to the river path. They passed the beer distributor where Asa had once, by some miracle, managed to get a part-time job. Although it had only lasted a week, it was one of the best weeks of Cole's life, at least the parts he could remember. They had to cross the abandoned railroad tracks on the Lehighton side of the river. Cole diligently looked both ways before crossing the track, even though you would have to be completely deaf not to hear one of those trains coming from miles away. The tracks were still frequented by extremely long freight trains and the rumblings from their engines shook the whole valley, usually in the middle of the night. They followed the dirt footpath leading to the river. Cole was done with the stalling. "So how do you want to do this?"

"I don't really know. I barely know how to think about it, let alone talk about it." Clara kicked a stone down the path. "Should we start with what we hear or feel and when?"

Cole didn't understand why the conversation was off to such an awkward start. It was like they had forgotten how to talk to each other. A couple years ago it would have been the easiest thing in the world.

"Sure. So, I hear like a humming and feel a vibration in my chest, like right here." Cole touched the little indent at the base of his neck. "But I don't hear it like an outside sound, it's like an inside sound. Like a little burp or when my jaw clicks."

"Yeah, same for me. It's like a droning sound that I can feel. I feel it a little lower than you do, though. And it has like a nervous energy about it. Like, it bothers me and makes me feel like I need to do something."

"Yeah, totally! Like when you go to do something and you forget what it was, but your body's like, 'hey, you're supposed to be doing something right now!'"

"Um, we should probably keep our voices down." Clara looked behind them.

"Okay. When did you first start to feel it?" whispered Cole.

"I'm not sure. I think was a few weeks after our last birthday."

"Same. But it took me a while to realize it was only when you were around. At first, I thought it was related to what I ate. I even thought it was beer for a while, which ruined a few weekends."

"Aw, you poor thing."

They were almost to the riverbank. Cole heard the faint gurgling of the fast and rocky Lehigh River. After a small bend in the trail, they came to a clearing of sand and smooth stones along the river. The kids in the town called it "the beach" and it was a favorite drinking spot. The beach was picturesque from a distance, with the rushing white rapids and surrounding tree-covered hills. Up close it was less than idyllic; broken beer bottles, litter and dog crap were common.

Cole and Clara carefully walked to the edge and took seats on a couple of the larger boulders. Cole picked up a flat, round rock and skipped it into the water. It did two jumps then disappeared into the rapids.

"I guess we should talk about when we feel it, specifically," said Clara.

"When we're together, duh. Can we just get to the cool stuff? Like the soccer stuff?"

"No, let's just first—"

Cole cut her off. "Why are you so stressed out about this? It's awesome. We should be happy, but you're so mopey about it."

"Happy? Are you kidding me? How do you think this is going to turn out? Do you think we're going to be on the local news and then do tricks for the crowd at the Allentown Mall?"

"Well, since you asked, my plan is to be an international soccer star, and I figured we'd fight crime on the side." Cole flashed a huge smile.

"When exactly will we be doing all this crime fighting?"

"All the time—whenever we're together."

"You know we're almost never together, right? I mean, I think this might be the longest we've been together outside the house in years."

"That's not true." Cole couldn't think of a specific example, but he was sure she was exaggerating. "We're always together."

"We're not. You're always playing sports or hanging out with your friends. Anyway, that's beside the point. We're not about to go to school, do homework, do all your sports stuff and then have time left to play Batman and Rob—"

"I call Batman!"

"—and Robin in the middle of the night. And we'll be going off to college in a couple years, likely different ones."

"Ouch. Sports could get me into a good school, you know." Cole skipped another rock into the river. "But it must be meant for some purpose. We were given it for a reason. Why not use it to help people?"

"Don't be naïve. If anyone finds out about this, they will E.T. us so fast you won't know what hit you." Cole looked confused. "You know. *E.T.*, the movie. The government will come and take us and all our family away and they'll do tests on us and keep us secret. They'll probably try to turn us into weapons or decide we're too dangerous to live."

"Maybe we're not the only ones. Maybe there are others like us."

"Have you ever heard of anything like this? We're not in a movie. This is real life. Do you think some freak show X-Men are going to come ask us to join them?"

Cole shrugged. "Maybe, why not?" He imagined himself posing next to Wolverine and Storm in a kick-ass black and yellow uniform.

"Get real. It's just us. No white owl is going to come and chuck save-the-dates at us."

"Huh?"

"Harry Potter . . . Invitations . . . Whatever, you know what I mean."

"Okay, okay. Relax. Let's just get back to talking it through."

Clara lowered her voice. "No, seriously, do you get it? We can't tell anyone and we can't let anyone find out. Not even mom and dad."

"Fine. I'll keep it a secret. At least until we know more."

"*And* we agree first," said Clara.

"Yeah, fine. You're such a drag sometimes." *All the time, lately.*

Cole looked down to find another skipping rock. There were no good ones within reach so he stood up from the boulder to look around. Clara brushed a plastic keg top into the water with her foot and watched it float away down the river.

"So, what happened last night?" Cole skipped another rock.

"It, I mean, the hum, translated a word for me—like from Spanish."

"What?! That's awesome! How's it work?" Cole turned from facing the river to look right at her.

"I don't know how. I just concentrated on it. See why I'm worried? It's more than just soccer."

"I could tell something happened. The hum gets weaker after it's used. Can we figure out a cooler name for it? Hum is kind of boring."

"I know it gets weaker. That's why I go to your stupid games. Otherwise, I'd just have to avoid you. It gets too intense some-times."

"Then it builds back up over time."

"Yeah. Have you tried anything other than kicking the ball?"

"No, just that. And it doesn't work every time. I can't control it—at least not yet. Oh, and I also pulled a whistle from Mr. Ray's throat—or at least I think I did. Have you tried anything else? Other than cheating on Spanish homework?" Cole snickered.

"Hey, I didn't mean to. And, no, I haven't done anything else."

"Should we?" proposed Cole.

"I don't know. Ugh, I hate this." Clara shifted where her foot was propped up the boulder so she could rest her forehead on her knee.

"Oh, come on. Don't be such a Debbie Downer. People would kill to have this."

"That's what I'm afraid of."

"C'mon. One little thing."

"Okay, okay, just one thing."

"Woohoo. So how about we try to skip this rock all the way to the other side, okay?" Cole held up a piece of coal that had been shaped into a smooth disc by decades on the river floor. "I'll throw and we'll both focus on the hum, which will soon have a much cooler name."

On their first try, the piece of coal hopped only twice and didn't even make it halfway across the river. They tried several more times before giving up. The longest attempt was only four hops to the center of the river. Neither of them felt any change in the hum so they concluded it was a failed effort. Cole tried to get Clara to do something else—move some driftwood back into the water, knock over the beer bottle on that stump over there, make that blue keg top levitate—but she refused. Cole was too hungry and tired to push it, so they headed back up the path toward home.

"Good talk, thanks." Cole looked both ways as they crossed the train tracks.

"Yeah, good talk. Remember, don't tell anyone," said Clara.

"Got it, got it. I won't get us *E.T.*'d. By the way, I never knew you were such a movie buff."

"Just trying to speak your language, bro."

EIGHT

see you now, Mother. There you are. Hidden in the shadows of my face. There, in the flickering candlelight. You have your mother's eyes, they say. But I don't really, do I? I picked this color to match yours from old photos. You have your mother's eyes, they say. Out of the blue. Without warning. They decide when it's time for me to think of you. They must think it's easy. Breezy. To think of your dead mother. At any time. Walking down the street. Waiting outside dad's office. The doormen at Gran's. They think it's okay whenever they want. They think it's okay to hit me with a truck. Like I don't have enough going one. Like I don't have something happening inside me. But I did choose these eyes. I could have picked contacts with a different color. But I chose these because I'm you. I'm all that's left of you. That's why I'm here, Mother. To be you. To protect you. To avenge you.

NINE

On their way to school the next morning, Clara realized that she had never gotten around to finishing the Spanish homework that they had started Saturday night. She had been so exhausted after their talk by the river and all the skipping stone concentration that she napped until dinner. She wasn't sure what Cole had done all night, but she guessed that it probably wasn't homework related.

On their walk to school, he didn't seem too concerned about being unprepared for Spanish, explaining to Clara that they probably wouldn't have a quiz that day. That gave Clara some comfort. It was too late to do anything about it anyway because Spanish was their first period class.

Clara took her assigned seat in the back left of the class, feeling worried again. She seemed to recall a high incidence of quizzes on Mondays. Again, there was nothing she could do about it and one quiz wouldn't impact her grade that much. Cole entered the classroom and, after a few fist bumps with his friends, ambled toward his seat in the center of the room. As he sat down, he glanced back at Clara with raised eyebrows and showed her his crossed fingers. At that moment, Mr. Donovan came in and immediately started writing on the blackboard, which meant a quiz and the whole class groaned. Cole looked back at her again and grimaced. She sighed and rolled her eyes. *Typical*, she thought.

As Mr. D wrote the quiz on the board, Clara noticed Cole looking all around the room. *What is he up to now?* His gaze eventually settled on the ceiling, making him look like a total goofball. She looked up to see what was so interesting. *Oh no*, she thought. Cole was staring right at one of the sprinklers poking down from the ceiling. She looked around the room at all the books, papers and electronics, including a cage full of laptops used for pronunciation exercises. She gave a loud fake cough to get his attention. Almost everyone turned except for Cole. He just kept looking up at the sprinkler. It was a terrible idea, even for Cole. Failing one quiz was no big deal. She was sure he failed quizzes all the time. It wouldn't be worth all the property damage. But then it occurred to her that *she* never failed quizzes, even in Spanish—he was doing this for *her*. She coughed again but no luck.

Cole kept staring straight up at the ceiling. A few classmates noticed and started snickering. One of Cole's buddies shoved his shoulder to get him back to the planet, but Cole ignored him. Clara would have to play defense and try to stop him. She focused on the hum, but she had no idea what to do beyond that. She couldn't think of how to use it to stop something from happening. She gave up and just hoped it wouldn't work. Then suddenly a corner of one of the large white tiles of the drop ceiling jumped up and then banged back down into the frame. Dirt and dust rained down on the students just under the tile. A few people in the class squealed and Clara jumped up from her seat. "No!" she said loudly. The room went silent and everyone turned to look at her.

"Miss Lund, is there problem?" Mr. D had turned slightly, still holding the chalk against the blackboard. "You all know it's just squirrels."

The class response was a uniform "ewwww." The school did in fact have a squirrel problem, which everyone knew and complained about. It wasn't uncommon to hear them scratching away in the walls and ceilings.

"Um, sorry, Mr. Donovan. It's just, I mean, I have to use the restroom," said Clara. Sighs and whispers danced around the room.

"I'm sure it can wait until after the quiz. Nice try, though."

"It can't actually, um, woman problems." Clara knew that would work, as much as she didn't want to say that in front of the class. A couple guys giggled and some of the girls scoffed.

"Fine. Make it quick."

Clara gave Cole a narrow-eyed glare as she left the room. She was furious. He tried to use it to get out of one measly quiz, right in front of everyone, while obviously looking right at the damn thing that was moving. It was reckless. He wasn't taking it seriously. She thought he understood from their talk just how dangerous that could be. It was exactly the type of thing that would get them *E.T.*'d. She quickly walked down the hall, slowing down only after she could no longer feel the hum.

Too mad to go back to class, so she went downstairs to Ms. Campbell to see if she could get a note for cramps or something. She would just apologize to Mr. D later and offer to do a make-up assignment. She avoided Cole for the rest of the day. It wasn't difficult since they didn't have any other classes together and Clara preferred to eat lunch alone in the auditorium rather than stress out about where to sit in the cafeteria.

By the end of the day, she had calmed down a little. After all, she reasoned, Cole had attempted to trip the sprinkler for her benefit. The intention was good, if not the execution. While Cole was at soccer practice, she studied in the school library and then waited at the bench by the east gate so they could walk home together. The days were getting shorter and it was almost dark by the time she saw him walking across the field toward her. He smiled when he saw her.

"Hey, guess I missed the sprinkler, huh?" Cole let out a laugh.

"That wasn't funny. We'll get caught if you pull crap like that." She shoved her book into her backpack and got up from the bench to walk next to him.

"Oh, c'mon. There was nothing wrong with that. No one would have figured it out."

"You were staring at the ceiling like a moron and then the ceiling jumped. It doesn't take a brain surgeon to be suspicious of that."

"Really? You think?"

"Yes. I'm sure some were wondering. One more incident and people will start to talk. Or at least they'll start calling you the squirrel whisperer."

"I'd like that." Cole added a little skip to his step. There was a rattling in his pocket as he walked.

"What is that annoying noise?"

"Oh, sorry." Cole moved a metal whistle from one pocket of his royal blue LHS sweatpants to the other and the noise stopped. A group of kids ran out from one of the porches and chanted "Cole! Cole! Cole!" as they ran by and then darted into an alley.

"So, do you have any idea why we have the Super Surge?" asked Cole.

"Huh?"

"The hum—I'm trying out a new name. Is it related to our eyes?"

"That's a dumb name for it. But I was wondering about our eyes too. It must have something to do with them."

"They're from the baby thing, right?"

Clara sighed—they had discussed that hundreds of times over the course of their relatively short lives, but it never seemed to sink in. "Yes, the eyes are a side effect of the fertility treatment, but Uncle Ted can't figure out why and it's very rare." Uncle Ted was their father's older brother, the esteemed fertility specialist, Dr. Theodore M. Lund of Mount Sinai Hospital in New York City.

"So maybe Adler has the Super Surge too then," said Cole. Adler was their cousin, Uncle Ted's son.

"Please stop calling it that."

"He was from the fidelity treatment too, right?"

"*Fertility* treatment. Seriously, what is wrong with your brain?"

"Oh, whatever, shut up. Have you talked to him recently?"

"No. He's way too cool for me now," said Clara. "But we can ask him over Thanksgiving break."

"I hope he has it too. That would be awesome. We might just have an X-men group after all." Cole made some dorky gesture with his arms that Clara assumed had to do with comic book heroes or something lame like that.

"Doubtful. Hey, listen to me. No more funny stuff with the hum, okay? I'm serious. Just stick to soccer," said Clara.

"And basketball. It will be basketball season soon."

"Fine. And be subtle about it, okay?"

"Okay. What about you?"

"What about me?"

"When are you going to use it? You want to use it too, right?"

"Not really. I guess I'll use it a little for Spanish homework." She didn't like using it, she didn't even like thinking about it. It was scary, dangerous and a distraction. It was certainly not part of the plan. She wished it would just go away. But it was nice to have something to talk about with Cole—just too bad it took supernatural forces to bring them together. "And we're not going to try anything new without talking first, right?"

"Oh c'mon. Why?"

"You know why. Promise me."

"Fine. You used to be fun, you know."

"Just trying to keep us alive. Sorry if that's not fun."

"Hey, dumbass," yelled a raspy voice as they walked by the pizza place. Cole waved back at the woman Clara recognized as the owner. Clara quickly averted her eyes so she didn't see her gross scar or greasy hair.

"How do you put up with her?" asked Clara.

"Sal? Aw, she's a sweetheart . . . once you get to know her."

They walked the next block in silence. At home, their father was cooking at the stovetop, decked out in some sort of full-body suit of light tan leather with long tassels hanging down the sides of the trousers and even longer tassels hanging down under his arms. On his feet were fur-trimmed moccasins that laced up over the trousers almost to his knees. On his head was a fur cap with a raccoon tail hanging down his back. Their mother was sitting at the kitchen table reading the newspaper, her elbow on the table and her hand on her forehead, shielding her eyes from the sight of her husband.

"What the—?" said Clara. Cole was laughing and clapping.

"Oh, hello children. Like my duds?" Mr. Lund raised his arms to show the full display of his underarm tassels and turned to face them in the doorway.

"That is awesome!" Cole ran over to give his dad a loud high five.

"Please don't encourage him," said Mrs. Lund, not looking up from her paper.

"Seriously, what the heck is that?" asked Clara.

"Why, this is what I will be wearing on our Lewis and Clark expedition. It is a near exact replica of what Captain Lewis wore when they departed the Mandan Villages." Mr. Lund stood up straight, put his hands on his hips and gave a proud look to the kitchen ceiling.

Clara just looked at him, astonished. "It's truly hideous."

"Maybe, but it's authentic," said Mr. Lund.

"Ugh, that word again. It's not 1804. If you want to be authentic, go get syphilis. Just don't wear that monstrosity," said Clara.

"No, thank you," said Mrs. Lund to her paper, presumably at the thought of her husband with a sexually transmitted disease.

"Dad, I think it looks very rustic. It will look even better after a few weeks on the trails," said Cole.

"Thank you, son." Mr. Lund turned back to the spinach he was sautéing on the stovetop.

"Is it even safe to be near an open flame in that thing?" asked Clara, noticing the tassels swaying with every stir.

"Eh, guess we'll find out." Mr. Lund grinned at Clara.

The debate over Mr. Lund's expedition attire continued through dinner and into the night. In the end, Mrs. Lund won again with "If you wear that thing, I'm not going."

III

Thoralf, a prominent merchant in the village, hosted a meeting of the Dímuner men to discuss arrangements for Gudrid the Fire-Eyed's upcoming Freya ceremony. As was the tradition in those pagan times, upon the first full moon following the fifteenth birthday of a young woman, her village would host a celebration in which she would be presented to interested suitors. The suitors would bestow gifts and court the young woman until she made her choice. Beginning with the Freya ceremony and ending when the maiden made her decision, the celebration was to be lavish with much food and mead flowing in order to show the prosperity of the community and the good luck that the young woman would bring.

News of Gudrid's ceremony travelled far and wide on account of her beauty, and prominent suitors from around the world were to descend on the small island along with their entourages. The Dímuner merchants were under pressure from the leaders in Tórshavn to give a good impression of the Faroe Islands to the powerful foreign suitors even though it was expected and hoped by many that Gudrid would choose Thurandur. Thurandur was the handsome son of the Faroe Islands' largest landowner, Thorbeorn, who owned most of the island of Eysturoy and even large tracts of land in Norway. It was felt that a lavish ceremony was still necessary so that Thurandur would not lose interest. While Thurandur was not a Dímuner, he was nevertheless the local favorite because it was understood that Gudrid's beauty presented a rare opportunity to bring outside wealth and status to the island, and at least Thurandur was Faroese and not a complete foreigner. Even Gudrid's parents approved of the match with Thurandur, despite Thora's occasional gripes that she would suffer dull-eyed grandchildren. She consoled herself that at least Estrid and Sigmundr would one day give her pure-blood Dímuner grandchildren with glinting eyes.

Under normal circumstances, a simple Freya ceremony would not necessitate a meeting of the Dímuner men, but Gudrid's ceremony could not be simple: it would require the outlay of significant resources, and they also had to account for the tribute. For as long as anyone alive could remember, the people of Stóra Dímun and, a long time ago, Dímun Lítla, paid tribute of great quantities of produce and livestock to the Greymen, who came to the island each year on a pilgrimage. The Greymen were gifted in the magic arts and were known shapeshifters. They considered Stóra Dímun to be sacred ground and visited the island in late summer to worship and practice their dark arts. Some years they did not come until autumn and some lucky years they did not come at all.

The tribute strained the food supply of the island. Even in good harvest years, the stock left over after the tribute often ran out before the winter's end. That year's growing season had been particularly weak due to large storms that lingered over the Faroe Islands for weeks at a time. There would not be sufficient food for both the tribute to the Greymen and the festivities to follow Gudrid's ceremony.

The older men at the meeting feared the Greymen. Some of them claimed to be old enough to remember when Glints lived on the now-deserted Dímun Lítla. It was said that many years ago the people of that tiny island refused the Greymen the tribute. In retaliation and to set an example for other tributaries, the Greymen cast a curse on the land. Afterwards, no crops grew on Dímun Lítla and in time it was abandoned. The older men argued for reserving the limited provisions available for the tribute and canceling Gudrid's Freya ceremony. They did not want the Greymen to curse the land of Stóra Dímun.

The younger men at the meeting did not believe the old wives' tales of Dímun Lítla. They wanted to stand up to the Greymen and doubted that their magic was any more than the stuff of fairy tales. The men of Stóra Dímun were strong and they were used to being attacked and defending their homes from Viking raids sailing from the east. Why should they cower at these supposed sorcerers sailing from Iceland in the west, asked the younger men.

After much debate, it was voted that they would hold Gudrid's ceremony in accordance with the tradition and, in doing so, would uphold the honor of their people in the eyes of the foreign visitors. It was noted that Thurandur was rich and powerful and had accepted the new Christian religion. It was said that he was even building a church on his family's estate on Eysturoy. If Gudrid's ceremony was successful and she wed Thurandur, as all expected, the Dímuner would have access to Thurandur's resources and the power of the new religion to fight the Greymen and release the Dímuners from the burdensome tribute once and for all. At the very least, Thurandur could help them buy replacement provisions before the Greymen arrived. The elder men argued that this plan only worked if the Greymen did not arrive until after the wedding and if the new Christ god was indeed stronger than the Greymen's ancient magic. The younger men were willing to take that risk, but they also agreed to keep a small reserve of food and mead so that they had at least something to present to the Greymen in the unlikely event they came earlier in the year than usual. The reserve provisions would be stored in one of Thoralf's warehouses near the harbor.

TEN

After three and a half hours cramped up in the back seat, Cole's legs were stiff and the car was only just approaching the Lincoln Tunnel. It usually took about two hours to get that far, but it was the Wednesday night before Thanksgiving so the heavy traffic was not a surprise. It was late, about quarter after nine, but it was still bumper-to-bumper in both directions.

The drive was quiet. Their parents were taking a break from discussing their packing list. Early in the drive, Clara had yelled at them that they had six months to figure that out. Cole didn't understand why she cared. She'd been listening to her headphones the whole drive. Cole didn't pay attention to them. He was focused on looking out the windows, otherwise he would get carsick.

Inching their way down the long, curved ramp to the tunnel entrance, Cole noticed that Clara was staring at the skyline. He wondered what she was thinking about. She loved the city and was probably thinking about everything she wanted to see in the next two days, probably some "hot" new musical or a special exhibit at the Googooheim, or whatever. Maybe she was wondering, like he was, why the Empire State Building was lit up orange that night.

"Glad we're not going in the other direction," said Mr. Lund, again.

"Uh-huh." Mrs. Lund was half asleep.

The traffic was bad all through Midtown and didn't ease up until they got into the 70s on the Upper East Side. They'd be staying at Uncle Ted's apartment on Park Avenue because Gran was having some work done on her guest rooms. When they reached Uncle Ted's building at 93rd and Park, one of the doormen recognized them and opened the gate. The building took up the whole block. There was an ornate gated tunnel for cars to enter into the building's central courtyard. The car pulled around the circular driveway in the courtyard, stopping at Uncle Ted's elevator lobby—each corner of the building had its own entrance and elevators. One of the doormen rushed over with a cart to help unload the car. Cole looked around the quiet and tranquil space. It was a stark contrast to all the honking and road rage they had endured over the past few hours. The courtyard was landscaped with English ivy and boxwoods that stayed green all year long. In the center was a small fountain with a life-sized, copper statue of a heron. The fountain was running, even in late November, and its peaceful gurgling added to the oasis-like effect.

Cole's father made some small talk with a doorman while two others helped unload the car. Mr. Lund had grown up in the building and knew most of the doormen and the superintendent. Uncle Ted had taken over their childhood home after Grandpa died and Gran moved into a "more manageable" apartment on Fifth Avenue. Before Uncle Ted moved in, he had the place completely gutted, changing it from a classic pre-war penthouse to a cold, modernist nightmare, at least in Cole's opinion. Clara seemed to like it for some reason. She thought it was very "downtown," whatever that meant.

The four of them squeezed into the tiny elevator. Uncle Ted's housekeeper, Sylvia, met them in the private landing. Sylvia had been part of the family's staff for many years, having started back when Cole's dad was only ten years old. She greeted them warmly and gushed over how grown-up Clara and Cole looked. She asked Cole if he was still a Spanish whiz and she tested him with some small talk as she giggled away at his answers.

The apartment was just as Cole remembered it. The rooms were large with very little furniture and what furniture there was looked uncomfortable. Everything was white, black or grey. Even the art on the walls was cold white on black geometric patterns. The stark, minimalist look clashed with the old red brick and wrought iron fencing of the wraparound terrace seen from every window.

"I'm really sorry, but the doctor and Mister Adler are not here tonight." Sylvia was visibly embarrassed that the hosts weren't there to greet them. "Doctor L is working late at the hospital and Mister Adler is out for the evening."

"That's okay, Sylvia. Don't worry about it. You're here and that's all we need." Cole's dad gave her a kiss on each cheek. "Do you know which rooms we're staying in?"

"Of course, of course, I'll show you to them now. I have towels ready and the beds are all made. Just make yourselves at home," she said, although Cole didn't think it was possible for that apartment to feel like a home.

—

The next morning, Clara, Cole and their parents got ready for their annual Thanksgiving jog around the Central Park Reservoir. Sylvia was sipping fresh coffee in the kitchen and made a big fuss about their running gear. She explained that Doctor L and Mister Adler were still asleep but would probably be up by the time they got back from the run. Cole invited Sylvia to come along with them. She blushed and shook her head, waving them away with both hands. "You're still loco, Cole."

"Ugh, this is going to suck," said Clara as they waited for the elevator.

"Don't forget, this was originally your idea."

"Yeah, when we were like eight. Who listens to an eight-year-old?"

"C'mon, kids. It will be fun. It's not a race and some fresh air will do you good," said Mr. Lund.

"Fresh air? What are you talking about? We basically live in the woods."

"No one is forcing you to come, Clara," said Mrs. Lund.

"That's right. You can choose loserdom if you want." Cole laughed and gave Clara's shoulder a little shove.

Team Lund started out at a light jog, exiting the building's little tunnel onto the clean Park Ave sidewalk. They jogged west on 92nd Street, passing lovely brownstones that had once been chopped up into various apartments. Now, many had been, or were in the process of being, combined back into single-family mansions. They took a left on Fifth Ave, jogging past the old Carnegie mansion, which was now some artsy museum, and then cut into Central Park at 90th Street. They crossed the East Drive, then the Bridal Path and then ran up the stairs to the running loop around the reservoir. They ran two-by-two, with their parents in front and Cole and Clara keeping pace behind. The windows of the buildings on the west side of the park glowed with the reflection of the rising sun.

Their pace was pretty slow for Cole, who probably ran ten times as far in the course of one practice, but he could tell from Clara's heavy breathing that it was a challenge for her. By the time they were rounding the north side of the reservoir, she was basically panting, which was unsurprising given her only exercise was doing yoga DVDs by herself in the basement. *She really needs to join a team*, thought Cole.

As they made the turn, the Midtown skyscrapers came into view and Mr. Lund, as had become a tradition, started telling them about each building, its history, its main tenant, what apartment just sold for such and such millions, and so on. Cole made the occasional acknowledgment of his father's insights, but he was more interested in the various ducks on the water. Some were small and black with white bills. One was multicolored with a cool pattern and Cole thought it might be a Wood Duck. Asa would be pumped, but probably annoyed that he couldn't shoot at the wildlife in Central Park.

As they turned down the west side of the reservoir, Cole's dad pointed out Uncle Ted's building, the very top of which was just barely in sight. Then he pointed to Gran's building, farther south on Fifth. They all knew all of this, of course, but Mr. Lund couldn't help himself. Clara just looked straight ahead, gasping. They rounded the path to the south side and even Mr. Lund had to take a break from talking to focus on running.

They were on the home stretch. With only a few hundred feet left, Cole felt a sudden dip in the hum. He looked over at Clara who had a sneaky smirk on her face, and then he watched in astonishment as she took off in a sprint. It took him a couple seconds to realize what was going on. When he did, he too dashed off in hot pursuit, following her as she weaved between their parents, booking it back to the 90th Street exit. She wasn't going very fast but had enough of a head start that Cole couldn't catch up to her. As she broke through the imaginary ribbon at the path exit, she raised her arms in the air and their parents cheered in the background. Clara stopped and hunched over with her hands on her knees. Cole joined her shortly after and they both gasped and groaned.

"Cheater!" Cole gave Clara a smile as he pulled the front of his sweaty shirt in and out to cool off.

"Hey, I learned it from the best," said Clara.

Their parents also raced to the finish, with Mrs. Lund winning easily. Mr. Lund joined his children in their red-faced struggles to breathe while Mrs. Lund looked pretty much the same as she had when they left.

"Are you sure you're ready for our trip?" Mrs. Lund asked. Mr. Lund couldn't answer and just waved her away.

On the walk home, Cole thought about how glad he was that Clara had used the hum. They hadn't used it in a while and the vibration was getting a little intense. While it had been a great asset during soccer season, it was proving less useful in basketball. He just wasn't that good at basketball, so he wasn't put in the games very often and rarely had the ball. The times he did have the ball were too short-lived for him to focus on the hum and use it. It did help with free throws though, but he wasn't going to become a basketball star by waiting around to get fouled and getting single points here and there.

When he went through a dry spell in basketball, he'd have to remind Clara to use the hum for Spanish homework, which she would do reluctantly. He also felt her use it during quizzes a couple times. It seemed that Clara just didn't like using the hum. *What had she called it? A dangerous distraction? Distraction from what?*

He was glad she thought to use it on her own this time with the run, but it was slightly annoying that she had used it in a new way after she had made him promise to not do that without consulting her first. Cole decided it wasn't worth getting into a fight over her double standard. She was in a good mood after her victory and he didn't want to mess that up. He wanted to start using the hum more anyway. *We really need to think of a cooler name for it*, he thought as they crossed Madison Avenue on the way back to Uncle Ted's apartment.

ELEVEN

I missed you, Mother. I've been away. Well, in bed mostly. But my mind has been away. My body, the feeling, it's too much to bear. So, my mind has been going away. It goes to dark places, where it can think what it thinks. Can feel what it feels. Can call out the evil all around us that we're not allowed to see, to say, in the light places. In the dark places it can be said. And there it is agreed. It is known. So that's where my mind goes when the feeling is too much. And that's almost always. And I think that I could stay there, in bed, in the dark places with dark thoughts until the end. When we're finally together. But if I leave, then they win. We can't have that, can we, Mother? I must stay and try. Try to find answers. Try to search in the darkness for answers, for a solution, a way to rid the world of them. Every last one. But not today. Today I must be out of bed and out of the darkness because we have visitors. Sylvia made me promise. She said you'd want me out of bed. That you'd want me to see your family. What does she know? Nothing. And she's one of them.

TWELVE

After the run, they chatted with Sylvia in the huge spotless kitchen overlooking Park Avenue. Clara thought the kitchen was amazing. The walls were like the white side of a solved Rubik's Cube, with each square opening up at the touch of a finger to reveal a cabinet or some other function. In the center of the kitchen was an island, a large rectangle of white marble lined on one end with black wire barstools. Clara sat at one of the stools, fully enjoying the latte that Sylvia had made for her, unprompted. Uncle Ted had a cappuccino machine that apparently only Sylvia could figure out how to use. Sylvia joked that it was her job security.

"Well, hello, family!" Uncle Ted tucked a folded newspaper under his arm as he entered the kitchen. "I'm so sorry for not being here to welcome you last night. And not just because Sylvia has been giving me the evil eye all morning."

Sylvia scoffed and said something in Spanish under her breath before leaving the kitchen. There were hugs all around. Clara watched as Uncle Ted and her mother hugged. Their hugs were always a little longer than the typical hug, reflecting the shared sadness between them. Uncle Ted's late wife, also a Clara, was Mrs. Lund's sister. Back in the day at Penn, when Clara's parents first started dating, they set up a blind date between their younger siblings. Clara's dad's brother, Uncle Ted, also a Penn man, hit it off with Clara's namesake aunt, then a freshman at Bryn Mawr. The two couples eventually got married and were to live happily ever after, but then Aunt Clara died from complications during their son Adler's birth. That was nineteen years ago, but Uncle Ted and Clara's mom still shared a certain tenderness whenever they were together. It was touching, especially to Clara who felt a connection to the namesake she never got to meet.

Clara lifted the large white mug of latte up to her bottom lip and inhaled the warm, rich air. Her lungs felt recovered from the run, but not the rest of her body.

"Why don't you two go wake up that lazy son of mine?" Uncle Ted suggested. Cole's furrowed brows and tight lips suggested he wasn't thrilled with the idea of waking up their cousin.

"Let's go." Clara tugged on Cole's sleeve.

"Okay," he sighed.

Adler's bedroom was down the hall of the north wing.

"Um, can we just leave him alone? I don't want to bother him. He's probably hungover." Cole's whispering was so low that Clara could hardly hear him.

"Stop being a wimp. It's just Adler." Clara waved her hand dismissively and then yelled, "Wakey, wakey!" as she knocked on Adler's door. Cole cringed.

There was no answer. They waited a few minutes then Clara knocked again, even louder this time. She reached for the doorknob.

Cole grabbed her arm to stop her. "Aah, what are you doing? Let's just leave him alone."

"Seriously? Why are you being such a baby?" Clara twisted her arm free and opened the door.

Through the bedroom window they saw that Adler was awake and having a cigarette on the terrace. Cole let out a sigh of relief. The hum changed frequency slightly. Before Clara had a chance to fully process that, she felt Cole grab her shoulder.

"Holy crap. Did you feel that?"

"Yeah."

Clara didn't know what else to say or think. She definitely felt something. Even though she logically acknowledged the possibility of Adler also having the power, she hadn't let herself believe it. It was now certain that Adler had at least some connection to it.

Adler suddenly turned to look at them. He squinted, presumably to see through the glare of the glass. He gestured for them to join him on the terrace. Adler's room—suite, rather—was huge, with a king-size bed, a separate sitting room, a walk-in closet and an en suite bathroom. The decor was the same as the rest of the house, with no hint that this was the bedroom of a nineteen-year-old boy. *This is the life*, thought Clara.

Adler was tall and skinny, so skinny that his pale, almost ivory, skin appeared to be stretched between his angular bones. He had dark circles under his deep-set eyes. The last time Clara had seen him, he had had their same light brown hair, but he had since dyed it to platinum blond and cut it very short on the sides, leaving the top long and floppy. He was wearing tight black jeans and a red hoodie. Clara thought he was beautiful.

Adler didn't turn to look at them when they joined him on the terrace. He just stared out at the view, stone-faced. Unlike the rest of the apartment that looked out onto Park Ave, Adler's suite and its adjoining terrace faced north. The building wasn't very tall, only fourteen stories, but it was at the top of Carnegie Hill and had a commanding view to the north of East Harlem and, farther in the distance, the Bronx. He took a long drag of his cigarette. Clara and Cole looked at each other, not sure what to do.

"Is everything okay?" asked Clara.

"I don't know. Does it look okay?" Adler raised his chin slightly toward the view, which was dominated by rows and rows of dark brick public housing towers. Cole and Clara exchanged confused looks.

"Look what they've done. Look at the decay, the filth, the crime, the drugs," continued Adler. "Look how they hang their dirty laundry and stupid flags out the windows. Go back to that island shithole, if you love it so much." Adler took another drag and leaned forward. "Look how they scurry in and out of their towers and bodegas like rats. How they shit on everything like disgusting, fat pigeons."

From the expression on Cole's face, Clara could tell that Adler was saying something shocking. She heard the words Adler was saying, but she wasn't paying attention to their meaning. Instead, she was captivated by his face, marveling at how the slightest change—a twitch of a muscle, a narrowing of an eyelid—could convey such passion, such rage. Adler had always said shocking things: one had to in New York to be heard—to matter. And Adler mattered.

"Dude, snap out of it. That's not cool." Cole's cheeks were red.

Adler slowly turned to look at them. "You're right. I just have a lot on my mind." He flicked his lit cigarette over the side.

Cole looked mortified and leaned over to watch it fall to the street. "Dude, you could hit someone."

"Possibly. Life is full of risks. More for some than others." Adler stepped back from the low, brick wall and brushed off the front of his sweatshirt. "So how are you guys? Sorry I've been hiding out here. I'm really hungover and can't even deal with the real world right now."

"Don't worry about it." Clara gave him a hug.

"Good to see you, man," said Cole, adding "I think," under his breath. Cole offered his hand to Adler who weakly extended his, palm down. Cole grabbed it and gave it two firm shakes. Adler winced.

"Pfff, men," said Clara. "So, how's it going? How's college?"

Adler was a sophomore at Penn, studying Art History. He had never been a particularly dedicated student, but he was a Lund. Their grandfather, also a Penn man, had been a renowned orthopedic surgeon who had helped design various artificial joints and prosthetics. He made hundreds of millions in royalties and donated a ton of money to the university to build a science building, now known, alliteratively, as Lund Lab. Clara hoped to also be a beneficiary of that legacy, but she still needed to get good grades and do well enough on the SATs, particularly coming from their crappy high school.

"I'm taking some time off. Philly just isn't my scene."

"I hear ya," said Clara. She caught Cole rolling his eyes.

"So, what do you do all day?" asked Cole.

"A little of this, a little of that. I'm mostly working on my art." Adler often referred to "his art," but Clara had no idea what kind of art he did. "Mainly just trying to relax. I'm having some medical issues."

"Oh no. What's going on?" asked Clara.

"Let's go inside. It's cold out here." Adler walked to the door leading back to his room.

"What the heck was that all about?" Cole whispered to Clara as they followed, presumably referring to Adler's little rant about the housing projects. Clara didn't know what to say so she just shrugged.

Back inside, they settled onto the L-shaped couch in Adler's sitting room. He put his hand over his chest and took a deep breath, as if gathering his strength to speak.

Clara broke the silence. "So, what's the medical issue?"

"It's hard to describe. It's like a fluttering in my chest, like a vibration," said Adler. Cole and Clara exchanged wide-eyed looks. She signaled for Cole to say something, but Cole shook his head.

"It's like I can hear it but not really," continued Adler. "No one can figure it out. Dad thinks it's hypochondria."

"We have it too!" Clara immediately realized she sounded way too excited. She felt like a little kid who had just blurted out a secret that just couldn't be held in any longer. She didn't like losing her cool like that, especially in front of Adler.

"What?" Adler turned to look at them. They both nodded. "I don't understand."

"We have the same thing," said Cole.

"Well, what is it? Have you been able to stop it?" Adler sat up in his seat, for the first time giving them his full attention.

"No, we can't stop it, but we can make it fade a little. Have you tried to do anything with it?" asked Clara. She was now doing her best to sound really chill about the whole thing.

"Yes," said Adler. "I've tried everything: pulmonologists, neurologists, ENTs, acupuncture, even fucking leeches!"

"No, like do something *with* it." Clara could feel herself getting too excited again. She had put more emphasis on the "with" than was necessary. She felt childish.

"I don't follow." Adler flopped back into his seat in frustration.

Cole stood up. "Here, I'll show you. Do you have a basketball?" Adler just looked at him like he was a crazy person.

Clara waved at Cole to sit back down. "Okay, forget that. Here, see that picture?" She pointed to a large-framed black and white photo of Angkor Wat. "See how it's a little crooked?"

"Yeah, so what?"

"Try to fix it," said Clara.

"Fuck you. You fix it," said Adler. Cole snickered.

"No, I mean from here. Like with your mind." Clara started moving her right hand up to point to her temple, but she stopped herself. *Stay cool, Clara*, she thought.

Adler turned to Cole. "Is she for real?"

"Yeah, just try it." Cole gave Adler an excited grin.

"You guys are on crack."

"Shut up and try it," said Clara. "Just think about moving the frame while also focusing on the feeling in your chest."

"Fine." Adler adjusted in his seat to better face the photo and squinted his eyes at it. "See, nothing. You guys are messing with me. It's not funny, I'm really sick."

"Just try again and really focus. It's not easy," said Cole.

Adler shifted back to face the frame. He leaned his face a little forward and tightened his lips. The muscles in his jaw bulged as he clenched his teeth. He gave up, exhaled, relaxed his face and slumped back into the couch.

"Try again, loser," said Clara.

Adler sat up. He took a deep breath and stared intensely at the frame. His mouth stretched into a tight grimace, his nostrils flared and his cheeks began to turn red. He wasn't breathing. His face got redder and redder. The dark circles under his eyes were almost purple. A vein bulged from his forehead. He shut his eyes and began to yell at the frame, baring his white, perfect teeth. He slowly rose up to a standing position and as he did, his yelling got louder and louder. Cole and Clara exchanged concerned looks then turned back to watch Adler. By then, he was standing, yelling at the top of his lungs, fists clenched at his sides. Then suddenly, Clara felt the hum recede. A split second later the glass in the frame shattered and shards of glass flew at them on the couch. Clara and Cole yelled out as they ducked and covered their faces with their arms. Adler fell back onto the couch and then slumped forward with his head down between his knees. The picture frame, now glassless except around the rim, swung a little on the nail and then crashed to the floor. Clara slowly lowered her arms to look around. The couch was covered in bits of glass, but everyone was okay. She looked over at Cole to share a look of relief.

Adler had the hum. It wasn't just a Cole and Clara thing. It wasn't just a Lehighton thing. It was also an Adler thing, a New York thing, a Penn thing. It could be part of Clara's real life; it could be part of the plan. She clapped her hands and giggled and, for that moment, didn't care about seeming cool.

"Holy crap." Adler slowly raised his head.

"Yep. We call it . . . The Force." Cole used a wispy, dramatic voice and waved his hand across his face Jedi style.

"No, we DON'T!" yelled Clara. "You're such a dork."

IV

Like most young men from Stóra Dímun, Sigmundr Brestirson daydreamed about how he would one day defeat the Greymen and free his people from the tribute. To that end, Sigmundr had studied the Greymen for years, collecting stories and rumors, mostly from the learned men of the great temple in Tórshavn. Traders from Iceland, where the Greymen were then based, and Norway, where the Greymen had originated, also shared with Sigmundr their tales of the Greymen and their powers. It was said that the Greymen could shapeshift into any animal, cast evil curses, control the weather, control the tides, turn rock to silver, cure diseases, start fires, control minds, move mountains, melt glaciers and so forth. Given the variety of fantastical stories that Sigmundr had heard over the years, he questioned if any of it were true at all. There were, however, two consistencies about the Greymen that he heard again and again: Only one of them had the power and, by killing that man, the power would be transferred to the slayer.

Sigmundr conveyed these stories and his ideas on defeating the Greymen to his oft companion, Estrid Beinedottir. Estrid shared in Sigmundr's enthusiasm for ridding the island of the Greymen. Generations ago, the Greymen had built a small stone cottage at the base of the steep cliff at the northern point of the island. The cottage was built just above the high tide line, on a small rock outcropping that had been formed many centuries ago when part of the cliff face had fallen into the water. In hushed voices, the Dímuners referred to it as the Snow Cottage on account of the accumulation of white bird excrement fallen on the roof from the fowling cliffs above.

In accordance with the true law of the Faroe Islands at the time, the outcropping was considered part of Estrid's father's land because the cliffs were part of his estate. It was said that the Greymen built the Snow Cottage there because it was a particularly magical location and that inside they stored sacrifices and paraphernalia to use in their dark magic ceremonies while on their pilgrimages to Stóra Dímun. All Dímuner fisherman avoided the north point out of fear that a curse would take hold of their ships. It was also rumored that any lundi captured from the cliffs directly above the Snow Cottage would bring bad luck to whomever ate them. This hurt demand for Beine's catch in the village, but Sigmundr would help him sell any overstock of birds in Tórshavn, where the merchants were less superstitious. Estrid was eager to rid her family's land of that specter.

Estrid, like Sigmundr, questioned whether the Greymen indeed had any powers at all. To test that, they had long ago planted a small vegetable garden on the far side of Dímun Lítla. The garden grew nicely and they took that as proof that the Greymen had not actually cursed the land of that small island leading to its abandonment, as the old story went. That garden still grew years later and had since become a planting ground for exotic herbs and flowers grown from seeds that Sigmundr collected from his trading partners from all over the known world. Many of the plants of the garden could not survive the harsh North Atlantic winters of the Faroe Islands, but Sigmundr carefully gathered the seeds and clippings each autumn and replanted the garden each spring. In favorable weather, it was not unusual for Estrid and Sigmundr to take day sails out to Dímun Lítla and spend the whole day in their exotic garden, hidden from sight of Stóra Dímun.

When Sigmundr learned of the decision to go forward with Gudrid's Freya ceremony festivities, and thereby leave insufficient provisions for the tribute, he decided that that year would be the best, if not the only, time to finally follow through on one of his ideas on how to defeat the Greymen.

On the warm summer day before Gudrid's ceremony, Sigmundr and Estrid spent the morning concocting a plan at their garden on Dímun Lítla. Later that day, they sailed back to Stóra Dímun with a pouch full of dream thistle leaves.

THIRTEEN

Cole helped clean up the broken bits of glass by using one artsy magazine to sweep them into another artsy magazine, which he then carefully carried to the wastebasket in Adler's bathroom. Clara and Adler decided that the most plausible explanation to give Sylvia was that Cole broke the picture while roughhousing. Cole reluctantly agreed to take the blame, but he didn't really understand how he could have been roughhousing by himself. It was likely that Clara and Adler didn't really understand what roughhousing meant.

While he was mostly glad that Adler had the hum too, he was still disturbed by Adler's creepy little monologue about East Harlem. He wondered if it was a good idea for someone who had thoughts like that to also have the power. Clara was also getting on his nerves, and not just for how little she helped with the broken glass. She was now gushing all over Adler for having done something so dramatic with the hum. *It was her lame rules that prevented them from trying cool stuff like that*, thought Cole. And for someone who considers herself so cultured, she seemed totally unphased by Adler's racist rant. Cole needed to get some fresh air. He grabbed his coat and headed down to the street.

When he got out to Park Avenue, he wasn't really sure where to go. He decided to walk north to East Harlem, as a sort of "screw you" to Adler. After a few blocks of fancy buildings, he crossed 96th Street, the border between the Carnegie Hill section of the Upper East Side and Spanish Harlem. At 98th Street, Park Ave split in half and the Metro North trains running underground from Grand Central Station shot noisily out of their tunnels onto tracks built between the two sides of the street. Cole stopped to watch the trains for a few minutes. When he and Adler were little, they used to go there with their dads to watch the trains. They would try to get the conductors of the south-bound trains to blow the horns and wave, which worked with varying degrees of success.

After 98th Street, Cole stayed on the east side of Park, which headed downhill until the trains were several stories above the street, running on an old stone platform. Little tunnels in the stone allowed cars and pedestrians to head east or west on the cross-town streets. The buildings weren't fancy anymore. The blocks switched between public housing developments and aging, brick walk-up apartment buildings.

There were not many people out and about, it being Thanksgiving, but those who were out were just going about their business like everyone else in the city. Cole didn't see anyone scurrying like a rat or shitting on anything like a pigeon, in Adler's words. He saw old dudes hanging out with their friends, young dudes hanging out with their friends, old ladies lugging groceries, a middle-aged guy heading somewhere with flowers. He saw mothers with their strollers and large diaper bags and kids of all ages, some on bikes and scooters.

At 115th Street, he came to the open-air Latin music venue situated under the tracks. When they were pre-teens, he and Adler used to sneak up there to listen to the live music and see the "sexy dancing." They weren't allowed in but would grab onto the chain-link fence with both hands and peer through it at the ladies dancing around in tank tops that barely held in their big jiggling boobs. Cole and Adler liked the music too and would hum it and dance a little on their way home.

It was closed today. Cole couldn't tell whether that was because it was Thanksgiving or if it was always closed during the colder months. All the signs were in Spanish, which he tried to read, but none seemed to answer that question.

Cole peered through like he had done in what felt like a different lifetime, back when the only things that mattered were hanging out with Clara and visiting Adler almost every other weekend. It was a simpler time, but he didn't want to go back. He couldn't go back. Adler was practically a stranger. Even Clara seemed to be slipping away, but he wouldn't let that happen—he would find more time to spend with her, he'd make more time. As he pulled his face away from the fence, he caught a glimpse of his watch. He had to hustle back to get ready for turkey dinner at Gran's.

By the time Cole got back to the apartment, Clara and Adler were already dressed up and ready to go. They were sitting on the couch in the living room and Adler was letting Clara sneak sips of his martini. Although Adler was only 19, Uncle Ted and Sylvia had long given up on trying to stop him from drinking. For as long as Cole could remember, Adler had pretty much free reign of the apartment and what few rules there were he broke regularly without consequence. On one visit when Cole was twelve, Adler, who was only fourteen, had stolen a pack of cigarettes from Sylvia's purse. The two of them hid on the terrace and tried to light one, but the wind was so strong that they used up the whole box of matches without getting a single drag. Sylvia later discovered them in the kitchen trying to light up on the gas stovetop. She calmly pulled the cigarettes from their lips, snatched the pack off the counter and walked back down the hall, shaking her head and mumbling in Spanish. It seemed that not much had changed— not that Cole was any saint, but at least he had enough sense to not break the law right in front of his parents.

Cole went straight to his room to get changed. He put on the hand-me-down tweed suit given to him by his dad for the occasion. He hated dressing up and this suit was particularly itchy on his legs, but it made Gran happy for them to look nice, so he would suck it up for one meal. He heard Uncle Ted yelling down the hall that they were getting ready to leave, so he quickly put on his shoes and ran to join the rest of the crew. Adler looked him up and down when he got to the foyer.

"Nice suit," he said, showing his teeth that were somehow whiter than his skin. He was in a tight-fitting charcoal suit with a crisp white shirt, no tie and a dark red pocket square.

"Nice makeup," said Cole.

"Thanks." Adler batted his unnaturally dark eyelashes. They cast shadows down his skinny face, darkening his pale skin that otherwise looked like the white shrink wrap of a dry-docked motorboat.

Clara then caught up with them, a little out of breath. "I almost forgot my coat. Where have you been?"

"Just went for a walk," said Cole. Adler went ahead to get in the first elevator.

"Here. I convinced Adler to give you his driver's license. Now you can buy smokes for Asa." Clara handed the I.D. to Cole.

"Oh, okay. Thanks, I guess."

He took a close look at the license. The picture of Adler was taken before he had dyed his hair, so Cole thought it was a close-enough likeness. Cole could always say he had gained weight if anyone ever asked why his I.D. picture looked like a skeleton with eyeballs. He put the license in his pocket next to the whistle. *Too bad Adler isn't 21 yet.*

"He feels it all the time. Like he never gets a break." Clara was whispering right into Cole's ear, probably more loudly than she realized.

"Jeez, that must suck."

"Yeah, and we decided it must have something to do with our eyes or the fertility treatment." Clara divulged that revelation as if it were some big scoop.

"Makes sense," said Cole. He didn't get this "we decided" stuff—hadn't he and Clara already figured that out? He was ready to be back in Lehighton. He had forgotten how Clara made every visit to New York into the Adler Show. Despite that, he was happy that there was someone else with the power and that Clara was finally loosening up about it, but those two BFF's sure were being annoying.

"So do you think everyone with the eyes has the hum?" Cole hit the elevator call button.

"Seems like that so far," said Clara.

"Hey, didn't you meet someone else with it? She was here for the eye tests—from England?"

"Ireland."

"Right, right. Uncle Ted asked you to show her the town while she was here. Oh, and then later you were emailing her for help planning that nerd-fest Dublin poetry tour." Cole pushed the elevator down button again. "She was cute, you should call her."

"'Cause she was cute?" Clara snickered.

"No, to find out if she has the hum."

"Er, she was weird."

"We were fourteen, everyone was weird. C'mon, just do it. There's nothing to lose."

"She was a triplet."

"Oh, then you *definitely* need to call her. Have them visit us."

"You're a pig. But fine, I'll email her when we're back home. She probably doesn't even use the same email address by now."

"Worth a shot. And sorry I said that about the poetry tour. It was actually pretty interesting."

"I know it was. And you can drop the dumb jock act. That might make you cool in Lehighton, but it doesn't work in New York City."

The elevator door opened and they went down to join the rest of the family.

Their parents didn't like to talk much about the fertility treatment, but over the years, Cole and Clara had been able to piece together at least some of the story. Uncle Ted was still in medical school when he and Aunt Clara started trying to have a child. After a few years of failure, they used Cole's grandfather's connections to get consultations with the leading fertility specialists, but none of them could determine the problem. Both Uncle Ted and Aunt Clara seemed to have fully functioning reproductive parts and yet they could not conceive, no matter what method they and their medical team tried.

Uncle Ted, meanwhile, decided to focus his studies on fertility, eventually excelling in the field and developing a unique treatment that was able to work for him and Aunt Clara. The science was beyond Cole, but it had to do with splitting the "chrono zones," or something like that, and then putting them back together again. On top of that, there was some part of the treatment that changed the genetic makeup of the inside of the womb. It was a complicated and expensive procedure that was considered an option of last resort and only for the very wealthy because no insurance companies covered it.

Cole's parents had also faced the same issues when they started trying to have kids. This led to speculation that, whatever the issue was, it must be genetic given that Cole's mother and father had mostly the same genes as Aunt Clara and Uncle Ted. At first, Cole's parents were nervous to try the procedure because Aunt Clara had died from pregnancy-related complications, but the consensus of the medical team was that her death was unrelated to the treatment. The full story of Aunt Clara's death was still a mystery to Cole and Clara, despite their many attempts to pry the details from family members. Anyone they asked would just get nervous and quickly change the subject.

Cole's parents eventually overcame their worries and decided to go for it and—*voilà*—Clara and Cole were born without any issues. Twins and triplets were a common outcome because many aspiring parents decided to just pay for one treatment for multiple babies rather than go through the cost and effort more than once. A potential side effect of the treatment, however, was that in very rare instances the babies were born with peculiar irises. Their eyes glowed in direct sunlight, like the eyes of a raccoon or cat caught in headlights at night. This side effect happened with Adler, Cole and Clara and only a handful of others. No one could explain why this happened. There wasn't even a plausible theory advanced, despite countless studies and tests. Fortunately, the eyes were easy enough to hide with sunglasses or colored contacts—that is, when they didn't get knocked out by some douchebag on the soccer field.

By the time they all got down to the courtyard of Uncle Ted's building, a light rain was falling. The doormen gave them umbrellas for the walk to Gran's on 85th Street and Fifth Avenue. Clara was already griping about taking a cab, but everyone shot that down. Cole figured her legs were probably still sore from all the cheating that morning.

When they got up to Gran's apartment, Ida, Gran's housekeeper, greeted them, took their coats and wet umbrellas and showed them to the sitting room. Gran was reading in an armchair next to the fire. Classical music was playing, which was always the case in Gran's apartment. She rose and opened her arms to receive their hugs, beckoning them forward with flits of her thick-knuckled fingers. A navy-blue skirt suit loosely draped Gran's tall and slender frame. Her hair was white and tied back in a short ponytail and she wore tortoiseshell reading glasses, the corners of which were attached to a string of little pearls that hung down in front of her cheeks and around the back of her neck.

"Welcome, welcome. Happy Thanksgiving, everyone," she said. "Have a seat and we'll have some hors d'oeuvres while the table is set." She made a sort of snapping-pointing gesture to someone in the hall behind them. "Any drinks?" Another staff member came into the room and took beverage orders as people found seats. Cole gave Gran a big hug and kiss and then snagged a seat on a couch near a window overlooking Central Park.

"So, Ma, is that a new doorman downstairs? He seems nice," said Uncle Ted.

"Yes, I already slept with him," said Gran.

"What?!" said everyone within earshot.

"I said I already spoke with him . . . about the creaky elevator door."

That was a typical exchange with Gran. Before their grandfather had died, he was nearly deaf and Gran just got into the habit of saying whatever she damn well pleased and just correcting it if she got caught. She hadn't broken the habit, even many years after Grandpa's death.

Cole saw something out of the corner of his eyes. A cool-looking hawk was flying over the park. He watched it until some trays of food appeared. After a half an hour of Cole stuffing his face with stuffed mushrooms, Ida entered the room and suggested they take their seats for dinner. The dining room was Cole's favorite room in the apartment. It was large with great big-windowed doors that opened up to a small terrace overlooking the park and, beyond that, the buildings on the West Side. The long table was positioned east to west and there was no chair at the western end so that everyone could see the view of the park, which was particularly stunning during sunsets. The walls were a dark wood about halfway up. On the top half of one wall was a painted country scene with rolling hills on which spotted dogs and horses with their elegantly dressed riders chased a fox. Painted on the other side was a lake scene with willow trees and two black swans. Every year, the first thing Uncle Ted would do after sitting down was to ask Gran when she was going to paint over that "hideously old-fashioned painting" and this year was no exception.

"I don't know. Ask your brother, he's getting the apartment and all the money when I die," said Gran with obvious delight.

"Speaking of the apartment, how is the work going on the guest rooms?" asked Cole's dad.

"The what?" Gran furrowed her brow, perplexed.

"The work on the guest rooms," said Mr. Lund more loudly, referring to the reason they were staying at Uncle Ted's.

"Oh, I made that up."

"What?!"

"I made a mix up," said Gran. "The start date . . . I thought it was this week, but they don't start until Monday."

"Uh-huh," said Mr. Lund.

"So, what is everyone doing during their stay in the city? Any museums? Shows? Reservations at the 'it' restaurant?" Gran asked the group.

"Well, unfortunately, we need to head back tomorrow," said Cole's mom. "Cole has a basketball game tomorrow night."

"Oh no, that's terrible," said Gran. "So much travelling for just a day. And I though Cole wasn't any good at basketball." No one bothered to say "what" that time—it was true. Cole was looking forward to baseball season; he thought the hum would be perfect for hitting.

"Well, there's still time to do something tonight. You should go out on the town." Gran used her napkin to point in the direction of downtown before unfolding it onto her lap. Naturally, she wouldn't expect them to go out anywhere north of 85th Street.

"Clara and I are going to a gallery opening in NoMad," said Adler.

"Where? Is that some new-fangled neighborhood like Tri-bee-cah?" asked Gran.

"Maybe." Adler rolled his eyes and Clara giggled.

"And then we're going to a club in Brooklyn where Adler's friend is spinning." Clara leaned forward as she spoke as if that was the best news ever.

"Spinning means disc-jockeying," said Uncle Ted, who was always trying to be in the know.

"Sounds interesting. What about you, Cole?" asked Gran.

"Oh, uh, I'm meeting a friend from Philly in Midtown." That was a lie, but the last thing he wanted to do was hang out with Clara and Adler at a snobby gallery and, come to think of it, he hadn't been invited.

Ida brought out the Thanksgiving feast. Cole was still hungry, even after all of the appetizers in the sitting room and was pumped for some normal-sized food. The table fell silent other than the clinking of silverware.

"Oh wow, look. It's a red-tailed hawk." Cole's mom pointed at one of the French doors. It looked like the same hawk Cole had watched earlier. It was right in front of the terrace, gliding on an updraft that made it look like it was floating in place. Its eyes and neck were moving constantly, checking out the scene below from all angles.

"Oh, yes. Aren't they beautiful?" said Gran. "Their nests make a bit of a mess, but I've been lucky so far this year."

"Did you know that they can live for over twenty years?" said Cole's mom.

"You should see the Wanamakers' terrace—twigs and feathers everywhere. But they eat rats and pigeons, so it's a net positive," continued Gran, ignoring her daughter-in-law.

The hawk dove a little out of sight and the table fell back to eating. Then suddenly Cole felt the hum dim. He looked up at Clara, who simultaneously turned to look at him. They both shook their heads slightly.

"Eeek," screamed Gran, shielding her eyes. "That's disgusting!" Everyone looked to see what was happening.

On the terrace wall, right in front of the table, the hawk was perched with a flailing pigeon clenched in one of its talons. Through the glass doors came a sickening, pained cooing sound as the pigeon struggled. The hawk looked straight into the room and started digging out the pigeon's insides with its beak. Feathers and blood stuck to the hawk's face as it pulled white and pink guts from the still-alive prey. The hawk switched the pigeon from one talon to the other. Now dead, the pigeon's head hung down loosely.

Cole looked around the table. Everyone was grossed-out. It was kind of funny until he looked at Adler. He was watching the hawk closely and his facial coloring was almost the same red as his pocket square. Cole realized that Adler was doing it—he was using the hum to control the hawk. Cole's mother calmly got up from her seat, opened the door and shooed the hawk away. Adler turned from the terrace and caught eyes with Cole. Adler opened his mouth slightly. Cole was expecting him to smile, but instead he made a biting motion, his gleaming white upper and bottom teeth clicking together loudly. Cole quickly broke eye contact and looked down at his plate. Chills ran down Cole's back. *When had Adler become so creepy?*

"Thank you, dear," said Gran to Cole's mom. "I can't say that the turkey looks very appetizing now. Any objections to moving on to dessert?"

They all agreed.

After dessert, Cole felt full and tired. He was having trouble staying awake during the goodbyes, but he made sure to give Gran a hug and kiss and let her know how nice it was to see her. He apologized for having to pull everyone away for his basketball game and she made him promise to "score a few hoops" for her.

"Will you all be going to see your other grandmother for Christmas? What do you call her again? Llama?" Gran asked.

"Amma," said Clara. "Yes, we'll spend winter break with her."

"Is she still a crazy hippie up there in Maine?" asked Gran.

"What!?" said Cole's mother.

"Is she still happy up there in Maine? I don't know how she deals with that cold all the time. I would just freeze to death."

"Yes, she still likes it." Although his mother hid it well, Cole could tell that she was getting annoyed.

On their way to the elevator, Gran called out, "Oh, and Adler, Clara, dears, have fun with your sinning tonight."

"Spinning," corrected Adler.

"That's what I said."

FOURTEEN

other. Mother. Everything is going to be okay now. The country mice showed me what I am. I can break things. I can rip things open. I can shatter and kill. I'm special. I knew it. You knew it. It will let me do what I was meant to do, what I need to do. I almost gave up, Mother. But you believed in me. You never gave up on me. Like I'll never give up on you. Never. Not until they're all shattered, ripped open, dead.

FIFTEEN

The drive from Lehighton to Amma's house in Prouts Neck, Maine usually took about seven hours, but it would probably take them nine given Christmas holiday traffic. Clara didn't mind the drive. She looked at magazines and read books and enjoyed some quiet time. Cole hated long car rides. He couldn't read or concentrate on anything inside the car without getting carsick. He was also a little too tall to be cramped up in the back seat for long periods. Fortunately for Clara, as his back seat partner, he wasn't much of a complainer. She admired him for that quality.

Clara was looking forward to a relaxing winter break of reading, roasting marshmallows on the fire and hot chocolate. She was relieved that finals were over and she thought she had done okay on most of them, except for Spanish, per usual. She had used the hum a little during the Spanish final this year, but she was in a bit of a "catch-22." If she did too well on tests, she would be moved to the next level up and wouldn't be with Cole, so no hum. Using the hum to advance to a class she couldn't handle without the hum would screw her over. She used it just enough to get in the B grade range—Penn would probably be okay with that, for a Lund. Cole didn't use the hum at all for Spanish because of something having to do with a whistle and cheating being wrong. When she had asked him why cheating at sports was okay but on tests wasn't, he just said "whistle exception." She didn't know what that meant.

While driving through Hartford, it began to snow and Clara's dad started talking about the Lewis and Clark trip, to no one's surprise. Their parents were excited to be up in Maine during the winter so they could try out some of their new cold-weather hiking gear. Part of their trek would go through the Lemhi Pass in the Rocky Mountains, which could be snow-covered even in the summer. Mr. Lund had gone a little overboard buying snow hiking supplies, including "the latest in snowshoe technology." It hadn't snowed yet in Lehighton and he was itching to try them out. For a good part of the day after the snowshoes arrived, he had walked around the house in them while Mrs. Lund yelled at him to not scratch up the floors. He tripped on them going up the stairs at least twice. When he extolled the virtues of their high-tech design to Clara, she couldn't resist saying, "Hey, what happened to being authentic?"

A few hours later, Clara awoke with a jolt as the car turned onto the gravel driveway leading to Amma's house. The driveway meandered a bit through the woods, where the ground and bare trees had a light dusting of snow. There was a fresh set of tire tracks. They weren't the first to arrive. Clara's mom had two brothers and a sister, not including the late Aunt Clara, and each had their own families. It would be a full house, like every Christmas.

Amma's house was on a small bluff, overlooking the ocean beyond. The house was hulking and solid. Its exterior walls were covered with weathered, cedar shingles, complemented by cream-colored trim around the doors and windows. There were five gabled windows on the second floor and four dormer windows poking out from the slanted roof on the third floor. The ocean-facing side of the first floor had a screened-in porch that led to a glass-enclosed sunroom with awe-inspiring views of the rocky beach. On clear days, you could see two small islands in the distance, Bluff Island and Stratton Island. Today they were hidden behind a curtain of snow-filled air.

Clara felt a wave of calm wash over her from simply looking at the house. While it wasn't really her style, having been built over a hundred years ago, it was one of the few constants in her life. Since birth, Clara had spent every Christmas and summer there—except for the summer when they moved to Lehighton—and it was a comfort that nothing about the house ever seemed to change. The furniture was the same, the color of the paint on the walls was the same, the rippled views from the old windows were the same, the smells of wood and dust and fireplaces were the same. The secret set of stairs, the cozy nooks, the tiny doors to tiny closets were all the same. And that let Clara feel like she could always be the same, she could be that same naïve little girl, hanging out with her brother and making her fondest memories. She didn't have to be jaded or cool or clever or sarcastic or sophisticated—she could be carefree and blissfully ignorant of the impending changes of growing up, and growing apart.

Various family members ran out to greet them as they stood shivering in the cold. Clara saw smoke rising from one of the three chimneys. She was excited to plunk herself down in front of the fireplace. She walked up the stone steps to the house. As she saw Amma in the doorway, snowflakes landed on her eyelashes. She opened her mouth to catch some on her tongue.

Amma pulled Clara in for a hug. Clara thought Amma's hugs were the best. Amma was not thin. She had large breasts and was often dressed in a very soft cable-knit sweater, which together made her hugs the coziest place in the world. Clara lingered in the hug with closed eyes.

"Everything okay, Honeybee?" asked Amma.

Amma had called Clara "Honeybee" ever since the summer before she and Cole turned seven. A bee had found its way into Clara's bathing suit. She panicked, pulling off the suit and running to the house stark naked and screaming. She had still gotten stung, but more clearly she remembers getting an extra scoop of ice cream that night.

"Yes, I'm great, Amma. Just happy to be here with you."

"So glad to have you here, dear."

Amma looked her in the eyes and moved a strand of hair out of Clara's face, tucking it behind her ear with a grandmother's practiced care. Amma's own hair was long, curly and dark grey. It was somewhat wild, which was how she liked it. One strip of hair on the left side of her face was dyed a deep purple. Keeping an arm around Clara's shoulders, Amma led her into the house. Clara went up to her room to settle in.

Clara's room was the one she had stayed in since she was little. It was on the third floor and looked out at rocks that jutted into the ocean like fingers. On the ocean-facing wall, there were three square windows, the middle one slightly larger than the others. Like all the rooms on the third floor, its ceiling slanted in parts. In the short walls under the eaves were little doors leading to crawl spaces that she had often turned into a secret cave or an underwater lair. She used to share it with Cole until they were about nine, when he decided that he wanted to stay in the room on the other end of the hall with his male cousins.

Clara looked out the center window. It was starting to get dark outside. The beach was covered in snow and contrasted starkly with the dark, stormy ocean. She opened the window a little and put her face down to take a deep inhale of the cool sea air. A few snowflakes flew into the room, melting before they could land anywhere. On the windowsill was an old black scallop shell that she had placed there ages ago. It was still there, right where she had left it. That reminded her to check on her rock collection under the bed—still there. Nothing ever changed at Amma's house. It was perfect.

The dinner bell was ringing, which meant everyone had to report to the kitchen to help prepare the meal. She bolted down the stairs. The last ones to the kitchen always got stuck with the crappy jobs, like peeling garlic or cutting onions. Clara was the first to arrive and got the best job of all: helping Amma measure out the spices.

The kitchen was old-fashioned, with a massive wrought iron wood-burning stove that hadn't been used in decades. Meal preparation was a boisterous affair of catching up and reminiscing about past Christmases and summers at the house. With so many different conversations going on, they almost had to shout to be heard, which just led to even louder shouting.

Once the measuring was done, Clara was assigned to set the table, which was another desirable job, especially if your ears needed a break. The dining room was a long and narrow room at the back of the house. The windows faced the woods—no need to waste an ocean view on a room so rarely used. It had a long wooden table that showed its age and the chairs were mismatched. The room's trim was painted a dark turquoise. Clara wasn't sure if that was something Amma had done, which would make sense, or was original to the house. The house had been in the family for generations. Maybe the love of turquoise was genetic. If so, Clara was thankful that the gene had skipped her.

When dinner was ready, there was a second ring of the bell. Various cousins carried in the food and everyone sat around the table. Once all were settled into their seats, Amma proposed a moment of silence for Aunt Clara, as was the custom. Then the conversations picked up where they had left off in the kitchen. Amma asked how Teddy and Adler were doing and about Thanksgiving with Grandma Lund. Uncle Ted and Aunt Clara used to come to Christmas at Amma's, but now Uncle Ted spends it with his mother. Adler had only come to Amma's house once in his lifetime and that was only for a week during the first summer after he was born. Clara gathered that it was just too painful for Uncle Ted to be around them without Aunt Clara.

Although Amma didn't get to see him much, she regularly wrote letters to Adler. Clara knew because she had once seen the large bin where Adler stashed all the letters—there must have been thousands of them. Amma liked to write Cole and Clara letters too. Clara loved getting them in the mail but, admittedly, she had fallen a little behind in writing back. Maybe that would be one of her New Year's resolutions, she thought.

After dinner, they gathered around the fireplace in the living room. The roasting of marshmallows was going to be saved for the next evening, Christmas Eve. Clara's mom took a seat at the old upright piano and took song requests. They sang and talked and laughed for hours. Eventually, cans of beer started to materialize and it seemed like it was going to be a longer night for some, including Cole, who was sneaking sips from the older cousins. Amma said her good nights, saying how happy she was that they were there, and headed up to bed. Clara followed shortly after to read in bed for a while.

She could see the near-full moon and its reflection on the ocean through the left-most of her room's three windows. When she was just about to switch off the lamp on the nightstand, she felt the hum and heard a faint knocking on her door, accompanied by a poor attempt at a whisper.

"It's me. Cole."

She opened the door. "What's up?"

"Hi, sorry, just wanted to say goodnight."

"Goodnight. Is the party still going on down there?"

"Not really. Darren and Margaret are still playing cards, but everyone else went to bed." Cole leaned toward her, lowering his voice to an actual whisper. "I don't think any of them have it." He smelled of beer. "I didn't feel any change and no one is acting different."

"Yeah, I agree. Guess it's still the fertility treatment then," said Clara.

"Anyway, sweet dreams, sis." Cole gave her a hug and turned down the hall to his room.

"Thanks. You, too." Clara shut the door and turned off the light. The moonlight coming through the windowpanes lit geometric sections of the comforter in cool white light. She climbed into bed, put her head on a bright spot on one of the pillows and fell asleep.

———

Clara woke up early the next morning. It was still dark out, but the sky behind the islands was beginning to glow. She knew Amma would be up and Clara was looking forward to some alone time with her, and some coffee. Downstairs, she found Amma sitting at the table in a small room off the kitchen that Amma called "the project room." She held a folded newspaper in one hand and a mug of coffee in the other.

"Good morning, Honeybee. Did you sleep okay?"

"Yeah, pretty well. You?"

"Yes, thank you. Although I don't need much sleep these days." Amma shrugged her shoulders and took a sip of coffee. "How are you, dear? You seem a little quiet—Cole too."

"I'm fine. Still not adjusting to life in rural PA, I guess. And Cole is always a little grumpy during basketball season. He's not very good at it."

"Well, just remember you can always talk to me. And don't worry too much about adjusting. You can't force that—just let it happen in your own time." Amma put her hand on Clara's shoulder. And you'll be going off to college in a couple years anyway. Penn, I suppose?"

"Maybe," said Clara.

"Have you heard about this terrible gale force wind gust in New York?" Amma held up the paper and pointed at it with her mug. "It blew in all the windows on one side of a public housing tower—eleven dead, three of them children." Shaking her head, Amma rested the paper back on the table and continued reading. "Just terrible. And the weathermen can't figure it out—there was no other damage in the whole city."

"That's awful. Can I grab some coffee?" Clara was not about to have a current events discussion without first getting her caffeine fix.

"Of course. Help yourself," said Amma. "99th and Lexington—that's not far from Adler and Teddy." Amma raised her voice slightly so Clara could hear her from the kitchen.

As Clara stirred the cream into her coffee, a terrible thought jumped into her head. "Yeah, that's just a few blocks from them. Which side?"

"Sorry?"

"The windows, which side of the building?"

"Hmm, I don't remember it saying." Amma moved her face closer to the paper. "Oh wait, here it is—south, the south side. Amma took off her reading glasses and looked up at Clara with furrowed brows. "Why, Honeybee?"

"No reason. Just curious." Clara walked back into the project room, trying her best to push the thought out of her mind. *It's just a coincidence.*

"Only in New York could the high-society Lunds live near a public housing project. What an amazing city." Amma unfolded the newspaper and a page of car ads fell onto her lap. "Have you and Cole started driving yet?"

"No. We haven't gotten around to applying for our learner's permits."

"Why not? You're seventeen. When does Pennsylvania allow permits?"

"Sixteen."

"So, what's the holdup?"

"I don't know. I guess we haven't needed it. We walk to school. And our parents certainly aren't pushing it on us."

"You really should do that. If you wait too long, you'll be in college and it will be harder to find time to learn."

"We've done a little. Like the short drives on the driveway here last summer. And I think Cole has done even more—he has a few friends with cars."

"Hope he's being careful with that. Here, dear, have a seat."

Amma pushed away some papers that were on the table so that there was a spot for Clara's coffee. The entire table was covered with handwritten notes and scribbles. A stack of books was on the floor next to Amma's chair.

"What's all this? The latest project?" Clara asked.

"Ah, yes. I am attempting to translate this book."

Amma reached down to the stack next to her and with both hands pulled up a large, old book and plopped it down on the table. The impact made a thud and blew a few pieces of paper off the edge that fluttered to the floor. The book was a familiar sight to Clara because it was usually displayed prominently on one of the bookshelves in the living room. It was bound in dark brown leather that was dried and cracking. On top of the leather, in tarnished metal, was an intricate design of unidentifiable animals with long, intertwined limbs, tails and tongues. Within the metal design were indentations, often where the animals' eyes would be, that seemed to have once held stones or gems.

"You're translating the family bible? Why?"

"Funnily enough, it's not really a bible. I don't know why we've been calling it that for generations," said Amma. "Look, it's written in runes." Amma opened to a random page and pointed. Clara gave her a puzzled look. "Runes, like old Scandinavian writing . . . Old Norse, like what they spoke in Viking times."

"I thought we were Irish." Clara leaned in to get a better look at the open pages. The writing was an odd stick-figure-like pattern and there were elaborate, colorful drawings at the corners and margins of the pages.

"Yes, me too," said Amma. "From what I've been able to translate so far, it's a history of a group of men who are protecting a magic power."

Clara's face felt flush at the words "magic power." Could it be a coincidence that there has been a book about a supernatural power in her family for generations and then she, Cole and Adler end up with a power?

"What kind of power?" Clara tried to sound casual.

"It's hard to say. So far there is some telekinesis and shape-shifting. Unfortunately, it seems like we only have the third volume in a series, so I don't have a lot of background." Amma picked up a few pages of notes from the table and stacked them in a certain order. "Also, I'm not translating exactly from the beginning to end. It's been a really tedious process. I have to look up each rune letter to translate it into our alphabet, which leads to a less-than-perfect word in Old Norse, which I then have to translate into English." Amma continued to gather and stack pieces of paper as she spoke. "It can be quite painful, so I skip around to parts of the book that look interesting, like ones with pictures."

"Any guess how old it is?" asked Clara.

"Well, I'm not sure but there are references to Vikings, so probably somewhere in the ninth to twelfth centuries."

"Wow, that's old."

"Stop making fun of your grandmother's age," said Clara's dad as he walked into the kitchen.

"Oh, hush," said Amma.

"Happy Christmas Eve, ladies," Mr. Lund said from the coffee machine.

Clara wanted to know everything about the book and the power in it, but she didn't know how to get it all out of Amma without drawing suspicion. She had to talk to Cole about what to do.

"Well, we should probably go be social," said Amma, easing her way up out of her chair.

"Ugh, with that guy? Do we have to?" Clara had raised her voice loudly enough to be heard by her dad over by the coffee pot. Amma put her arm around Clara's shoulders and they giggled their way into the kitchen.

V

Gudrid's Freya ceremony attracted five prominent suitors, most of whom were attended by their retinues. The harbor teemed with large ships and the island bustled with foreign visitors. Thoralf was given the responsibility of formally welcoming the men and to see to their needs and comfort while on the island. The villagers offered up rooms in their homes and set up tents in the nearby pastures to accommodate the overflow. The suitors themselves were given lodging at the modest homesteads of the larger landowners. The island was abuzz with excitement.

On the morning before the ceremony, word spread throughout the island that a mysterious sixth suitor had arrived, and the Dímuners' excitement grew.

That afternoon, the ceremony took place on the grassy common in the village not far from the harbor. The six suitors lined up in a row facing the platform that had been constructed for the occasion. Each suitor held in both hands his gift for the maiden, as was directed by custom. The Dímuners, the suitors' retinues and spectators from other Faroe Islands gathered around, most facing the backs of the suitors so that they could have the best view of the platform. The crowd was boisterous, cheering and singing songs as they waited for the ceremony to begin.

The first suitor was the local favorite, Thurandur Thorbeornson. There was much cheering from the crowd when he first took his place among the other suitors. Thurandur was strong and handsome. He wore the traditional Faroese garb of woolen trousers and a tunic with a red and white striped cape.

Two of the other suitors were powerful Viking chieftains. One was from Denmark and the other from Norway. Since their arrival on Stóra Dímun, they had done nothing but fight each other until their respective retainers pulled them apart. The Viking suitors had to be kept at opposite ends of the line and yet they still cursed and spat at each other from a distance.

There was an Irish suitor in a kilt and a Caliph suitor all the way from the warm sea. The Caliph wore a long robe of bright yellow silk and an unusual head dressing. His skin was dark and he was the favorite of the small children of the island.

No one could determine from where came the mysterious sixth suitor. He was tall, slender and pale and, like the Irishman and the Caliph, he did not speak the Norse language. He did not bring men or a ship, as far as anyone could tell, and his style of dress could not be identified. He wore a thick hooded tunic and matching trousers of vibrant blue fabric the likes of which had never been seen before on the island. Painted on parts of the fabric were white symbols unfamiliar to the Dímuners. Curiously, his feet were bare, which was presumed to be a tradition of his people for solemn occasions, as it was for some tribes in the Orkney Islands. Based on the color of his clothing, blue being the color of royalty in those days, it was agreed that he was a prince from some kingdom in the great continent to the southeast. He was referred to as the Blue Prince among the spectators, or the Barefoot Prince in private conversation.

SIXTEEN

ole woke up to a light knocking on the door. His cousins were already out of bed, except for Darren, who was snoring loudly in the lower berth of the bunk across the room. The thin walls of the house provided little defense against the hum, so he knew it was Clara knocking. Climbing down from his bed, he thought how particularly unpleasant the hum was when hungover. He opened the door a crack.

"Hey."

"Good morning," said Clara.

"What's up?" Cole saw from her wide, darting eyes that something big was on her mind. Her mouth was tight in a losing effort to hide a smile. She was almost bouncing.

"Can you come out here for a sec?" Cole looked down and remembered he was just in boxers. Shrugging, he opened the door wider and walked out into the hallway—everyone in the house was family, so no need for modesty.

"What's going on? You okay?"

"Yes. Fine. Good. Listen. Amma has a book." She turned back to scan the hallway, looking worried someone might overhear.

"Um, yeah. She has lots of books."

"No, I mean, the family bible. It's . . . not actually a bible."

"Okay, what is it then?" *Let's get to the point.*

"It's about a power."

"Wait, like our power?" he asked. Cole wondered if maybe he was still drunk.

"Shhh. Could you be quiet?"

"Sorry," he tried again. "Like our power?"

"I don't know. Maybe. She's only translated parts of it. I don't know how to get more info without sounding suspicious."

"So, you think if you ask Amma about a book she's translating that involves a power, she'll think you have a power?"

"Yeah, I guess."

"Good thing it's not really a bible, or she might think you're Jesus."

"Okay, smartass. So, what's your brilliant idea? Just bombard her with questions and then just say we have an unquenchable thirst for knowledge?"

"We should just tell her."

"What do you mean 'tell her'?"

"Just tell her. About the power and the stuff we can do."

"Are you crazy? She will freak out." Clara was almost yelling. Cole didn't understand why he was the only one who had to keep his voice down.

"Will she? I don't think so. She's into crystals and yoga and Buddha stuff. I think she'll be cool about it. Cooler than anyone else."

"I mean . . . I guess. If we wanted to tell anyone, it would be Amma." Clara furrowed her brows and froze in place. Her eyes looked through Cole, locked on the wall behind him.

He waved his hand in front of her face. "Earth to Clara. Wouldn't it be nice to tell someone anyway? And maybe the book *is* about our power and has some answers."

"Or maybe it's some fantasy novel that Amma's great-great-grandfather found at a flea market." Clara waved her hand dismissively.

"Maybe. But how will we know?"

"I need to think it over." Clara started pacing the hall.

"Okay, but don't ruin Christmas by being all pissy about it. We should just tell her and learn about the book and have a good time. It's what Jesus would have wanted."

"Shut up. Fine. I'll try to be in a good mood, but don't tell her anything until I've thought it through."

"Okay." He was looking forward to the day and wasn't going to let Miss Negative Nancy or his hangover ruin it.

Amma liked to save getting the Christmas tree for the day before Christmas so that the family could do it together. They would spend the whole day decorating the tree and the house, and baking cookies and pies and singing carols. This year there was the added bonus of a mystery book, potentially about their super-duper ultra-power. Cole wondered if Amma had a thesaurus. He really needed to come up with a cooler name for the hum and a thesaurus might help. That seemed like something Amma would have lying around somewhere.

Clara kept her promise to be in a good mood. She was downright cheerful at times, which was refreshing. She even volunteered to go into town with some of the other cousins to buy the tree. When the tree-collecting mission returned, triumphantly carrying their prize into the living room on their shoulders, Darren was making fun of Clara for not wanting to drive, even just down the driveway. Cole was relieved to see she was taking it in stride.

"Why do I need to learn how to drive? There's nowhere to go in Lehighton," she said, pushing the tree off her shoulder so that Darren and the other cousins staggered to the side before regaining their footing.

"Cole, are you going to end up chauffeuring Clara around like she's a New York Lund?" said a voice from the other side of the tree.

"Cole, my good lad, do drive Adler and me to the bowling alley. Chop chop," said Margaret from the couch in a terrible British accent.

"Hey, watch it," called Cole's dad from the kitchen.

"So, does anyone know what the deal is with Adler? Why doesn't he ever come here?" asked Darren.

"It's just too sad for them to be here without Clara," said Cole's mother.

"Adler doesn't seem sad. He seems angry," said Margaret. "And what about? I know it's sad, but what's he so mad about? Who is he angry at?"

Cole saw his mother and Amma exchange nervous looks. He was used to that generation being cagey whenever anyone started poking around Adler's birth story.

"Okay, enough of that," said Amma. "Get the tree up."

Cole and Clara were tasked with stringing the lights. Clara handed him the wheel of lights and he plugged them in. The room glowed with bright white light and the shadows of the branches danced around on the walls. He could feel the electric warmth coming off the luminous wheel. He handed it out to Clara and she began stringing the lights on a lower bough, walking around the tree, unwinding the wheel with one hand and positioning the string of lights with the other. They strung them around in loops. About halfway to the top, Cole heard a "psst." Through a space between the branches, he saw Clara peeking at him, the Christmas lights shimmering in her eyes.

"Psst."

"Yeah, I see you. What?"

"Let's tell her." Clara's barely restrained excitement reminded Cole of someone way too excited for the arrival of the guest of honor at a surprise party.

"Okay." Cole tried to match her enthusiasm. "When?"

"Tonight, after everyone's in bed."

"It's Christmas Eve."

"So what? Worried about getting on Santa's naughty list?"

"No. It just feels wrong. Fine, whatever."

"There's no reason to wait and Amma will be up."

"I already said fine."

"Honeybee, don't forget to crisscross in the opposite direction on the way back down," said Amma as she walked by.

"I know, I know," said Clara.

⁓

Later that evening, after dinner, the roasting of marshmallows and the singing of what seemed like every Christmas carol ever written, everyone started to say their goodnights and head up to their rooms. Clara snuck up behind Cole while he was washing his ice cream bowl and whispered that he should meet her in the hallway at eleven o'clock. He looked at his watch to see it was only ten.

"What am I supposed to do for an hour?"

"I dunno, read? Sing more carols?" she said with a laugh.

"Can't we just talk to her now?"

"No. We need everyone to be asleep. The walls are too thin here."

"How will we know everyone will be asleep in an hour?"

"Ugh, we don't. But some will be. You're so annoying. See you at eleven." Clara left the kitchen in a huff.

After a few rousing games of Solitaire, Cole tiptoed upstairs at eleven on the dot and met a jittery Clara in the third-floor hallway. She grabbed Cole's hand and held it as they walked down to Amma's room on the second floor. Cole knocked gently and stepped back as if he had just lit the fuse of a firework. Clara cringed and squeezed his hand.

"Oh, hello dears. Everything okay?" She squinted at them as she put on her glasses. She was wearing a deep purple nightgown with mother-of-pearl buttons. Cole noted absently that the second one down was missing.

"Everything's fine. We just wanted to talk to you about something," said Cole.

"I knew something was up with you two. Come in, come in."

Amma put her arms around them and led them into the room. It was basically the same as Clara's room just above except that the ceiling didn't slant and there were two square windows instead of Clara's three. Her bedframe was white-painted wrought iron and the springs below creaked when they climbed onto the green and white quilt. Amma put her legs under the covers and moved her knitting to the nightstand. Clara and Cole sat at the end of the bed, cross-legged. Cole felt like a little kid again, about to listen to one of Amma's stories. It was great. Then he remembered that *she* was going to listen to *their* story, and he got a little bit nervous.

"So . . . talk to me," said Amma.

Cole assumed Clara had some excessively conservative plan on how to present this to Amma. He looked over at her. She looked paler than usual and her eyelids looked dark and heavy. He gave her what he hoped was an encouraging look, a slight nod with raised eyebrows, and she quietly cleared her throat and sat up straight.

"So, um, we want to learn more about the family bible." Clara's voice cracked a little as she spoke.

"Cut the crap. What's going on?" Amma looked at Cole for an answer.

"We have a power," Cole blurted out.

"And we want to know if it's the same power as in the book." After she spoke, Clara immediately buried her face in the palms of her hands as if she just couldn't bear to see what was to come next.

"A power? What do you mean? What sort of power?" Amma spoke calmly as she repositioned the pillow behind her back. Cole was relieved—though not surprised—that Amma was taking it in stride.

"Well, it's like a buzz or a hum that we feel or hear . . . it lets us do stuff." Clara was mumbling though her hands.

"Honeybee, stop that. You can talk to me."

"We call it . . . the Droning," said Cole. He moved his hands like a magician. It was awesome.

"No, we don—" Clara paused. "Actually, that's not bad."

"Thanks. I've been working on it." Cole was pretty proud of himself and didn't feel the need to reveal his secret weapon: Amma's dusty thesaurus.

"But we don't call it anything," said Clara to Amma.

"Well, this is exciting. So, what can you do with it?"

And just like that, Amma believed them. Cole had known she would. She was like him in how he always believed there was magic in the world, even after the whole Santa thing was such a huge letdown.

"Well, I can read Spanish," said Clara.

"I would hope so, dear. You've been taking it since you were ten."

"No, I mean any word. If I concentrate, the letters move around and change into English."

"Interesting. And you, Cole?"

"I mostly use it for sports."

"That's no surprise, dear. Can you show me something?"

Cole looked around the room. "Here, hand me that button." Cole pointed to a circle of mother of pearl by the lamp on the nightstand.

Amma picked it up and leaned forward to hand it to him. He looked around the room and spotted a tarnished brass candlestick sitting on a windowsill. He pointed to it and closed his eyes to concentrate on the hum and the button and the candlestick and the hum and the button and the candlestick. He opened his eyes and tossed the button across the room. It landed perfectly into the little cup at the top where a candle would go, making a dull clink-clunk before coming to rest at the bottom.

"Wow," said Amma. "I thought you said he was bad at basketball, Honeybee."

"Hey," said Cole, offended. "I never have the ball long enough to use the power. But I'm great at free throws. But only when Clara bothers to come to games. It only works when we're together."

"Oh, and I can run," Clara added.

"Like, 'faster than a speeding bullet'?" asked Amma, making quotes with her hands.

"No, just, like, finish a run . . . at a normal speed." Clara lowered her head mid-sentence, and Cole figured she had realized how pathetic that sounded.

"I guess that's something, Honeybee. Good for you." Amma gave Clara an encouraging smile. "This is all quite amazing. Thank you for confiding in me."

"We can probably do more things too, but we're trying to be careful," said Clara.

"You mean boring," said Cole.

"So, what's next?" Amma wrung her hands together in excitement.

"Well, we were thinking that, since the bible has been in the family for a long time and it's about a power, maybe it's the same power," said Clara.

"That's a good thought. It would be quite a coincidence otherwise."

"Can you tell us a little more about what's in the bible?" asked Clara.

"Well, first, we should probably stop calling it the bible. Second, we should go down to the project room."

In the project room, Cole and Clara took seats at the paper-strewn table and Amma shut the door behind them. She rustled through the pages of handwritten notes, putting them into an organized pile. Sitting down, she put the book-formerly-known-as-the-family-bible on the table next to the stack of papers. She closed her eyes for a moment, took a deep breath and cracked her knuckles by weaving the fingers of both hands together and turning her hands palm out.

"Okay. Let's see. Where to begin?" she said. "So, Cole, as I told Clara earlier, the book is written in runes, in Old Norse, and I haven't really done a great job translating from the beginning. I skipped around a lot because some sections are really boring and not worth the effort. I also wasn't taking the translating that seriously because I thought it was just some mythical Icelandic saga that was just for fun."

"Which it still might be," said Clara.

"Quite true, dear." Amma tapped the stack of papers down on the table to straighten them and then started flipping through from the top. "The story is about a group of men who call themselves The Order of the United Power. 'United' might actually be 'consolidated.' The translation isn't that precise, at least not the way I do it. Since this is the third in a set of books, it jumps right in without any background. The book begins by chronicling the Order's travels around Norway looking for pilgrimage sites. Apparently, the power is stronger in certain places."

"Why is the family bible about Norway? I thought we were Irish," said Cole.

"That's what I said!" Clara's hand shot up to cover her mouth. "Sorry, too loud."

"I thought that too, dears. So far, the book takes place only in Norway and Iceland—no mention of Ireland. So, moving on . . ." Amma flipped through the stack of notes and pushed her reading glasses higher on her nose with her index finger. "The Order has a leader, or 'chieftain,' and then another man who has the power, who is never named. He's just called the 'Vessel.' I don't really get why the leader doesn't have the power—it must be some sort of checks and balances thing."

As Amma talked, Cole shifted uncomfortably in the wicker chair. He was really tired. This was interesting and all, but he wondered if maybe they could pick it up in the morning.

"Cole, honey, are you okay?" asked Amma.

"He's fine," said Clara. "Go on."

"So, the beginning of the book is basically just the Order sailing around looking for special places. The leader at that time was called Thorir the Explorer, for obvious reasons. The book describes—in excruciating detail—every single darn fjord in Norway, so I stopped and skipped ahead to a section with pictures."

Amma licked her finger and leafed through her notes. "Boring, boring, boring," she said as she turned each page. "Oh, this part was sort of interesting." She adjusted her glasses again. "This is when the leader was Thorgerd the Grey. There was a great battle with the Order's nemeses, two sister Viking chieftainesses—that's a hard word to say—and their army. The battle was a draw, but the Vessel was wounded and needed to be replaced. There is an elaborate ceremony to ordain someone as the new Vessel. I think the new Vessel gets castrated first. It says something like 'remove the orbs of Frey'—Frey being the male fertility god. And then the new Vessel kills the old Vessel, which apparently transfers the power."

"Wait, what? Killing someone with the power transfers the power?" asked Clara, alarmed. "If this is the same as our power, we really need to keep it a secret." She glared at Cole.

"Personally, I want to know more about why they are castrated," said Cole.

"Uh huh." Amma was concentrating on her notes, not Cole. "Much later in the book there's another battle with the Viking sisters and the ladies burn down the Order's headquarters, called Twin Halls. Girl Power! Am I right?" Amma looked up at Clara, who just shrugged. "But the Order's leader and the Vessel escaped with a few other followers and they fled to Iceland and built an exact replica of Twin Halls. Anyway, that's much later, I should try to stay in sequence."

Cole struggled to keep his eyes open and wondered how Clara was still so awake. Also, how can she go from never wanting to talk about the power to staying up all night talking about something that is maybe—just maybe—related to it?

"Oh, oh! This! Yes, this will help us figure it out." Amma excitedly opened to a section of her notes. "Way back when Ulf the Wise was the leader, he had his Vessel create—or conjure, I guess—a place where each new Vessel could go to learn how to use the power. From what I can tell, it's like a room in the Vessel's mind, like a dream, where the power is stronger and he can train himself to use it. It's called the 'temja rum' or 'training room.'" Amma opened the book and started flipping through the delicate pages.

After finding what she was looking for, Amma turned the book to face Cole and Clara. "Look. See that?" She pointed to a drawing of what at first looked like a big flattened out "Y." When Cole focused, it revealed itself as a corner and ceiling of a room, the lines of the "Y" being the edges where the walls met. About midway up, there were symbols on both walls close to the corner. The symbol on the left wall was a slanted, upside-down "V," like the first two lines when writing a capital "N." The symbol on the right looked like an "M" with a squished "X" in the middle, like two little pennant flags with their points touching.

"See that, kids? That's how the Vessel gets to the training room. Those runes spell 'um,' which means 'in.' We can try that and if you get in, we'll know it's the same power."

Amma looked around the project room for a suitable corner. She pointed to the one behind Cole and motioned for them to get up and move the table and chairs back. She grabbed a pencil from the table, looked at the point, then put it back down.

"Ah, I know." Amma got up to go to the kitchen. Clara and Cole exchanged puzzled looks.

"Don't get your hopes up, Clara. This all sounds too crazy." Cole yawned as he spoke.

"I know, I know. But what if?"

Amma returned with a baggie of thick sidewalk chalk, which reminded Cole of coloring beach rocks when they were little. He used to throw his finished rocks as far as he could into the ocean and imagine the lobsters and starfish at the bottom admiring his artwork. Clara used to keep her finished rocks in a cloth-lined box like they were delicate eggs. *I bet she still has that box full of rocks hiding somewhere in her room*, thought Cole.

Amma pulled out a purple piece of chalk and held it above her head like the Statue of Liberty's torch. "I don't want to permanently mark up the walls—your great-grandfather painted them. This will clean right off." She walked over to the corner and carefully drew the runes on the walls near the corner just above her head. The sound of the chalk on the wall sent a shiver up Cole's spine. Amma stepped back excitedly with her arms out to her sides. Nothing happened.

"Now what?" asked Clara.

"Hmm, I don't know." Amma walked back behind the table to look through her notes. "It just says to write the runes and enter the training room."

"Enter? Like how?" asked Cole.

"It doesn't specify. Just try a few things," said Amma.

Clara approached the corner cautiously. She raised her hands and started pressing the walls in various directions and angles. She tried pressing one wall with both hands, as if it would rotate around like a revolving door. She tried knocking. First once, then three times. She even said "open sesame," but nothing happened.

Then she just walked into the corner face first. Her forehead bumped the corner with a thud. Cole giggled and she told him to "shut it," her voice muffled into the corner. Amma continued to flip through pages looking for clues while Clara backed away rubbing her forehead. The three of them then sat in silent thought for a few minutes, all facing the corner of disappointment.

"Maybe we need to try to open it with the hum—I mean, the droning," said Cole.

Clara agreed, so for a few minutes they tried using the power to open the room. It didn't work.

"I really need to go to bed." Cole looked at his watch. It was Christmas already.

"What if it's like the train station in *Harry Potter*?" said Clara. Cole and Amma looked at her blankly. "You know. The track they get to by running into the wall, full speed. Try it." She was looking at Cole.

"Who, me?" he asked.

"Yeah."

"Why?"

"Aren't you this tough jock? You don't want me to get hurt, do you?"

"No, but it's your idea." He could hear it in his own voice that he had already given up. He backed up to ready himself to run at the corner. *Just do this and then you can sleep.*

"Now remember, you can't hesitate or slow down at all. Just go right at it like it's not there," said Clara.

"Oh, I don't know. Be careful, Cole," said Amma.

Cole took a deep breath, closed his eyes, lowered his head, and ran full speed at the corner. He hit it hard and bounced back, falling down into a seated position on the floor. The impact and Cole's pained groan were loud. The force on the walls shook a nearby hutch and a plate fell forward and smashed on the tile floor. Cole slumped forward, holding his head in both hands.

"Oh, and Adler can break picture frames," Clara said to Amma.

"Adler has it too?" Amma frowned, looking somewhat concerned. "Well, maybe that's a good thing. Maybe it will give him some direction."

"Is someone down there?" Mrs. Lund's voice echoed down the living room stairwell. Cole and Clara froze and looked at Amma in a hushed panic. Amma put a finger over her mouth.

"Yes, honey. Just me," called Amma.

"Everything okay? I heard a crash."

"Yes, yes. Everything's fine. I just dropped one of my books. These hands aren't what they used to be."

"Okay, try to get some sleep, Ma. It's a big day tomorrow."

"I will, honey. Sweet dreams."

"You too."

They waited a few minutes in silence.

"We better wrap things up for the night," whispered Amma.

"Yeah, I guess." Clara was not hiding her disappointment.

"I'm okay, by the way. Thanks for asking." Cole was still hunched over on the floor. His head hurt, but mostly he was exhausted.

"Oh, yes, sorry dear. How is that hard head of yours?" Amma walked over and tousled his hair.

"You two head up to bed. I'm going to look through my notes a little more," said Amma as she hugged them.

Clara went over to the fireplace. Turning around, Cole saw she was holding a charred piece of kindling in her hand.

"What's that for?" whispered Cole.

"I want to try one more thing. Let's go to my room."

"Oh, c'mon. I'm way too tired. Can we please do it tomorrow?" Cole knew he sounded whiney, but he didn't have the energy to care.

"It will just take a second. I promise."

After creaking their way up to the third floor, Clara shut her bedroom door behind them and looked around. Because of the slanting roof, there was only one corner that was tall enough for them to stand in. She walked over to it and used the charred end of the kindling to write the "in" runes.

"They didn't have purple sidewalk chalk in the Viking Age. Let's just try this. One more time," said Clara.

"Fine, but I'm not running into it." Cole walked over to the corner and started pushing and knocking around quickly, going through the motions so it could all be over for the night. He walked into it forward, then walked into it backward. When nothing happened, he rested his back against the corner.

"Can we be done? It's not working. It's just a fantasy book."

"Just wait a sec—I'm thinking. Did we try everything we did downstairs?" asked Clara.

Cole, still leaning his back against the corner, sighed and closed his eyes. He could almost fall asleep standing there, he thought. With his eyes still closed, he leaned his head back into the corner. Then he felt something cold on the back of his head. It was very cold, like ice water. It flowed through his hair and chilled his scalp. His head kept slowly leaning back and the cold waterline moved its way forward on his scalp, to the top of his ears and then to the top of his forehead. As his head went back, his body felt stiff, as if it were a board swinging upward with a hinge at his head. He couldn't open his eyes, he couldn't call out, he couldn't move and he couldn't tell which way was up or down.

The frigid water flooded his ears with a swish and washed over his closed eyes. Then it reached the top of his nose and filled his nostrils. It was extremely painful, like when he would forget to hold his nose when jumping off Amma's catboat into the icy Maine ocean water. The waterline was moving ever closer to his mouth and he didn't know what to do. He was about to drown. He took a deep breath just before the waterline moved across his lips, down his chin and down his neck. What was he going to do? He couldn't hold his breath forever. Was he going to drown to death in the corner of Clara's bedroom? How would she explain that? He was panicking and slowly started to let out some air. Drowning is the worst way to die, he thought, because you are the one who takes the breath that kills you. It's cruel to make your body sabotage itself like that. He started to feel faint. His mind wandered. He thought about his short life, his parents, Clara. He thought about Amma and how sad she would be, how the house would never be the same for them. He thought about Asa and other friends back home. He thought about Molly at the Weissport Dunkin' Donuts, and her tight sweaters. He wondered why he had never asked her for her phone number.

It was time. He couldn't hold his breath anymore. He let out what little air was left in his lungs and took a shallow breath. The cold water swelled into his mouth and down his windpipe. He gagged and coughed. And coughed again. And then he realized that the coughing was working to clear his lungs, or maybe he was breathing the water, he wasn't sure. All he knew was that he wasn't dead. He remembered that he had eyes and tried to open them. It worked.

He was in a dimly lit room that was cold and damp. It was a small room, maybe fifteen by fifteen feet. The windowless walls were made of stacked stones, except for the one behind him, which was just a solid sheet of grey rock. To his left was a small fireplace, with a small fire burning, the room's only source of light. A loud, rolling, rumbling sound seemed to come from all directions just outside the walls, as though a subway train was circling the room. The sound built upon itself, louder and louder, just to the point when Cole considered covering his ears, but then it faded off, to slowly begin its build again.

In the dim, flickering orange firelight, he made out that the ceiling was made of log beams and dark thatch that glistened in their dampness. In front of him was a rectangular wooden table with long benches on either side. On the tabletop was a stack of smooth, flat river stones that reminded him of the beach in Lehighton. They were the perfect shape for skipping. There were four, stacked largest to smallest and all were a dark grey except for the smallest, top-most one, which was white.

There was a wooden door in the wall across from him. He walked over to investigate. The door had elaborate metal hinges, slightly tarnished, that were half the width of the door. The hinges were in the shape of slender, unidentifiable animals, maybe lions, like on old English flags in movies. He tried to think of where he had seen something like that before, and then it hit him: the cover of the family bible. The door didn't have any knob or lock. He tried to open it, pushing at first, then pulling with what little grip his fingertips found in the seams between planks, but it didn't budge. He tried to peek out through cracks around the doorframe, but it was shut up tight. Looking back across the room, he saw that the same "in" runes were carved into the walls in the corner from which he had arrived.

Sitting down on one of the benches, he leaned his elbows on the table and propped his chin on his palms. Then it occurred to him that he wasn't tired anymore. He was wide awake and he felt the hum, even with no Clara in sight. Of course, since the training room was just a figment of his mind, Clara was technically right next to him, back where his corner-leaning body was, but there was something different about the hum in the room. It was stronger and somehow felt cleaner. It was a comforting feeling, rather than the nervous energy the hum usually produced.

"So now what?" he asked out loud.

He looked at the stack of stones. There must be some training lesson to be learned with them, he thought. But what was he supposed to do? He figured he was supposed to knock down the stack, so he began to focus on the hum while looking at the stack of stones. *Hum, stones, hum, stones, hum.* He visualized the stack knocking over. *Hum, stones, hum, stones*—then it happened. The stones fell over to the side and the top two rolled off the table onto the floor. He could barely hear them hit the floor over the rumbling from outside. Even though he had used the hum countless times in games, it still gave Cole a jolt of excitement. Seeing it in action, moving inanimate objects, without the pretext of a good kick or skilled free throw, was even more exhilarating. It was all hum. He moved those stones with his mind—just his frickin mind. *Well, I guess that's it*, he thought. He gave his hands a proud dusting off, one against the other, signifying—to his audience of no one—a task expertly completed, and stood up.

He walked over to the corner with the runes, leaned his back against the corner and tilted his head. This time the water was warm, almost hot. It burned a little as it worked its way down his head and hurt like hell when it filled his nostrils. While he knew from the way in that he probably wouldn't drown, it was still hard to take that breath of hot water. Like before, he coughed and gagged as the water filled his lungs until, once again, he was breathing the warm water like it was air. When he opened his eyes, he was back in Clara's room. A wave of exhaustion came over him. He leaned forward, putting his hands on his knees for support.

"I really need to go to bed," he said, with some effort.

"Okay, okay, thanks for giving it another try. Maybe we can try some more tomorrow," said Clara.

With that, Cole realized that she didn't know anything had happened. All she must have seen was him leaning his head back and then coughing. No time had passed at all. He considered for a moment: *If I tell her now, I'll have to explain the whole thing in detail and, likely, have to wait around for her to try it too, or, if I wait until the morning to tell her, I'll finally get to go to sleep, but it would be an asshole move to make her wait when her heart is so set on it.*

"Yeah, let's get some sleep." Cole stood up and walked toward her door. She opened the door for him.

"Sweet dreams and Merry Christmas," she whispered as he walked into the hall.

"Thanks, you too," Cole whispered back from halfway to his room. "Oh, and Clara . . ."

"Yeah?"

"It worked!" he said with a huge grin.

Clara's jaw dropped and she started to speak, but Cole raised his finger to his mouth as he opened the door to the male cousins' bedroom. As he walked into the dark, snore-filled room, he looked back at her. She was standing in her doorway giving him the finger.

SEVENTEEN

Sure, it felt good. And it did dim the feeling for a little bit. But what good does that do in the grand scheme of things, Mother? A few dozen of them cut by the windows blowing in? It's a pittance. A drop in the bucket. It's not big enough. I need a plan. Something bigger. Something on a grand scale. I will find it, Mother. Don't you worry. I will find it and I will get them.

EIGHTEEN

Clara's first waking thought wasn't about coffee or about how little she had slept; it was about the training room and Cole's whispered "it worked" that had echoed in her ears for hours until she had finally fallen asleep. She sat straight up in bed and looked at the corner where it happened. The ashy runes were still there—it wasn't a dream. For the first time in recent memory, waking up on Christmas morning felt like it was supposed to feel, with the excitement of a little kid, knowing that there were piles of toys from Santa downstairs.

This Christmas morning wouldn't have any toys waiting for her under the tree, but there would be the training room: answers, meaning, connections. Their power wasn't just some freaky medical anomaly from the fertility treatment. It was old and real and had a story and could be trained. That is, unless Cole was just messing with her, but that wasn't really his style. He knew she would probably kill him if he had lied to her about something that serious—not that he took it as seriously as she would like. She got out of bed, put on a flannel robe, glanced back at the rune corner and went downstairs.

Downstairs, most of the family was already in the kitchen and a chorus of "Merry Christmas" filled the room as she entered. To Clara's disappointment, there was a crowd waiting for the coffee maker to finish brewing the next batch. Cole sat at the table with a cup of orange juice. He still didn't like caffeine. *How on earth can he survive a morning without any coffee*, she wondered.

She took the seat across from him. Their cousins were talking about the Christmas when little Cole slipped down the stairs in his footie pajamas and said the F-word, which he had then just recently learned. That story was always a crowd favorite. At the time, he was so worried he would be moved to the naughty list and not get any presents that he ran right back upstairs and got into bed so that he could start the morning over. Come to think of it, Clara couldn't think of a time that Cole had used that word since then.

"Good morning!" Cole looked up from his orange juice, a coy twinkle in his eyes.

"Morning." She glanced back at the coffee pot to check the status—it would still be a while.

"Sleep well?" he asked.

"Not really. Could I speak with you when you have a moment?" Clara was already losing her patience with his overly casual schtick.

"Yes," he replied without moving.

"Now?"

"Sure." Cole didn't move but looked up at her expectantly.

"In private!" *Get the hell up*, she thought.

"Oh, of course." Cole smirked and slowly rose from his chair. It was clear that he was enjoying driving her crazy.

As they walked out to the living room, Clara overheard Margaret saying, "Those two are weirdos."

Clara and Cole walked over to the far end of the living room, right by the windows facing the ocean.

"So, did it really work?"

"Yes. It was crazy. I drowned and was in a cold room and—"

"Shhh!" Clara cut him off as their parents came into the living room, each with a coffee in one hand and a plate with a chocolate croissant in the other. "Let's meet in my room after I get some coffee."

"Okay." Cole looked slightly disappointed that he couldn't get the whole story out. Clara didn't feel bad—he could have easily stayed up a few extra minutes last night to tell her instead of rushing off to get his beauty sleep.

They went back to the kitchen and when Clara's coffee was finally ready, she gave Cole a subtle nod. Once upstairs, Cole sat down on her bed and explained what had happened. Clara paced the room as she took it all in. When he was describing the stones on the table, something outside caught Clara's eye through the window. A couple of large bushy pine trees were moving slightly and large clumps of snow were falling off of their branches. She moved to the window to get a better look. The pine trees were close together at the bottom and the lower branches were shaking wildly like a large animal was trying to pass through them. It wasn't unusual to see a bear or moose in this part of Maine, but rare to have them wandering around out on Prouts Neck.

Suddenly a person burst through the branches. It was her father, fully decked out in winter hiking gear, including ski goggles. He had on his new snowshoes and was taking large, awkward duck-like steps across the field toward the beach. He stopped, dramatically shaded his goggled eyes, and pointed out to the islands as if he were a toddler playing explorer. Clara rolled her eyes and looked away. She was too embarrassed for him to keep watching.

"Sorry, I got distracted. How many stones were there?"

"Four, I think. All grey, except the top one."

"And nothing happened when you knocked them down?"

"No, should it?"

"I mean, I would think there'd be some indication when the training is over. There has to be more to it than knocking down a pile of rocks."

"Hm, I guess. I can't think of anything happening. Maybe if I go back in there will be something else." Cole stood up to go to the corner.

"Don't even! It's my turn." She pushed him back onto the bed.

"Okay. The drowning part really sucks, by the way."

As Clara slowly walked across the room, her heart pounded in her chest. She was aware of every step, every minuscule creak of the floorboards, every breath, every pulse beating in her fingertips. She walked into the corner, turned around, and leaned her back against the walls.

"Good luck," said Cole.

"Thanks." She shut her eyes and slowly tilted back her head.

When the back of her head hit where the corner would have been, she felt the icy water rush through her hair. Cole wasn't kidding that the water was cold. It moved down her head and face, as expected. She instinctively took a breath right before the waterline crossed her mouth. She considered holding her breath, but what was the point, she reasoned. She took in a deep breath of the frigid water and coughed uncontrollably for a few seconds before opening her eyes.

The room wasn't what she was expecting from Cole's description. For one, the walls of the room were made out of wood, not stone. There wasn't a rumbling sound outside, but instead the sound of a baby crying uncontrollably. The arrangement of the room was pretty similar though. There was a fireplace to the left, the only light, and a rectangular wooden table in the middle with four stones stacked as Cole had described. There was a door in the wall across from her, but the door was painted a dark green, like Starbucks green. She turned to confirm that the runes were on the corner behind her. They were there, but written in charcoal rather than carved into the wall, like in Cole's room.

She sat down at the table and tried to focus on the stones. It was hard to think with the sounds of the baby crying. She occasionally thought she heard an adult woman whimpering, which was creepy. She tried to tune it out.

It seemed to Clara that something should happen in the room when the training was completed. Like you get a point somewhere or at least an encouraging ding sound like on a game show. She concluded, therefore, that the task was more than just knocking down the stack of stones. It must be something more difficult, but what? Perhaps it had something to do with the white stone, she thought. Maybe the challenge is to knock down the white stone and not the others. It was worth a shot. She lowered her head, shut her eyes, and tried to focus on the hum and not the baby's wails.

Cole was right that the hum was stronger and felt cleaner somehow. Once she was tuned in on the hum, she looked up at the white stone and stared at it intensely. It wobbled a little. She squinted her eyes and clenched her teeth, trying to fuse her focus on the hum and the white stone. The top three stones toppled over. The white one rolled off the table and onto the dusty floor in front of the fireplace. She walked around the table, picked it up and stacked the stones back in order. She did that a few more times, sometimes knocking just the top two, another time the top three again, and even once she knocked down the whole stack. On maybe her eighth or ninth try, she managed to knock down just the white stone. She was pretty frustrated by then and the force of the hum sent the white stone flying right into the fire. It hit the smoldering wood with a sizzling thud.

When the white stone hit, she noticed a flicker out of the corner of her left eye and looked over. In the corner to the right of the corner she had arrived from, there were glowing, golden runes. They were different symbols from the "in" runes. On the left side, the symbol was an "X" with two lines connecting the top in a point. On the right side was an "R" except the round part of the top of the "R" was two lines making a point.

Clara wanted to go back to tell Cole what happened, but she was also excited to go on to the next level of the training. She figured she should use the hum to translate the new runes before she dove headfirst, literally, into the unknown. Concentrating on the hum and the two golden runes, the symbols turned into an "O" and an "R" and then changed into the word "out," with the "U" written across the corner. Clara rolled her eyes. *In and out—not very original, guys*, she thought. She then assumed the position with her back against the corner and headed out. When she was done coughing out the warm water, she opened her eyes to find Cole and her bedroom in front of her.

"Pretty cool, huh?" he asked. "It's crazy—all I see is you leaning back and then coughing."

Clara looked around the room, confused. She wasn't expecting to be back there. She expected another room with another training task. Turning back to look at the corner, she saw the same "in" runes.

"Everything okay?" asked Cole. "The drowning is the worst, right?"

"Yeah, yeah. I'm fine. I just . . . just wasn't expecting to be back yet."

Clara went on to explain her experience in *her* training room, how she thought she had completed the task and how the new runes showed up in the other corner. She detailed how her room was different from his.

"Maybe it will be a new task when you go back," offered Cole.

"That's a good point. Let me see." Clara walked back to the corner but when she leaned back her head, it just hit the wall with a muffled thump. Nothing happened. *That couldn't be it, could it?* she wondered.

"Maybe it needs to reset, like after a certain amount of time," said Cole. "Here, let me try."

Clara sat down on the bed while Cole walked over to the

corner. He backed into it and leaned his head back and then coughed a couple times.

"My room was the same as before. I stacked up the stones and knocked the white one into the fire . . . on the first try, thank you very much."

"Bravo."

"The gold letters showed up, like you said. Should I try to go back in?"

"Sure, knock yourself out."

He took a step forward then stepped back into place and leaned his head back. "Nothing," he said. "It must need some time."

"Uh-huh." Clara massaged her temples as she considered what to do next.

"Don't look so worried. This is exciting. There's a book about our power, and there's a way to train it. We're much better off than we were yesterday."

"I guess."

"You disagree?"

"No, you're right." Clara tried to heed Cole's encouraging words, but she couldn't help but be disappointed. The room and the stones were not enough; she needed more.

"We'll figure it out. Let's just take a break for now and try to enjoy Christmas." Cole gave her a pat on the back. "It's what Baby Jesus would want."

Clara just rolled her eyes and got up from the bed to go back downstairs. From the racket coming up the stairwell, it was apparent that the party had moved from around the coffee pot to around the fireplace in the living room. When they were almost to the bottom of the stairs, Cole pretended to fall down the stairs and yelled "Fuck!" The room exploded in laughter, except for Amma who just shook her head disapprovingly.

"Baby Jesus, my ass," said Clara under her breath.

Clara tried to have a nice Christmas. She mostly succeeded, but it was hard for her to stay in the moment. Her mind kept wandering back to the training room and the book. She speculated on what the next task might be, if there was a next task, and she wondered what other useful nuggets might be in the book. While cleaning up after dinner, she couldn't help whispering to Amma that they had gotten the training rooms to work and that they would tell her all about it later. Amma gave Clara a big smile and they agreed to meet in the project room after everyone went to bed.

When Clara told Cole about the plan to meet up with Amma later, he declined to participate.

"I've drowned four times in the past twenty-four hours. I need a break and a good night's sleep."

"You sure? It won't take that long."

"You can tell her without me and we'll catch up in the morning. Maybe try the rooms again," he said while walking up the stairs.

"Okay." Clara was reluctant to tell Amma without him there, but she couldn't bear to wait a whole night.

"Sweet dreams," he said from out of sight up the stairwell.

"Thanks. You too, and don't trip. Those stairs can be treacherous."

⌇

After impatiently waiting until the house grew still and quiet, Clara snuck down to the project room. She told Amma all about how they had managed to get into the rooms, the details of her experience and what she could remember from Cole's description. Amma took frantic handwritten notes as Clara spoke. She agreed with Clara that stone stack couldn't be the full extent of the training and that the rooms must need to reset somehow. She also wondered if maybe they had to do something out in the real world to get the rooms to reset. While Amma looked over her translation notes, Clara flipped through the book. With Cole two stories above, the hum wasn't available for her to translate any of it, but the pictures were interesting. She studied the picture of the corner and the "in" runes closely, but didn't see any clues about what should happen next.

"Hold on," said Amma. "Cole entered the room Christmas Eve night, right?"

"Yes, and?" replied Clara. From the tone of Amma's voice, Clara could tell she was onto something.

"And you did it the next morning?"

"Yes."

"Was it light out?"

"Yes. Why does that matter?"

"Well, my notes say it has to be at night . . . but let me check something." Amma reached out her hands for the book and Clara quickly passed it to her across the table. It was heavy. Amma flipped through a few pages, stopping to examine the bottom section of one page, looking back and forth between the book and her notes.

"Here . . . here, see these runes?" Amma pointed to a jumble of symbols in the book.

"Sure."

"This says 'after the moon,' which I translated, based on good authority, to mean 'at nighttime.' All the scholarly books say that's what it means. But maybe the Order is more literal, maybe they meant like actually after the moon, the full moon." Amma looked up from the pages and gave Clara a wide-eyed, hopeful look.

"Why would the moon have anything to do with this?"

"Honeybee, this is about a magical power. We have no clue what it has to do with. Why not the moon?" Amma stood up and left the project room, returning a few seconds later with her laptop. She opened it up and started typing. "Look, the internets say there's a full moon in two days. Maybe the room resets after that."

"I guess. It's a plausible theory." Clara wanted to believe, but it just seemed too far-fetched. *What next, will we need Mercury to be in retrograde?* she thought.

"Or maybe it resets overnight. Just keep trying it out," suggested Amma.

"Okay. Would it be possible for me to look at your notes and the book? I want to try to learn as much about the power as I can."

"Of course, dear. Help yourself to anything in here and when you're back home I can mail you my translations as I complete them," said Amma. "Oh, I guess you can just use the power to translate it yourself. In that case, I can Xerox a few pages at a time at the General Store and mail you the copies."

"That would be awesome." Clara stood up to give Amma a hug goodnight. "You're the best. Sweet dreams, Amma."

"You too, dear."

When Clara woke up the next morning, the first thing she thought about was trying the training room again. She turned over in bed and looked at the runes on the wall. The pink light from the rising sun cast disjointed geometric shadows around the room. So much had changed in the past few months. Her perception of the world and her place in it was completely different now. Now she had a power. Right over there, in the corner of her room, a room that never changed, she could go to an enchanted place in her mind, maybe in another dimension, and practice a superpower. There was actually magic in the world. Looking around at the glowing light, slowly changing from pink to orange, crisscrossing the room in dusty rays, she wondered how she could have ever doubted that.

There, in that already magical house, talking openly about the hum with Cole and Amma, connecting the dots to power's story, it was easy for Clara to get caught up in it all. Her initial fears and reservations—the *E.T.* worries—were still there, but now she felt more intrigued than panicked. Cole's question from months ago echoed in her head: *What do you want?*

Coffee.

Down in the kitchen, Cole sat at the table sipping his boring orange juice. When he saw her, he stood right up and cut off her beeline to the coffee pot. "Let's get it over with," he whispered. Clara didn't understand why he was being so grumpy—that was usually her job. Yes, the drowning part wasn't pleasant, she admitted, but it was worth it. She poured her coffee and they went up to her room where she told him about Amma's full moon theory, which he didn't doubt for a second. Clara marveled at his apparent inexhaustible supply of optimism, annoying as it was at times.

"Who should go first?" asked Clara.

"Doesn't matter to me. You can go if you want." Cole sat down on the edge of the bed, presuming her answer.

Clara's heart was racing again. Her skin felt hot and heavy. The thought of another disappointment, another thump on the back of her head, made her nauseous. She felt dizzy and her coffee mug was shaking to the point of almost spilling. She put it down on the nightstand and sat next to Cole on the bed.

"I can't do it. I'm too nervous. You go."

"Suit yourself."

Cole stood and walked to the corner like he walked up to the free throw line: slowly, confidently, projecting an awareness that what he was about to do mattered a great deal to the people watching. *Just go already*, thought Clara. He turned slowly, closed his eyes, leaned his head back, and then started coughing uncontrollably. Clara jumped to her feet and ran toward him.

"My turn. Move over." Grabbing his arm, she pulled his hunched, coughing body out of her way.

Clara took over Cole's spot in the corner and turned, quickly, but gracefully, to lean her back against the walls. She closed her eyes and braced for the frigid liquid about to permeate her hair and envelop her scalp. Slowly leaning back her head, its motion was stopped by a bump against the room-temperature walls. *Just give it a second*, she thought as she held in position. Then she heard something: a slight, barely perceptible change in Cole's coughing. The cough was changing into a laugh. She shot open her eyes to see Cole's stupid smiling face staring back at her.

"You asshole!" She ran at him and shoved his chest with both hands.

He stumbled backward, tripped over her open suitcase on the floor and fell on his backside, catching himself with his elbows, laughing all the way down. In her rage, Clara used the hum to swing open one of the small doors to a crawl space under the eaves and it whacked his shoulder and then clipped the side of his head.

"Ouch. Okay, okay, I'm sorry." He grabbed his shoulder and rolled on the floor away from the door. "Jeez, relax."

"That's not funny."

"It was a little. Admit it."

"No, it wasn't. This isn't a joke."

"Not everything has to be so serious. Lighten up." He rubbed the side of his head, still lying on the floor.

"You don't get it. This is important."

"You used to not even want to talk about it. Now it's *oh so important*?"

"Yes. The book changes things."

"How?"

"I don't know. I guess, I guess it makes it more real. Like there's a story to it. It has a history—rules, uses that we can learn. It has meaning. And with Adler having—"

"Right, of course," said Cole as he rolled his eyes.

"What?"

"Now that Adler has it, it's cool and worth your time, right?"

"No. But him having it helps. Before it was just some scary thing that only the two of us have. It's not just some elaborate hallucination we're having from all the coal in the Lehighton water supply. With Adler having it, we're not the only ones and, now with the book, we know it's been around for a long time, it has a story. The book gives it a certain intellectual element."

"Huh?"

"The book gives it parameters, rules, dimension. We can learn about it, study it, practice it, train in the rooms—hopefully."

"You're the only person who can make a superpower sound like homework." He looked up at her. "So, you're not worried about it anymore?"

"No, of course I'm worried about it. How can you not be? I have no idea what this will mean for our lives. Almost every scenario I can think of ends badly. Sorry to disappoint," she continued. "But you know I'm right. We get caught and our whole world changes: no parents, no home, no school, no friends." *Not that I have to worry about that last one.*

"Yeah, yeah. *E.T.*—I know."

"The safest bet is to never use it, but that's not going to happen, is it? It's too tempting. We just need to be extremely careful and use it sparingly. No sprinkler shenanigans. Stick to what we know and what we learn in the book—and the rooms, if we ever get back in."

"So now what? The rooms still aren't working." Cole pulled a silver whistle from his pocket and started tossing it from one hand to the other.

"I guess Amma's full moon thing is our only hope."

"It sounds like a good theory to me, but what do I know?"

"I wonder if we can each just go in once during the moon period or if the rooms close on certain days no matter what." The flying whistle caught Clara's eye. "Could you stop that? It's distracting."

"Oh, sure. Sorry." He put the whistle back in his pocket.

Suddenly, a new thought occurred to Clara. "We should see if Adler can get in now to see if it's based on certain days."

Cole let out a sigh. "Um, I don't think we should tell Adler."

"Tell him what?"

"About the book . . . and the rooms."

"What? We have to tell him. Why wouldn't we?"

"I'm just worried about his state of mind. The whole terrace thing still bugs me."

"Still? That was nothing. You know how he is—he'll say anything to get a reaction. And he thought he was dying."

"He called the people in Harlem rats."

"*And* pigeons. Pigeons aren't so bad."

"Um, yes they are. And then the hawk eating the pigeon thing. I'm telling you he has issues."

"We're not sure he did that."

"I'm sure. The freak made a biting face at me."

"A what?"

"Like this." Cole bared his teeth and clicked them together a few times like he was trying to take a bite of hot pizza without burning the roof of his mouth. "Like a total weirdo."

"Oh, please. You're being paranoid. We were eating dinner. He probably had a carrot in his mouth or something." Clara imagined Gran's Thanksgiving spread as she spoke: no carrots. "Anyway, he's family and the only other person with the power."

"Look, can we please just wait to tell him? See what we find out in the rooms."

"If we ever get in again," said Clara. She wanted to stay positive, but it was hard work.

"And if he's acting normal the next time we see him, we can reconsider. Please? It's important to me."

Clara thought on those three words. They were heavy with deeper meaning: I'm your brother, your only sibling, I don't ask you for much, you rarely do anything for me, but this—this one thing—is important to me, you owe me at least this. *But what about me?* thought Clara. *Aren't I owed something? For being left alone, abandoned? What about what's important to me?* Clara took a deep breath. She didn't know what was important to her, but that didn't change the fact that it never seemed to matter to Cole.

"Okay, but I think you're making a big deal out of nothing," she said finally.

"Thanks. I hope it's nothing but let's be sure."

For a few moments, they sat there on the bed in silence. Clara's first thought was that she wanted him to leave, but then was grateful he didn't. They were spending time together. The hum was bringing them closer together. She wondered if that would last once they were back home and he had his sports and buddies to pull him away.

"Now what?" asked Cole.

"I guess we wait until after the full moon."

"And let's try to enjoy our vacation." Cole left the room.

Clara flopped back on the bed, looking up at the slanted ceiling. There were a lot of things to think about, worry about, but none were in her control. She would have to take Cole's advice: wait and try to enjoy her time here.

By the time she was pouring her second cup of coffee, it was snowing heavily and it did so on and off for the next two days. The snow was the wet and clingy kind that made beautiful winter wonderland scenes outside the windows. Beautiful as it was to look upon, the cold and wet reality of it meant that no one wanted to leave the house. There were no trips into town, no walks around the Neck, no visits to or from the few year-round residents. The whole family just lounged around, reading their books and playing cards and old boardgames with missing pieces. It was a lot of time together with no breaks or change of scenery.

Clara usually liked lazing around, but she had something on her mind: the moon. The passage of time, the rotation of the planets and the earth's lone moon spinning around it, were not things she normally thought about. But now they obsessed her. Every shadow from the sun, every opportunity to look up at the sky, every high and low tide, made her think about the full moon and if—a big if, in her view—the rooms would change the next morning. "After the moon . . . after the moon . . . one more day to go," she found herself whispering as she paced around the house. But one more day was too long. She needed progress. She needed something to happen, an outlet for the nervous energy coursing through her veins. She paced into the seldom-used card room on the far side of the dining room and she saw it: the phone, just hanging there on the wall above the tangled mess of its green rubber cord. She picked it up and dialed.

"Hello?" said a raspy voice on the other end of the line.

"It's me."

"Me who?"

"Clara."

"Clara who?"

"Clara, your cousin. Stop being an ass."

"What is that horrific area code?"

"Huh?"

"That 207 mess."

"Oh, it's Maine. We're up at Amma's . . . for Christmas."

"Don't you have a cellphone?"

"No. I told you that like ten times over Thanksgiving."

"But still?"

"Yes, still. Listen to me. I have something important to tell you."

"You're a lesbian. I knew it!"

"No. Just shut up and listen."

Clara wanted to be pacing around the room as she talked but the tangled cord kept her close to the wall. A few seconds is all it would take to untangle the cord by holding it and dropping the phone to spin itself free, but she didn't want to do that. She didn't want to take her ear away from the phone for even one second. She wanted to hear every reaction, every gasp, every thoughtful silence inspired by what she was about to tell him. Adler was going to get it. Adler would understand. Unlike Cole, who was content to have some amorphous power fall from the sky with no explanation as long as he could do his little sports tricks and be a second-rate superhero, saving the world one cat-stuck-in-a-tree at a time. Adler would appreciate the significance of the book and the rooms, how they give the hum meaning, history, shape. The power belongs to something bigger, something important, and now so do they. And Adler will understand, even if Cole doesn't. Heck, even superheroes need origin stories.

Cole couldn't really have expected her to keep the book and the rooms hidden from Adler. He has as much right to that knowledge as they do. She's giving him information about what's already inside him. *How can that be wrong? Not doing it is what would be wrong—cruel, almost.*

"Fine. This better be good."

"It is. Trust me."

"Then get on with it."

"Okay, so we're up at Amma's in Maine."

"We covered that already."

"Right, so Amma has a book."

"Fascinating."

"It's called the family bible. You might know it. It's usually on the bookshelf to the right of the living room fireplace."

"I haven't been up there since I was a baby. You know that."

"Yeah, sorry. I'm just excited. So, the book isn't a bible, it's about a power."

Adler gasped at exactly the right moment. "Our power?"

"Yes."

"Go on."

"So, the book is from Viking times and is about a group of men in Norway who have the power—well, one of them has the power." Clara went on, telling Adler everything she could remember Amma telling her about the book and the Order. Adler listened intently, every so often adding an encouraging uh-huh or a thoughtful hmm. It was exactly what she wanted; she couldn't get the words out fast enough."

"Hey, slow down. Take a breath."

He was right, she was going too fast. She felt saliva building up in the corners of her mouth. She took a deep breath and licked her lips.

"Sorry. I'm excited. There's a lot, a whole book." Her heart was racing. She really was excited. It had been a while since she had been truly excited about something and it felt good.

"Okay, but let's pump the brakes and take it step by step. How do you know it's *our* power?"

"Oh, this is the best part. So, a part of the book describes a room, like in your imagination, where you go to practice using the power. Cole and I tried it and we got in."

"Got *in?*"

"Like one second we were in my room here and the next I was in like a wooden cabin or something. It's amazing. Well, you kind of have to drown to get in, but then you're in this room and the power feels better, like stronger."

"Stronger?"

"Yeah. And there's a table with stones and if you—"

"Breathe."

"Right, and if you knock the top stone off with it you go out a different way."

"Stones? That's it?"

That's it? Typical Adler trying to act all unimpressed. That too-cool-for-school act isn't going to work on me. "For now, I mean, I think there will be new tasks later, we just haven't been able to get in again. Amma thinks we have to wait until after the full moon, which is tomorrow."

"How's it done? I should probably try it out—see what all the fuss is about."

Fuss? You're lucky I even told you. "I'll email you the details later. I'll need to take pictures of what to write on the walls."

"Huh?"

"You get in through a corner of room and you need to write runes in the corner first. I'll give you all the details later."

"Why not right away?"

"I'll try, but I have to borrow someone's phone."

"Sooner the better. I have plans later."

"I'll try my best."

"Please do, but I wouldn't want to take you away from your busy schedule of sitting around in long johns sipping hot chocolate and doing jigsaw puzzles of lighthouses."

"Hey, some are of kittens in baskets, thank you very much."

"Oh, pardon me, then. Anything else I should know?"

"There's a lot. I'll put it all in the email. Oh, and don't tell Cole I told you." Clara's stomach felt hollow as she spoke. She didn't want to say that, but the fact that she felt the need to say that gave her second thoughts that maybe it had been wrong to break her promise to Cole. No matter how she wanted to rationalize it, to talk herself out of trouble, she had promised him and broke the promise. She hadn't lasted even two whole days. *What's done, is done.*

"Why?" asked Adler, adding under his breath, "Not that we talk anymore."

"It will just stress him out. You know how uptight he can get."

"Cole? Your goofball brother, Cole?"

"Yeah. He gets worked up about this sort of thing. Let's just keep it between us for now."

"If you say so. We weren't going to talk anyway."

"Thanks. Oh . . . one other thing." Clara pulled the phone away from her ear and looked at it. Its white buttons glowed faintly from some light source inside, otherwise hidden by the phone's dark green plastic casing. She took a deep breath, squeezed shut her eyes, returned the phone to her ear and braced. "Did you hear about the wind that blew out the windows in East Harlem?"

"Of course. It was right up the street."

"Did you see it happen?" A few seconds passed without an answer. "Adler? You there?"

"Sorry, what?"

"Did you see the wind gust?"

"Yes . . . Hey, so sorry but I need to head out. I just realized I'm really late for brunch. Shoot me that email and we'll pick it up after I go in. Okay?"

"Okay, but—" The phone clicked into a dial tone.

Clara dropped the phone to untangle its cord and then hung it back on the wall. She felt a sense of relief having told someone who truly appreciated the significance of the book. Breaking her promise to Cole dampened her mood somewhat, but they were going to tell Adler eventually anyway. She just jumped the gun a little. *Rationalizing again—I know it was wrong and I need to own it.* And, of course, the wind gust thing wasn't really resolved, but did that matter? Even if he had done it, it was probably an accident and only a few windows. He's learning about the power, just like they are. He just needs to be trained on how to control it—all the more reason to tell him about the rooms. Clara went back to waiting and pacing and trying, in vain, to enjoy her vacation.

Before dinner on the second day of waiting, when the moon was to be full, she asked Amma where the moon would be rising. Amma pointed to the north of the islands and then, through the course of the evening, Clara took every opportunity to look in that direction in the hopes of seeing the moon's white glow through the low-lying snow clouds. She had Cole come to her room to try again that night, but it didn't work. She had insisted on going first to avoid another incident.

"*After* the moon," she reassured herself. It would work in the morning, *after* the moon. She really wished that the translation was "after the *full* moon," but it wasn't. She saw that as a gaping hole in Amma's theory, but she pushed that out of her mind. That theory was all Clara had to hold onto. Cole, perhaps seeing how stressed out she was, kindly offered to wake up extra early the next morning to try the rooms again. He then and there set the alarm on his watch for 5:00 a.m. as proof of his dedication to the cause.

Clara opened the curtains and crawled into bed, adjusting a pillow so she could watch the windows while lying down. Somewhere out there, behind the snow clouds, was the full moon, moving along its course. Was it resetting the rooms as it sailed by, cranking and clicking gears in her mind to ready the next task? It had to be; there were no other leads. Thinking about the moon and the hope it represented, Clara pictured it pulling her through the night sky. Her mind was racing and sleep eluded her. She wondered about all the unknowns. *What if moonlight had to shine on the runes? What if they had to say some magic words? What if "after the moon" meant to write the word "moon" before the "in" runes?* Other girls her age were probably spending these days considering which Christmas presents to return and what to do for New Year's Eve. After hours of her thoughts jumping from one worry to another, she had to try to sleep. She had to let the moon float away and drift back to its hidden universe behind the clouds.

A little after five o'clock the next morning, Clara woke up feeling the hum, followed by a light knocking on the door. It was Cole, unexpectedly keeping his promise to get up extra early. She yawned and pulled her stiff body up out of bed to open the door.

"Good morning, sunshine!" His demeanor overflowed with good cheer.

"Ugh, Jesus, how long have you been up?" Clara yawned and rubbed her eyes.

"Just got up. See?" He blew his morning breath in her face.

"Ew. You're disgusting." She fanned the putrid air away from her face with both hands. "But thanks for getting up early. Mind if I go ahead and try?" Clara nodded her head toward the rune corner.

"Go for it. Fingers crossed."

Clara took a deep breath and slowly walked across the room. *This is it.*

If this didn't work, she was out of ideas about what they should do next. She turned around and leaned back against the walls of the corner. "Here goes nothing," she said, closing her eyes and slowly leaning back her head. Her scalp itched with anticipation. Would it be a devastating thump or an exhilarating arctic plunge?

To her great relief, she felt the icy chill soak into her hair and work its way around her head. When it covered her mouth, she didn't bother to hold her breath. Pulling the liquid deep into her lungs, she embraced the panic of her body as it fought for air. She coughed unceremoniously and opened her eyes.

She was back in the training room. Although she was ecstatic about her return, she was instantly disappointed when she saw a stack of stones in the same spot on the table. She had also forgotten how disturbing the crying baby and moaning woman sounds were. She wondered why her mind couldn't have just given her the rumbling train sounds like Cole's room.

On closer examination, the stack of stones was different. There were now five and the white one was in the middle, with two larger grey ones below and two smaller grey ones above. She sat down at the table, propped her elbows on it and rested her head in her hands to think about what this next challenge might be. She didn't feel tired anymore. It seemed that the better, cleaner hum had a way of waking her up and putting her in a good mood.

Contemplating the white stone's role in the prior task, she reasoned that this time probably also had something to do with moving it. She tried knocking it into the fire again. On her first try, the top four stones fell over, a couple rolling off the table onto the floor. She looked over at the other corner and was not surprised that the "out" runes hadn't shown up. She found the stones that had fallen to the floor and restacked them in the same order.

She tried again and the top three stones fell. As she tried various ways to move the white stone, she concluded that the task must be to knock the white stone with such force and precision that the two stones above it just dropped down onto the stack below, like a pulling-the-tablecloth trick. She made several attempts without success. Eventually, she stood up with her fists clenched to the sides, like Adler breaking the frame. That worked a little better, but it still took about four tries before succeeding. When the top two rocks fell with little clinks and wobbled slightly before coming to rest in the stack, Clara saw the flicker of the gold runes out of the corner of her eye. She walked over, drowned in warm liquid and—*poof*—was back in her room with a cough or two.

"Yes!" Cole pumped his fist in the air, like he did after hitting a free throw.

"It worked!" She bounced on her tippy toes and then ran over to hug Cole. She told him about the task and how hard it was for her.

"Pfff, that sounds easy. I got this." Cole did some strange, cocky duck walk over to the corner. "I bet it will take me one try. Ready? Time me." Cole pointed to her watch as he moved to the corner.

"Are you for real?" said Clara.

"Yeah, time me. Ready?"

Clara stared at him blankly, blinking in dismay.

"Oh, oh, right, duh, never mind."

Once again, Clara found herself rolling her eyes at a male family member. Cole coughed and it was over for now, until the next after the moon.

VI

Gudrid Beineson's Freya ceremony began with horns sounding over the harbor, in keeping with the tradition of the time. Gudrid walked out onto the platform wearing the ceremonial white robe and green cape. On her shoulders she wore copper oval brooches that had been passed down from her grandmother on her mother's side. Her female friends, including her sister, Estrid, also wore white robes and gathered on either side of the platform, which was purposefully arranged so that the maiden faced the sun to give full spectacle of her glinting eyes.

One by one, the suitors announced themselves and presented Gudrid with gifts. Thurandur offered a large chest of iron tools and bowls. The gift was obviously intended for distribution to the community and it elicited cheers and applause from the spectators. The Viking from Norway presented a barrel of hazelnuts and walnuts, both prized delicacies of the time. The Irishman presented a golden harp that he strummed to the delight of the spectators. The Blue Prince presented a small whistle of brightly polished silver and curious design. Holding it between thumb and forefinger, he brought it to his mouth to demonstrate its use. With breath of force, the instrument produced a loud shrill that caused the spectators to wince and cover their ears. The Caliph presented three large rolls of shimmering silk. The Danish Viking presented a small chest full of silver coins. Upon seeing the make of the coins, the Caliph cursed and hissed at the Dane and it was understood that the coins had been plundered from his Caliphate.

Gudrid thanked the suitors with fair words and mirth. She said the traditional prayer to the old gods. Thurandur was then asked to lead a prayer to the new Christ god, which he did, over the grumbles of the Dímuner elders.

NINETEEN

Cole's alarm went off and he immediately whacked his head against the wall. After almost a month, he was still getting out of bed on the wrong side. When they had returned to Lehighton from winter break in Maine, Clara had asked if he could move his bed over to the wall closest to her room so she could use the hum while he slept. He had agreed and they rearranged his room together. He still wasn't used to it.

Following their return home, Clara stayed up late most nights, reading Amma's notes or using the hum to translate the photocopied sections of the book that Amma was sending her periodically. She also started to practice using the hum. Her favorite drill was to get out their old Hungry Hungry Hippos game and use the power to move the balls around the plastic bowl-like board. She had recently told him that she was getting good at moving one ball to one side and all the others to the other side. She thought that was pretty close to practicing the stone stacks without having to go find stones in easily stackable shapes and to keep restacking them after every misfire.

Cole once made the mistake of saying Jenga would be like practicing the second task of moving out the white stone while keeping the others stacked. Several times that night he had been jolted awake by the loud, clunking wood sound of a crashing Jenga tower. Eventually, he had crawled out of bed, pulling with him his blankets and pillows, to sleep on the floor on the other side of his room. Clara must have felt the hum fade and he heard a faint "sorry" through the wall.

Cole rubbed his head where it had struck the wall. He had managed to hit the same exact spot that he had the day before, so it really hurt. *Why is it taking me so long to get used to this new setup*, he wondered. He knew it had been almost a month since they had gotten back because it was going to be a full moon that night.

A full moon apparently happens about once a month. He was learning a lot about the moon, now that Clara was obsessed with it and the training room and all things hum-related. She even bought a phases-of-the-moon calendar poster for her bedroom and religiously crossed off each day that passed. That night was the full moon, as Clara had reminded him several times.

Tomorrow he would have to wake up extra early to do the training rooms before school. He had agreed to do it on two conditions. First, he would get to go into the training room first. Second, Clara would come to his basketball game on Friday night. Clara reluctantly agreed to those terms, as Cole knew she would. There was no way she could handle waiting until the weekend to do the rooms, which was Cole's alternative proposal. In retrospect, Cole realized he probably could have asked for more. Maybe Clara would have done his chores for the week.

Next time, he thought.

After the whole training room discovery and completion of the stone tasks, Cole realized that the hum could actually be more useful in basketball than just helping him shoot free throws. He could also use it to change the trajectory of the other team's shots, causing them to miss the basket. It was a challenge to do it in a subtle way, but the stone tasks had inspired him. The trick was to move the ball just as it hit the rim or the backboard.

Moving it in the air was too obvious and would definitely raise some eyebrows. A few weeks ago, when he first tried it at a game, Clara realized what he was doing and she got up in a huff and stormed out of the gym. She later told him she thought what he was doing was wrong.

She explained that it was one thing to use the hum to make yourself better, but quite another thing to use it against other players. She said it was like using the hum to make everyone else fail on Spanish quizzes, no matter how much they studied, so that the curve would give her the better grade. Cole thought she had a point, but he still liked to win. Of course, using the hum to win that way didn't give him any credit personally for the win, but winning made the team happy and put everyone in a good mood. Friday's game was against Jim Thorpe, so he really wanted to win, one way or another.

When he got down to the kitchen, Clara was reading a paper and sipping her coffee. He wondered how she could drink something that smelled like tar and burnt nuts. As expected, the first thing out of her mouth was that the full moon was that evening. *No kidding, good morning to you too*, he wanted to say but didn't. He poured himself a glass of orange juice and rescued an old, cold slice of pizza from the back of the fridge before taking a seat across from her. She folded the top of the paper slightly to peer over at him.

"Is that your breakfast?"

"Yes. So what?"

"How old is it?"

"I dunno. It tastes fine."

"You're not going to warm it up?"

"No. Just read your paper so I can eat in peace."

As he gnawed on the last bite of damp, chewy crust, he heard Clara make a slight gasp on the other side of her newspaper.

"You okay?"

"What?"

"Are you okay? You made a sound."

"Oh. Yeah, I'm fine. Just burnt my tongue a little." She put the paper down on the table. "Hey, we better get going to school. We're running late." She stood up and slung her backpack over one shoulder.

Cole thought her cheeks looked a little flushed and her brows were furrowed. She must have burned her tongue pretty badly, he thought. "Okay, let me grab some more OJ. I'll meet you on the porch in a sec."

He took a cool swig of pulpy orange juice straight from the carton and turned to leave. As he passed the kitchen table, a headline in Clara's newspaper caught his eye: "Crane Collapse on E. Harlem NYCHA Community Center, 7 Dead." *So sad*, he thought as he hustled to meet Clara on the porch.

Walking across the square, they talked about what the next training task might be. Cole joked that they would have to juggle the stones or balance them on their noses, but he got the vibe that Clara wasn't in much of a joking mood.

———

When Cole got home after school that evening, he entered the kitchen to find the table covered in old-timey gadgets and instruments. The instruments were so large and stacked so closely together that he barely saw his mother sitting at the far side of the table. He could see just the top of her head, which was shaking disapprovingly as she looked up from her paper at the stacks of tarnished widgets and faded wood boxes and other dusty contraptions.

"What's all this?"

"Ask your father," said Mrs. Lund.

"Ah, Cole. Just the man I was looking for." Mr. Lund appeared from the hallway behind Cole. "Like my new toys?"

"What are they?"

"These are close approximations to the instruments that Lewis and Clark used on their expedition—the cutting edge of technology at the time."

"What are they for?"

"Good question," said Mrs. Lund without looking up from her paper.

"Well, son, a big part of the Corps of Discovery's mission was to record their location, draw a map of the area explored and collect scientific specimens of local flora, fauna and minerals. These are the instruments they used to do that. They didn't have GPS or new-fangled smart watches back then—heck, they didn't even have dumb watches." Mr. Lund let out a laugh.

"Cool. What's this one do?" Cole placed his hand on an old wooden box about the size of a basketball.

"Believe it or not, it's a compass." Mr. Lund opened the lid of the box to reveal a tarnished brass dial.

"Why is it so big?"

"That's the best they could do back then."

Cole's dad walked around to the other side of the table and picked up a dusty gadget that looked like a large metal "A" with a semicircle connecting the bottom and a swinging piece in the middle. As Mr. Lund pulled the contraption toward himself, it knocked against what looked like a small telescope, which tipped over onto other instruments that toppled onto others, creating a chain reaction. Mr. Lund frantically scrambled to set the instruments back in place. Once order was restored, he held up the A-shaped contraption and declared it to be "the most important one." Mr. Lund explained that Lewis and Clark had used something like it to measure the angle between the horizon and certain stars to determine their location. "It's called a sextant."

"SEX-tant?" Cole chuckled.

"Yes, that and the chronometer, which is somewhere around here, were used together." Mr. Lund scanned the table, either not getting Cole's joke or not wanting to acknowledge it. "We should go test it out on a clear, moonless night," he continued, still searching for the chronometer.

Cole noted that yet another family member was planning things around the moon. He half expected his mother to declare that she would only eat cheese on half-moon days.

"Cole, you should have some dinner. There are some leftovers in the fridge," said Mrs. Lund. "Asa is already eating downstairs."

"Okay, thanks. But didn't you say you were looking for me?"

"Oh, right, any chance you could help me move these downstairs later? For some reason, your mother doesn't want them on the kitchen table."

"That's odd," said Cole as he rummaged through the fridge. "I think they look great there."

Cole ate dinner with Asa in the basement, did some homework in the dining room and then helped his dad carry down the instruments. When it was time to go to bed, he looked for Clara to say good night and found her looking out a window in the library.

"Good night, sis," he called in through the library door.

"Full moon tonight." She didn't turn away from the window.

"I know, I know."

"Don't forget to set your alarm for six. Training rooms first thing in the morning."

"Ugh, you're like a broken record. I don't know why you're so worried about waking up early. It's the one thing that *literally* takes no time to do."

"I know, but we'll need extra time to talk about it." She finally turned away from the window to face him.

"Hey, talking about it wasn't part of the deal." Cole shot her a sly smile, feeling pretty good about his expertise at messing with her.

"Just go to bed already." She turned back to the window to look at the moon.

"I love you, sis. Sweet dreams."

"Uh huh. You too." Cole briefly considered asking her which she loved more, him or the moon, but he decided against it, figuring that he probably wouldn't like the answer.

Cole's alarm went off just as Clara was knocking. *So much for being fashionably late*, he thought. They had previously decided to do the training rooms in Cole's bedroom because it had a free corner. All of the corners in Clara's room were taken up by either books or shelves displaying her many travel photos, mostly of Paris. Cole thought all the black and white Eiffel Tower pictures were pretty cheesy, but never said anything.

Clara walked in without even acknowledging him. She took a crumpled paper towel out of her pocket and unwrapped it to reveal a charcoal briquette that she had pulled from a bag in the garage.

"Um, good morning," said Cole, his voice loud with annoyance.

"Oh right, good morning." She used the briquette to write the "in" runes on the walls. "Go ahead. You're first."

Cole let out a big yawn and leisurely walked to the corner, enjoying Clara's frustration with his glacial pace. Facing the corner, he raised his arms and made stretching groans. He slowly turned around only to see Clara rushing at him full speed with her hands out.

"Just go, dammit," she said, shoving him back into the corner.

Cole laughed and leaned his head back. The water sensation felt particularly cold and he thought to himself how drowning in ice cold water was an extremely effective way to shake off the sleepies.

When he opened his eyes, with a cough or two, he was back in his dim and damp stone training room with the same old rumbles from outside. The hum was crisp and comforting. He found it funny to think it was only his third time there. He had replayed the experiences so many times in his mind that it felt like he had been there a thousand times. It was a relief not to see a stack of stones on the table. In its place was a single, unlit cream-colored candle held upright in a tarnished pewter candlestick. He immediately understood the task at hand. This time, figuring out the task was the easy part, but he feared that figuring out how to actually light the candle would be difficult.

He took a seat on one of the benches and examined the candle. Staring at the wick, he focused on the hum and said "fire" while thrusting his fingertips toward the wick like a magician. The wick didn't so much as twitch. *Worth a shot*, he figured. His attention drifted to the fire in the fireplace. He sat up straight so he could see it on the other side of the table. He let his thoughts linger on the flames, how they moved, how their colors constantly changed, how they danced around, casting living shadows on the stone wall behind. The pulsing embers below the flames glowed orange and red. Closing his eyes, he visualized fire in his mind: the roaring fires they had gathered around at Amma's over Christmas and the accompanying marshmallows. The thought of marshmallows would have normally made him feel hungry, but it didn't. Come to think of it, he didn't remember feeling hungry at all the last times he was in the room. A place where you're never hungry or tired. *Everyone in the world should have a training room,* he thought.

Realizing he was losing focus on the training task, he opened his eyes to stare at the wick again. His mind went back to marshmallows, unsurprisingly. Clara and his cousins liked to roast marshmallows just above the flames so that they got "golden" or whatever. Not Cole. He liked to put his marshmallows right down into the flame until they caught fire. The blue inner flame would work its way around the marshmallow as he twirled the stick. He wouldn't stop twirling until the entire marshmallow was charred black and then he would blow it out like a birthday cake candle. He loved biting into the crunchy, ashy outside to get to the gooey sweet insides.

Again, his mind was wandering off the task. He refocused on the wick, but the image of the blue fire stuck with him. Maybe that's what he should focus on. Putting his face up close to the candle, he peered right at the wick and squinted his eyes, focusing on the hum and imagining a blue fire dancing on the wick. *Hum, wick, blue fire, hum, wick, blue fire, hum, wick, blue fire,* over and over.

Then the very tip of the wick began to smoke. He squinted his eyes even more tightly and channeled the hum right to the top of the wick where the smoke was rising. He saw a faint flicker of blue light, which became a blue, low-lying flame that then rose into a full-fledged yellow and orange flame, working its way down the short wick and resting on top of the wax. "Hell, yeah!" he yelled out with enough force that his breath accidentally blew out the short-lived flame. *Crap.*

Quickly looking over at the exit corner, he was relieved to see the "out" runes there in glowing gold. He stood up and walked toward the exit corner, but stopped himself to look back at the candle on the table. He didn't want his training room burning down, if that could even happen in that imaginary fifth dimension, or wherever the hell he was. While walking back to the table, he licked his thumb and then pinched the hot wick to make sure it was out for good. He then left through the warm waters of reality. Opening his eyes, he saw that he was coughing right in Clara's face. Her eyes and mouth were tightly shut as she grimaced in disgust.

"Oh, sorry," he said. "But, on second thought, you're kind of in my personal space."

Clara nudged him aside and, in a single fluid motion, turned and leaned back into the corner as if she were doing a backflip off a diving board. A split second later, she coughed and said, "Well, that was easy."

Cole just shrugged. *She's such a showoff.*

TWENTY

I tried the training room thing that Clara wouldn't shut up about. I was trapped in some dreadful shack. It was a joke, Mother. A waste of my time—flitting stones about like a child. I can do that in my sleep. What I want to toss are buildings, neighborhoods. Toss them into the fire. Burn them to the ground. Erase them from the earth.

TWENTY-ONE

Walking home from school, Clara looked in the wrong direction at the wrong time and caught a glimpse of that stupid, decaying, pink stuffed bunny in the hoarder's backyard. She had managed to avoid noticing it since before they left for Maine and its condition had noticeably deteriorated in those five weeks. This time, the sight of the matted pink fur didn't drop kick her into a state of helpless despair. The town still sucked balls, of course, but now she had other things going on, things to look forward to. For example, she was currently looking forward to calling Adler when she got home. He had probably already done the candle task by then and she was sure he'd be pumped about it. Conjuring fire was definitely more his speed than the stone tricks.

No one was home. Good. She grabbed the cordless phone and ran up to her room. She organized the photocopies from the book that Amma had sent and set them next to her translation notes on the floor in front of her. Maybe they should be reorganized. Perhaps she should sit on the bed and not the floor. That would give her the wall to focus on as she talked. She dialed.

"Hello?"

"Hi. It's me. Clara. Your cousin."

"I know. What time is it?" Adler's voice was phlegmy.

"Three seventeen."

"In the morning?"

"No. The afternoon. Were you asleep?"

"Yeah. I had a late night. What's up?"

"I got some more pages from Amma and wanted to talk about the room. Did you do it?"

"Ye—" He coughed several times. "Hold on, I need a cigarette."

"Okay." Clara heard some rustling, then the distinctive clicks and squeaks of the terrace door. Then all she could hear was wind, car horns honking and sirens blaring in the distance. *Ah, New York*, she thought. Then the line went dead. "Hello? Adler?"

"Can you hear me? It's loud out here—I put in my earbuds."

"Yeah, I hear you fine now."

"Good. So Amma finally sent some new pages, huh? I hope they're more useful than the Viking sisters and sailing crap from your last call."

"Yeah, there's some good stuff in this set. But first let's talk about the task. Pretty cool, huh? I mean *hot*." Clara faked a laugh.

"Don't be a loser. You're better than that."

"Sorry." Clara didn't feel that sorry. She mostly felt flattered that Adler—cool, sophisticated, artistic Adler—thought she was better than that. It didn't really matter what "that" was, as long as he thought she was better than something. A complement from him was rare, and it had meaning. She was better. She was above it. "So, starting the fire. Pretty cool, right?"

"Yeah, it was fine."

"Just fine? I thought you'd like that one."

"I did. It's just . . . well . . . are they supposed to be difficult? These tasks are super easy."

"It wasn't that easy. Um, I mean, it was—but I think they'll get harder."

"I hope so. I've started just staying in the room and making up my own tasks, bigger ones."

"Like what?"

"Whatever I think of. Like this time, the candle left me uninspired so I set the whole room on fire—the walls and floors and ceiling and table, everything." Adler took an audible drag of his cigarette.

"You didn't get burned?"

"No. Flames were all around me and I didn't even feel warm."

Chills ran up Clara's back and neck, but she didn't know whether they were from fear, jealously or awe. She considered that inciting that combination was probably Adler's goal in every aspect of his life.

"Anyway, what's new in the pages Amma sent?" he asked.

"Give me a sec."

Clara flipped through her notes again. She was determined to give a professional presentation this time. She was disappointed with how she handled their last call. She had jumped around too much between topics. She had failed to adequately convey the significance of some key intel, like the battles with the Viking sisters and the Vessel-killing ceremony that transferred the power to the next Vessel. She wasn't surprised that Adler wasn't as into the Viking sister stories as Cole, but she was convinced that he would have had more appreciation for the power transfer had she done a more systematic job presenting the material, rather than jumping around from one story to another.

The highlight of her last presentation was her A-plus job answering his question on what happens if two people kill the Vessel at the same time—do they both get the power? She was pleased with herself for having had an answer at the ready and immediately citing the Order's experiments on that subject. The two killers in the Order's experiment had ended up with no power at all, but generations later, the power arose in direct descendants of both killers. Clara theorized that the power was cut in half, lying dormant in the killers' genes until combined with the other half, also dormant, in the other killer's genes. Of course, the Order summarily executed all descendants of the killers so that the half-power wouldn't be lurking around unchecked. That wouldn't have jived with the Order's control issues.

Adler had been satisfied with that explanation and prompted her to move on, without so much as a "thank you for being so on top of that point." Clara guessed that she shouldn't have been expecting any praise given that the rest of her presentation had been such a disaster. With this new set of pages, she was determined to be less scatterbrained. After all, she's better than that.

"Okay, ready? This time I'm first going to tell you the stories in the pages and then we'll talk about what they mean. It will be like Bible study."

"Jesus Christ, you need to get out of Pennsylvania. How the hell do you know about Bible study?"

"From movies, relax. Ready?"

"Let me go back inside." Following the familiar sounds of the terrace door, Adler announced that he was ready.

"Alright, so in this story, the Order is sailing—sometimes rowing—around a cluster of islands off the northern coast of Norway."

"Oh god. Is this another boring as hell sailing story?"

"No. Now shut up. As their ship passed between two small uninhabited islands, the Vessel called out and the leader ordered the rowers to halt the ship. The Vessel sensed the power, but there was no one in sight. They rowed the ship around the islands and found a small fishing boat and in it was a skinny old man with a long white beard." Clara stopped to turn to the next page of her notes. "Still with me?"

"Yes, but barely conscious."

"What's new? So, the fisherman flashed them a toothless smile and the Order demanded that he come aboard. He obligingly rowed his small boat alongside the Order's ship and then, with great effort, climbed the rope ladder up to the deck. The old man was out of breath by the time he got on board. He tried to greet them, but, without a word exchanged, the Vessel ran him through with a harpoon."

"Ha! That's awesome."

"Why do you always like the creepiest parts?"

"Because I'm not a boring loser. Go on."

"The man died instantly, but the Vessel announced that he did not feel an increase in the power and he still sensed it in their midst. That part is important, remember that."

"I can't, I'm asleep."

"Good. The leader then ordered some men down to search the fishing boat. Besides the usual fishing tools, they found a net full of small silver fish. Outside of the net, wriggling and gasping for breath, was a large sturgeon. One of the men grabbed the sturgeon and lifted it above his head, revealing its flat and white underbelly and whiskered snout. 'Lunch!' he yelled up to the men on board. The leader looked alarmed and yelled at the man to hold the fish tightly and bring it on board."

"And then they made fish tacos and whipped out the frozen margarita machine."

"Shut it. When the sailor was on board, the leader told him to drop the fish on the deck and step back. 'Show yourself,' said the leader to the fish as it flopped around. 'Clever ruse, but this is not the time of year for sturgeon in these waters.' The fish flipped its tail and flung itself into the air. While airborne, it transformed into an old, haggard woman with long grey hair. She landed hunched over with her skinny legs slightly spread and her hands on the deck in front of her."

"You can spare me the senior citizen erotica, thanks."

"Shhh. It's almost done. The old woman rose and opened her mouth to address the leader, but, as with the old man, before she could get out a single word the Vessel had thrust the harpoon into her back."

"For the win!"

"The Vessel announced that he felt the power get stronger and the leader was satisfied to continue on their way. The men unceremoniously dumped the old couple's bodies overboard and then raised the sails. Okay, so that's the end of part one, for today. What have we learned?"

"That you have a monotone reading voice?"

"C'mon, seriously. This one is important."

"I know it's important." Adler's voice was loud and stern. "I'm not an idiot. When someone with the power kills someone else with the power, it gets stronger. It's clearly important—it's probably one of the most important things I've ever heard in my entire fucking life."

"You don't have to yell at me. It's hard to tell if you're paying attention with all the smartass commentary."

"Sorry, sorry. I just got excited. What's the next part? I'll need to head out soon."

"Okay, I'll read quickly . . . in my most monotone voice, now that I know how much you love it."

"Thanks. Just give me a sec to head out for another smoke." The phone went quiet for a few seconds. "Okay, ready."

"So, after dumping the two bodies overboard, the Order sailed to the nearest village on the mainland to look for any family members of the fisherman's wife. In canvasing the villagers, the Order discovered that the fisherman and his wife were well-known and it was whispered that the wife knew dark magic. The couple had one child, a son who had ventured to Trondheim at a young age and had become a great Viking chieftain. With that information, the leader then referred to the Order's records—I think that means one of the earlier volumes in the same series as Amma's book—and confirmed that they had already killed a Viking of the same name not far from Trondheim. That's it for the second part."

"I liked that one. Short and sweet."

"I won't question your appreciation of the importance of that part of the story.

"That the power passes down genetically and that the Order's mission is to hunt down and kill everyone with the power so the Vessel gets stronger."

"I'm so glad to see you've been paying attention. And, come to think of it, the genetic passing probably explains why the new Vessels are castrated before the ceremony. Cole will be relieved to learn it's just that."

"Have you told Cole all this?"

"Not yet. He's been pretty busy. Maybe he'll have some time this weekend."

"Why tell him at all?"

"Huh? Why not?"

"Why stress him out? You said this stuff gets him worked up. Why give him something to worry about when he's having fun with his whole big-man-on-campus thing?"

"But—"

"No but. He doesn't need to know this stuff. Why complicate his simple life, his simple mind?"

"But we're trying to figure out why we have it. The passing down through genes seems important."

"Okay, you can tell him that. But don't burden him with the thing about killing others with the power to get stronger. Knowing that would just make him paranoid for no reason. Let him enjoy high school. It will probably be the best years of his life."

"But he already knows that it transfers on death to the killer."

"And that's probably weighing on him. Has he been acting down or sad lately?

"I don't know. It's hard to tell with him during basketball season."

"Why give him yet another thing to dampen his spirits? He can't handle things like we can. He's not like us."

Clara considered for a moment. Adler was making some good points. Cole didn't need to know all that. He didn't really care about the Order or the power's rules. It could be just between her and Adler. Just them. It could be their thing.

"I guess you're right. Okay, I'll just tell him the genetics part." *Another promise to not tell someone something. Maybe I'll do a better job this time.*

"It's for the best. And sorry I snapped at you before. You're a good friend for telling me all this."

Clara let Adler's kind words wash over her: she was a good friend. She had a friend. But his next words brought the warm and fuzzy feelings to an abrupt halt, like a swift kick to the gut.

"So still nothing about twins?" he asked.

It was a perfectly reasonable question. From anyone else it wouldn't have struck Clara as particularly noteworthy, but from Adler it hit hard, it stung, it burned. He had asked it the last time too and it still hurt just as much. No, she hadn't found anything in the pages about twins, but Adler didn't really care. He was making a point: that, unlike him, Clara needed someone. She needed Cole around to be powerful. She required a crutch to hobble down the street, while he was free to walk and run and fly away on his own. By asking that, he was reminding her of where they ranked. He was first because he was always powerful, whereas she, and her conditional power, played second fiddle. But she had a power he would never have: she could turn it off. With a few steps in the right direction, she could be normal whenever she wanted. She could escape the power's constant buzzing in her ear like an eager mosquito urging her to use it, to act. She was thankful for that, but she had to admit that a part of her was jealous of him. *Fear, jealousy and awe.*

"No. Still nothing about twi—"

"FUCK YOU!"

"What?!" Clara heard the terrace door swing open again, but louder and faster than before.

"Sorry, not you. Some asshole thugs are blaring gangster rap out of their car. THIS IS FUCKING PARK AVENUE, ASSHOLES. TAKE THAT SHIT BACK UPTOWN!"

"Adler, chill out. You can't say things like that."

"You don't understand. You don't know what it's like to have *them* always around. Always ruining everything. Keeping you in constant fear. You wouldn't get it—everyone there is the same."

"Hey, that's not cool. You need to relax." Clara could picture the faces Cole would have made if he had heard that. "What's your problem?"

"*My* problem? You want to know *my* problem? Well, you're not ready to hear it. No, not precious Clara and Cole. Amma and the rest of them want to protect your delicate little brains and keep you in some fantasy world where bad shit doesn't happen. I'll tell you my problem when you've grown the fuck up and grown a pair."

"Look, I don't know what you're talking about and I think it's a good time for us to hang up, but just tell me one thing."

"What?"

"You wouldn't do anything to hurt anyone, would you?" There was no answer. "Adler, answer me. You wouldn't use it to hurt anyone, right?"

"Sure, whatever."

"Good. So, I will call you when I get the next set of pages. In the meantime, try to chill out and have a drink, or ten, or whatever it is you do every night."

"Fine, but ask Amma to pick up the pace with the pages. This is taking forever."

"I know, I know. Bye."

"Bye."

Clara flung herself back on the bed and stared up at the ceiling. She was angry with him, of course, for saying stupid stuff and being a racist or whatever on earth was going on with him, but that was just Adler being Adler, right? He had always had a volatile personality, prone to outrageous comments, mainly for shock value and to add a little drama and danger to his carefully crafted persona. She wasn't going to dwell on it. He'd get over it and be back on the planet by the next time she called. She wanted to think about something else, she wanted to let other words marinate in her mind: "you're a good friend," he had said—before dropping the twins bomb. Adler, whose friends were supermodels and D.J.'s and artists, considered her a friend, not just a cousin, not just some family member he had to put up with, but a friend. She couldn't remember her last friend. She had had a few friends in Philly, but she was always with Cole back then, and maybe they were really his friends. She hadn't kept in touch with any of them, and what were their names? *I seem to remember a Heather*, she thought. But now she had her own friend. He wasn't Cole's friend at all, because Cole is "not like us." Adler was *her* friend.

"Clara, do you have the phone in there?" Clara's mother called in from the hallway.

"Hi, mom. Yeah, I have it." Clara swung her legs around off the bed and brought the phone to her mother.

"Here you go. Everything okay?"

"I hope so. I need to call Ted and make sure he's okay."

"What's wrong?"

"I heard in the car that there was a high-rise fire near the hospital this morning and some Mount Sinai employees got hurt helping residents escape." Mrs. Lund dialed as she spoke.

"Oh no. That's terrible."

"Yeah, it was a housing project with outdated fire safety equipment. Nine deaths confirmed already—just awful." She paced the hall with the phone up to her ear. "Hi Sylvia, how are you? Have you heard from Ted?

Clara watched as her mother's face relaxed and seamlessly shift into a smile.

"Oh, thank god. Sorry I didn't call earlier, I just heard about it on the radio. Such a shame." Mrs. Lund held the mouthpiece and whispered to Clara that Uncle Ted was okay, as if she couldn't tell from the one side of the conversation. Walking down the stairs, Clara's mom continued her call with Sylvia and Clara returned to her room.

It's just a coincidence, she told herself.

When Cole came home from practice later that evening, Clara was doing homework in the dining room with her back to the entry hall. She heard the faint creak of the floorboards as he crept up behind her.

"Hey, genius, you can't sneak up on me anymore," she said without turning.

"Oh, right. The hum. Duh. Here, I have a present for you."

In front of her, on top of her A.P. Chemistry textbook, he placed a piece of lined loose-leaf paper with a crude drawing of two people. They had circular heads and thick legs and arms, like the tracings of gingerbread man cookies. The figures each wore the same clothing, a one-piece pants and long-sleeve shirt getup, drawn over with perpendicular lines of yellow, pink and blue highlighter. One figure had long hair, the other short, and written above their heads were the words "Super Twin Duo."

"What the heck is that?"

"It's us—when we're superheroes. I made it during study hall."

Clara laughed, picking up the paper to examine it. "You are truly a crazy person."

"What? It's awesome."

"Super Twins Duo? You don't need the duo."

"Huh?"

"Duo means two. Twins already means two. It can just be Super Twins."

"No way. Duo is a cool superhero word, like Batman and Robin."

"What's with the hideous stripes?"

"That's plaid."

"*That* is plaid?"

"Yeah. I thought since we're from the mountains, our uniforms should be like plaid flannel. It would be cool and funny."

"We are *not* from the mountains. And there's no way I'm wearing a costume."

"It's a uniform."

"Whatever, I'm not wearing one."

"Are you going to fight crime like that?" he asked.

Following his eyes, she looked down at her grey sweatshirt with the word "Maine" in white letters across the front. "No, I'll put something nice on. Like slacks and a blouse." She smiled.

"Great, so we'll be Super Cole and Business-Casual Girl—real intimidating."

"Oh, I forgot to tell you, I finally heard back from Rose. She has the hum too."

"Who?"

"Rose, the Irish girl. Remember, a while ago, you said I should contact her? I had an old email address that she doesn't check often. Man, she is still a total weirdo."

"Oh cool. So, with Adler, there's four of us. We can be the Fantastic Four."

"I'm pretty sure that name is taken. But Rose is a triplet and her sisters also have it."

"Hm, that's six. That seems like a lot for the same uniform."

"No costumes! But I would love to see you try to get Adler into a plaid unitard."

"I really hope the next task will be something useful for helping people."

"You could set the bad guys on fire."

"Um, I was thinking we'd capture them and turn them over to the police for a fair trial."

"Where's the fun in that?"

"I mean, ropes coming out of our hands would be really useful."

"Look, if you want to be Spiderman, just admit it. Drop the ropes B.S. and just say webs."

"Okay, okay, I admit it. Webs would be awesome."

When their laughs subsided, they sat in silence for a few moments.

"You don't really think any of this is going to happen, do you?" asked Clara.

"What do you mean?"

"The helping people, fighting crime—it's not happening. You know that, right?"

"Why not?"

"Cause we're not going to suddenly start hanging out all the time and fighting crime by night. We're too old to be dreaming about being superheroes when we grow up."

"We have the power for a reason. We should use it."

"We're not little kids running around the yard with pillow-case capes. It's time to grow up."

"Isn't this what you wanted? To go back to a simpler time, when we were always hanging out? Now we can. We have a proj-ect we can work on together."

"It's too late for that. We've changed. I've changed."

"So, what do you want now?"

"I'm not sure yet." She really wasn't sure. But she knew that if she was going to risk getting caught using the hum, jeopardiz-ing her freedom and her life, it would have to be for something more momentous than what Cole had in mind. It would have to be on a much larger scale.

"Well don't count out superheroes yet. I'll wear khakis and a button-down, if you want."

Clara gave a small laugh and handed the paper back to Cole. "It's a nice thought though, thanks."

He took the paper, making an overdramatic pouty face and turned to leave the dining room.

"Oh Cole, Super Twins Duo . . ."

"Yeah?"

"The initials are S.T.D.—you should put that on front of the costumes."

"Aw, crap."

VII

In the days following her ceremony, Gudrid was careful to give equal time to her six suitors, as was expected. During the day, she would spend time with each of them, even the ones that did not speak the Norse language, taking hikes in the hills, horseback riding, sailing and so on. Then each night a different landowner hosted the festivities at his estate. On the third day, the Caliph and his men abruptly departed Stóra Dímun. It was said that he did not feel that Gudrid was interested in him and that he was still angry about the Danish Viking's stolen coins. On the fifth day, a rumor spread that Gudrid had been seen kissing Thurandur on the deck of his longship.

Later that day, Thoralf announced that Gudrid would be declaring her decision the next morning. Knowing that it would be the last day of festivities, and that it was all but certain that Gudrid would choose Thurandur, that evening's festivities were held in the village square, not far from the harbor. There was much merriment on the island and the mead flowed swiftly until the barrels ran dry. Music filled the air and the Dímuners and their guests taught each other their traditional dances. By early evening, the Dímuners and their visitors were drunk and exhausted. That is when they heard an unwelcome call from the western hilltop.

"Grey sails!" cried the lookout.

TWENTY-TWO

About two weeks after the fire-starting task, it was a no-moon night. That's what Cole liked to call it, mostly because it drove Clara crazy. "*New* moon! *New* moon!" she would gripe. That didn't make any sense to Cole. You don't call an empty glass new water—it's no water. If you want to call it a new moon when a sliver of the crescent shows up, that's fine, but not when nothing is there.

It being a no-moon night, their dad had convinced Cole and Clara to go with him to test out the sextant, which Cole still thought was a funny word. Mr. Lund never did find the chronometer, though he eventually admitted that it served the same function as a wristwatch, despite being the size of a microwave. In order to maximize the visibility of the stars, which was apparently necessary for the sextant, the plan was to go down to the beach along the river to get away from the light pollution from the town. "Yeah, it's a regular Times Square around here," Clara had said.

The three of them bundled up, left the house and headed east toward First Street. A chorus of "Cohhhl" rose from the gazebo, which was crowded with shadows and glowing orange dots from cigarette tips. Cole looked up at the sky. It was a clear, crisp night. He thought they could see the stars just fine from up here in town, but his dad was on a mission and there was no point in trying to discourage him.

They made their way to the dirt path leading to the beach. It was dark and the pine trees along the path made it look like a spooky tunnel. As they entered, Cole made ghost sounds until Clara elbowed him in the side. Well before they reached the river, Cole heard its rushing and gurgling, which grew louder and louder as they approached. When they arrived at the beach, their father looked up at the sky and at the black peaks surrounding them. Cole also looked up and marveled at how many stars there were. In the distance, a faint glow hovered in the sky above the town and Cole admitted that his dad may have had a point about the light pollution.

"Here, Clara, hold this." Mr. Lund handed her the sextant. "Don't drop it. It's very fragile," he added as he fumbled with an old notebook.

"Okay. I wasn't planning to drop it."

"Alright, now, Cole, take this . . . and this." Mr. Lund handed Cole the notebook and then a pencil.

"Aye-aye, Captain," said Cole enthusiastically. Cole heard a faint rumbling sound coming from the north.

Clara gave Cole a slightly surprised look. "Did you actually know this was a nautical instrument?"

"I did not," said Cole.

"Okay, now Clara, hand me the sextant and—see these numbers here? I'll let you know when to call them out. Cole, write down the numbers that she calls out." The rumbling was getting louder and it was clear that a freight train was coming down the active tracks on the other side of the river.

"Why do I get the writing job?" Cole complained.

Clara called out the numbers on their father's signal and Cole wrote them down in the notebook. At first, Clara had to raise her voice slightly to be heard over the train. By the time she was reading out the last numbers, she was full out yelling, and the train wasn't even in sight yet.

"Now what?" shouted Clara.

"Now we wait an hour and measure it again to see how much the stars have moved," said Mr. Lund.

"You mean, how far *we* have moved." Clara was still shouting to be heard over the train.

"Technically speaking, yes." Mr. Lund cupped his hands around his mouth to amplify his voice.

"So, you'll be able to tell where we are based on these numbers?" shouted Cole. "Can we move a little closer so we don't have to yell?" As he spoke, Cole gestured with his arms and the three of them huddled close together.

"Um, so I won't really be able to tell where we are, because, well, the measurement is supposed to be against the horizon, not mountain tops, and this thing probably hasn't been calibrated for a hundred years, but I'm still going to see where it puts us. It will be fun." Clara looked at their father blankly and Cole gave him a pat on the back.

Finally, a bright light appeared on the trees upriver and began working its way toward them. The freight train turned a corner revealing its gleaming headlights. The rumbling sound intensified until it felt like the whole valley was shaking around them. Of course, that was also a good time for the conductor to blow the horn, which was earsplitting.

The three of them crouched down, covering their ears and, for some reason unknown to Cole, Clara started yelling. A few seconds passed and Cole, observing their ridiculous, huddled, ear-covered squats in the middle of the rocky shore of the not-so-mighty Lehigh, began to laugh. Soon, Clara and their father giggled uncontrollably too. Eventually, the horn stopped, but the rumbling went on with the same intensity. The freight cars just kept coming and coming, even long after the engine had disappeared along to the southern curve.

"Maybe we can just do a half hour," shouted Mr. Lund as he lit up his digital watch. He was answered with eager nods.

After the extremely long train and its sounds had disappeared around the bend, they completed their second round of measurements and headed back to the path. As they started through the woods, Cole heard a rustling sound up ahead to their left, like someone walking through dead leaves. Approaching the pine tree tunnel, he heard the sound again. Clara rushed next to him and grabbed his arm.

"What's that?" she whispered.

Cole looked in the direction of the sound. Through the darkness and the multitude of thin trunks of leafless trees, he saw a standing figure. It was a man, about Cole's height, wearing sweatpants and a sweatshirt with the hood over his head. The hood obscured his face in shadow. Cole thought it kind of looked like an LHS sweatshirt, but he couldn't tell for sure. The man was facing them, standing extremely still.

It was the stillness that got to Cole and sent shivers up his spine. The figure's only movement was a slight raise in his shoulders with each breath. It was as if he had gotten caught trespassing on the property of a shot-gun-wielding centenarian and he thought that if he stayed really still he might get mistaken for a tree. It wasn't working. Cole fought his instinct to run away, for Clara's sake.

Mr. Lund, walking a few steps ahead, greeted the figure casually. "Hello there, lovely evening we're having."

The figure didn't move or respond. Mr. Lund just kept walking and Cole and Clara followed. As they got closer, Clara squeezed Cole's arm even harder and he felt a change in the hum. Suddenly, the figure let out a soft groan and hunched forward. Cole realized that Clara was using the hum to throw things at the mystery man.

"Hey, what are you doing?" said Cole.

"I don't know. He's freaking me out," whispered Clara.

"Just leave him alone."

"Let's get out of here." Clara let go of Cole's arm and ran ahead to catch up with their father.

Cole kept walking, trying to play it cool and not look at the creeper. Cole noticed that his shoelace was untied but ignored it and kept walking into the pine tree tunnel section of the path. By the time Cole cleared the tunnel, Clara and his dad had already crossed the tracks and were halfway up the hill to the beer distributor. Feeling back in civilization and sufficiently far from the hooded woodsman, Cole knelt down to tie his shoelace. Just then he heard rustling in the trees behind him. Another chill went up his back and he froze in fear.

"Hey," said a somewhat familiar voice. The hooded man could be Asa or someone else from school just messing with him, he assured himself. But why? Why in the middle of the night, down by the river? Cole was freaked out. He didn't dare look back and focused on his shoelace.

"Cole, don't open the door," said the voice.

Goosebumps ran up Cole's legs and arms—the man knew his name. *And what door? We're outside, you freak.* Giving up on his shoelace, Cole ran across the tracks at full speed, stopping only after rejoining his family. He never looked back. For the rest of the walk home, "don't open the door" ran through his head, over and over. What could it mean? What prank did Asa have planned for him? Was it even Asa? There were plenty of guys at school who would want to prank him, especially during basketball season when he was a bit of a joke. When they got to their house, Cole lingered a little behind to let his dad open the front door, just in case.

For the rest of the night, Cole couldn't shake the creeped-out feeling. Every little unexpected sound made him jump. Clara seemed a little off too, but she seemed more sad than jumpy. When it was time to go to bed, they went up to their rooms together. Cole asked her to open his door for him. It wasn't his most manly move, but he knew that if it were Asa messing with him, he wouldn't do anything bad to Clara. When she agreed to open his door without even questioning why, he knew that something was bothering her. She just walked over, opened the door and turned to go to her room.

"You okay?"

"Yeah, I'm fine," she said without looking back. She sniffled.

"You sure? Look at me." She turned to face him. Her eyes were red and watery. She was holding back tears. "Seriously, what's the matter?"

"I used it to hurt someone. It's what I was afraid of from the beginning. And I did it without a second thought."

"Don't worry about it."

"I just pelted some poor old river hermit with rocks, just because I had the willies. What's next?" Her voice was shaky and angry.

"You were startled. It's not your fault."

"Whose fault is it then?"

"Nobody's. We're just getting used to it. You'll control it next time."

"Will I? It was just a man in the woods. What if next time it's something really scary? I could kill someone," she said. "And to think, I wasn't even worried that I would be the one. I was so sure *you* would misuse it one day and get us into trouble." She let out a little laugh through her tears. "But it was me . . . me." She wiped the tears from her cheeks with the palms of her hands.

"You're being too hard on yourself. It's not a big deal. You'll feel better in the morning."

"I don't know."

"Seriously. It was a mistake. You don't need to cry."

"That's the thing. It wasn't a mistake. I meant it. And I'm not crying because I feel bad—I'm crying because I *don't* feel bad. It felt good—I liked it. That's what's upsetting."

"You're making a bigger deal of it than it is. You're just not yourself."

"What does that even mean? Who am I really?"

"Look, you're getting worked up. It was a stressful night and you just need a good night's sleep. I'm still creeped out too." Cole considered telling her that the man had talked to him, but he decided against it. That would probably just stress her out even more. It was certainly stressing him out more.

"Yeah, you're probably right."

He could tell she just wanted the conversation to end so she could go to bed. "Sweet dreams, sis."

"Night," she said, shutting her bedroom door.

Cole went into his room and got ready for bed. It took him awhile to fall asleep. He kept running through all the possibilities of which classmate might want to mess with him. It was a pretty long list, not because he had a lot of enemies but because he was also a bit of a prankster and what goes around comes around.

He didn't feel Clara use the hum at all that night. She was usually up until all hours using it to practice or translate the photocopies of the book. Almost every morning, she would update Cole on what she had read, but it was clear he wouldn't get any updates the next morning. He'd probably have his morning OJ in silence instead of the usual stories about the mysterious ways of the Order or great battles with the Viking version of Xena warrior princesses. He thought most of the stories were pretty boring, but he sure did have a thing for those badass Viking sisters.

TWENTY-THREE

I t was easy enough to get the list from father's office. I thought good-ol' Marty would let me waltz right into the hospital offices. You probably knew Marty, Mother—the fat old security guard on the Madison Ave side. Always with the same old "I knew you when you were this high" bullshit. He chased me for a bit but it worked out. Nothing a little shove down the stairs couldn't fix. Anyway, the list has some tasty morsels in it. The Coolidge brat has the eyes, Mother, and maybe the power. The world won't miss her, that's for sure. There are twins in Westchester. Is that double the pleasure? There are even triplets in Ireland. I met one of them once. A long time ago. She was odd, but intriguing. Think of it, Mother. Three times the power at one go. I need to get stronger. Then my path will become clearer.

TWENTY-FOUR

Clara's mouth burned as she pulled in large gulps of her coffee. Yes, she was running late and Cole was yelling at her to hurry up from the porch, but she wasn't about to face a day of school without a full mug's worth of caffeine running through her veins.

"Okay, okay. I'm coming."

"Come on. What took you so long?" Cole was already on the sidewalk as Clara locked the front door.

"Sorry, I overslept. It took a while to fall asleep." She had spent a couple hours analyzing the incident in the woods and dissecting her hot and cold relationship with the hum. She had used it to hurt someone and that frightened her, but it had also made her feel strong. She was a force to be reckoned with, not just some impotent, friendless loser scurrying to the auditorium to eat lunch alone. Although so very obvious in retrospect, it had not previously occurred to her that by having a power, *she* was powerful.

"I slept pretty well," said Cole, picking up his backpack as she caught up to him. "So, what were the names of the Viking sisters?"

"Not sure. I haven't seen their names in the book yet. Why?"

"No reason. Just curious."

"You know they've been dead for a thousand years, right? I get you're into skinny girls, but actual skeletons might be taking it too far."

"Hey. Not cool. I was just wondering." He laughed and shoved her off the path that cut across the square.

They speed-walked in silence until a gruff voice boomed at them from across the street.

"Hey look, it's dumb and dumber."

"Morning, Sal. Any shifts open this weekend? I could use some cash."

"Why don't you ask prissy pants there to lend you some? I bet she has a wad of cash stashed away somewhere. And I bet I can guess where from the look on her face." The force of Sal's laughs caused her to lean forward, putting her hands on her knees until she caught her breath.

"So, no shifts then?" asked Cole, unphased.

"Not yet, but I'm sure one of those doofuses will flake on me. I'll let you know later in the week."

"Thanks."

"God, I hate her," said Clara, picking up their already brisk pace.

"Just let it go. She's harmless."

As they approached the house with the stuffed bunny in the backyard, Clara looked up at the road ahead and then quickly over her shoulder. No one was out on the street except them. No witnesses. No rumors. It was time. *I am powerful.*

Clara swung her backpack around on one shoulder and pulled out a stack of Spanish flashcards. She fumbled with the cards in her shaky hands until the rotting pink mound of fur came into view down the narrow space between the houses. Slowing down just enough that Cole wouldn't notice, she stared at a grey lump at the base—maybe it was once the bunny's cute little cotton tail—and focused on it and the hum. Recalling her technique in the training room, she focused on the hottest part of a flame, which she knew from A.P. Chem was the blue part. She imagined a pulsing indigo light dancing around the grey lump, smothering it like how Cole preferred to completely ruin perfectly good marshmallows by charring the living crap out of them. *How can he eat those? It's like licking an ashtray.*

Pulling her thoughts back to the bunny, she again pictured the hottest heat on the lump. Suddenly, the faintest flicker of blue appeared just under the lump and it grew into a small flame. As Clara walked, the bunny moved out of view behind the next house.

"Hey, what was that?" asked Cole from several paces ahead. "The hum changed."

"Just me." Clara jogged a few strides to catch up. "I needed some help on this card." Clara slightly lifted the top card from the pile.

"You're cheating on your own flashcards? That's pretty sad."

"Your layups are what's sad."

"Ouch."

Before entering the school's east gate, Clara turned to look back at the town. Rising above the grey rooftops was a pillar of dark smoke and she heard a faint siren starting up in the distance.

Your childhood is over, she told herself. *It's time to let go and grow the hell up.*

When Clara got home that afternoon, she was disappointed to not find a new letter from Amma. It had been almost a week since the last set of pages. She was getting impatient and called Adler to commiserate.

"Hey."

"Hey, it's Clara."

"I know."

"What's that sound?"

"What sound?"

"That thumping sound. It's like club music."

"Oh, yeah. I'm at the gym."

"And it's blasting club music?"

"Of course—it's a nice gym."

"Want me to call you back later?"

"No, now is fine. I'm not really working out."

"What are you doing then?"

"Just looking at people. Hold on, let me get to a quieter spot." The thumping base in the background faded slightly. "Okay, that's better. Before you get started, I have some news. So, after our last call about the Vessel getting stronger after killing the fisherman—"

"It was his wife."

"Whatever. I, um, *borrowed* the list from my dad's office."

"What list?"

"The list of kids born with the eyes. You know, in case we want to get stronger."

"So, they can come join us?"

"Uh, sure. So, get this, Thalia Coolidge is on the list."

"Should I know who that is?"

"Yes. Daughter of Jaime Coolidge . . ."

"Like related to the president, Calvin Coolidge?"

"I don't know—who cares about that? Jaime Coolidge is the founder of Core Bank. He's one of the richest, most powerful people in the city. You've really never heard of him? He's on the board of directors at the hospital with Gran. And her mother is from a Greek shipping family, so Thalia is like the richest six-year-old on the planet."

"How would I know any of that?"

"Everyone knows that. Everyone."

"How many are on the list?" Clara caught herself nodding her head to the beat of the gym music.

"I think about twelve. I don't have it with me. There are twin boys around your age in Sleepy Hollow. Did you know that was a real place? It's right up the Hudson, near the Tappan Zee."

"Yes. Everyone knows that. Everyone." Clara felt pretty pleased with herself.

"And there are triplets in Ireland. Three for one!"

"Oh, I—" Clara cut herself off before revealing that she knew one of the Irish triplets. "Never mind. Where are the others?"

"They're scattered all around, San Fran, Boston, London, Oslo, if I remember correctly. So that's my contribution. You can go ahead with the pages."

"Huh?"

"Go ahead . . . with the new stories from Amma's pages."

"Oh. I don't have any. She hasn't sent anymore."

"What? Then why are you calling?" Adler's voice was loud and breathy with exasperation.

"I don't know. To talk—see how you're doing?"

"I'm doing fine. Call when you have more pages."

"Wait, wait, hold on. I'm ready to talk about it—your issues with Harlem. I'm ready." *I am ready. I'm powerful and ready to act like it.*

"What makes you think you're ready?"

"I just am. I can handle it."

"Tell me, what's the most interesting thing you've done with the power? And no, your Spanish nerd shit isn't interesting."

Clara thought back on her uses of the hum. It was mostly Spanish, but she had a few good ones. "So, besides the translating and the stuff in the rooms, I've used it to run—"

Adler interrupted her with a loud, exaggerated yawn.

"I'm not done. I've used it to pelt someone with rocks."

"Why?"

"Huh?"

"Why did you pelt them?"

"Because he was creeping around the woods. I got scared."

"Fear isn't a good reason. It's too easy. What else?"

"Well, I set fire to—" Clara paused to think of the best way to phrase it. "I set fire to someone else's personal property."

"What was it?"

"Why does that matter?" Torching the bunny had been a major symbolic act for Clara, but Adler wouldn't appreciate the deeper meaning.

"Tell me."

"Fine. It was a stuffed animal."

Adler belted out a single "ha" and then said, "Look, you're not ready. You might never be and that's okay. But I had high hopes for you. You have the potential for greatness."

"I don't even know what I'm supposed to be ready for." Clara felt like a mouse being toyed with by a cat. Remembering Thanksgiving, maybe a hawk was more fitting.

"Ready to hear the truth—why I'm the way I am, and my new project. You and I could change the world."

"How? What am I supposed to do? Why are you messing with me?" Clara wanted to reach through the phone and strangle him.

"Don't worry about it. Just call when you have more pages. I need to go."

"Wait, I was thinking I could come visit this weekend. There's a bus that leaves from right across the square."

"My weekend is full. Just call with pages."

"But Adl—" The call cut out. Clara gripped the phone so tightly she thought it might crush like an empty soda can.

For the rest of the evening Adler's words replayed in her head—his coy phrases, his games, his bullshit aura of mystery. She considered getting on the bus just to go kick him in the nuts and get right on the next return bus. But at the same time, she wanted to be "ready"—whatever the hell that meant—and she wanted to change the world with her friend, to use the power to make great things happen.

What do I need to do, she wondered.

VIII

At word of the approaching Greymen, the two Viking suitors and their men, all drunk and staggering, prepared their ships and fled Stóra Dímun for their homelands. Greymen and Vikings were no strangers to each other. Thurandur and most of his men also departed for the northern Faroes, but he left a representative to accept Gudrid's hand on his behalf should that be her decision. The other non-Dímuner Faroese also left for their respective islands. The Blue Prince and the Irishman stayed where they were, perhaps not knowing any better. Estrid and Sigmundr, who had been too busy talking to each other to fully partake in the mead, ran to Brestir's farm to collect a pitchfork and the dream thistle tea, which was dark and potent after five days of brewing. Racing the arrival of the Greymen's large ship into the harbor, Sigmundr and Estrid ran back to the village. They snuck into Thoralf's warehouse and poured the dream thistle tea into the mead barrel of the tribute reserve.

As with prior years, the Greymen brought with them many large and fierce warriors who quickly subdued what little resistance the Dímuners offered. Being as tired and impaired as they were, many Dímuners thought it unwise to engage in a fight and they instead rested on the hope that the small tribute reserve would somehow satisfy the Greymen and avoid their dark magic.

The Greymen and their warriors gathered up all the people on the island and corralled them onto the common. The leader of the Greymen ascended the platform and glowered down at the drunken throng. He wore a long gray woolen robe with no adornment other than a thin silver necklace from which hung a small glass vial caged in intricately etched metal. The vial held a dark liquid that quivered at the slightest motion.

Raising his voice above the whimpering crowd, the leader demanded silence and that the tribute be presented for inspection at once.

TWENTY-FIVE

Cole gave Sal a wave from across the street as he and Clara walked by on their way to school. Sal was sweeping the sidewalk while somehow also smoking a cigarette and talking on her cellphone that was smushed against her face by her large shoulder. With almost every part of her body in use, she acknowledged Cole's wave with only a quick raise of her eyebrows, one of which was cut in half by the scar.

As they continued on their way to school, Cole felt a change in the hum, followed by a clang from across the street. Turning toward the sound, he saw that a metal lid had fallen off a trashcan and into Sal's path. Distracted by her various activities, she stepped on it and it slid away from her, causing her legs to do a split as she tried to hold herself up with the broom. Her phone fell to the sidewalk and, losing her grip on the broom, she fell forward onto her knees. The cigarette stayed firmly in place between her thin lips, even as she cursed and groaned all the way to the ground.

"What the hell, Clara?" Cole scowled at her before running across the street to help.

"Motherfucking trashcans! I swear to god they'll be the death of me," said Sal from the cigarette-free side of her mouth.

"Are you alright?" Cole grabbed one of her solid arms to help pull her up.

"I'm fine, thanks. But look at my fucking knees?" Sal pointed at her torn jeans that revealed pink and red scrapes on her knee-caps. "Now I'll never win the swimsuit competition!" Sal cackled and took a drag.

"Seriously, are you okay? That was some fall."

"I said I'm fine. Thanks for helping me up, hon." She kicked the lid hard and it skidded across the sidewalk, hitting the brick wall of her restaurant with a clatter. "You better get going or you'll be late."

Cole picked up the broom and handed it to her before crossing the street. Clara was just standing there, looking straight ahead in the direction of school. She started walking before he got to the sidewalk.

"Hey, that wasn't cool. What's your problem?" Cole ran a few steps to catch up to her.

"She's a bitch to me. She deserved it."

"She's like that with everyone. Don't take it personally."

"Well, someone needs to teach her a lesson."

"You think that taught her a lesson? You think she'll be like, hey, that trashcan lid wants me to be nicer to people?"

"Whatever."

"Seriously, we really shouldn't use it like that. What if she had fallen on her head?" Cole pulled his lucky whistle out of his pocket and displayed it on the palm of his hand. "See this? This is the whistle that nearly killed Mr. Ray. I used the hum to hit him, then I used the hum to save him. We decide how to use it: good or bad. It's our responsibility to make the right choice. The whistle reminds me of that."

"How is all your cheating to win games good? Isn't it bad for the other team, or for sportsmanship in general?"

"True, but I allow myself one little exception for sports."

"Well, my exception is taking down fat bitches."

"Yikes. Do you hear yourself? You need to relax."

"I'm just saying, what's good or bad isn't always black and white. It's all relative. You think a sports exception is harmless, but what about the kid on the other side trying to get a sport scholarship? You think tripping the pizza lady is bad, but see how nice she was to you when you helped her up? Maybe she'll start to appreciate the people around her more."

"That's B.S. and you know it. Weren't you the one so worried about the dangers of the power? Now you're knocking people down in broad daylight. What changed?"

"I did. I'm starting to appreciate the benefits of it. Like you said, we were given it for a reason and should use it."

"I meant a *good* reason, not to hurt anyone who happens to piss you off."

"She doesn't *happen* to piss me off. She intentionally does it almost every day."

"That doesn't make what you did okay. Look, we're bound to have slipups. We're only human—I think. I'm just saying we need to be thoughtful about how we use it. Being impulsive could be dangerous. Something tangible, like a whistle, might help remind you to make the right choices—it works for me." Cole tossed the whistle into the air and, in one fluid motion, caught it and put it back in his pocket.

"I'm not you."

"No kidding."

A few days later was the February full moon. With the morning after falling on a Saturday, Cole didn't have the leverage with Clara to get any concessions for him to wake up early. She knew he would want to do the rooms at some point in the morning, so she had played it cool.

Cole was between the end of basketball season—which had

finally come, to his great relief—and the beginning of baseball season, for which he was almost counting down the seconds. He was confident that the murmur would be a great asset in baseball. Murmur was his current name for the hum, but Clara wasn't a fan. "It already feels like a heart condition—let's not name it after one," she had said when he first came up with it. He knew it wasn't perfect, but he was determined to keep trying.

By the time Cole went down to the kitchen to get his morning OJ, Clara was already sitting at the kitchen table sipping her coffee and reading a newspaper.

"Good morning, my dear sister."

"Morning." Clara glanced at him above the paper. She didn't have her contacts in and her eyes glinted in the sunlight coming in through the kitchen window. He rarely saw her like that and was a bit taken aback at first.

"Lovely morning."

"Indeed."

"Any plans for the day?" Cole poured his orange juice.

"Oh, nothing much. I'll probably just head to Jim Thorpe for at least some semblance of civilization. You know, the usual," said Clara, from behind the paper. "You?"

"Just hanging out. I'm covering a shift at Sal's later," he said, adding, "the pizza place," after Clara gave him a look.

"Sounds good."

"Yep."

"Uh huh."

"Are we done?" asked Cole.

"Yes." Clara gave him a sly smile. She stood up and they both ran to the living room and up the stairs.

Having gone first the last time, Cole agreed to let Clara go first. She didn't hesitate: she walked right over to the corner, turned around, leaned her head, coughed surprisingly little and that was it. She was getting good at drowning, thought Cole.

"Well, good luck, brother," she said.

"What is it?"

"I'm not telling—where's the fun in that? You'll have to figure it out like the rest of us."

"Us?"

"Just go."

Now that he had started the pattern, he couldn't help but
think about Molly from the Weissport Dunkin' Donuts every
time he went in or out of the training room. *Is that now what I'll
think about when I'm actually dying?* he wondered. Would his last
thought be of a light blue cable-knit sweater on a girl that the
most he'd ever said to was "two Boston creams, please?"

Once Cole had drowned his way into the training room, the
first thing he noticed was the rumbling sound. He kept forgetting that there was a sound in the room. In his memories, which
he had rerun countless times, it was always silent in the room
except for the crackling fire. In his last three times in the room,
he had gotten used to the noise pretty quickly; it had just faded
into the background, which is probably why he kept forgetting
about it. The room was the same as last month except that in
the place of the candle was a small birdcage, also pewter like the
candlestick had been.

The birdcage was bird-free and the little gate to it was open.
Cole sat down on the bench and looked at the cage for a few
seconds until he heard a faint scratching sound from the rafters
above. He looked up. Peering down at him was the face of a little bird. It was about the size and coloring of a sparrow, but its
head and neck were a faded red. Cole and the bird stared at each
other for a couple of seconds. The bird tilted its head slightly, as
though wondering who Cole was and what he was doing there.

"Hi, birdie," said Cole. The bird tilted its head in the other
direction, then turned around on the rafter to reveal its tan tail
feathers. Suddenly, Cole saw something white falling down right
at him and he shifted to the side just in time to avoid getting hit
in the face with bird excrement. He was not fast enough to avoid

it altogether though. A white blob had landed on his shoulder and a cloudy liquid ran down the sleeve of his shirt. "Why you little . . ." growled Cole as he rose from the seat and swatted at the rafter where the bird sat just out of reach. The bird chirped and flew to another rafter in the corner. From there, it turned to look back at him. Cole searched for something to throw at it, but there was nothing. He really wished the stacking stones were still around.

Cole tried to refocus on the task at hand. It was pretty obvious that this month's challenge was to get the stupid bird back into the cage. He had to use the murmur to get the bird to do that. *Clara is right*, thought Cole, *murmur is not a good fit*. Anyway, he had to use the hum, but how?

It couldn't be that hard, Cole assured himself. Adler was controlling birds by his second time using the hum. A vision of Adler and the hawk creepily staring at each other while the hawk ate the pigeon guts drifted through his head. Cole tried staring at the sparrow. It just looked back at him and turned its pea-brained head to the side like a jerk.

Cole tried to concentrate on the hum and the bird and the cage, over and over like he had done for moving the stones. He tried that for about fifteen minutes without success. At one point he thought it was working, but the bird was just flying back to the other rafter to take another dump on him. Cole darted out of the way in time, but the droppings hit the table in front of him and splattered onto the front of his shirt. He yelled at the bird again and it just chirped and flew back to the corner. *How could there be nothing in the whole room to throw at that little asshole?* Maybe he could just use the hum to knock the bird against a wall a little, Cole wondered. At that thought, the bird straightened up, shifted its feet and then chirped. The bird looked nervous. It didn't turn its head to the side. It just looked straight at Cole, as though it was worried about what Cole was going to do. *Interesting*, he thought.

"Hey bird-face, if you don't turn your head to the side and stand on one leg, I am going to use my power to toss your stupid little body into the fire," said Cole to the bird.

The bird complied. Cole didn't need to control the bird, he realized—he just had to incentivize it to do what he wanted. The bird understood what Cole's power could do to it and, so it seemed, could read Cole's thoughts. Cole smiled and then thought, *listen bird, unless you want to be reduced to a red splotch on that stone wall behind you, you better get into that cage right now!* The bird leapt from the corner rafter and flew right into the cage at top speed. Cole shut and locked the little gate and then the glow of the "out" runes flickered in Cole's peripheral vision.

After he warm-drowned himself back to his bedroom and caught his breath, he immediately looked down at his shirt where the bird crap had landed. The shirt was clean.

"That little shitter got you too, huh?" asked Clara.

TWENTY-SIX

It would seem that people don't appreciate the dangers of living across the street from a zoo. Even rich people, Mother. Thinking nothing bad could ever happen on Fifth Avenue even when just across the street wild animals are pacing their cages, wishing for nothing but to escape and eat a bunch of Upper East Siders. After I broke the glass, the snow leopard was more than happy to comply with my instructions. Being stronger feels better, Mother. It's less jittery. More focused.

TWENTY-SEVEN

After speed walking home from school, Clara immediately checked the mail for a letter from Amma. It had been almost three weeks since the last letter and Clara was becoming impatient. It was almost as if Amma had better things to do than sit in front of a Xerox machine all day. Clara couldn't think of what an old lady, alone, in still-frigid Maine could be doing with her time that was more important than making her only supernatural granddaughter happy. She really wanted to call Adler, but, after last time, she wasn't about to try that without some pages to report. Thankfully, a letter had arrived in the mail that day, though it wasn't as thick as Clara would have liked.

Dear Honeybee,

Your mother told me about that nasty cold you had last week. I hope you are feeling better. It reached up to fifty degrees here on Tuesday and some of the big snow piles are somewhat diminished. Everyone in town is excited for spring to finally arrive. They say it was one of the snowiest winters on record, which does not sound right to me. Everyone was out and about in the relatively nice weather. Unfortunately, there was a line at the copy machine at Prout's General so I was only able to copy five pages. The book gets enough curious looks without people also rolling their eyes at me for taking too long at the machine. The copies are of some of the early pages that I skipped translating, but I think it's more sailing around the fjords in Norway. The Order seems to love writing about sailing trips. Let me know if you find anything interesting.

Which reminds me, I have some good news on the book. I think I found some people who can help us locate the other volumes. I discovered on the World Wide Web a place in Iceland that studies old Norse books like ours. It is the Árni Magnússon Institute for Viking and Medieval Norse Studies. It is in Reykjavík and is affiliated with the University of Iceland. From what I can tell, it is highly respected. After Gail Robinson taught me how to dial internationally (you met Gail last summer at yoga class), I called to see what kind of impression they gave me and they were really nice and sounded smart (although their accents are a little funny). I sent them a letter asking if they know of our book or any other related volumes and I enclosed photocopies of a few pages. You would not believe how many stamps I had to put on the letter. I have not heard back yet, but it is pretty exciting. Even if they can't point us to the other volumes, I'm sure they can help in other ways, such as figuring out how old the book is. I will write you as soon as I hear back from them.

I am glad you are taking such an interest in translating the book, but do not forget to be a teenager. Relax and have a little fun. You should get outside and try to make some new friends. I know it is not easy to connect with people there, but what about the coffee shop you like so much? Does anyone your age hang out there too? What is the name of that town again? John Thorn? And how is that Aca fellow?

Well, I need to head into town for yoga class. We have a yogi visiting all the way from Varanasi! I miss you and

cannot wait to see you this summer. Our first summer with-
out your parents! I will write again soon, and yes, I will send
more pages.
    Love,
    Amma

P.S. Have you talked to Adler recently? He hasn't written me
back in weeks.

There were a lot of things that Clara didn't like about Amma's letter. For one, sending copies of only five pages was frus-
trating. What are the chances that there will be something wor-
thy of reporting to Adler in only five pages?

Second, Clara didn't appreciate the preachiness about getting
out there and making friends, or other nonsense like that. What
happened to saying she didn't have to worry about it because
she'd be going off to college in a couple years? Clara suspected
her mother was pushing that line to Amma behind the scenes.

They don't understand the type of people I am dealing with here,
Clara thought.

The third thing she didn't like about the letter, and the most
concerning, was Amma sending pages out into the unknown
world. Who were these people at the Arni Institute, or whatever?
Could they be trusted? What if the book was some great lost
work of pre-medieval literature that would be newsworthy, or
would somehow draw attention to them? It was out of character for Amma to be so reckless. *She is getting old though*, thought
Clara. Maybe she's not thinking things through as carefully as
she used to.

Clara would have to give that more thought and maybe ask
Amma to not do anything like that without consulting her first,
but, for now, she had pages to translate. After unsuccessfully
searching for Cole in his usual spots around the house, she reluctantly accepted that she would have to put the translating on

hold until he got home. In the meantime, she would actually try to do some homework. Schoolwork had not been a priority of hers since Christmas break, as shown by her recent grades. How could she be expected to care about Pre-calc or A.P. Chemistry when she had a superpower and was about to change the world with her cousin?

Clara tucked the letter under her arm and went into the kitchen, where her parents were sitting around the table having an early dinner. She made herself a plate of food, telling them that she would need to eat in her room because she had a lot of homework. Her dad said something encouraging about the importance of junior year grades, which she acknowledged with a deflecting, "I know, right? That's what I keep trying to tell Cole."

She felt Cole get into his bed a little after nine o'clock. She stopped writing her English paper mid-sentence and got to work translating the new pages. Amma was right that the pages were mostly the Order sailing around, as they loved to do, but there was one interesting tidbit tucked away at the bottom of page four. While the Order's ship was moored off the coast of Flotta in Orkneyjar—now the Orkney Islands, according to Wikipedia—a large rowboat full of Pictish fighters from the nearby islands approached undetected. It was early morning and the Order and its warriors, including the neglectful night watchman, were fast asleep, several of them on the deck to escape the heat. When within striking distance, the Picts silently launched a barrage of arrows, killing many on the deck of the Order's ship, including the Vessel. Rather than retaliate and massacre the fighters and decimate all of the nearby settlements, as was the Order's usual M.O., they immediately hoisted the sails and returned to their headquarters, Twin Halls, on the outskirts of the village Vágar in Lofoten.

Clara looked up Vágar on her computer, but it didn't seem

to exist anymore, but Lofoten was still around. It was a large archipelago in northern Norway, the online pictures of which entranced Clara. The islands were slender, snow-peaked mountains rising right out of the sea. It looked like a landscape that Elsa from *Frozen* would have created in one of her moods.

Arriving home at Twin Halls, the leader went straight to East Hall. It was the first time the book had mentioned East Hall. Most of the Order's activities were in West Hall, or at sea, of course. After the leader's visit to East Hall, there was a new Vessel without any explanation except directing the reader to "refer to the *Chronicles of East Hall*." They then returned to the ship to hunt down the Pictish archer who would then have had the power from killing the prior Vessel.

The East Hall story was definitely worth reporting to Adler. The Order went there when they needed a new Vessel—it could hold the source of the power. Clara tried to anticipate Adler's questions. "But the Viking sisters torched the Norwegian Twin Halls," he'd likely say, to which Clara planned to explain that the Order build an exact replica of Twin Halls in Iceland after fleeing the Viking sisters. "But we don't have the *Chronicles of East Hall*, this story raises more questions than it gives answers," he'll say. "But we now know something significant happens there and we know the power comes from *something*, not just passed down genetically," was her planned reply. She was ready. She snuck downstairs to retrieve the phone from its base on the kitchen counter. It was a little after midnight, but Adler would still be awake—heck, he'd probably be up for another five hours at least.

"Hello?" Adler hiccupped mid-word.

"Hey, it's me."

"Who?"

"Clara. Are you drunk?"

"No." He took a quick breath, clearly intended to stifle a hiccup. "I've only had a few martinis."

"How many?"

"One, two, three, four, five." There was a faint clinking sound after each number.

"Jesus. Five martinis could get a rhino drunk."

"I'm not a rhino. Do you have pages?"

"Yes, but first I want to talk. I'm ready to hear what's bugging you and your plans to fix the world."

"You? Ready? Pfff."

"I am. I made someone fall."

"Oooo, so imp . . . impressive. How?"

"I slid a trashcan lid under her foot when she was walking. She almost did a split. You would have cracked up."

"Why?"

"Because it was funny. She's really fat."

"No, I mean why did you do it?"

"Because she's a bitch. She's rude to me and deserved it."

"If Jennifer Lawrence was mean to you, would you trip her?"

"God no, of course not."

"Why not?"

"Because she's Jennifer Lawrence—she's allowed to be rude to me."

"Why is she allowed?"

"Because she's amazing. I'm a nothing compared to her. She can be rude if she wants."

"So, tell me, why was it okay for you to trip that fat lady? Being rude apparently isn't enough. What else?"

Clara thought for a moment, trying to figure out what Adler was getting at. "Well . . . I guess . . . cause she's a nothing compared to me?"

"Don't ask me. Look into your heart."

Clara closed her eyes and took a deep breath. "Yes. Because she's beneath me—she's a disgusting animal, a worthless piece of white trash." Clara gasped at the words she heard coming out of her mouth. *Is that really what's in my heart?*

"That's the most honest thing I've ever heard you say." Adler took a slurpy sip of his drink. "Maybe you are ready after all. Do you want to hear it now?"

Clara was having second thoughts—if that hate-filled version of herself was who she had to be in order to be "ready," she wasn't sure she wanted to hear what came next. Part of her wanted to hang up, grab a stuffed animal off the shelf and curl up under the covers. But she had come too far to turn back—her evolution had begun. She had already built the chrysalis around herself and going back to a naïve caterpillar hiding under a leaf was no longer an option. Sure, she might not emerge as the majestic monarch butterfly or beautiful blue morpho that she once thought she'd become, but it was time to emerge, in whatever form she was meant to take. And with Adler at her side, she wouldn't be surprised if she broke through and unfurled her wings as a shrieking bat or a fire-breathing dragon. It was time to scratch the skin of the cocoon and let in a sliver of light, or darkness.

"Go ahead."

"Hold on."

Clara heard the rapid, tinny beat of a martini shaker. "Are you sure you need another?"

"No, but I want one," said Adler, followed by the breathy hissing sound of his first sip.

Clara could picture his wide, contorted mouth as he tried to breathe in the top layer of the martini, his white incisors resting on the shallow glass rim.

"Mmmm, that's good."

"Can we get started? It's late—for some of us."

"So, my mother didn't die during childbirth—she was murdered."

Clara gasped. She knew there was something fishy about Aunt Clara's death, but she wasn't expecting that. "Aunt Clara? How? Why?"

"When she was walking to the hospital to have dinner with my dad. She went the long way to pick up his favorite empanadas to surprise him." Adler's voice quivered as he spoke. Clara had never heard him like that before. Something was just under the surface, like at any moment he could burst out sobbing or yelling or even laughing. "While she was walking to the hospital on 102nd, crossing Park Ave through the tunnel under the tracks, they attacked her—a gang of thugs, animals. She was eight months pregnant and they slit her throat, they left her—and me—to die in the filth, rats scurrying all around us."

The thought of Aunt Clara, serene and beautiful in old photos, pregnant and dying alone in a dingy pedestrian tunnel was too horrible to believe, but Clara believed it. Yes, Adler liked to say shocking things, often with total disregard to the truth, but he wasn't lying about that. Clara could tell from his voice and, after over five martinis, he probably couldn't have lied about it even if he had wanted to.

"Oh my god. Adler. I'm so sorry, I didn't know any of that."

"Of course not. You're not supposed to. Much easier for dad and the rest of them to say it was childbirth—so everyone can secretly blame the little baby, the baby that didn't want to be born into that, to be born out of a dead mother. Life from death."

Clara thought back to all the times she and Cole had tried to get more information about Clara's death, all the furtive glances and abrupt subject changes. Now knowing the circumstances, Clara didn't blame them for keeping it a secret. What could they have said? When could she have handled the truth? Never. *It would have been better to never know.*

"That's terrible." Clara scanned her mind for something else to say. "They should have told us," she lied. Her throat felt thick with his pain. "Were you born out on the sidewalk, all alone?"

"I don't think so, but who knows? You can't trust anyone." His voice was back under control, forceful and even.

"I'm so sorry, Adler."

"It's okay. I will win in the end."

"Oh, did they find who did it?"

"No, but that doesn't matter—they all did it."

"What do you mean?"

"All of them, the Blacks, the Latinos, they're all part of the same problem."

Clara gasped and momentarily pulled the phone away from her ear to look at it in disbelief. He was going too far. She wasn't going to let that slide. "Whoa, hold on. See, that stuff is where you lose me. How is it anyone's fault except who did it? You said they don't know who it was. It could have been anyone, any race."

"Have you been to East Harlem? It wasn't any race."

"There are bad people in every color and in every part of the city. And even if the people who did it were Black or Latino, they are products of systemic problems—poverty, drug addiction, no access to mental health treatment. It's the whole system that needs to change. That's where you should focus your energy."

"I totally agree. The problems are systemic. They need systemic solutions."

The way he lingered on the s's like a snake made her skin crawl. He took another audible sip of martini and Clara imagined a slender forked tongue darting from his mouth, caressing the bottom of the shallow glass to fondle a sunken olive.

"Yeah, through education, tolerance, access to basic services."

"Don't be naïve. That's just bullshit rich white people say to feel better. The problem is the difference, the visible difference—and human nature, of course."

"I don't understand. And I don't think I want to." Clara was unsure of the right thing to do: Should she hang up or stay on to try to convince him he's wrong?

"Humans have evolved to process differences, to categorize them, rank them. It's instantaneous, subconscious. Like, if Margaret barged into your room holding a gun, what would be your first thought?"

"Um, I guess I'd wonder what she's doing here and if she's okay."

"Right, now what if it's a Black guy?"

"That's not fair—I know Margaret."

"Fine, then think of some white chick you don't know."

"That just highlights *my* issues, what I need to work on to be a better person."

"Are you fucking kidding? It's survival, it's human nature. You can't *work* on it. Just like you can't work on breathing carbon monoxide or drinking cyanide."

"So, what then?" Clara felt the clenched muscle in her jaw pressing against the phone.

"Get rid of the differences."

"Like genocide?"

"But with a noble purpose."

"You've lost your mind. You better be on some major personality-altering drugs right now because this isn't you. You're not like this."

"John Lennon understood. He got that differences are the root of all the violence in the world." Adler cleared his throat and began to sing. "*Imagine there's no countries. It isn't hard to do. Nothing to kill or die for. And no religion, too. Imagine all the pe-po-woo-oh. Living life in pea-ee-ee-e-ece.* See, the differences cause the problems. Because we're humans, we need to get rid of the differences to be at peace. The same goes for race."

"That's not what he meant. You need to stop. Just thinking about that is wrong. You need help."

"It's what I'm meant to do. It's my purpose—the reason I was born that way, the reason I have the power. I will find a way. I'm getting stronger every day and I feel it's out there, some grand solution, some targeted disease or something to prevent their procreation. It's out there, somewhere—a spell, a curse. *You might sa-aa-y I'm a dreamer.*"

"Adler, listen to me, you can't talk like this. I know you like the whole shock-value thing, but this is too much. It crosses too many lines. I know it's just talk—drunken, insane talk—but you need to stop. It's wrong."

"Is it just talk or is it why I have the power? Why the power is on our side."

"Hey, there is no our side. I'm not on team Crazytown. And what if the power is on the non-psychopath side too?"

"It's not. You already figured out that the power is genetic. It's on the white side."

"What if white people with the power stop you?"

"Like who? You? You and Cole? Ha! You two country mice are weak. You're still flicking stones around and kicking balls to get points on the scoreboard. You're nothings."

"Jesus Christ, Adler. Can you hear yourself? This isn't you. You need to talk to someone."

"I'm talking to you. You said you were ready."

"You need to talk to a *professional*." Clara heard a gasp then a crash.

"Shit, you made me spill my drink. Now I need to make another."

"This isn't funny. I'm really sorry about Aunt Clara, but you're directing that energy to the wrong place." Clara heard a few metallic clinks.

"My energy is directed to the right place . . . this shaker."

"Why don't you give the drinks a rest. You're clearly drunk based on the bullshit coming out of your mou—"

Clara was cut off by the sound of the shaker. It was louder this time, as if he were holding it right up to the phone. The rhythmic sound kept going and going. She tried to yell his name over it, but there was no answer. After a few minutes, she lost her patience and hung up. She looked at the phone in disbelief—had that conversation really happened? Had that really been Adler?

Of course, five and a half martinis are a lot, plus whatever pills were in the mix. And it was probably emotional for him to tell her about Aunt Clara. Maybe that just opened up the floodgates to every negative thought he had ever had about the whole ordeal.

He couldn't possibly have meant what he said, she told herself.

She decided she would call him back the next day, to make sure he had sobered up and was back on the planet. They would talk about the new pages and then brainstorm ways they could actually make the world a better place. *He just needs direction, that's all.*

When she called him after school the following day, there was no answer. She tried again late that evening, but again, no answer. The next morning, she called the apartment phone and Sylvia said he was asleep, but when she tried later that day, Sylvia said he was out for the night. She tried his cellphone a few more times, but then gave up. He would talk to her in a few days, after the next training room, she reasoned. He wouldn't be able to resist talking it over with her and then bragging about how he stayed in the room to do a bigger and badder version of the task.

When the morning of the next training room arrived, Clara awoke to Cole knocking on her door.

"Alright, alright," she grumbled.

"Are you okay? It's a room day and we need to leave for school soon."

"Relax, I just overslept. I'll be right over. Whose turn is it to go first?"

"Mine. Hurry up."

When she entered Cole's room, he was already in position, his back leaning into the corner. He gave her two thumbs up, leaned his head back and immediately started coughing up a lung. *He's not getting used to it*, she thought. *What a wimp.*

"Ugh, that was creepy," he said once he caught his breath. He wiggled his body like he had the heebie-jeebies, then flicked his hands like he was trying to fling off invisible mud. "Have fun."

"What is it?" asked Clara.

"No, no, you have to figure it out just like the rest of us," he said, punctuating the end of his sentence with air quotes.

"You used to be the nice one." She moved into position in the corner.

When she got into her training room, the anticipated moaning woman sounds from outside were more like screams.

"Hello?" Clara called out in a loud voice.

The screams faded immediately, but she still heard the usual baby crying and the woman whimpering. *What the hell is going on out there?* She wondered. Was that supposed to be her psyche or something? Why oh why couldn't she just have a train sound like Cole?

She scanned the room. On the table was a mirror in a silver frame, propped upright with the help of a little stand in the back, like a picture frame. After checking the rafters for any shit-birds, she sat down on the bench in front of the mirror and looked at her reflection. She should probably do something about her hair before she went to school, she thought.

Sitting quietly and pondering what the task could be, she picked up the mirror with both hands and peered into it. Was she supposed to go into the mirror, like into another dimension or something? Wasn't she already in another dimension? Going into the mirror seemed like a bit much, even for that whacked-out place. The simplest guess was that she had to change what she looked like. She thought about whom she should become. She could change into her mother or Amma or Gran, but that thought was a little vexing given that she would probably turn into them one day anyway. She put the mirror back down on the table. The fireplace on the opposite wall cast a wavering shadow from the mirror, the edge of which fell in a vertical line down the right side of her face. It reminded her of the nasty scar on that awful pizza lady's face—Sam, or something like that. She knew who to become.

Clara concentrated on the clean, crisp hum of the training room and thought about the pizza lady. Clara imagined her lugging trash cans from the back alley, lit cigarette dangling from her mouth. She thought about her thinning, oily hair, her large fleshy shoulders, her greenish arm tattoos. That succeeded in making her a little nauseous, but Clara's same pale, scarless face, looked back from the mirror.

She decided to take a different approach. There always seemed to be a little trick with the tasks, like convincing the bird to do something, rather than forcing it to. She would think about what it would be like to *be* the pizza lady, not just look like her.

What would it be like for her to see people look at her, to feel their judging eyes on her scar? Would they stare? Would they quickly look away? Would she care? Could she care? Or would she just do her best and move on?

Clara looked in the mirror. It was still her face. She closed her eyes and touched her face where the scar would be. She imagined what it would feel like: hard and fibrous, and yet sensitive to the touch. She reached her hand to her head and imagined tiny moist tendrils running through her fingers instead of her long, dried-out hair.

How would she feel about her hair? Would she worry about what people thought? Or would she just accept that age is a bitch and she worked in a pizza place all day so oil was a part of the deal?

She tried to imagine having a big strong body that could lift two full trash cans at once and could intimidate the likes of Cole and Asa to keep them in line while at her shop—her shop that she built and ran like a boss. Clara started to feel good and proud. She was free from the cares about appearances that she and many other girls her age thought about constantly. She was flesh on bones, a lot of bad ass, tattooed flesh on bones and all those effers would just have to deal with it.

Clara opened her eyes and found the pizza lady staring back from the mirror. She examined her round and scarred face in the mirror for a few minutes then looked down at her huge knockers and gave them a good shake. She reached down to touch her large round knees, feeling the braille of tiny scabs along the scrapes from her fall, when that stuck up bitch sister of Cole's wouldn't even cross the street to help her up. She raised her big arms and flexed her biceps. "Fuck yeah," she yelled out loud, smiling with her yellow, missing-tooth smile.

Sal, she remembered. *Her name is Sal.*

IX

At the demand of the Greymen's leader, Thoralf and his associates staggered to retrieve the few crates and barrels of provisions that had been reserved for the tribute in the unlikely event that the Greymen arrived earlier in the season than usual. The unexpected having come to pass, they looked upon the meager stacks in the corner of Thoralf's warehouse with fear and heavy hearts.

Returning to the common, they placed the scant tribute in front of the platform. The Greymen and their warriors scoffed and roared at the measly offering. The leader grew red with anger at the pittance, especially infuriated considering the blatant evidence of lavish consumption all around the village.

Looming above on the platform, the leader scolded the weak and weary Dímuners who gathered around, whimpering helplessly. He raged that an example would need to be made of their insolence and that the great sorcerer would arrive shortly to teach them a lesson they would never forget. Thoralf climbed up on the platform and pleaded with the leader to show mercy. At the leader's signal, a warrior fetched an axe and delivered to Thoralf a blow to the neck that took off his head. His head rolled off the platform and into the gasping and wailing crowd. At that, the Irishman promptly requested permission for himself and his men to take leave of the island, which was granted by the Grey-men, who could understand the Irish language.

The Dímuners, huddled together along with the only remaining suitor, the Blue Prince, observed that the Greymen often looked toward the harbor in anticipation of the arrival of their sorcerer. It was known that the sorcerer did not travel to Stóra Dímun on the ship with the rest of the Greymen, but instead materialized in the Snow Cottage by means of black magic. He would then sail to the village harbor on a small sailboat moored near the cottage in advance. The Greymen and warriors looked concerned that the sorcerer had not yet arrived.

"Where is the Vessel?" grunted one of the warriors.

At that moment, a point poked out of the shallow water of the beach next to the harbor. The point grew longer and longer and soon revealed itself as the tusk of a spotted narwhal that was purposefully beaching itself on the sand. Once on dry land, the narwhal shapeshifted into a tall, thin man, wearing a long grey robe like the other Greymen. He walked up from the shore, dripping wet and with a pink circular bruise on his forehead where the tusk had been. When he arrived at the crowded common, he yelled at the other Greymen that his sailboat had been missing.

When the sorcerer saw the pitiful tribute and looked at the gluttonous spectacle before him, it was resolved among the Greymen that a curse was in order. The Dímuners begged and sobbed for forgiveness, but their pleas were ignored.

Estrid and Sigmundr watched the disappointing scene from the roof of Thoralf's warehouse. As the sorcerer prepared for the curse, Estrid sighed that it would be too late for their plan to save the island. Sigmundr encouraged her to not give up hope, to put their plan to the stake. "We can undo the curse once we have the power," he assured her.

TWENTY-EIGHT

ole tapped the bat against his cleat to knock off some of the dirt. The dirt fell to the ground in little cleat-shaped clumps, like thick slices of Swiss cheese. It was the top of the ninth inning and Jim Thorpe was leading seven to five. Four of Lehighton's runs were thanks to Cole's three homers earlier in the game. Their fifth run had just come in when Asa hit a double, batting Carl Snider into home plate. The spectators were still on their feet and cheering when Cole moved into the batter's box. Even Clara was standing and clapping in her usual spot high up in the bleachers, all alone. She liked to read books during games, breaking only to watch Asa's and Cole's turns at bat.

Cole looked at the scoreboard out of habit. He knew the score, that there was one out already, and that a home run now would tie up the game. He readied his mind to use the hum to control the placement of the ball and the impact and arc of the hit.

The pitcher gave the catcher a few hand signs and Cole got into position, the umpire crouching down behind him. Then the catcher stood up and moved a couple paces to the right and the pitcher pitched the ball high and well outside the batter's box. They were intentionally walking him.

No, no, no. They can't do this, Cole thought.

There were some boos from the Lehighton fans. Cole panicked and looked up at Clara. She shrugged. He gave the pitcher a nasty look, or as much of a nasty look as Cole could give. There wasn't enough time to try to control the pitcher like the bird in the training room, if that even worked on people. The pitcher threw another ball. Now the count was two balls, no strikes. Cole had to think fast. As the pitcher threw the next lob, Cole focused on the hum and had the ball curve in flight toward him but not enough to be too obvious. At the same time, he ran forward and wildly swung up toward the ball, connecting with the very tip of the bat.

The hit was a line drive toward first base, but Cole used the hum so that the ball rose just out of reach above the first baseman. As he ran toward first, he watched the ball to keep it in fair position.

Asa rounded third and then scored. The crowd was jumping and screaming. Once the ball landed in fair territory, way out in right field, he put all his energy into rounding the bases. It would have been easy enough to screw with the throw of the outfielder, but that would go against Clara's rules and there were still a few more games he wanted her to attend. As he rounded third, heading to home plate, the first baseman caught the ball and turned to throw it to the catcher.

Cole booked it as fast as he could and dove headfirst toward the plate, stretching his gloved hands out in front of him as far they could go. As he landed and slid safely to the plate, the crowd erupted. He had tied up the game, but all he could think about was the pain in his leg. He had forgotten to take his lucky whistle out of his pocket and had landed on it hard. *That's going to leave a mark*, he thought as he stood up and dusted himself off.

By the time Jim Thorpe was up to bat in the bottom of the ninth inning, Lehighton had taken the lead, eight to seven. The Jim Thorpe pitcher was their second batter and he made an explosive hit directly at the Lehighton shortstop, who freaked out and ducked instead of catching the ball. The batter made it to second base. Cole was out in left field. He heard a rustle in the bushes next to the field and saw a squirrel digging for something in the dirt. Looking at the squirrel and then over at the back of that jerk pitcher who had tried to intentionally walk him, Cole had an idea. He was going to have a little fun.

As soon as Cole used the hum, Clara shot up from her seat to see what he was up to, squinting and shielding her eyes from the glare of the field lights. The squirrel walked out onto the grass and did a few little hops out to center field. It then turned toward second base, slowly crawling in the direction of the infield. There were some laughs and pointing from the spectators. The Lehighton infielders and the Jim Thorper on second base turned to see what was causing the commotion behind them.

About ten feet from second base, the squirrel stopped and started flicking its tail. It looked up at the Thorper, opened its little mouth to show tiny, white, pointy teeth, and let out a sort of high-pitched grunt, like the sound a bird would make if it could bark. It made the noise again and then started bounding toward him. He took a few quick steps back with his hands out in front of him. The umpire blew his whistle and waved his arms around to pause the game. The squirrel picked up its pace toward second base and the Thorper started running backward. The squirrel, squeakily grunting the whole time, kept gaining on him until the Thorper himself was squealing and running at full speed toward his team's bench. The squirrel cut him off and next had him running circles around the field, yelling and screaming. It reminded Cole of that time when Clara had a bee stuck in her bathing suit.

Laughter erupted from the bleachers and Cole could see that even Clara was enjoying the spectacle. As the kid passed the Lehighton bench on one of his frantic laps, Mr. Ray ran out and jumped in front of the squirrel, like he was playing man-to-man defense. Mr. Ray's heroic act reminded Cole of his whistle pledge and he called off the squirrel. It scurried back to the bushes through left field and Cole imagined himself giving it a little high five as it passed by. The game resumed and Lehighton made three quick outs for the win.

Thinking about it after the game, Cole regretted the squirrel stunt. It was exactly the type of thing he didn't want to do anymore. Messing with people like that is what almost killed Mr. Ray and the whole point of carrying around the whistle was to remind him of that. He felt bad, though not enough to skip going out with his teammates to celebrate.

After some pizza at Sal's, the team headed down to drink at the river beach. He hadn't been down there since the hooded hermit had freaked him out. He still got the willies whenever he thought about the mystery man and his warning to not open the door.

Which door, creep? Be more specific next time!

Asa, busy on his phone spreading the drinking plans to his posse, asked Cole to drive from Sal's to the beach path. Asa was always finding reasons for Cole to drive and he had a sneaking suspicion that Asa just got a kick out of how nervous Cole would get when behind the wheel. Cole figured it was good practice, so he usually went along with it.

After slowly rounding the square, Cole drove Asa's dad's old pickup truck down to the end of the road that led to the beach path. He pulled the truck into the grassy section and parked. He and Asa pulled the keg from the truck bed. Cole wasn't sure how Asa always managed to get his hands on cold kegs of beer or, for that matter, how he was paying for them. Maybe he still had a connection at the beer distributor, Cole speculated. They carried the heavy keg down the winding path, taking occasional breaks to rest their arms.

Reaching the beach clearing, Cole and Asa let go of the keg. It hit the ground with a tinny, stone-scraping crunch that drew the attention of the crowd already congregated at the meeting spot.

"You losers need to carry this the rest of the way," Asa called out.

Three freshmen jumped to their feet and ran over. When the freshmen returned with the keg, Asa lifted his beloved beer bong—a dirty car oil funnel that he had long ago shoved into a cut garden hose—over his head.

"Let's put the fun in funnel," he yelled. Everyone laughed and hooted and hollered. Cole thought that line was pretty lame, but Asa had a strong following with the younger teammates. He probably could have said anything and still gotten the same reaction.

The drinking was fast and aggressive. Cole took part in several keg stands. He much preferred those over the funnel, which he doubted had ever been cleaned after years of use. It wasn't long before Cole was feeling the beer and acting like an idiot along with his teammates. Some girls from school eventually showed up, unseasonably dressed in tank tops. While it was technically springtime, it was a particularly cold April with evening temperatures still in the 50s. The girls didn't seem to mind, but Cole could feel goosebumps on their bare shoulders when he put his arms around them to say a slurred, "Hello, ladies."

After a couple hours of heavy drinking and other shenanigans, a loud, deep voice yelled from the head of the path, "Everybody stay where you are."

Half-empty Solo cups pattered to the ground like the first rain drops of a summer thunderstorm. One person began to run toward the path at the other end of the beach and the rest followed in an almost instantaneous domino effect. They quietly ran down the beach, smushing together as they reached the narrow path at the other end. Cole was in the middle of the pack, doing his best to avoid the frenzy of swinging elbows and running feet that surrounded him. The only sounds were quick footsteps and heavy breathing. The girls were all on the track team and they squirmed through the crowd to take the lead and then disappeared around a curve. Despite his thorough inebriation, Cole was keeping up with the others. He didn't feel like he was running though. It felt more like he was constantly falling forward but catching himself with his legs just at the last minute before he truly fell down. That worked for a while until one of his legs didn't catch him when it was supposed to. He fell flat on his face and got a little trampled as the crew ran ahead, leaving him in their literal dust. There were no hard feelings in those circumstances. When it came to running from the cops, it was every man for himself.

Cole tried to get up, but a hand pressed down on his back and pushed him into the dirt. The hand was then replaced by a heavy knee.

"Stay down, punk," said a deep voice through gasps for air.

"Good evening, officer," slurred Cole. "Lovely night for a moonlit stroll, isn't it?"

"Save it, loser. There's no moon tonight," said the policeman. Cole was pissed at himself for not remembering that. Clara had even said "happy halfway day" when they passed each other in the hallway that morning.

"Hey, Murph. Go easy on that one. He's our star hitter," said another wheezy policeman as he ran by. Officer Murph just pushed down harder with his knee on Cole's back.

"Hear that, slugger? I'm supposed to go easy on you. What do you think of that?"

"Well, I agree." Cole tried to raise his face off the ground to get his cheek off of a particularly sharp pebble.

"Don't move." Murph pushed Cole's face back into the dirt. Then he pulled Cole's right arm back under his knee while he retrieved clinking handcuffs from his belt. The officer cuffed Cole's right wrist and then grabbed Cole's left arm to do the same. Just after he closed the handcuff around Cole's left wrist, the officer froze.

"Shit, shit, shit, shit," whispered Murph.

"What?" asked Cole.

"Shut up."

Cole's face was pointed toward the woods, away from the path, so he tried in vain to push up to turn his head. "What's the matter?"

"I said shut up. I'm serious. There's a bear." Murph's mouth was inches from Cole's ear.

"Brown or black?"

"Shut the FUCK up, you idiot. It doesn't matter." Murph's hot breath and spit landed on Cole's ear and temple.

"Um, it does," said Cole under his breath.

Cole felt Murph slowly shifting positions above him and then heard an unsnapping sound, presumably of Murph's holster. At that the bear let out a great roar that seemed to rattle the valley.

"Fuck this. I have a family. Sorry, kid." Murph jumped up and Cole heard him running and wheezing back down the path.

The bear growled and huffed. Cole stayed as still as he could, listening to the beast lumbering toward him slowly. Shutting his eyes tightly, he braced for the jarring pain of a claw swipe or the wet ache of a bite, slowly closing until the teeth broke the skin. It was hard to prepare himself without knowing where on his body the bear would strike. He thought about the story he had seen on the news earlier that day about the little girl who got mauled and killed by a snow leopard that had escaped from the Central Park Zoo. He wondered what she had been thinking when it happened. She probably thought the pretty kitty was coming to give her a nice cuddle. Cole didn't have that luxury; he knew the bear wasn't interested in some cuddle time.

When the bear reached Cole, it sniffed his hair and then his ear. He had thought the officer's warm breaths were annoying, but they were nothing compared to the hairdryer-force winds coming from the bear. He really wished Clara were around so he could convince the bear not to eat him. Without Clara, he was just like everyone else and was soon to be the bear's midnight snack. Cole clenched his teeth and squinted his eyes, preparing for his impending doom. The bear gave his neck and face a long, wet lick, turned and lumbered away.

Cole didn't move until the sounds of gravel and leaves under the bear's claws faded away completely. Even then he just laid there, cheek pressed against the dirt path, his heart racing. He was still pretty drunk and not entirely confident that he hadn't peed himself. After regaining his composure somewhat, he got up, which wasn't easy with his wrists cuffed behind his back. He had to roll over on his side and then scoot his knees under himself.

When he finally stood, he looked back in the direction the bear had gone to confirm that the coast was clear. Heading back toward the beach, he heard a twig snap in the woods to his right. His heart stopped. Was it another bear, maybe its cub or its girlfriend? Without making any sudden moves, he turned toward the sound and saw the same outline of the creepy hooded mystery man from his last visit to the beach. So, it couldn't be Asa, Cole concluded, given that Asa wasn't wearing his sweatshirt and was probably well upriver by now telling a dramatic story about how he had escaped the cops. Cole wanted to yell to the man, "Who are you and what do you want?" But he didn't want to risk calling back the bear. Instead, he just walked away down the path.

Walking handcuffed through the dark woods on a moonless night while drunk proved to be as difficult as one would expect. Cole fell several times and, thanks to the cuffs, couldn't catch himself. He was glad that he had moved his whistle to the pocket on his side that was not bruised by the slide into home plate, but by the end of his walk to the beach, it seemed that he would have two bruised thighs. When he got to the beach, it was still deserted. The squad would trickle back eventually, but it was too soon. The chase was likely still on, at least for some.

Cole kept walking to the next part of the path and through the pine tunnel and out to the abandoned train tracks. A cop car was parked next to Asa's pickup truck with someone hunched down in the driver's seat. Cole walked over to the driver's side window and saw Murph, he presumed, with his hat pulled down over his face. Cole knocked on the door with his knee and Murph jumped before registering Cole's presence. Looking relieved to see him, Murph rolled down the window.

"Can you take these off please?" Cole turned slightly to show the handcuffs.

"No, you need to come to the station." Murph opened the car door.

"Do you really want to explain at the station how you cuffed a high schooler and left him to a bear while you ran off with your gun?"

"Oh. But I—well, I guess not," said Murph. He turned Cole around and unlocked the cuffs. "Stay out of trouble, slugger." Cole didn't have the energy to respond. He brushed the dirt and pebbles from his clothes for the second time that day and headed up the hill.

Arriving at home, his bruised thighs burned when he walked up the few stairs that led to their porch. For a moment, he stood there and stared at the front door, remembering his first encounter with the river creep. As he did whenever he had a door to open and the time to think about it, the hermit's voice echoed in his head: *Cole, don't open the door.* Seeing no other choice, Cole reached out for the doorknob until the door suddenly opened by itself. In his drunkenness, it took him a few seconds to realize that Clara was opening the door from the inside. She pulled him inside.

"Where the hell have you been?"

"I got licked by a bear," said Cole in a daze.

"You're drunk."

"So what?"

"Amma sent a letter." Clara's voice was deep and serious.

"Yeah, what's new?" Cole could tell he was slurring a little. "What's the rush? That book hasn't been read for a thousand years. You can wait one more night."

"Her letter is in Spanish," said Clara.

"Why?" Maybe he was drunker than he realized, thought Cole.

"I don't know, but it must be important and you've been M.I.A. all night!" Clara grabbed his arm and led him toward the stairs.

"Hey, let go. You know Spanish."

"Not enough to translate a letter in Amma's chicken scratch. Just go to bed and I'll translate it while you sleep." She grabbed his arm again.

Cole had had a long day. It wasn't worth fighting over so he complied. After all, she was just asking him to go to bed, which is what he desperately wanted to do anyway.

"Fine," he said and marched up the stairs. "Did you hear about the little girl who got killed by a snow leopard in the Central Park Zoo?"

"No, that's terrible. Could you walk a little faster?"

"I wonder why her cat killed her but my bear let me live."

"Seriously, did you forget how to use stairs? How much did you drink?"

"Maybe rich people just taste better."

"Wait, what? She was rich?"

"Yeah. Lots of lawyers on the news."

"What was her name?" Clara opened his bedroom door and led him inside by his shoulder.

"I don't remember."

"Try."

"It was something to do with food. Good food." Cole plopped himself down on the bed. "I want to say taco."

"Huh?"

"Her name . . . taco something—Taco Cool Ranch, maybe."

"You think the girl's name was *Taco Cool Ranch*?" Clara's eyes widened when she said the words. "Coolidge? Thalia Coolidge?"

"Oh, yeah, that sounds right and ma—"

"Shit!" yelled Clara and she stormed out of the room.

"—makes more sense." Cole kicked off his sandy sneakers and crawled under the covers. "Mmmm, Cool Ranch Doritos. I

would kill for a bag of those right now," said Cole to no one before passing out.

The next morning, a Saturday, Clara read Cole her translation of Amma's letter over their morning coffee and orange juice.
Clara held her mug with both hands, but it still shook a little
whenever she took a sip. The skin around her bloodshot eyes was
dark and puffy. Cole was hungover and the bear incident from
the night before seemed like a distant dream. It was not their
best morning.

Clara took another sip of coffee and cleared her throat before picking up her notes to read them.

Dear Bee,

*I think I am being followed. At first, I just thought it
was my imagination, but now I am pretty certain. It started
about a week after I sent the pages to the Institute in Iceland.
I first noticed it when I pulled out of the driveway and there
was a car parked across the street near the Harris' driveway.
First of all, there is no parking allowed on the street. Second,
the man in the car seemed to jump and duck when I pulled
out of our driveway. Now I see that same car everywhere I
go and it is usually somewhere waiting on the street when I
leave the house. Then I noticed there is a lobster boat always
moored out by the islands. It never leaves. Other motorboats
come to it and people get on and off, but it doesn't budge from
its spot in front of Bluff Island. I occasionally see the glint of
binoculars pointing toward the house.*

*On Tuesday, I went to the supermarket and watched in
the rearview mirror as the car followed me the whole way
from the house. When I got into the store, I peered out the
window as two hipster type guys with dirty blond man buns
(I do not know why they are so popular these days) and grey
scarves got out of the car and came into the store behind me.*

I hid in the unmarked staff bathroom (which they let locals use) and overheard them ask the cashier if she had seen me come in. They had the same funny Swedish Chef accents as the people on the phone at the Institute. (Do you remember when we used to watch Sesame Street reruns together? Do you still have that Oscar the Grouch doll that you would never let me put in the wash? I digress.)

After the supermarket incident, I am truly convinced that they are following me and I am worried that they are after the book. But fear not. I smuggled the book out of the house disguised as a sheet cake for Gail Robinson's daughter's baby shower. (You met Gail when you came to yoga class with me last summer.) Gail is going to have the book shipped to you. We don't have to worry about Gail's discretion. She used to work for the CIA.

Please let me know as soon as you have the book. And re-member, whatever happens, do not tell your parents or the po-lice. We do not know what will happen to you if word gets out. I cannot wait to see you this summer. Only one more month!

Love,

Amma

Cole took a long swig of his OJ while he thought over the letter. He was worried about Amma. His instinct was to go right to the police, but he already knew how Clara felt about that.

"So, what should we do?" he asked, breaking the silence.

"Nothing. We just wait for the book," said Clara.

Cole could tell from a flicker in Clara's eye that she was mostly excited to get her mitts on the book, the full book.

"Aren't you worried about Amma? Shouldn't she go to the police?"

"Amma is a grown up. She's been through a lot worse than this and she can take care of herself. And no. No police."

Cole rolled his eyes. "Right, right. We don't want to get *E.T.*'d."

Amma's book arrived later that day. Cole found it propped up against their front door when he got home from a shift at Sal's. It was tightly wrapped in brown paper with no address or any other markings. *This Gail lady is pretty stealthy*, he thought.

Cole picked up the wrapped book and went inside. His parents and Clara were in the dining room turning it into a staging area for the Lewis and Clark trip. They still had a month to go before the trip, but he guessed he shouldn't be surprised.

"Shouldn't we start with a list?" Mrs. Lund asked.

"Makes sense to me," added Clara.

Mr. Lund didn't answer. He was deep in thought facing the corner of the room, looking at his snowshoes, his awesome tasseled leather jumpsuit, all of the old-timey instruments, including the sextant, and even a folded-up newspaper with a circled classifieds ad for Newfoundland puppies.

When Clara saw what Cole was holding, she jumped up and snatched the package out of his hand. She held it to her chest with her arms crossed over it, protecting it. From the look in her eyes, Cole figured she wouldn't be getting much sleep the next few nights.

———

After two weeks of the moon's crescent growing thicker and thicker, it shifted to a gibbous that grew fatter and fatter. Gibbous was a new vocab word that Cole had picked up from Clara. Now, it was a full-on full moon, and another training room morning arrived. Cole wasn't able to get any concessions out of Clara for him agreeing to wake up early. She just acted like she didn't care and then it turned into Cole trying to convince *her* to wake up early.

It was Clara's turn to go first. She went in and came out without even having to clear her throat. As to be expected, she didn't give Cole any clues about what was in store. She simply walked out of the corner, gave him a pat on the shoulder, and said, "All you, bro."

Cole went into the room, wondering what he would be thinking of during his future, actual dying breath. He still coughed and gasped after each corner drowning, continuing to find it really scary and unpleasant. He doubted he would ever be as nonchalant about it as Clara. *That can't be a good instinct to lose*, thought Cole. *She'd better stay out of the ocean this summer.*

In the room, the first thing he saw was the birdcage back on the table. He quickly backed up against the wall and tried to be as flush as possible to avoid any bird droppings. On a closer inspection of the room, including the rafters above, he determined that there was no flying crap factory to worry about this time. On the table, next to the birdcage, was the same mirror that was there in the last training. Just thinking about that last task gave him the willies, so he put it out of his mind. Looking at the two props, he considered what this task might be—it must be something involving getting a bird into the cage and him looking like someone else.

Oh crap, he thought. *I need to be the bird.*

Cole imagined that little brown and red asshole bird, flitting around and taking dumps on him. He did not want to turn into that guy. Probably any bird would do the trick, he reasoned. He had some trouble thinking up other birds. He wasn't much of an orthna—, orath—, bird-lover, whatever. He thought about the dirty, disease-ridden pigeons in Philly. He definitely didn't want to become one of them. The crows out front in the town square were kind of creepy and certainly too loud. Then it came to him: the seagulls up in Prouts Neck. For as long as he could remember, he had loved to watch the big fat gulls drop clams or crabs onto the rocks from high above to break them open. He would sit there on the beach and watch them for hours, assigning names to diligent gulls, and cheering for them with each drop. They would try over and over until finally the clam shell cracked open to reveal the gooey, flesh-colored innards. Then some other rude birds would swoop in and try to steal the prize from the one who had made all the efforts. *Birds are jerks*, thought Cole.

He knew from his last time in the room that it wasn't enough to just think about who or what he wanted to become. He had to imagine what it would be like to *be* that person or, in this case, a flying asshole. He started thinking about what it would be like to try to hold a giant clam in his mouth and soar up above the rocky coastline. He imagined opening his mouth and letting go of the clam, watching it spin in the air as it fell toward the wet, black rocks below.

The clam hit the rocks with a hollow-sounding thud and ricocheted into another rock before rolling back into the frothy water. Cole thought about how that must be very disappointing for the pea-brained gulls. He imagined swooping down to retrieve the clam and trying again. As he pictured that in his mind's eye, Cole felt a falling sensation and felt his arms being forced back behind him, not unlike when Officer Murph was cuffing him in the woods. When Cole opened his eyes, he was still facing the fireplace, but now he was looking at it from under the table, and somehow only seeing it with one eye. The other eye saw the back of a white and grey bird body—*his* bird body, apparently. Turning his head to look down at his feet with one eye, the view from the eye on the other side of his head swung up to view the rafters. The two images mashed together made him a little dizzy at first, but then his mind somehow organized them in a way that made perfect sense. His feet had flattened out into pinkish grey, three-pointed, webbed fans. He picked one up and moved it around, stretching and flexing it. He had to admit that the feet were pretty cool.

After remembering that he was supposed to be doing something up there on top of the table, he stretched out his neck so that his beak just reached over the edge of the table, barely touching the top. He wondered how he was going to get from the bench all the way up to the tabletop.

Yes, he could probably fly up, but he was not feeling inspired to figure all that out. In an extremely ungraceful combination of pulling himself up by his beak, flailing his wing arms and kicking his webbed feet, he made it up. There was a shiny thing propped up on the table. He waddled over to investigate. He looked at it, tilting his head from one side to the other.

Was that another room in there? It sure looked like another room. He got closer.

Hey, there's another bird in there. Why is he looking at me like that? What's his problem? Cole wondered.

That other bird seemed to be mimicking him. "Cut that out," he squawked, but the other bird just did the same thing. *I'll show him,* thought Cole. Waddling even closer, he pecked at the other bird, who met him blow for blow. Cole couldn't stand that asshole. He had to kill that bird, so he pecked at it with all his strength. The shiny thing fell down flat on the table with a loud clang and he jumped back with spastic, fluttering wings. He landed on his side with one wing stretched out in front of him.

What am I doing here?

As he rocked himself back to an upright position, one of his eyes noticed the cage. He remembered something about needing to get in the cage, but why on earth would he do that? It was something about the wall over there. He'd better just do it. He waddled over to the cage.

There was a problem: he was much bigger than the cage. Maybe it, whatever it was, would work if he just got his head in. He cautiously leaned down and put his beak and then the rest of his head into the tiny door to the cage. When he did that, some nice and shiny things showed up on the corner walls. He wanted those shiny things. Lady gulls would definitely like him if he had those gold shiny things over there. However, there was another problem: his head was now stuck in the cage. When he tried to pull his head out, the feathers on his neck got caught on the bars around the doorway. Boy, did it hurt to have his feathers pushed in that direction.

He pulled and pulled and even propped one of his cool webbed feet on the cage so he would have better leverage. He pushed on the cage with all his might until suddenly his neck feathers buckled back, causing excruciating pain, and he was freed from the cage—only to fall and roll backward. He landed on his back with his wings spread out and his webbed feet kicking above him. He did not know how to get out of that position. After a few minutes of rocking and trying various unsuccessful methods, he concluded that he would just have to move his wings up and down on the table, as though making a snow angel until he made it to the end of the table. At that point he would shimmy himself off the edge. Maybe he would figure out flying during the fall from the table to the floor.

Finally arriving at the edge of the table, his head and neck were hanging off the side with one of his eyes looking down at the floor. It was a long way down. He was worried, but he didn't have any choice. He moved his wings a few more times, scooching himself ever forward, until the moment when more of him was off the table than was on. He teetered on the edge and then toppled down headfirst toward the stone floor. During the fraction of a second while he was falling, a flicker of a thought came to him.

Wait a sec, he thought. *I'm not a bird. I'm a Cole.*

In that instant, he turned back into a teenage male human being, just in time to smash his face into the floor. His legs flopped forward violently and smashed into the table and then his shins scraped against its sharp, splintery edge as he melted into an injured groaning heap of tangled human parts on the floor. He rolled onto his back and rested for a moment, staring blankly up at the rafters.

Um, that was crazy, he thought. *And I didn't even get to shit on anyone.*

His skin around his mouth felt a little strange. It was sore and tingling. He stood up slowly, groaning all the way, and looked at his face in the mirror, which was now lying flat on the table for some reason. In a roughly diamond shape, the skin around his mouth was bright pink and raw to the touch. *That was about where the beak would have come out of his face*, he thought. As he peered into the mirror, he saw the redness starting to fade. He straightened himself and headed for the gold "out" runes in the corner. He had one last thought before the warm drowning to get back home: *Birds are the worst.*

TWENTY-NINE

The looks on their faces. You should have seen them, Mother. Totally confused and horrified and deeply hurt as it sunk in that their father, at least what looked like their father, was shooting them. Their expressions were priceless. What? No, I'm not. Don't say that, Mother. You know it's not true. Taking the power from twins was definitely a big bump. Cole and Clara are lucky they're family. But honestly, how long will that really protect them? We know me, Mother. I won't let anything stop me. Family or not. But first, I'm heading to Ireland. Triplets, Mother. Triplets!

THIRTY

Clara stood at the bow looking across the turbulent sea at the slender, jagged mountains rising above the crashing waves. Weary from their long journey, she and her crew were finally home in Lofoten. Passing through the sentinel mountains marking the harbor's mouth, she ordered a warrior to sound the horn in announcement of their arrival. The horn blared across the harbor and echoed off the surrounding peaks. The harbor horn answered and the wharf came alive with subjects preparing to receive Clara's mighty ship. The harbor horn answered a second time, an unusual gesture, perhaps in celebration of their triumphant return. The harbor horn blared once more. And again. Clara looked around the boat as sailors prepared the sails and uncleated the ropes.

The horn rang out again, then again, and again. She yelled at the warriors and sailors to make it stop. They ignored her, carrying on their various tasks around the deck. The horn grew louder, picking up a constant beat that grew upon itself as it reverberated off the mountains. The sound, the rhythm, they were familiar, but not there, not in Lofoten. They were from a dark place and they pulled her to it, like the Sirens, calling her to where she didn't want to go. The ship's bow stretched out in front of her and began to increasingly quiver to the beat of the horn until the quivering became so intense that the bow's deck shattered into a million splinters that scattered in all directions until they reconvened into nine wooden spheres that shot straight up into the sky, leaving her suspended in the air, high above the harbor's choppy surface. The sound grew more intense and as she reached up to cover her ears she was suddenly released from whatever force was holding her in place, freeing her to plummet feet first into the icy water. She screamed and reached her hand up. Her hand slammed down on the one thing that would silence the incessant harbor horn: the snooze button of the alarm clock on her nightstand.

"Holy crap," she said, pulling a pillow over her face.

The nauseating, swaying feeling of being on a dream boat eventually faded and she rose from bed to test out her land legs. After staying up until the early morning hours translating Amma's book—as had become her routine of late—and worrying about what Adler was up to, she really wanted to crawl back into bed to sleep a few more hours. But sleeping in wasn't an option that morning, even though it was a Sunday, because it was the big day—the day her parents were to depart for their Lewis and Clark adventure.

It was surreal to Clara that the trip was actually happening. They had been talking about it for so long that it had started to feel as if talking about it was all they would ever do. It was also surreal that they were leaving now, over three weeks before Clara and Cole would be done with school for the year. Their parents' college classes had ended a few days ago and their plan was to grade all their students' final papers on the drive out to St. Louis. Cole, who could get car sick from just reading the radio dial, expressed his astonishment at that plan.

They apparently needed to leave that day so that they would be in St. Louis in time to depart up the Missouri River on May

14th, the same day that Lewis and Clark's Corps of Discovery had departed in 1804. Clara knew all these dates and facts by heart, which she thought was a great waste of her grey matter. In one of Mrs. Lund's few concessions for the sake of "authenticity," she had agreed to that date, even if it meant leaving her two high-school-age children unsupervised for almost a month, and during finals no less. She agreed to this in exchange for Mr. Lund giving up his efforts to bring a rifle on the trip. Of course, rifles were indispensable to the original Lewis and Clark expedition, to hunt for food and fight hostile tribes, but times had changed and Mrs. Lund was not about to spend several months near a loaded gun.

She had also agreed because there had been a good reason for Lewis and Clark to have left that early in the spring: they wanted to get as far as they could before winter set in and halted their progress. While the Lunds didn't expect the trip to take longer than the summer, they were determined to complete the entire route and had made arrangements with their jobs to accommodate a late return, if needed. The trip was for research, after all.

On the one hand, the whole idea of being abandoned for more than three weeks—after which they would at least be under Amma's supervision in Maine—seemed to Clara like Bad Parenting 101. On the other hand, she and Cole had earned and enjoyed a fair amount of trust from their parents. Yes, Cole would go out and get drunk sometimes, but he was always back at a relatively reasonable hour and he wasn't that sloppy—usually. Clara was certainly responsible enough, perhaps to a fault—it's not like she had any friends to come over and trash the place.

Leading up to their departure, Mrs. Lund had been busy cooking meals that she froze in neatly labeled Tupperware. She had even rented an industrial-sized freezer for the basement, that was, by then, full of containers of frozen meals, a third of which were labeled "Asa."

Mrs. Lund had arranged for a driver to come pick up Clara and Cole and drive them up to Amma's house on the day after school let out for summer vacation. She gave Clara some cash and a credit card to use for emergencies and to buy groceries while they were in Maine so they didn't "eat Amma out of house and home."

Mr. Lund had prepared a spreadsheet of establishments, mostly national park visitors centers and, to Clara's surprise, a few rough-sounding bars, that the expedition might stop by along the route. The spreadsheet included timing estimates so that a message could be left at a particular place or two if they needed to be contacted. Clara was quick to point out that cellphones would have alleviated much of the logistical challenges of getting in touch with them, to which Mr. Lund proudly announced that cellphones would not work where they were going. So, in sum, Clara thought her parents were at least taking a responsible approach to their utterly irresponsible decision.

Waffle breakfast was already in full swing when Clara entered the kitchen and beelined to the coffee maker.

"But what about the gas station surveillance video? It puts him on the other side of town when it happened," said Mrs. Lund.

"There are at least ten eyewitnesses who saw it happen. It was broad daylight," said Mr. Lund.

"Can we talk about something else? The whole thing is creepy." Cole was looking down as he spoke, busy using his middle finger to fish a piece of orange juice pulp from the bottom of his glass.

"What are you talking about?" asked Clara.

"These horrible murders up in Westchester. A dad shot his teenage sons right in front of their high school. Just terrible," said Mr. Lund.

"But maybe he didn't do it. There's a lot of conflicting evidence putting him at other places at the same time." Clara's mother handed her a waffle-laden plate as Clara took a seat at the table.

"Well, somebody did it and half the school says it was him." Mr. Lund poured more batter on the griddle.

"Maybe he has an evil twin," said Cole.

"I know I do," said Clara.

"Very funny. But seriously, that could explain it. And the sons were twins, so it runs in the family."

"There's no evidence that he had a twin, but that's a good theory, dear." Mrs. Lund patted Cole on the shoulder.

"Very strange," said Clara as she pulled the mug of piping hot black gold to her lips.

"And who the heck knew Sleepy Hollow was a real place?" said Cole.

Clara gasped and sucked in a much too big and much too hot gulp of coffee. It burned her mouth and felt like hot lava slowly flowing down her throat. She coughed and held her mouth open in the hopes of letting in cool air.

"Are you okay, honey?" asked her mother.

"Yeah, I'm fine. Just too hot," she managed to say after some wheezing and fanning her tongue with her hand like some moron kid who ate a chili pepper on a dare.

But she wasn't fine. The wind gust, the crane, the fires, the snow leopard, and now Sleepy Hollow. Could they all really be coincidences? If they were Adler—that would mean he was actually doing it. By killing the rich girl and the Sleepy Hollow twins, he was taking their power and getting stronger. But he couldn't possibly be doing it.

A memory of young Cole and Adler dancing and singing down Park Avenue like a couple of goofballs flashed in her mind. She pictured his wide smile, his teeth perfectly white and unbraced, as he belted out some Spanish lyrics. But just above that smile, even in his happiest times, his eyes betrayed a sadness. Sure, she saw in that a sadness about his mother, but she also saw something else, a greater understanding of the world, a maturity, an acceptance of all experiences, good and bad. How they looked up to him back then. Even now, she looked up to him; he was artistic and deep and cultured and refined. He was everything she wanted to be. He was her idol and that would be hard to let go of, especially now when she felt so alone. Letting go would be too hard, maybe even impossible. But she wouldn't have to. Underneath all the talk, he is good—sad and hurting, maybe—but good. It was up to her to remind him of his goodness, to reintroduce him to the boy he was. *He's not doing anything. He is good.*

She had to talk to him, but he still wasn't returning her calls. She felt responsible, but what could she do? She just had to keep trying to get him and he would eventually answer. She was his friend, after all—he had to call her back at some point, he just had to. He's probably just busy with his art, like Sylvia had told her, and she was just being paranoid. He'll resurface and call soon. The creative process can be all-consuming for someone as passionate as Adler. *He will call and all of this will have an explanation*, she told herself. *He is good.*

⌒

After the car was packed and a few final lectures on home safety and responsibility were concluded, they all said, hugged and kissed their goodbyes. Clara could see her mom's eyes watering up, but she didn't break her cool, as usual. Mr. Lund, however, broke down into a slobbering, whimpering mess. So much so that his plan to take the first driving shift had to be aborted so he could sob in the passenger seat until his composure returned, which, by the looks of him, might not happen until at least Ohio.

The car drove off, the kayaks strapped to its roof. Clara and Cole stopped waving and sat down on the cement steps that led to the back door. For a few minutes, they sat there thinking in silence—well, silence other than the loud cawing of a crow perched somewhere in the trees above. Cole was leaning forward, using a twig to redirect some ants that had been marching in a row on the step. He scowled up at the trees and then the hum dimmed as the crow flew off over the house. "Birds," he sighed.

Clara sighed too. It was odd that their parents were actually gone. With Adler not returning her calls, Cole perpetually busy being cool and now no parents around, her opportunities for human interaction were looking pretty slim. At least she had the book, and lately it was pretty much all she had.

Clara wondered whether her parents would have still left had they known how poorly she was doing in school. She had cast all schoolwork aside while she prioritized translating the book. She had to use the hum to translate a word or two at a time and then write the English version in her notes. These she had organized in neatly labeled three-ring binders. It was time-consuming, and nothing short of an obsession. Whenever Cole was around, she worked on it, and when he was not around, she read and reread her notes, always looking for answers or clues about the power, its origins, its limits, its potential, etc.

Since Cole was somehow going about his normal life and flaking on her every time they had plans to practice the hum together because of a "hot date" or "big game" or "sick party" or whatever, the biggest chunks of time for her to work on the book were at night, when she could use the hum through the wall separating their bedrooms. She wasn't sleeping much, unless you count the times she had fallen asleep during classes. And, except for the walks to and from school, she was rarely outside, which gave her an even more pale and pasty look than usual. She was hardly eating. Her only consistent meal was the handful of vanilla wafers loosely wrapped in paper towels that someone was slipping under her bedroom door almost every night. Being vanilla flavored, she knew they were from Asa. That was the closest thing they had to an inside joke—he would still sometimes make little comments about her ordering "boring vanilla" ice cream on the day they met.

She accepted that her obsession with Amma's book was a problem, but she didn't feel inclined to do anything about it. It's not like she had other interesting things going on in her life, and the book was exceptionally interesting to her. She loved the stories—even the monotonous sailing around ones—the adventures, the history and the culture of the Order. She still hadn't found anything about twins, but that didn't matter. *It doesn't matter, right?* She was glad to share the power with Cole. She was lucky to be able to have a break from it when she wanted, unlike Adler who never gets a break—it could drive someone mad. *Sharing the power with Cole is a strength, not a weakness. It's good to need someone and to be needed.*

Her favorite leader of the Order was Ulf the Wise, who was not alive during Amma's volume, but the book still referenced him often. He was considered the greatest and wisest leader, having come up with the idea for her beloved training rooms and developing whatever the heck was going on in the East Hall that let them have the power available for a new Vessel. She also liked the battles. So far, they were mostly between the Order and the Viking sisters, but there were others. Not surprisingly, the Order was not very popular, but none of its foes seemed to understand the altruism of the Order's mission, which was to consolidate the power so it didn't run amok. And, as far as she could tell, they weren't doing it for some grand evil purpose, unlike a certain unhinged cousin had drunkenly suggested doing. Clara viewed the Order as doing a great service to humanity.

Cole wasn't convinced, given that they were primarily murderers. Whenever they had that argument, Clara would ask Cole to try to imagine a world in which the Order had not kept the power in check. Imagine sports games in which a third of the team had the hum, she would say. Or imagine getting cut off on the highway when one driver's idea of road rage was giving the finger and another's was flipping over cars with their mind.

The Viking sisters were kind of cool, she guessed—Cole certainly thought so—and she felt like she should be rooting for the kick-ass warrior women fighting "the Man" but she couldn't. The sisters and their large Viking army were vicious, heartless killing machines. There seemed to be no explanation for the sisters' furious attacks other than their pure bloodlust and a desire to steal weapons, ships and riches from the Order. Feminism be damned: Clara considered the sisters to be monsters, and she had formed that opinion even before reaching the part of the book when the cruel sisters burned the sacred original Twin Halls to the ground. Clara was not looking forward to reading about that, but she probably still had a ways to go in the book. In the month or so since Gail had sent it to them, Clara had translated a little over a hundred pages, but there were still hundreds more. She might never sleep again, Clara thought.

"Birds suck," said Clara, way too late.

"Yep," said Cole. "How many more days until the next training room?"

"Seventeen days." Clara knew that without even having to think.

"Okay. Let's try to stay out of jail until then."

"That's not funny. Let's not abuse their trust."

"Ugh, I was kidding. You can be so lame sometimes." Cole stood up from the steps and brushed the back of his shorts. "And can you get some sun? You're freaking me out."

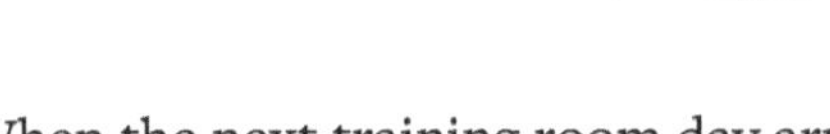

When the next training room day arrived, there were only seven days left of school before they would be on their way up to Maine for summer vacation. After their parents had left, Clara took on the role of nagging Cole about schoolwork, which in turn meant that she had to get back in the school game as well. She still stayed up late translating the book but buckled down and actually did homework in the early evenings. She had to do well on finals, given her slacking off in the middle of the semester, but she was feeling okay about it.

It was Cole's turn to go first in the training room. They were both up early and Cole was already brushing his teeth in the bathroom, humming the school fight song like a dork. Meeting in the hall, they walked together into his room and he threw a pile of dirty clothes from the rune corner to another corner. He got in position and headed in.

"Nope, nope, nope, nope," said Cole, coughing and shaking his head. "I'm not doing that."

"What?"

"There is no way I'm doing that . . . and you shouldn't either."

He ran out of the room and was out of hum range before Clara could get into the corner. Then she heard the front door slam shut downstairs. She just stood there, blinking, looking at the runes, then back at the open door of Cole's room. *What could be so bad to get that reaction*, she wondered. Without the hum, there was nothing she could do but get ready for school. She would have to catch up with him later and get the details.

But Cole seemed to be avoiding her. In Spanish, the only time she saw him during the whole day, he was quiet and sulking. She tried to ask him what was in the room, but he just brushed her off and said he would tell her later. After school, Clara sat at home waiting for later to come, but it didn't. Cole was once again M.I.A. and she wished her parents were around so they could worry for her. Asa wasn't around either, so they were probably out somewhere together. She shamefully used a pair of binoculars to check out the gazebo in the square, but didn't see anyone. While returning the binoculars to the basement, she grabbed a screwdriver and put it in her pocket. She went up to her room to do homework and, of course, spend some time looking through her translation notes on the book.

Cole came home very late. From her room, Clara could tell he was drunk from the banging and fumbling sounds coming from their shared wall. A loud thud followed by an extended silence, signaled to Clara that he had flopped into bed and promptly passed out. She got out of bed, carefully moved all of her framed Paris photos from the shelves in the corner and placed them on the bureau on the other side of her room. Then she took down the shelves, one by one, using the screwdriver from the basement to remove the brackets.

After taking a moment to gaze proudly at her very own clear corner, she wrote the "in" runes with organic eyeliner—she reasoned it was just overpriced burnt sticks anyway, so it should do the trick. It felt a little wrong to do a room without Cole, like watching the second episode of a show without the person you started it with, but she needed to know what was in there. *And Cole was being a jerk about it anyway, so screw him.*

Her training room was the same: same walls, same table, same fire, same moans and baby wails from outside. On the table was a wooden hammer, or maybe it would be called a mallet, Clara wasn't sure. She sat down on the bench and studied the mallet. It was large, about the size of one of Cole's baseball bats. The wood was old and dark. As she leaned forward to lift it up, something wet touched her leg. She squealed and jumped up from the bench. Inspecting under the table, she found an extremely cute grey and white puppy playing on the floor. She wasn't sure if it was a dog or a wolf, but a wolf somehow seemed more plausible under the circumstances. She lifted it up and placed it on the table as it nipped at her fingers with its tiny puppy teeth. Its eyes were bright blue and it made the sweetest little arfs as Clara scratched its neck and tummy.

The pup's attention turned to the mallet and it started gnawing at the handle and doing little funny half barks and then jumping back like the mallet was some playful foe. Then it dawned on her—she understood why Cole refused to do the task.

This one is a toughie.

Clara put the pup back on the floor so she could focus. How was she going to do it? It seemed like a big jump from the other G-rated tasks from prior months. Or was it? In the mirror room in March, she had to look like someone else. In April, she had to become some*thing* else. This time, she had to become some*one* else—she had to become someone who could do that task, someone cold, someone emotionless. It wouldn't be her. It would be someone else, she told herself.

She concentrated on the hum and thought about what it would be like to be someone who could do that task. She thought about all the brave men in the Order, how day after day they put aside their own lives and petty feelings. They could just be machines, doing whatever it took to advance the cause, to advance the greater good. She was sure they hadn't always wanted to do the things they had done, but they had been able to put themselves last, ignoring their perceptions of right and wrong, casting off any fears or doubts. They had to become empty shells, mere vessels, able to harpoon an elderly couple in the blink of an eye.

A few minutes later, Clara awoke from a hazy, sleep-like state. Her blurry eyes slowly adjusted to the flickering light of the fire. There was something itchy on her face, which she wiped at with her hand. It left a red smear on her fingertips. She stood up and saw a horrific sight: the road-kill version of the pup, lying on the floor, smashed in a puddle of blood. The mallet was on the floor next to the mess, one side of its head bloodied. Although the sight was nauseating, she didn't feel like she expected. She didn't gasp or cry or even feel bad. She hadn't done it, after all; it had been someone else. She felt the way she felt when she saw a dead baby bird on the ground after a fall from the nest. It was sad and all, but that's life sometimes.

Returning to her bedroom through the corner, she put the shelves back up, hid the runes behind one of the pictures and went to bed. She had one of the best night's sleep that she could remember.

～

After returning home from the last day of school, Clara discovered in the mailbox a letter simply labeled "Clara." There was no address, no last name, no stamp or any other marking. She opened it and saw from the signature that it was from Amma's friend Gail—that was not a good sign, Clara thought, and, another bad sign, it was in French.

Clara found Cole upstairs in his room packing for Maine. She wasn't surprised that he had left that until the very night before they were to leave. She went into her room, grabbed a notepad and started translating Gail's letter. Cole was moving around his room as he packed, which made the translation slow-going as the hum dimmed in and out.

Dearest Clara,

This is your grandmother's friend Gail Robinson. We met last summer when you came to yoga class. You were an inspiration. What I would give to be young again, and that flexible. As you know, your grandmother recently asked me to mail you a package that she snuck over to my house disguised as a sheet cake. A pure genius, that grandmother of yours. She told me that she thought people were following her and trying to get the package and asked me to send it to you. It was all very mysterious and exciting. It brought me back to my days in Clandestine Ops. More on that another time. She asked me to keep an eye on her and if anything should happen, I should write to you in French and, no matter what, not contact the authorities. As an aside, I am so glad that you finally switched from Spanish to French. I have been telling your grandmother for years that you should take French. It is such a beautiful language and it is the language of diplomacy, a career path that I think would suit you perfectly.

This morning, your grandmother did not show up for yoga, which never, ever happens. Naturally, I went over to her house to check on her and, I am sorry to say my dear, that I found the front door open and the house quite ransacked. It was clear that the intruders were looking for something, presumably the package: drawers and cabinets were emptied, pillows cut open, even the contents of the fridge dumped out onto the kitchen floor. There was no sign of your grandmother and, I am relieved to report, no sign of struggle or blood. My first instinct was to immediately call the police, but then I remembered your grandmother's solemn request that I not contact the authorities if anything should happen. I went around the house looking for any clues of what might have happened or where your grandmother might be, but I couldn't find anything definitive. One thing that did jump out, although it might just have been a coincidence, is that, among the scattered fridge and freezer items, were three blue plastic ice trays, sitting in a puddle of their own making. They were distinctly positioned in the shape of the letter "L." Perhaps your grandmother left that as some sort of clue. I have been thinking about it nonstop. Perhaps it stands for Lund and she was telling me to contact you. Maybe she meant Library Lane, so I have walked along that road a few times looking for clues but no luck. Maybe it has some significance with respect to the contents of the package. I will leave that for you to consider.

So, my dear, that is the troubling news that I have for you. I still have not contacted the authorities, but please write me back to confirm that is the right course of action, or inaction, in this case. I hope you and your grandmother are safe and I await your further instructions.

Your friend,

Gail Robinson

Completing the translation in sloppy handwriting, Clara froze, blankly staring, the pencil point still resting on the page. Clara's mind shifted from the effort to translate the words to the content of the letter. It was almost more than she could process. Their grandmother was missing. Her house, where they were headed tomorrow morning, had been totaled. The only clue was an "L" written in ice trays. And Gail, who had met Clara once was convinced that diplomacy would be a good career path for her. *And for God's sake, why was this being done over snail mail? We have a phone. We have computers.*

L, L, L, L, what could that stand for? Clara pondered. "L written in ice trays," she whispered to herself. *Ice tray L. Ice L.* She dropped the pencil, ran out of her room and poked her head into Cole's room.

"Don't forget to pack Adler's driver's license," she called in to him.

"Why? Did you take up smoking again?" Cole didn't turn around from his overstuffed suitcase.

"No," she said.

"Why then?"

"You'll see." She purposefully tried to sound mysterious. "Oh, and your passport," she added before slipping back to her room.

"Why?" said Cole, but she didn't answer. "Clara! Stop being a prick and tell me what's going on!"

Clara quietly ran back from her room and then jumped into the doorway in a failed effort to startle him. "We're not going to Maine . . . we're going to Iceland."

X

In preparation for the curse to punish the insolent Dímuners, the Greymen's sorcerer had a great fire kindled in the center of the common and ordered four warriors to press their shields upright into the ground next to him so that they formed a square. He bade no man speak and used a staff to score furrows into the ground, making nine concentric circles around the shield square. All the while he fell to chanting "the seed shall fail, the seed shall fail" over and over again. When the ninth circle was complete, he took into his hand dirt from inside the shield square and cast it into the flames. The dirt burned in a white flash and the fire was extinguished.

After the curse was cast, the Dímuners were ordered back to their homes for the night. They slowly left the common, eyes downcast and heads hung low. They knew not what the future held for their island, the only remaining home of the Dímuner people. The Greymen took over the tents left vacant by the fleeing Vikings and moved the tribute to the village square where they had a modest feast and quenched their thirst for mead after the long journey from Iceland. Feeling the effects of the dream thistle tea hidden in the mead, the Greymen retired to their tents and fell into a deep sleep.

THIRTY-ONE

“Did our parents tell you the change of plans?” Clara asked the driver.

Cole clicked his seatbelt and shifted uncomfortably in his seat. He didn't understand how she could seem so calm and natural.

“Uh, no miss,” said the driver.

“We're going to New York instead of Maine.”

“Oh, um, I would need to talk to your parents about that. You mother's instructions were very specific.”

“Well, you can't talk to them. They're hiking in the Midwest.”

“Well, I can't just take your word for it and drop you off all alone in New York City.”

“We won't be alone. Our grandmother is still in New York. She got delayed and hasn't left for Maine yet.”

“Er, I dunno.” The driver adjusted the rearview mirror to look at her.

“If you take us to Maine, you'll be abandoning us in an empty, spooky old house in the middle of the woods. Our grandmother is in New York. You'll see when we get there,” said Clara, feigning frustration. "And look, it's a much shorter trip and you'll get paid the same."

"Okay," said the driver. "But your grandmother better be in New York when we get there."

"She is, she is. Now let's get going."

Cole was amazed at how good she was at that. He would have been sweating and stammering the whole time. He was completely uncomfortable with the whole situation. He wanted to call the police. Their grandmother had been kidnapped. In the words of Clara, this wasn't a movie. In real life, you call the police when a family member is kidnapped. You don't fly off to Iceland with your superpower and try to confront the bad guys—you just don't. But Clara could be persuasive, as Cole and the driver had just witnessed. Whenever Cole suggested they go to the police, she played the whole "we don't want to get *E.T.*'d" card. It was becoming increasingly difficult to argue with that as they discovered more and more about what the power could do. Considering what they had learned over the past few months about the hum and its range of uses, even Cole had become convinced that getting abducted and weaponized by the government was the most likely outcome if they were to involve the authorities.

Cole was carsick before they even got to the highway. Since he was a captive audience for the drive, Clara used the time to work on translating the book, punctuated with the occasional "hmm" or "that's interesting." Cole was only mildly interested in hearing any more book stories. He had heard a lot of them and they were rarely useful for modern times, but if he ever found himself having to use the hum to navigate a Viking-era ship through a fjord on a starless night, he'd know where to look.

When they pulled up to Gran's apartment building on Fifth Avenue, a flurry of doormen ran out to greet them and help with their bags. Cole said hi to each of them by name and Clara gave him a funny look.

"How do you keep track of all *their* names?" she asked. Cole ignored her because he didn't like how she emphasized "their." She seemed to forget that those guys lived in New York City and spent most of their days on Fifth Avenue, whereas she and Cole were from the boondocks of PA. Which group was "higher class"? Cole didn't like her thinking that way. Nor did he understand why it mattered to her.

The driver opened his door slightly to avoid passing traffic and stood up, keeping one leg in the car. He called to one of the doormen over the car's black hood, "Hey, does their grandmother live here?"

"Yeah, who's asking?" said Junior. Junior's father John had also been a doorman at the building until he retired a few years ago. The driver shrugged, got back into the car and drove off.

"We weren't expecting you guys," said Junior. "Your grandmother is at a board meeting all afternoon."

Cole wondered how far ahead Clara had planned all of this.

"Oh, that's okay. We were going to surprise her. We're actually heading over to Uncle Ted's," said Clara.

"With all your bags?" asked Junior, looking surprised. "Should we get you a cab?"

"No, thanks. It's only a few blocks and our bags have wheels." Clara pulled up the arm from her bag and started wheeling it north.

"Are you sure?" asked another doorman. He was directing the question more to Cole.

"Yes, we'll be fine, Mark. Thanks, though," said Cole.

"Okay, we'll tell your grandmother you stopped by when she gets back," said Junior.

"Please don't. We want it to be a surprise when we come by later," said Clara.

They rolled their bags up Fifth and made the first right to head east on 86th Street.

"Are we really going to Uncle Ted's?" asked Cole.

"Yes."

"Why? Our flight is in less than three hours and I don't want to be rushing around the airport like crazy. You know how the traffic can be. If we miss this flight, we'll miss our connection."

"Calm down. We're not going to miss the flight. And if we do, there are plenty of redeyes to London."

"We should have taken a direct flight."

"I already told you—there weren't any direct flights available. Summer flights to Iceland are very popular. I pulled all this together last night, remember?"

"No dilly-dallying at Ted's, and there definitely isn't time for Sylvia to make you a chappucino."

"Cap-puccino. We'll be quick. I just want to see Adler. I haven't heard from him in a while and he's been acting odd lately."

"Lately? How can you tell?" asked Cole.

Looking north while crossing Madison Avenue, Cole saw in the distance the charred and crumbling shells of the housing development high rises that had been burned in the fires. There had been five similar fires in the last few months and the police still had no suspects. Cole had seen interviews on TV of residents in nearby buildings who lived in constant fear. Some on high floors even went so far as to buy parachutes. It was scary to think about.

Cole saw that the top of one of the buildings had partially collapsed, creating a grid of charred brick walls framing sky-blue rectangles that had once been windows. It was an eerie sight and reminded Cole of old movies with scenes of deserted cities that had been bombed during some old war.

"Look." Cole tapped Clara on the shoulder and pointed up toward Harlem.

Clara gave it a cursory glance. "Ugh, that looks terrible. What an eyesore."

"You mean it's so sad, right?" His voice was insistent.

"Yeah, of course. That too." Clara's flippant response disturbed Cole, but there were too many other things going on to dwell on it.

When they arrived at Uncle Ted's building on Park Ave, one of the doormen came out of the driveway tunnel to meet them.

"Well, hello, Mister Cole and Miss Clara. Good to see you again. I didn't know we were expecting you."

"Hi Angel," said Cole.

"No, we're not expected. We were hoping to say a quick hi to Adler . . . more of a surprise," said Clara.

"Adler? Oh, sorry, guys. He's not around. He left for Ireland a couple days ago."

"What?" Clara was almost yelling. "How? Why?"

"I think he said he was visiting some friends. Maybe a girlfriend?" Angel put a knuckle to his chin and looked up at the sky. "No, that's not right. Maybe he said friends that were girls."

"You're positive it was Ireland?" Clara stared at him with furrowed brows, as if the answer had some great significance that Cole could not comprehend.

"Yes, definitely. Joe, the super, is Irish and he made a big fuss about it."

"Shit! We need to go." Clara grabbed Cole's arm and pulled him to the curb, her other arm up hailing a cab.

"Bye, Angel. Nice seeing you. Tell Ted and Sylvia we said hi," said Cole.

"No! Don't do that. We were never here." Clara looked back at Angel as a cab pulled over in front of the building. "Got it?"

"Uh, yeah, sure," said Angel, turning back to the building.

"Cole, hurry up!" said Clara as Cole helped the cabbie load their bags in the trunk. When Cole and the cabbie were in their seats, Clara barked, "JFK, and step on it."

"You know, you don't need to be so rude to everyone." Cole was annoyed. "You need to chill. What's the issue with Adler going to Ireland?"

"Don't worry about it. The first thing I need to do at the airport is find an international payphone."

"Does that even exist?"

"It better—for everyone's sake."

Cole watched as the next set of travelers left the line, lugging their carry-ons toward the table while pulling out laptops and large baggies of toiletries. The space they freed up in the line was filled with the people behind them and it snaked its way back until it was Cole's turn to take a step forward. He was getting pretty close and still no sign of Clara. He scanned the airport for her. Nothing. He didn't really need to look for her anymore; he could simply just feel that she was not around, but looking for her was a habit he would probably never break.

The line moved up again and he started to panic. What would he do if he got to the front without her? He couldn't go through security and meet her because he had her ticket. Could he just wait at the front and wave people in front of him? Was that allowed?

He was in the last row of the line. That might be a good place to stop and let people pass—less likely to draw the attention of a TSA agent. Just before deciding to let the people behind him play through, he felt the hum and relaxed a little. He saw Clara coming down an escalator at the far end of the departures hall. She was just standing on the step, letting the escalator ease her down slowly to the floor like it was some toddler ride at an amusement park. *Hurry up and walk*, he thought.

Cole watched, mortified, as Clara cut through the line, ducking under the corral ropes, without as much as a single "excuse me." By the time she got to him, he was only four people from the front of the line.

"Where have you been? Look how close I am."

"I told you, I had to call someone."

"Who?"

"Rose, the Irish girl who also has the hum. She and her sisters are going to meet us at the airport when we arrive."

"Oh, cool. But why? Wait a sec, I thought we were going to Iceland, not Ireland. They're different, right?"

Clara sighed. "Yes. We're going to Iceland and they're going to catch a flight tomorrow morning to meet us there at the airport in Reykjavík."

"Which is in Iceland?"

"Yes. It's a short flight from Dublin and they'll arrive around the same time as our connecting flight from London."

"Got it. But why?" Cole took off his belt and put it in his backpack.

"Because I invited them. That's why I called. I figured this was a good opportunity for us to meet and talk about the power. It's not every day we're in Europe and maybe they can help us rescue Amma."

"And they were willing to come on such short notice?" Cole noticed that Clara's eyes were looking everywhere except at him. *What is her deal?*

"Apparently, they were planning to go to Iceland at some point this summer anyway, so they just bumped up their plans. I got the impression they go there a lot, like it's a party destination."

"Like Cancun?"

"Um, probably not," she said with a laugh.

"This is awesome—we're gonna be in a superhero gang. I just wish we had uniforms."

"I doubt they'll be into your superhero thing. Rose is weird, but not that weird."

"We'll see. So does this have anything to do with Adler being in Ireland?"

Clara's smile evaporated and she was suddenly very focused on looking through her carry-on. "No. It just gave me the idea to invite them . . . to meet us."

"Then why did you make such a big deal of calling them?"

"I just wanted to catch her before she went to sleep. It's really late over there."

"Hmm, okay. You know, sometimes you can be really weird yourself."

"Next," said the TSA agent.

Cole put his sneakers in a grey plastic bin and scooted it and his bag onto the belt. He walked through the scanner, which immediately beeped, prompting an agent in purple rubber gloves to administer a pat down. Halfway down, the agent pointed to Cole's left pocket and asked, "What's that?" Cole reached into his pocket and pulled out his lucky whistle just as Clara walked by.

"See you at the gate, weirdo," she said with a smirk.

After dozing off somewhere on the Heathrow runway, Cole awoke hours later to the bump of the plane's wheels hitting the tarmac. Looking out the window, he saw a flat landscape made up of bright green grassy fields, a grey sea and, beyond that, darker grey mountains rising out of a haze. *This is really happening*, he thought—they were really in Iceland. And they were there to rescue Amma. He wondered what his reaction would have been had someone come up to him on the first day of school and said, "by the way, on the first day of summer vacation you'll be on an island in the middle of the Atlantic trying to rescue your kidnapped grandmother. Have a nice day!"

Tired and jetlagged, Cole and Clara muddled their way through immigration and customs, eventually coming to rest at their flight's assigned baggage carousel. As they waited for their bags, Cole felt a change in the hum.

"Did you feel that?" asked Clara in a low whisper.

Cole nodded and they both started looking around. Standing by a baggage carousel a few down from theirs, Cole saw three girls about his age who also seemed to be looking around with a purpose. One of them stood up on the ledge of the carousel to have a better vantage point.

"I think that's Rose. She dyed her hair," whispered Clara. "I told you she's a freak."

Rose looked in their direction, hopped down from the ledge, and then she and the two other girls walked toward them. Cole was expecting the triplets to look the same, but their faces, heights and bodies were all slightly different. Even their hair was different, with one having long, straight blonde hair, another curly brown hair and the third with jet-black hair that was buzzed on one side. They were dressed in what Cole would consider goth style, wearing mostly black and often ripped clothing, and Doc Martin boots.

Rose, the black-haired one, was the most goth of all. She had dark eyeliner, a silver stud on the right side of her nose, a pierced lip with a ring that went inside her mouth and she wore a baggy, faded black sweatshirt that fell off one shoulder, revealing the shoulder strap of her bra, which was, of course, also black.

The brown-haired one wore a black tank top with a black and red plaid flannel shirt tied around her waist like she was in an early 90's Seattle grunge band. She smiled as they approached, drawing Cole's attention to the cute freckles on her nose and cheeks. The blonde one had a confusing look. She was also in all black, but the front of her t-shirt had a larger-than-life photo of Taylor Swift's face. If she was trying to look as badass as the other two, she was failing miserably.

"Hello, Clara," said Rose from a few steps away.

"Hi, good to see you." Clara put out her hand for a shake. Cole might have expected a hug under those circumstances, but he wasn't surprised that Clara took the more formal route. "Wow, you look different."

"Thanks. You look the same." Rose let out the slightest exhale that Cole read as disappointment. Rose put her phone in her pocket to shake Clara's hand. "And you must be Cole—I see the resemblance."

Cole was having trouble understanding Rose's thick accent, but it seemed at that moment that all attention was on him. "Hi. I'm Cole, Clara's brother." He was mainly talking to the brown-haired one.

"So, these are my sisters," said Rose. "That's Eileen there with the curls. And Aoife here has a picture of herself on her t-shirt in case she gets lost."

"Howya. Isn't my sister hysterical?" said Aoife, stepping forward to shake Clara's hand.

When Eileen approached, Clara again extended her hand but Eileen grabbed it and used it to pull Clara in for a hug. The hug lasted a few seconds, with Clara's face smothered in brown curls, until Clara gave Eileen a couple pats on the back with her fingertips. Coming out of the hug, Eileen grabbed Clara's shoulders in each hand and looked intently at Clara's face.

"It is so wonderful to meet fellow witches."

Clara giggled nervously. "What?"

"You have the power like us. We can feel it."

"Yeah, but we're not witches."

"Of course you are," said Rose, who was looking at her phone.

"Um, no—no we're not." Clara's cheeks were turning pink. Cole couldn't tell whether she was embarrassed or angry.

"Then how do you explain the magic?" asked Aoife who had to raise her voice to be heard over a flight change announcement.

Clara looked around nervously. "Look, okay, can we talk about it someplace more private?"

Out of the corner of his eye, Cole saw Clara's bag coming down the conveyor belt. He ran over to retrieve it, leaving the ladies to work out the details of their more private rendezvous.

After gathering their bags, Cole lugged them back to where Clara was standing. The triplets had already left to catch a taxi to their hotel. Since Cole and Clara didn't have any accommodations yet, the plan was to check into the same hotel and meet up in the triplets' room later. But first, much to Cole's surprise, they had to go rent a car, which explained why Clara had him pack Adler's driver's license.

"Can't we just take a cab to the hotel?"

"You remember why we're here, right?" asked Clara. "You think we're going to rescue Amma and then what? Run to the nearest bus stop and wait to make our escape?"

"I mean . . . I guess not. But I can't really drive." Cole was already feeling nervous about the prospect of getting behind the wheel.

"Well, you've driven Asa's truck a few times, which is more than I can say."

"But, like, don't they drive on the wrong side of the road here?"

Clara looked at him blankly. "Um, no. You need to get out of Lehighton more."

They found their designated car, a nondescript white compact car. Cole paused before opening the driver's side door. The creepy river guy's voice echoed in his head and this time Cole genuinely agreed—he definitely should not open this door. The next thing he knew, Clara was out of her seat yelling at him over the roof of car. "Earth to Cole. Might I remind you that we are on an important mission to save our grandmother." Once again, Cole saw no choice but to open the door.

Getting out of the rental parking lot was a harrowing experience. Asa's dad's old pickup truck did not have much umph, whereas Cole felt like the slightest tap on the acceleration sent their little rental car careening forward at warp speed.

"Just be thankful it's not a stick shift," said Clara as she looked down at her handwritten directions to the hotel.

"Wait, what? Was that a possibility?"

"It's what I was expecting—this *is* Europe."

"Jesus."

The car jerked and bucked as Cole inched it out of the parking spot and down the ramp to the exit. Clara complained that he was going too slowly and then the next second complained that he was going too fast. She grabbed the back of her neck dramatically and sometimes clenched the handle on the door with both hands like the bar on a rollercoaster. Her lack of composure was not helping Cole's stress level. At her every gasp or yelp, he would jerk the wheel or slam on the brakes, leading to even more gripes from the passenger seat. His hands were tight and sweating at two and ten on the steering wheel, pulling his body forward in his seat so his chin almost touched the top of the wheel. Finally, the lot's exit came into view and Cole slowly proceeded, trying to get as close as possible to the booth to hand the attendant the car's paperwork through the window. Off by a long shot, Cole had to open his door and walk a couple paces to hand the man the papers. The lot attendant rolled his eyes, handed back the papers and said "Good luck" in strongly accented English.

When they finally reached the hotel, Cole handed off the car keys to the valet with a great sense of relief and accomplishment. They had reached their destination, the Hotel Kvosin, in downtown Reykjaviík, despite several wrong turns, a lot of honking and Icelandic curses being hurled at him from passing cars. He didn't remember the scenery at all, only Clara's increasingly frustrated navigational commands and a few near misses. Now he could finally relax and take in his surroundings.

First of all, he noticed that it was cold. The day had looked bright and sunny from inside the car, but the air had a crisp bite that made Cole question his packing choices. It was what Amma would call "window weather," best enjoyed from indoors. In fact, it wasn't that far off from the weather they might have expected for an early June morning in Maine; winter was still there but had loosened its grip just enough to let in the slightest hope of spring. The second thing Cole noticed was that the hotel and most of the other buildings on the block were painted white and made of wood or some type of textured metal that looked a little like the aluminum siding that was popular back home. He had been expecting all the buildings to be made of stone.

The hotel was small, by U.S. standards, maybe eight stories at most. Across the street was a squat little church that was clearly very old despite its obviously fresh coat of white paint. The church's slanted roof was an appealing green, like a muted version of oxidized copper.

The outside of the hotel also looked old, although not as old as the church, but the interior was renovated and had a minimalist decor that reminded Cole of Uncle Ted's apartment. As to be expected, Cole didn't like it and Clara loved it.

When they checked in, the concierge told them the triplets' room number, as they had instructed him. Much to Clara's embarrassment, she had had to explain to the triplets at the airport that she and Cole did not have cellphones and they would have to get in touch with them the old-fashioned way, by calling their room's landline or even stopping by in person. The agreed-upon plan was for Cole and Clara to go to the triplets' room in a couple hours where they would order room service for dinner.

While Cole was exhausted from the harrowing voyage to the hotel, meeting the triplets had given Clara a burst of nervous energy. She paced around the small hotel room, frantically unpacking her bags and putting her clothes in the dresser drawers and rambling off questions and theories to Cole. Lying down on his assigned bed, he tried to tune out her incessant questions. Clara threw one out after another: "Can they do the same things with the power? Do all three of them need to be together to use it? Do they know about the book or the training rooms? Why on earth do they think they're witches?"

"What about Amma?" interrupted Cole.

"What about her?"

"Like, what's our plan?"

"I don't know. I guess we'll need to find that institute, but I'm sure it's closed by now."

"Should we go anyway? Get the lay of the land? Look for clues?"

"Let's just focus on the triplets for today—see what we can find out from them and if they'll help us. We can investigate the institute first thing tomorrow."

Cole wondered whether he should have just called the cops when they first learned Amma was missing. Clara went back to pacing around and firing off questions about the triplets.

"Why does any of that matter?" Cole tried to use his most calming tone. He took a deep breath through his nose. The air was dry and smelled crisp with hotel-strength cleaning products.

Clara didn't answer but just kept rambling on, going down one rabbit hole after another. She even suggested that they turn into roaches and go spy on them, but she self-rejected that idea, acknowledging that the triplets would likely be able to feel that they were present.

"Who gives a crap?" he yelled, finally losing his cool. "We—are—here—to—FIND—AMMA."

"No shit. I want to find her just as much as you do, if not more. But what are we supposed to do now? The institute is our only lead and it's after business hours. If we click with the triplets, they can help us. We don't know what we're dealing with. It's better to have allies." She flicked the wrinkles out of a t-shirt with a loud snap before laying it out on her bed for refolding. "If you have a better plan, let's hear it."

"I don't have one. But I can't just sit here and do nothing. I need to start looking."

"If wandering around aimlessly will make you feel better, go for it."

"It's better than nothing." Cole pushed himself up out of the cozy bed and dug out a sweatshirt. Outside the hotel, Cole walked around the old church and cut across a small, well-manicured square, heading in the direction of a bustling intersection flanked by cafes and shops. He walked quickly, his heart still racing with frustration at Clara's lack of urgency. Arriving at the intersection, he paused at the corner, looking down the two busy streets leading from the openness of the square to cut narrow corridors between quaint three-storied buildings with A-frame roofs. To Cole, both roads looked the same. Neither one had a more or less chance of leading to Amma—in all likelihood both had an equally zero percent chance of that outcome. But Cole couldn't just stay in that room and he couldn't just stay standing at that corner either. He would let fate decide. He closed his eyes and slowly counted to ten. When he opened his eyes, the pedestrian crossing light was green to the right, so Cole went right.

He walked down the road for a few blocks, weaving through clumps of tourists stopped on the sidewalk to look down at their phones. Walking by a bakery, he slowed his pace to let the buttery, bready air linger in his nostrils. His stomach growled, but he didn't have any money to do anything about it. He considered turning back to the hotel to grab some cash, but then he would have to figure out how to exchange it and he didn't really feel like seeing Clara who was probably still rambling on and on. His stomach could wait until room service with the triplets. At that thought, he caught a glimpse of curly grey hair that turned right, disappearing around a corner. *Amma?*

Cole sucked in a last deep breath of bakery air and ran ahead to follow the hair. Arriving at the corner, he was disappointed to discover the hair attached to a body that was not Amma's. It was a skinny old man with curly silver hair cut to a length just above his bony shoulders, on which hung a baggy tie-dyed tank top. It was an odd fashion choice for the temperature, but not as odd as the haircut. The length and the curls fluffed it out around the sides so that from the back it looked like his head was shoved up a doll's grey ruffled hoop dress.

Having no other plan, Cole followed the old man, taking various turns here and there, all the while Cole's eyes fixed on the man's hair that swayed side to side as he walked, like an upside-down dry mop. When the man ducked into a bookstore, Cole decided to let the intriguing character escape. Cole continued walking and he realized that he was back at the same square near the hotel, having accomplished nothing in the quest to find Amma. Dejected, he crossed over to the square and took a seat on a park bench.

Clara was right, he thought. *There's nothing we can do today except join forces with the Irish girls.* Closing his eyes for a moment, a wave of exhaustion washed over him and his stomach growled. He shifted his butt forward to uncomfortably rest his head on the back of the bench. Looking up at the sky, he fought the heaviness of his eyelids. A rush of panic jolted him upright. Before him, maybe ten feet away, stood the tank-topped old man, his back to Cole.

"Hello?" said Cole, but there was no answer. "Are you okay?"

The man slowly began to turn around and as he did it was revealed that the hair continued around to the front of his head—no face, just hair all the way around, indeed in a full mushroom-top shape. Terrified, Cole jumped back and fell onto the ground. Scrambling to his feet, he watched the man continue to turn around, all the way around, round and round, and as he turned, the hair began to grow. It cascaded over his wrinkled shoulders, down his torso and down until his faded jeans and dirty sandals were completely covered in grey curly hair. The man had transformed into a spinning, elderly Cousin It. The hair continued to grow and as he spun it wound itself around his body and brushed along the ground as it simultaneously grew longer.

Suddenly, the man began to shrink and as he got shorter the circle of spinning hair grew around him. He shrunk and shrunk until his body was completely gone and all that was left was a spiraling, expanding mat of hair, looking like an aerial view of a hurricane. Then the eye of the storm sunk down into the ground, becoming a churning funnel, pulling the spinning hair down, deeper and deeper. From the depths, Cole heard a faint voice, but he couldn't hear what it was saying. It was a woman's voice. *Amma?*

Drawn to the voice, Cole stepped forward onto the spinning mat. As his foot touched down, countless strands of dry silken human hair threaded between his toes and tickled his ankles. *What was happening?* With each step, his legs strained to free themselves from the living tangles. When he finally reached the edge of the funnel cone, he was out of breath and sweat was dripping down his face. Propping his hands on his knees and leaning down to look into the hole, he felt the sweat change direction on his face. It ran forward toward his nose until a darkness appeared in the inside corners of his eyes. Closing one eye, he could see that it wasn't sweat dripping down his nose: it was blood. Thick drops of dark blood fell from the tip of his nose into the whirlpool. As each drop struck the surface, it dyed the hair purple and a streak of purple hair grew from each spot, following the swirly course down the drain. Nine drops fell in all, creating nine concentric spirals spinning around and around.

"Amma!" he yelled into the hole.

The voice called back unintelligibly. The hypnotic spirals drew Cole closer.

"Amma, please! I don't understand. What is ecky sofany?" *Is it a clue?* wondered Cole.

The voice answered with the same sounds, *ecky sofany*. Cole stared down at the spiraling whirlpool of grey and purple hair. His heart raced, his breaths quick and shallow. He had to do something. He had to save her. Closing his eyes, he pulled both hands into fists, raised his right arm over his head and placed his left fist by his waist. He calmed his breathing enough to shout, "I'm coming Amma!" just before diving, Superman-style, into the hole.

Cole's eyes shot open to the sight of a gloved hand waving in front of his face. It belonged to a female police officer in a black uniform.

"No sleep," she said, smiling. "No sleep in the park."

THIRTY-TWO

I almost gave up. No, I did give up, Mother. I had searched that pathetic excuse of a city for days. Wandering the streets. Searching directories. Scouring the internet for addresses, clues. Talking to strangers, like a loser. But nothing. I threw in the towel and went to the airport. Sullen and angry. I don't like to fail, Mother. You know that. I was on my way back to New York but then I felt it. Right there in the airport. Dim, but there. And then I saw them—one, two, three—in the distance. I backed away so they wouldn't sense my presence. I waited, then found out their destination. I'll be on the next plane to Iceland, Mother. This is going to be fun.

THIRTY-THREE

"Here goes nothing," said Clara just before knocking on the door of the triplets' penthouse suite.

"These must be some rich-ass witches," Cole whispered.

"Shhh. We're already late."

"I said I was sorry. It's not my fault I fell asleep."

"It isn't?"

When the door opened to reveal their gigantic room, it indeed appeared that the triplets were well off. The room was, more accurately, a large apartment. Clara could see a full modern kitchen, dining room, living room, a huge TV, and a large balcony facing the green roof of a church.

Brown Hair greeted them and led them into the kitchen where Rose was sitting at the countertop, speedily typing something into her phone with her thumbs. Blonde Hair was out on the balcony having a cigarette, her long hair blowing dramatically in the wind. Rose looked up from her phone to say "Greetings, kindred spirits." The sun from the glass door to the balcony shone on to her face and her eyes flashed back at them, catching Clara by surprise.

"Oh, you don't wear the contacts?" said Clara.

"The what?" asked Brown Hair.

"Contact lenses . . . to keep your eyes normal looking." Clara took a seat at the large kitchen counter.

"Why would we do that? Our eyes are awesome," said Brown Hair.

"Our sun goddess eyes are enchanted. Don't hide your goddess power," said Rose.

"Especially you, love," said Brown Hair to Cole with a wink.

Brown Hair pulled five bottles of beer from the fridge. She handed one to Rose and one to Clara and Cole. She waved one at Blonde Hair on the balcony, who nodded. Cole sat down next to Clara and took a quick swig.

"Thanks, I needed that." Cole looked at the beer label. "You wouldn't believe the crazy dream I had," he said to Clara under his breath.

Clara looked at the ice-cold beer in front of her, its brown glass dotted with condensation. It looked delicious, but drinking didn't feel right—not with Amma missing. But there was nothing they could do about Amma until tomorrow. Today's objective was to bond with the triplets, right? And Cole was drinking. *And I am thirsty after all the travelling—traveling we did for Amma. It's not like we didn't do anything today.* Clara took a long swig of beer. Its bubbly goodness cooled her mouth and throat. *That was the right decision.*

Clara couldn't figure out how the triplets had had time to go grocery shopping, shower, get changed and generally look amazing, other than their questionable fashion choices. Speaking of fashion, Blonde Hair opened the balcony door to join them and Clara was amused to see yet another Taylor Swift shirt, this one a tight black tank top with the singer's name scrawled across the chest in bright red letters.

"Aoife, they wear contacts to hide the glinty eyes," said Rose, not looking up from her phone.

"Why?"

"I know, right? That's what I said," said Brown Hair.

"Here, look." Cole squished his fingers into his eyes and pulled out the contacts. Brown Hair moved him into the sunlight. Keeping her hands on his shoulders, she looked deep into his eyes and smiled.

"They're beautiful," she said. "You're the prettiest sun goddess in Iceland."

Clara saw Cole's cheeks blush. They all looked at Clara, as if it were her turn to take some dramatic stand against conformity and toss her contact lenses off the balcony or something.

"Uh, no thanks. I'll keep the contacts," she said, shaking her head.

"So, are we going to talk about the gift or what?" said Rose.

"Relax, Rose. We're working up to it," said Brown Hair. "But she's right, we don't want to be cooped up in here longer than we have to."

Clara looked around the sprawling suite, unsure how it could ever feel cooped up.

"So, when did you first realize you were witches?" asked Blonde Hair.

"We're not witches," said Clara in a frustrated tone. "And neither are you. It has nothing to do with witchcraft—it's obviously the fertility treatment."

"We *are* witches," stated Rose, matter-of-factly. "And what makes you the expert on what it has to do with? We've been playing witches since we were little girls and now our spells actually work."

"We're happy to turn you into toads, if you need more proof," said Brown Hair.

"That's ridic—" started Clara until Cole cut her short with a tug on her arm.

"Can I talk to you for a sec on the balcony?" His mouth was pulled tightly into a fake smile. He led her by the arm to the balcony door and they went out into the glaring sun and biting wind. "What is your problem?"

"What? We're not witches. They're being stupid," said Clara.

"How do you know we're not witches? And what difference does it make to you? They can be whatever they want."

"But witches are lame. I don't want the power associated with some corny Hermione worshippers."

"I don't think they're those kinds of witches."

"They're not any kind of witches," said Clara. "They're just like us. It's not witchcraft, it's genetics."

"You're probably right, but just let them have it. You're not going to convince them and we want their help to find Amma," said Cole.

Clara thought on that for a moment. "I guess you have a point. But I stand by my position that witches, all types, are lame."

"Good, but nobody really cares about your personal views on the coolness of witches."

Clara stepped back, a little surprised by Cole's out-of-character snarkiness, but Cole continued.

"Just try to focus on what we can learn from them, how they can help us save Amma. We're here for *Amma*. Remember?"

"Oh, *I* remember. Just make sure *you* remember when you're not napping or flirting."

When they returned inside, the triplets were just finishing tequila shots. Brown Hair and Blonde Hair shook their heads, howled and slammed the table with their hands, whereas Rose barely reacted. Brown Hair poured two more shots for the twins. Clara and Cole looked down at the tiny glasses of golden liquid and then looked up at each other. A beer hadn't fazed Cole, but doing shots was a different story: it was celebratory, incongruous with the worry they were feeling about Amma. They exchanged a look. *Right or wrong, we are making this decision together. Befriending the triplets is in Amma's best interest. Neither of us needs to feel bad about this. We promise to not judge each other.*

They took the shots.

Clara put on her friendliest tone. "Sorry about before. I didn't get much sleep on the red-eye and I'm a little cranky."

"So, we first noticed the power in early fall of this year. I started using it in soccer," said Cole, clearly eager to get the conversation back on track.

"He means football," said Clara.

"I just used it a little to improve my game. Not that I needed it. I mean, I'm pretty good without it anyway," said Cole.

Clara rolled her eyes. "What about you?"

"Well, we first used it a couple years ago when Aoife broke up with a boyfriend," said Brown Hair. "As a joke, and for old times' sake, we held a séance and were going to burn a bucket of his old stuff. As we were chanting, the bucket just burst into flames without a match or anything. It was awesome."

"It was transformative," said Rose.

"He died in a fire, by the way." Everyone looked up at Blonde Hair in horror. "Kidding," she added with a sly grin.

"I started a fire once too." Clara tried hard not to sound too competitive. "What other types of things can you do?"

"Eh, standard witch stuff. We can move things, do curses—not all of which work," said Rose.

"Oh, and we can turn into cats," said Brown Hair.

"We can communicate through the spirit dimension," said Rose.

Cole and Clara looked at each other and then at Brown Hair for an explanation.

"We can talk to each other without speaking," she explained.

"That's a good one. We should try that," said Cole to Clara. A moment passed and then all three triplets let out a little chuckle. Cole glared at them suspiciously.

"This is so great. I'm so happy we were all able to meet each other," said Brown Hair, smiling. "And in one of our favorite places."

"Come here often?" asked Cole with a raised eyebrow and smarmy voice. His joke fell flat.

"We used to, before my sisters became nerds. There's great craic here." Blonde Hair did a little dance with her bare shoulders. "We need some music."

"Crack?" asked Cole. He turned to Clara and gave her the wide-eyed, fearful look of someone realizing that everyone around them was a hard-core drug addict.

"It means fun," said Clara.

"Since when?"

"It's an Irish expression." Clara rolled her eyes yet again.

"We're part Irish, I think," Cole said to the sisters like a loser.

"I've never met an American who hasn't said that to us," said Blonde Hair as she poured another beer into a glass.

"Rose, on our call you said you were planning a trip here anyway?" asked Clara.

"Nerd stuff!" said Blonde Hair as she fiddled with a portable speaker. Rose gave her a look so stern that Clara half expected her to be replaced by a toad with bright red lipstick and a tiny blonde wig.

"Sorry, mind if the three of us talk in private for a moment?" Rose put her phone down on the counter.

"Sure, we can go out on the balcony." Cole started to scoot back his stool.

Brown Hair giggled. "You don't have to go anywhere. Just give us a minute."

The triplets quietly exchanged glances and slight nods until Brown Hair spoke. "Well, we have this old book."

At the word book, Clara knocked over her almost-empty beer bottle. It didn't break, but clinked as it fell, bouncing a few times on the marble countertop. *Could it be?*

"Sorry, go on," said Clara, carefully placing the bottle upright on the counter. Her hands were shaking.

"We have an old book from our grandfather. We think it's a book of spells, but it's in some old language," continued Brown Hair. "Rose, what did your professor say?"

"He thinks it's Old Norse . . . written in runes."

Clara could hardly breathe. They had the power and an old book written in runes. It had to be one of the Order's books, maybe a different volume. She placed her palms flat on the counter to quell the shaking.

"Right. He said we would need to find some expert in Norway or Iceland to figure it out. We picked Iceland because we've been here before and it's super fun," said Brown Hair.

"And the guys are hotter," added Blonde Hair.

Clara wasn't sure what to do next. She didn't have time to think it over and the tequila shot was starting to kick in. She decided to throw caution to the wind and take a risk.

"We have a book like that too," she said, much to the apparent shock of everyone in the room. The triplets were shocked at the interesting development and, presumably, Cole was shocked that Clara decided to show their cards so early.

"Seriously?" asked Brown Hair. The triplets exchanged glances. Clara assumed they were once again talking to each other in the spirit realm or whatever.

"Yes. Would you mind going down and getting it?" Clara said, looking at Cole, who moped away to the door. Feigning calmness, Clara turned back toward the triplets. "Can I see yours?"

Blonde Hair went down a hallway off the living room area and returned with a wooden box with a black pentagram painted on the top. She handed the box to Rose who mumbled an indiscernible prayer and ceremoniously opened the lid. From deep inside the box she pulled out an object about the size of Amma's book that was draped in light blue silk. She unwrapped it and held up the book. Clara felt her heart racing. It was the same style as Amma's book: same materials, same intertwined metal animal design on the cover, same spots where it looked like gems had once been. Clara tried to play it cool and act like she would have if it were just some old book with chicken scratch in it.

"Ours looks just like that. This is an amazing coincidence," said Clara.

Rose scoffed. "There are no coincidences."

"Can I look?" Clara held out her hands, which were still trembling. There was a pause and then Blonde Hair took the book from Rose and gave it to Clara. Cole walked back in and Clara used the hum.

"Hey, what was that?" asked Rose.

"Oh, sorry. That was me. I sometimes use the power to improve my eyesight. I'm totally farsighted," Clara lied.

She didn't want the triplets to know that she could translate the book and certainly wasn't ready to reveal what she and Cole already knew about the Order and the training rooms. She opened to the first page of the book and her heart skipped a beat. There was no volume number reference like there was in Amma's book. The title caption simply read, "The History and Teachings of the Order of the Consolidated Power." It was the *first* volume. It could potentially answer Clara's countless questions about the origin of the power and the beginnings of the Order.

Holding the first volume in her hands was more than Clara could handle. Her heart was racing and her palms were sweaty. She needed to calm down. She imagined herself snatching the book, running out of the room, and running all the way to the airport. Or maybe she could just turn into an eagle and fly back to Lehighton with the book in her talons. She needed to chill. She asked if anyone else wanted another shot and everyone was game.

"Does anyone in Iceland know that you were coming with this book?" asked Cole after he stopped grimacing from the shot.

"Eh, I don't think so," said Brown Hair and the other two confirmed by nodding their heads. "There's only one university in this whole country, so we figured we would just show up and ask around."

"Whatever you do, don't do that," said Clara.

When she had called Rose from the airport, she hadn't mentioned anything about the book or Amma, just that they were going to Iceland for a short vacation and it would be great to meet up. She had wanted to feel them out before revealing too many details. But now was the time, and the beer and tequila had sufficiently loosened her tongue.

"This book was our grandmother's and she was calling around trying to find experts to help her with it. She found some institute here in Reykjavík. Cole, do you remember the name? Muggleson or something?" She turned to Cole who shrugged and shook his head. "I have it written down somewhere. Anyway, she sent them some photocopied pages and next thing she knows she's being followed. Then her house was ransacked and they kidnapped her."

The triplets gasped.

"That's brutal!" said Blonde Hair.

"We're here to rescue her." Cole proudly puffed out his chest.

What a dork, thought Clara.

"We'll help you," declared Rose.

"We will?!" The other two looked quite taken aback.

"It's our destiny," said Rose. Her voice had a far-off, smoky quality.

"Rose, can we talk about this first?"

"What is there to talk about? These are kindred spirits who need our help."

"Our Iceland trips are supposed to be fun, not finding Miss Daisy," said Blonde Hair, who had finally figured out how to use the wireless speaker and was bopping to the beat of club music.

"Aoife, Rose is right," said Brown Hair. "We're connected to them and they need us. And if these kidnappers are after their book, they might come after us one day too. We should act as a team."

"Yeah, superhero gang. How do you guys feel about plaid?"

"We're witches, not superheroes," said Rose to her phone.

"Right, right, of course." Cole had a goofy look on his face and Clara figured he was imagining all of them in his silly costumes, punching bad guys with the words "POW" and "WHAM" floating above them.

"We would certainly appreciate your help, but we don't exactly have a plan," said Clara.

"Well, let's get one," said Brown Hair. "But not tonight. It's time to hit the pubs."

Cole glanced out the windows at the bright blue sky. "What time is it?" He looked confused. *Time to look at your dorky wristwatch*, thought Clara.

"It's nine thirty at night. Welcome to Iceland, bitches!" Blonde Hair raised her arms so that her annoyingly perfect stomach showed from under her t-shirt. She chugged the rest of her beer and slammed the bottle down on the counter.

Clara felt a little bad going out on the town when Amma was being held captive somewhere—in the best-case scenario—but the buzz from the shots and beers was making it easy to rationalize. The opportunity to make the responsible choice had long passed. *What's done, is done.* She was more surprised that Cole was willing to go out drinking under those circumstances, but the twinkle in his eye whenever he looked at Brown Hair made it clear that his brain was no longer the organ making his decisions.

Following the triplets' lead, the newly-formed superpower crew cut down a path behind the church and across a little square with a manicured lawn and old statues. Clara couldn't help but think about the town square back home, even though the Lehighton square was about four times larger and ten times shittier. She thought about Asa putting his arm behind her in the gazebo right after she had first used the hum. She wondered where he was and hoped that he had found the jar of wet nuts that she had left on the basement couch as a joke.

"So, what do you guys call the feeling?" asked Cole, more loudly than Clara liked.

"I call it the gift," said Rose.

"Um, I dunno," said Blonde Hair. "I guess I just call it the feeling. Or whatever one of them called it last." She gestured to Rose and then noticed that Brown Hair had fallen behind while typing in her phone. "Craic on, Eileen! What do you guys call it?"

"We've tried a few names, but we keep going back to the hum. It's super boring, I know," said Cole.

Brown Hair caught up with them and fell in next to Cole.

"What do *you* call it?" Cole asked her.

"I call it the whir. It just feels like the sound made by something spinning around. It's dumb."

"No, it's perfect," whispered Cole, looking her right in the face.

Clara could never figure out Cole's taste in girls. Blonde Hair was clearly the prettiest, but Cole didn't always go for the prettiest ones. He was more interested in something else that Clara could never quite put her finger on. It was some sort of combination of confidence and playfulness—big boobs didn't hurt either.

After the square, they made a few more turns and then the triplets cheered when the bar came into view down a narrow pedestrian street.

"Where are you from in Ireland?" asked Clara.

"Dublin," answered one or more of them.

"And you come all this way to go to a bar called The Dubliner?" asked Clara.

"Yeah, we like it. What of it?" said Brown Hair.

Cole further proved his dedication to the conquest of Brown Hair by running ahead to hold the bar door open for her. He never opened doors for Clara or even their mother. In fact, it often seemed like he was falling back so that someone else would open doors for him.

The inside of the bar was like any other Irish pub that could be found in any other town in the world. The walls and furnishings were made of varying dark woods, and it smelled of old beer and cigarettes with just a hint of vomit. There were mirrors with old-timey Guinness ads painted on them and an occasional shamrock here and there. They sat down at the bar and Brown Hair ordered a round of shots and beers. Clara sighed. They hadn't eaten dinner and there seemed to be no plans to eat. She would regret doing shots later. Blonde Hair went over to the jukebox and it wasn't long before a Taylor Swift song was playing.

"Turn that shite off," growled a heavyset man at the other end of the bar. Clara didn't recognize the accent, but it wasn't Irish or Icelandic. "Nobody wants to hear that American slut," he roared, saying the words "American" and "slut" with equal disdain.

Clara watched Rose and Brown Hair exchange nervous glances and then look toward Blonde Hair. She had turned from the jukebox to face the offender. She leaned forward slightly, her arms at her sides, her hands in clenched fists. Her face was cruel, yet somehow beautiful in its coldness. The look alone might have killed the hater had he bothered to look up from his beer.

A moment later Clara felt a change in the hum and then instantly the two back legs of the man's barstool snapped, seemingly under his weight. The barstool and its occupant careened backward, the man's shoulders and head hitting a low table behind him. His fall broke the tabletop off its pedestal, flipping up everything on it. Pint glasses full of beer and plates of bar food came crashing down onto him just after he hit the floor. He groaned loudly and rolled over onto his side, broken glass crunching under his weight. The bartenders and a bouncer rushed over to help the man up and escorted him out of sight, perhaps to an ambulance. Before he was even up off the floor, the jukebox switched itself mid-song and started playing "Shake It Off."

XI

With the Greyman and their warriors well under the influence of the dream thistle tea and the sun finally set, Sigmundr and Estrid retrieved the pitchfork from Thoralf's warehouse and crept among the tents searching for the sorcerer. In the largest tent, beyond the sleeping warrior sentinels slumped down on either side of the opening, they found the sorcerer on a straw mat at the foot of the leader's bed. Both men snored vigorously. Sigmundr accidentally scraped his pitchfork against a warrior's shield that was propped up against a tent post. Sigmundr and Estrid froze in fear, but the leader and sorcerer were undisturbed.

They tiptoed to the sleeping sorcerer and loomed over him. Sigmundr held the pitchfork just above the sorcerer's chest, sharp prongs pointing down. Sigmundr asked Estrid to come over and hold the handle but she refused. She whispered that Sigmundr should do it himself. Sigmundr explained that they had to do it together so that they would both get the power. Estrid agreed and together they delivered the death wound deep into the sorcerer's chest. He opened his eyes and died silently.

As they turned to take leave of the tent, Estrid noticed a large sack next to the leader's bed. It was full of large, intricately decorated books. The leather covers were inlaid with silver and gold in a pattern of slender animals with interlaced appendages. The eyes of the animals were depicted with valuable gemstones. Though neither of them could read, Estrid and Sigmundr conspired to take the sack of books. Just a single one of the gemstones could buy enough food to fill the Dímuners' stomachs for the long winter. They absconded with the sack of books and ran up the hill to Beine's estate on the northern tip of the island.

THIRTY-FOUR

Cole was both relieved and disappointed that Eileen wasn't next to him when he woke up. He had a vague memory of kissing her on the dance floor of a club, but he wasn't a hundred percent confident that it had actually happened. He didn't remember how they got back to the hotel, so he was also relieved to see Clara in her bed. She had definitely let her hair down and had spent most of the night flirting with one of the bartenders at The Dubliner, who had met up with them at the club after his shift.

Cole wasn't as hungover as he would have expected, though he figured it would catch up with him later. For now, he mostly felt guilty for having gone out and had fun while Amma was being held captive in god knows what condition. Cole resolved to get his act together and focus on what was important. He opened the shutter covering their room's only window. "Wakey wakey!" he shouted at his grumpy twin.

~

Over the hotel's continental breakfast, Clara, Cole and the triplets tried to devise a plan to find Amma. Clara confirmed in her notebook that, based on Amma's letters, the prime suspects were the Árni Magnússon Institute and Icelandic hipsters with man buns and grey scarves.

A glance around the hotel dining room, combined with his hazy memories from their night out on the town, convinced Cole that the man-bun clue was not going to be very useful. It seemed like almost every man in Iceland had long hair, and a bun was somehow a completely acceptable style option. Cole would have loved to see one of them try to rock that look in Lehighton. He also wasn't sure how useful the grey scarf clue would be. While he couldn't remember seeing any grey scarves specifically, they seemed like something that would be commonplace in the Nordic hipster wardrobe.

Before breakfast, Clara had learned from the concierge that the institute, which Cole kept referring to as the Muggle Institute, was located in the University of Iceland's main library building. According to Clara, the university library also acted as Iceland's equivalent of the U.S.' Library of Congress, where, Cole presumed, congressmen kept the books they liked to read during lunch breaks. Having no other leads, the super friends decided their first mission should be to stake out the library to see what intel they could gather.

To Cole's dismay, the library was not within walking distance of the hotel. That meant Cole would have to show off his driving skills to their new companions. He did not want to embarrass himself in front of them, especially Eileen, but it seemed he had little choice in the matter. After Clara called him out for stalling, he finished his third croissant and the five of them piled into the white compact.

Cole wondered whether there was any way he could use the whir to be a better driver, but he couldn't think of how—plus, his likewise-gifted passengers would feel what he was doing.

Clara took the passenger seat and pulled out the handwritten directions from the concierge. Eileen offered to use her phone to navigate, but Clara insisted they do it the old-fashioned way because it was more "authentic." Cole held in a laugh and wondered where his parents were at that moment—maybe kayaking authentically on a raging river somewhere, although he had no clue what time of day it might be in the Midwest.

"By all means, don't let us rush you," said Clara.

"Huh?" Cole emerged slowly out of his kayaking daydream. "Oh, right. I'm ready."

"Good. So . . . how about starting the car?"

"Right."

It appeared that none of the triplets had noticed that he had no idea what he was doing. Rose, who seemed to be constantly looking down at her phone, probably wouldn't notice if he drove right across the square and knocked down a few statues. Unfortunately, it wasn't Rose he was worried about. After a few careful turns at Clara's direction, a huge building came into view in the distance at the end of a main thoroughfare. It looked like a 300-foot-tall NASA shuttle made out of tan stone.

"Whoa. What the heck is that thing?" Cole looked back at the road just in time to avoid driving up on the sidewalk.

"It's the main church," said Eileen. "Don't you guys know anything about Iceland?"

"No, why would we? We're Americans," said Cole, who immediately received a punch in the arm from Clara.

"Another phallic monument to the Christian patriarchy," said Rose.

"I don't know," said Aoife. "From certain angles, I think it kind of looks like a giant vagina."

"You would," said Eileen. Cole snickered.

When they got to the library, it became clear that the church was not the only funky building in Reykjavík. The upper floors of the library were bright red and looked like a giant shoebox.

The lower floors were less wide and mainly glass, giving the impression that the shoebox was hovering in the air. Feeling more confident in his driving skills, Cole relaxed a little and promptly clipped a car as he pulled into a parking spot. He was sure his face turned the same color as the upper floors of the building. At least he hadn't left a mark on the other car.

"Are you coming?" said Clara.

"Craic on," yelled Eileen, already halfway to the library entrance.

Clara ran ahead to catch up with the triplets. Cole also picked up his pace until he felt the familiar flick of a loose shoelace against his leg. He stopped to tie it, propping his foot up on the bumper of a nearby parked car. When he turned to continue on his way, he saw a figure leaving the library from a side door on the left. It was moving quickly toward the parking lot, a man—tall, thin and maybe in his thirties. He had shoulder-length blond hair, some of which was loosely gathered into a bun.

Something was trailing behind the man like a cape—a long scarf loosely draped around the back of his neck. It was a silky material that made its deep grey color look like pewter. A man with a bun and a grey scarf! Cole looked at Clara and the triplets but they had already gone into the library and were out of sight.

In a panic, he frantically looked back and forth between the library and the man. Was he one of the bad-guy Amma-abductors? He didn't know what to do. Out of the corner of his eye, Cole saw a tall black van enter the parking lot. The van's horn honked and the bad guy raised his hand. Increasing Cole's sense of panic, it occurred to him that the van was coming to pick up the man and their only lead would drive off. Cole took a deep breath and accepted what he had to do to fulfill his superhero destiny: follow that van. He sprinted back to the rental car.

Besides all the curse words running through his head, Cole thought how this was one of the few times in his life that he really, really wished he had a cellphone. He got to the car at about the same time that the van pulled up next to the man, who hopped into the back sliding door. Cole fumbled with the keys as he tried to figure out which button unlocked the doors.

"Shit, shit, shit, shit, shit," he whispered to himself. Finally in, he put his seatbelt on, started the car, gave a hard bang with both hands on the steering wheel, yelled one last "shit" at the top of his lungs and put the car into reverse. Pulling out of the parking spot, he hit the same car as he had on the way in, this time definitely leaving a mark. Too bad—he had to focus on his mission to follow the van and save Amma.

Fortunately, there was a fair amount of traffic at that time of day, so Cole could maintain a manageably slow pace while still keeping up with the van. How slow exactly Cole couldn't tell because the car's speedometer seemed broken; it was showing speeds much faster than he could have possibly been going. It was also helpful that the van—a Mercedes, to Cole's confusion— was oddly tall so that it was easy for Cole to keep track of it. At some point he drove right by the large church and Cole could see what Aoife meant; with the view of the spire blocked by the roof of the car, the church did have a certain vagina vibe to it.

After about twenty minutes of stop-and-go city driving, the black van turned onto a highway. Cole tried to keep calm, re- minding himself that he was an old pro at highways, having al- ready driven one on the trip from the airport. The van didn't seem to be in any particular rush, so Cole was able to keep up with it by driving at a reasonable pace in the right lane.

As he got farther out of the city, the landscape opened up and at times looked almost moonlike. Off in the distance ahead of him, well beyond the more immediate grey rolling hills and bright green pastures, were large snowcapped mountains. After a while, the highway narrowed to two lanes and fed into a tunnel. Cole's confidence deflated. The width of the lanes provided very little margin for error and the opposing traffic in the lane to his left was whizzing by at high speeds. The tunnel was pretty dark and he couldn't figure out how to turn on the car's headlights. Making matters worse, the car behind him noticed that he didn't have his lights on and so was flashing its headlights and honking. Many of the cars heading toward him also wanted to be good Samaritans by flashing their headlights, turning the tunnel into some terrible strobing, pulsing nightmare—not unlike his vague memories of the dance club from the night before.

It soon became clear that it was not a short tunnel. It wouldn't be a quick experience that would suck but at least be short-lived, like ripping off a Band-Aid. He would have to endure this tunnel. He would have to experience it and survive it. He had to stay in his lane and ignore the other cars. On and on it went, by far the longest tunnel Cole had ever seen. He didn't think Iceland was even that big and started to question where it would let out. Still, the tunnel went on. At least he didn't have to worry about losing track of the black van. It remained four cars ahead, as it had been at the start of the tunnel and would be at the end, if there was an end.

Indeed, there was eventually a literal light at the end of the tunnel. After his eyes adjusted to the glare of the white sky, Cole relaxed as the highway expanded back to four lanes with a generous shoulder. The highway ended at a traffic circle and almost all of the cars took the first exit that, according to the signs, led to a place called Borgarnes.

All of the cars, that is, except for the black van, which continued around the circle until the second exit toward Akranes. The road was no longer a highway but just a simple asphalt road running between bright green fields. To the left was the ocean with some hazy mountains in the distance. Cole couldn't tell whether the mountains were on smaller islands or were just other parts of the main island that jutted out into the sea. Along the road, there were occasional large farmhouses, usually painted white with bright red roofs. Straight ahead, the lush, green farmland ended abruptly at the foot of a large rock formation. It was larger than what Cole would call a hill but not quite big enough to be considered a mountain. Up ahead, Cole saw where the roadway was carved into the rock. It climbed about mid-way up, turning to the left toward the ocean. It hugged the cliff wall and rounded to the other side. He was not looking forward to driving on that precarious roadway. There weren't even guardrails. He tried not to think about it and just focused on the road right ahead of him—and the van.

The van took the curve along the cliff and Cole followed. His fingers ached from how hard he was gripping the steering wheel. On the other side of the big rock, the road gradually descended down to go along a rocky beach, passing so close to the water that sections of the asphalt were wet from sea spray. To Cole's dread, after less than a mile of beach, there was another huge rock outcropping, practically identical to the one he had just survived. No choice but to keep going. Around the bend of the second mini-mountain, the road didn't descend but thankfully moved about twenty feet inland from the precipice. A farm came into view to the inland side of the road to the right. Sheep grazed, unconcerned that they were a few feet from a hundred-foot drop into the sea.

Straight ahead was a large pine forest. Cole realized that he hadn't seen any trees since he got to Iceland, other than those in the city squares. He wasn't even sure he had seen any vegetation that was dark green, given that all the fields were the bright green of new crops. The pine forest looked dark, dense and creepy, and like the perfect place for the secret lair of Nordic villains. The van entered the forest via a driveway just beyond a grey mailbox. Cole couldn't exactly follow the van down the driveway, so he pulled over onto a patch of gravel. He looked back at the driveway and considered his options.

He had two options. One, he could return to the library and tell the ladies that he had found the kidnappers. They could all come up with a well-reasoned plan to ambush the hideout and rescue Amma. Or, two, he could go investigate now, planless and alone, and snoop around the pine forest. But he had no way to defend himself and there was no way for anyone to ever know what had happened to him if things turned out badly.

The choice was obvious.

Cole walked up and down the edge of the forest looking for a spot where the pines weren't quite so thick and tangled. He would just need to barge through and deal with the branches and needles—sharp and long, like the pine trees along the beach on Prouts Neck—as they came at him. He checked the car for something he could use to cover himself, but there was nothing. He would have to man up and prepare for a few unpleasant scratches. He cupped his hands over his eyes and walked into the wall of needles. He tried not to make any sounds, but it was near impossible not to hoot and holler as various parts of his body were pricked. He tripped over a low branch and, afraid to uncover his eyes, he fell onto his elbows. The impact against the ground caused his hands to force his head back violently.

Opening his eyes, Cole found that he was inside the forest. The thick canopy above gave it a dusk-like quality. What little light there was had a golden tinge from the layer of copper-brown, dried-up needles blanketing the ground. Cole stood up and examined his hands. They were covered in little scratches and he expected his face looked the same. He was also covered in dried needles from his fall, revealing another hazard of pine trees: sap. Every part of him was sticky, but it smelled amazing.

He walked deeper into the forest. He noticed how quiet it was. It seemed that the thick floor of needles was absorbing all sound. He couldn't even hear the crashing waves far below down the cliff wall. It couldn't be that far off to his left. He also didn't hear any birds, which was eerie for a forest.

After a while, he came upon what appeared to be a trail. The needles on the ground weren't quite as thick and there were occasional patches of visible dirt. He decided to take the path in the direction that seemed more likely to lead deeper into the forest.

The trail meandered through the silent golden woods until it led through a break in the pines. It was along the very edge of the cliff. Cole did not consider himself afraid of heights, but walking along the narrow path, squeezed between the sharp trees and a few hundred-foot drop to certain death was terrifying. He tried to see what was at the bottom of the cliff, but couldn't quite bring himself to get close enough to the edge. Since he was already covered in scratches, sap and pine needles, he saw no harm in getting a little dirtier by lying on the ground, stomach down, and shimmying his body so just his head protruded off the ledge. That position felt safer to him.

Maybe he *was* afraid of heights, he told himself as he gazed down at the waves crashing against the rocks far below. He felt dizzy and closed his eyes. While he could escape the view, he couldn't escape the sounds of the crashing waves and the brisk sea air shooting right up into his face. There was also a disgusting, old-fish, bird-shitty smell that managed to overpower the piney sap smell. The dizziness lifted a little, and he opened his eyes again. Only a few feet below him and to his right, jutting out from the cliff face, was a small ledge, on which stood two birds. They were about the size of the pigeons back home, but they were more stocky, almost muscular, if that was possible for birds. The tops of their heads and backs were black and their faces and bellies were a brilliant white but their most striking feature was a large orange and yellow striped bill that was almost the same size as their heads. Cole thought they were pretty cool-looking. They peered up at him, tilting their heads to the side, and made little grunting noises that sounded more like the braying of a sick horse than anything one would expect from a bird.

"Hi," said Cole.

Hundreds of feet below were jagged rocks at the water's edge. They must have been part of the cliff face once. Over time, maybe centuries, the cliff wall was crumbling off into the ocean. It seemed anyone's guess when it had last happened, or when it would next happen. With that thought in mind, Cole decided it was time to move on, so he said goodbye to his new friends, carefully scooted himself away from the edge and stood up to continue his mission. He stuck close to the right side of the path, as far away from the edge as possible without being pricked by the pines. Soon, the path veered away from the cliff and back into the forest through a slight opening in the branches.

After a while, the trail eased slightly downhill and Cole came upon a large clearing in the forest that formed a small valley. It was dominated by two long structures made of dark wood, parallel to each other, with only a few feet in between them. They were single-storied, almost sunken looking, with asymmetrical peaked roofs. Without leaving the cover of the trees, Cole walked to the right to get a better look and there, parked in front of the building to the left, was the black van.

He momentarily froze at the sight of it, but after assuring himself that it was unoccupied, he gathered up his courage to continue his survey of the structures. The off-centered pitch of the roofs and the placement of the doors were mirrored between the two buildings. Even from that distance, Cole could see that the wooden exterior was intricately carved with unidentifiable animals with interlocking limbs, tails and tongues. The animal pattern, also mirrored between the two buildings, reminded Cole of the cover of Amma's book.

Two long, mirror-image buildings right next to each other, in Iceland, and carved with the same patterns as on Amma's book.

"Twin Halls!" Cole whispered to no one. Amma wasn't kidnapped by some academics who just really, really wanted her book—she had been kidnapped by the Order. The Order still existed and apparently was still up to its old shenanigans.

Clara is going to freak when I tell her about this, he thought. *Assuming I live to see her again.*

The hall to the left seemed to be where all the action was. In addition to having the van out front, light came through the slats of the closed shutters and two of the three chimneys were spewing smoke. By contrast, the hall on the right was completely lifeless. Its windows were dark and the shutters were boarded up tight by pieces of lumber nailed on in crisscross patterns. The chimneys were smokeless and everything about the building just seemed colder and dustier than the one to the left.

Cole heard faint voices as two men came into view from between the halls. They were large men holding large guns. It had never occurred to Cole that guns might be involved somehow. The men were moseying around, presumably patrolling the premises, and having a heated conversation in what Cole assumed was Icelandic. He thought about how the responsible choice at this time would be to leave and go back to the car.

He waited until the men wandered out of sight behind the right hall and then crept forward, out from behind the tree line. Understanding that he probably didn't have much time before the gunmen's patrolling rounds led them back, Cole sprinted down the hill as fast as he could. When he reached the left hall, he dramatically aligned his body against the wall, as if he and his jeans and royal blue sweatshirt could somehow camouflage with the dark, old wood.

He crept along the side of the building, trying to peer through the seams between the closed shutters of various windows. He couldn't see anything useful. About halfway to the other end of the building, one of the shutters creaked when he pressed his face against it to look inside and then it opened slightly when he moved away. He used his fingernails to pry it open even more. Not wanting to open it too much, he pressed the left side of his face against the fully closed shutter so that he could look through the cracked-open right shutter with just his left eye. He didn't see much in the room immediately beyond the window, but he was able to see into another room through an open doorway. He could tell that a TV was on somewhere in that room and he saw at least two men sitting in folding chairs, the TV's blue light flickering on their smiling faces and their shiny silk scarves. To the side of the doorway, he saw just a sliver of the back of a woman, but it was enough. The woman was heavyset and had a shock of purple in her long curly grey hair. *Amma!*

He gasped at the sight of her, surprised and relieved that she was alive and well. He had found Amma. That crazy idea—Clara's crazy, wild, international goose chase of an idea—was actually coming true. No authorities, no getting *E.T.*'d, just getting on a plane and finding their grandmother—as simple as that. Only one step left: the rescue. *This superhero thing is actually happening.*

One of the men stood up suddenly, catching Cole off guard. Startled, he abruptly pulled away from the window, knocking a shutter that banged against the outside wall. He could hear men yelling in Icelandic from inside the building. Other voices were shouting as well, probably the gunmen. Cole turned and sprinted up the hill.

As he neared the tree line, two shots rang out and he dove, hands first, into the pines. He stayed on the ground without moving and waited. After a few minutes, which felt like an eternity, he adjusted his position so he could look down at the halls. From what he could see, no one was looking for him. The gunmen were talking together, and the van was still parked in the driveway. Maybe they hadn't seen him and those were just warning shots. He gathered up the courage to stand up and get back to the trail. Having potentially been shot at, he decided that it was definitely a good time to return to the car—for real this time.

He ran back along the trail, except for the part along the cliff edge, which he carefully walked. Back at the car, he took a moment to look out at the vast ocean and tried to organize his thoughts. He was exhausted, physically and mentally, and he still had to do the drive back to the library, through the never-ending tunnel of doom. He would probably have to stop along the way to ask for directions at least once. As he started to turn the ignition, something broke the surface of the water. It wasn't even that far out—a large black and white whale. The whale shot straight up until its white underbelly broke the surface and then it flopped itself sideways back into the water, leaving in its wake a dramatic fan-shaped spray of water that shimmered in the white sunlight.

Cole had never seen a killer whale before in his entire life, but no one was there to share the experience. He gazed out again at the sparkling ocean as the ripples left over from the whale's jump radiated out and dissipated. He then closed his eyes and leaned his forehead against the steering wheel.

THIRTY-FIVE

Mother, I finally found the triplets. But you'll never guess how. I searched for a while. This town is bigger than I was expecting and these sisters are quite wily, it would seem. But then, who do I see sleeping in the park? I'm in Iceland, remember. Who do I see sprawled out on a park bench, head back, mouth open like a buffoon? Your dear nephew, Cole. Mister All-American himself. Snoring away until a cop woke him. Surely no coincidence, so I followed him and cased his hotel. Then they came out together. Cole, Clara and the triplets. Bingo. Jackpot.

THIRTY-SIX

"Let's give him five more minutes," said Clara. The trip-lets were milling about the library's entrance hall, skimming flyers and looking at bulletin boards. Clara scanned the parking lot nervously. *He probably just stopped to tie his shoelaces and got turned around, or maybe he went in another entrance,* she told herself.

When the five minutes had passed, Clara could no longer stall the mission. "Okay, okay, let's go. He'll just have to catch up with us."

"Should we be worried?" It was Brown Hair, of course. By then it was obvious to everyone that the crush was mutual.

"No. He's fine. He pulls this sort of crap all the time. He'll show up in a couple hours saying he went to look for a snack or something."

"You guys should get mobiles." As usual, it looked like Rose was talking to her phone.

"No shit," said Clara under her breath.

The plan was for each of them to investigate one floor of the library and then reconvene at the entrance in an hour. They agreed it was best to not ask anyone for help just yet, at least not until they had a better understanding of the facility. Per Brown Hair's suggestion, the floors were assigned alphabetically by name. Clara had the second floor. She didn't understand how a name that sounded like "Ee-fah" could start with an A, but it wasn't worth the conversation.

Based on the exterior of the library, Clara had been expecting a super cool, minimalist, modern interior. She was disappointed. While the first floor, part of which she had to walk through to get to the central staircase, had a somewhat contemporary, open-concept computer lab space, the second floor was just rows and rows of bookshelves. She was a little surprised by that and then surprised that it surprised her—it was a library after all. On the second floor, she picked a random aisle to walk down, occasionally looking at the section labels or a few book titles here and there, although most were in Icelandic. Even though this had largely been her idea, she wasn't really sure what she was supposed to be looking for. Maybe a room with "The Árni Magnússon Institute" over the door. Maybe a hidden shelf with all the other volumes of Amma's book just sitting there for the taking. Maybe some man-bunned hipsters sneaking around dark corners. Or maybe nothing. *What was the plan if they came up empty handed?* she wondered.

She snaked up and down the rows aimlessly for a while before reasoning that she should be more systematic in her approach. She decided to find the beginning and work her way up and down each row. The problem was that she had gotten herself so turned around that she didn't know where a logical beginning would be.

While looking for a spot that would work as a beginning, she came upon a wall with a glass door. A sign taped to the door read, below some Icelandic words, "Please keep door closed at all times. Rare book room is climate controlled." Intrigued, Clara tested the door and found it unlocked. She went in. The room was dim, with the only light coming from glass display cases that wrapped around the room at waist height. Above the cases, the walls were covered in bookshelves with the books safely locked behind intricate wrought-iron gates. The air was still and dry and the old parchment smell was overwhelming. The door clicked closed behind her and she walked forward to examine the old books in the display cases. Many of the books were presented open, presumably to particularly important or beautiful pages. Clara took a deep breath. The style of the artwork in the books was familiar. It was the same as in Amma's book.

The margins were filled with fanciful paintings, reflecting the scene in the book, animal designs, swirling vines or geometric patterns. They were not, to Clara's disappointment, written in runes but instead used what she recognized as the Icelandic alphabet: mostly the same as the Latin alphabet used in English, except for a few peculiar letters.

While a little bummed that the books were not the long-sought other volumes of Amma's book, they could at least lead to clues about the time period. Clara cursed Cole for not being there so she could try to read them. She settled for reading the descriptions affixed to the cases, helpfully provided in English. The descriptions were mainly saga-this and saga-that. The most prominently displayed and perhaps the largest of the books was called *Egil's Saga*, noted as being from or about—Clara couldn't tell—Borgarnes, Iceland. The book was open to an early page showing a painting of an ugly man with an American football player's build. He was wearing a red shirt and a green and blue cape draped over his shoulder.

Clara scanned the other cases, noting the various tongue-twister Icelandic names and locales. In a far corner was a case under a placard reading "Foreign Sagas." Having lost interest in obscure Icelandic place names, Clara walked over to investigate. The display case held three sagas from or about Norway, one from or about Greenland, one from or about the Orkney Islands, and two from or about the Faroe Islands.

One of the Faroe Islands books, called the *Dímuners' Saga*, caught her eye. In the margin of one of the open pages was a picture of a woman. Clara hadn't seen any women in the other sagas on display. She was clothed in a long white tunic and wore a green cape that was fastened by brown oval brooches on her shoulders. What struck Clara most were the woman's eyes: the pupils were white in the center and there were little lines coming out of them, which gave the impression that they were glowing.

Clara leaned down to have a better look, putting her face close to the glass. Just then, the door clicked shut and she jumped up, startled. She turned quickly to find a tall man standing by the door, his dark shape silhouetted by the brighter light coming in through the glass door behind him. As he walked toward her, she was able to make out his features. She was immediately struck by a single thought: *Damn, he is hot.*

His eyes were a striking pale blue, contrasting with his bushy black eyebrows and black hair cut that was short on the sides. A slight space between his front teeth accentuated the utter symmetry of his face. His nose, eyes and lips were petite, his skin, a creamy pink. The dim light of the rare book room was too weak to reveal a single scar or blemish or pore, if any existed at all. Moving her eyes across his tiny chin and down to his pointy Adam's apple, Clara glimpsed a silky grey scarf hanging around his neck, just inside the collar of his jean jacket. He was one of those rare beauties who could pull off a denim jacket post-high school.

"Where is your brother?" He spoke casually in a thick Icelandic accent, but his question put Clara on alert.

"Um, do I know you?" Clara subtly scanned the room for something she could use as a weapon. Everything was secured behind bars or under glass.

"No. Where is he?"

"None of your business. Who are you?"

"That doesn't matter. Bring the book to the sun voyager at midnight. You give us the book and we give you your grandmother."

The grey scarf, of course, thought Clara, getting increasingly nervous. *He's one of the kidnappers.* She backed away until her butt hit a display case. Without the hum or a weapon, trying to fight him and his jean-jacket-filling muscles would be risky. The safest bet was to stay calm and gather information.

"Is she okay?"

"Yes, she is great. We love her," he said, momentarily breaking his cool demeanor. "She does talk a lot, though."

Clara couldn't believe she was having this conversation with her grandmother's kidnapper. She raised her eyebrows expectantly.

"So, um, do you want to grab lunch or a drink?" he asked.

"What?"

"Grab some food?" He flicked his head slightly to the side to move some of his dark hair away from his eyes. *Those eyes.*

"Like a date? Are you kidding me?" Clara couldn't believe the gall of this man.

"Yes. Why not?" He looked confused. Clara presumed that his confusion stemmed from having never been turned down before.

"Well, because you fucking kidnapped my grandmother. Get the fuck out of my face, you shithead," Clara yelled. The man was visibly taken aback and he slowly walked backward, reaching back with his hand until it grabbed the doorknob.

"Sorry," he said, lowering his head as he opened the door to leave. "We haven't had to do anything like this for hundreds of years. It's not what I expected when I joined."

Clara responded by giving him the finger. He looked back at her with offended, puppy dog eyes and then he was gone and the door clicked shut.

Clara was furious. Just because he was handsome, he thought she would overlook the kidnapping of her own grandmother and go out with him? She was glad Cole wasn't around in her state of rage because she feared she would use the hum to burn the whole place to the ground. On the other hand, she was relieved that they had an actual lead and knew that Amma was alive and in Iceland.

Clara waited a few minutes, just staring at the glass door, then left the rare book room to go find the triplets and, hopefully, Cole. *But what does "sun voyager" mean?* she asked herself. *It must be some cryptic riddle.* As she wandered around looking for the stairs, she pondered this question. Sun probably stands for the east, where the sun rises, she mused. And voyager maybe means some form of transportation. Perhaps they are to meet at the eastern end of a train line, or something like that.

Finding the goth sisters in the vast library proved futile, so she decided to wait in the entrance hall until the designated meeting time. While waiting, she concocted other theories on the meaning of sun voyager, including the possibility that a ship in the harbor had a planetary name or maybe there was an old sundial somewhere in town.

When the triplets finally all gathered in the hall, Clara explained what had happened and started to offer her theories on the sun voyager riddle. They all laughed.

"The Sun Voyager is a famous statue," said Brown Hair. "It's right by the water."

"You're the only person within a thousand kilometers who doesn't know that," said Blonde Hair.

"Other than Cole." Brown Hair piped in.

"Speaking of . . . have any of you seen him?" Clara tried to play it cool and not seem embarrassed by the Sun Voyager thing.

"No, and the car is gone," said Brown Hair.

Clara looked at her in surprise. "How do you know that?"

"I checked before I went upstairs."

"Oh, right." Clara considered whether she should have thought of doing that too. There was too much swirling around in her mind to decide whether to be frustrated with Cole or worried about him.

"I need a nap," said Rose to her phone.

"And I need a drink," said Blonde Hair.

Sunlight shining through the glass wall of the library entrance hall shone on Blonde Hair's eyes, which glinted back at Clara and reminded her of the picture of the woman in the rare book room. Clara had intended to investigate the book in case the woman's eyes had some connection to them, but she forgot in all the excitement of the encounter with the cocky kidnapper. She would try to look it up later. *Daminer Saga or something like that, from the Faroe Islands,* she reminded herself.

"Let's grab a taxi back to the hotel," said Brown Hair. "Cole will figure out to meet us there and it is near the mysterious and elusive Sun Voyager." The sisters snickered and they all headed out to hail a cab.

About an hour and a half later, there was a knock on the triplets' hotel room. Blonde Hair was having a beer on the balcony and the other two were off taking naps. Clara jumped up and ran to the door. *Thank god.* The relief of seeing Cole overwhelmed her and she gave him a big hug that almost knocked him over.

"I have huge news. Where the hell have you been?" she said, breaking the hug with a frustrated shove. "And why are you covered in dirt?"

"It's sap. But guess what."

"What?" She was in no mood for games.

"I found Amma."

XII

When they arrived at Beine's estate, Estrid and Sigmundr were out of breath from their uphill run from the village carrying the large sack of books stolen from the Greymen. They hid in the barn and quickly tried to practice their newly gained powers amongst the livestock. They were not able to cast any spells or shapeshift or do any magic at all.

"It is not working. I do not feel any different," said Estrid.

"Nor do I," said Sigmundr.

"What are we going to do when they wake up? We did not consider the possibility of not receiving the power. We cannot fight them and we cannot undo the curse," she said.

"We will hide here until they leave the island," said Sigmundr.

"We cannot hide. They will kill all of our people and burn down the houses until we are found. We must leave the island and they must see us fleeing so that they are drawn away."

"How? They have warriors guarding all the ships in the harbor."

Then Gudrid entered the barn complaining of the noise at such a late hour. Estrid explained to Gudrid what had transpired. Gudrid was angry at them for taking such a risk, but she was willing to help her sister.

"The Barefoot Prince has a sailboat hidden in the brush near the northeast beach," said Gudrid. "It is small, but it might outrun the Order's ship to the northern islands with a fair wind and enough of a head start."

"How do you know he has a boat?" asked Estrid.

"He showed it to me. We sailed around the island in courting. It barely fit the two of us. He is a kind and gentle man. He will help you if I ask him."

"Where does he sleep?" asked Sigmundr.

"He does not sleep. We will find him awake in the village," said Gudrid.

At that, Gudrid, Estrid and Sigmundr started to leave to go find the Blue Prince, but Sigmundr stopped Estrid from going. He told her it was too dangerous for her to go with him and instructed her to hide the books and stay on Stóra Dímun. He would come back to her if he survived the escape, he explained. Estrid reluctantly agreed but convinced him to take with him one of the books so that he could barter the gemstones if needed.

THIRTY-SEVEN

"So, what's the plan?" asked Aoife. "Sun Voyager at midnight for the book swap?"

"I don't want to give up the book," said Clara. "Why don't we just storm Twin Halls and rescue Amma now?"

"Em, we're happy to help but nothing too risky," said Eileen. "We're not missing *our* grandmother."

"What if you three do the swap and Clara and I go to Twin Halls at the same time," suggested Cole. "That way, if it's a trick and they just plan to take the book, we can rescue Amma from Twin Halls. And there will be less of them there because they'll be at the sun thing."

"Fewer," whispered Clara.

"We're in. We agreed to help. It's our destiny," declared Rose. The other two sisters made whiny sounds.

"Not again, Rose. You can't keep putting us in harm's way." Eileen scowled at Rose but snuck another wink at Cole.

"At least not without consulting us. Remember what happened last time?" Aoife flashed the back of her right forearm.

Eileen leaned over to Cole and whispered. "Rose once had us help a homeless man find his dog because its name was Star—she has a thing for stars. And, well, the little twinkler ended up biting Aoife's arm when we were pulling it out of a dumpster."

"And how did all that work out in the end?" Rose was looking down at her phone, seemingly unphased by her sisters' attempted revolt.

Aoife blushed and looked at the floor. "Fine, I guess."

Eileen again leaned in toward Cole's ear. "She's still dating the doctor who gave her the stitches." Eileen then raised her voice for the benefit of the others. "I guess that plan seems fine. The Sun Voyager is a pretty open spot. They won't try anything there."

"But I don't want to give up the book." Clara was adamant.

"It's for your grandmother, ye wagon," said Aoife.

"Could we make a copy of the book, like with the power?" Everyone nodded at Eileen's interesting proposal.

"Worth a shot," said Cole.

"A séance!" Rose stood up dramatically as she spoke. "And there are five of us—that's perfect!"

Cole looked over at Clara and caught her rolling her eyes. Rose disappeared down the bedroom hallway and moments later returned with a black duffel bag. She pulled out several thick black candles and some red yarn. "Move the dining room table so we can all sit on the floor."

"We really don't need to do all this," said Clara.

"Are you a witch?" asked Rose.

"No."

"Then don't tell us how to do a séance."

"None of us are witches. We can do it without all this ceremony," said Clara. "It's stu—"

"Clara!" said Cole, cutting her off. He scowled at her. She got the message and let it go.

With the floor cleared, Rose had everyone sit in a circle on the floor. Cole put Amma's book in the center, having retrieved it from their room downstairs. As Clara moved to take her seat in the circle, he saw her stealthily take the triplet's Volume I book off the kitchen counter and place it on the floor just behind where she sat down. Rose arranged the candles in a circle around Amma's book and lit them with a bright green plastic lighter that she pulled from her back pocket.

"Do *not* light that book on fire," said Clara. Rose just glared up at her and went back to lighting the candles.

"Aoife, do you have your eyeliner?" asked Rose. "I still can't find mine." Aoife tossed a black pencil thingy to Rose across the circle. "So does anyone know what the number two looks like in runes?"

Cole looked at Clara, who was next to him, but she just shook her head.

"It's probably just Roman numerals," Clara offered. "Why?"

"Okay, thanks. Roman numerals it is," said Rose. "Cole, lean your face down a little bit."

Holding Cole's chin in her left hand, Rose wrote the Roman numeral for two on his forehead with Aoife's eyeliner.

"Oh, come on," said Clara.

"Let it go," said Cole out of the side of his mouth. "Just roll with it."

Rose then handed the eyeliner to Cole, who greatly enjoyed writing the numeral on Clara's forehead. He even added a little spiral flourish on the end of the top connector line. When everyone had their forehead markings, Rose took the red yarn and handed it out with instructions to hold here or there so that in the end the yarn made a five-pointed star, each of them holding a point.

"Now, what do we chant?" Rose asked their little coven. Cole noticed Clara subtly scoot the Volume I book under her butt with her hand that wasn't holding the yarn.

"What, you can't think of a Xeroxing spell? What kind of shite witch are you?" said Aoife.

"How about 'double, double, toil and trouble'?" said Eileen.

"Oh, cool! Like the Olsen twins' movie. I love that one!" said Cole.

Clara shielded her eyes with her free hand. "Or *Macbeth*," she said, shaking her head slowly in apparent disappointment.

"That's perfect." Rose put her free hand on Cole's shoulder and the others followed suit to create a circle. The circle with a five-pointed star matched a tattoo on Rose's wrist that Cole had noticed earlier. Rose closed her eyes and started the chant. The others joined in and Cole even heard Clara's reluctant voice playing its part. Clara was probably right that it was unnecessary. He focused on the whir and their objective of making a duplicate of Amma's book. He let the chanting fade into the background of his mind and imagined two books while heightening his awareness of the whirring in his chest. Then he heard one of the triplets let out a scream and he opened his eyes.

"Feck, feck, feck, feck," said Aoife.

"Rose, what do we do?" asked Eileen in a panic.

Confused at first, and still just seeing the one book in front of them, Cole looked in the direction that had caught the triplets' attention. There, on the floor a few feet from them, was another set of . . . them. There were identical copies of each of them, sitting in the same formation, holding the string, marked up foreheads, Amma's book, candles, everything. Cole and Clara shared a troubled glance and quickly stood up.

Their five duplicates looked equally confused by the situation, or more so, perhaps. Their quiet confusion seemed to turn into fear as they looked around. They cried out and moaned, as if they didn't quite know how to speak. They slowly dropped the red yarn and stood up, some using the back of the nearby couch to pull themselves up, others helping each other to stand. Their legs were wobbly, like those of newborn horses. When Clara's double stood up, Cole saw that under her was also a double of the triplets' Volume I. Cole watched as Clara tried to get her double's attention. When their eyes finally met, Clara made a kicking motion with her foot. The Clara double furrowed her brows and then awkwardly kicked the double of the triplets' book under the couch. No one else seemed to notice any of that in the chaos.

"Rose! What do we do?" asked Eileen.

Aoife was crying and mumbling something.

"I don't know. Just keep calm." Rose didn't sound calm at all.

Clara scrambled into the kitchen. The doubles were all backing away, going deeper into the living room area. Cole slowly approached them, palms facing down as though calming a skittish animal. That appeared to work with Cole's double, who stopped moving backward. The female doubles now had their backs against the wall and were still moaning, though also forming some odd words. Cole continued to approach his double, careful not to make any sudden movements or sounds.

"We have to kill them," yelled Clara from the kitchen.

Everyone, including the doubles, looked back at her. She was holding a large knife above her head. One triplet said, "You're right," while another one yelled "No," and the doubles' moans intensified such that Cole could barely hear himself think. His double froze with fear and then started to retreat back to the others, but Cole reached out his hand to stop him. When Cole's hand touched his double's arm, the double popped just like a bubble, silently, with little trails of liquid flinging about.

"Touch them!" Cole called out to the others. He ran forward to the wall and gently touched Eileen's double's shoulder, as tears streamed down her cheeks. She didn't pop. "It has to be *your* double," he added. Hand still on her shoulder, Cole looked Eileen's double in the eyes and told her it would be okay. Then the real Eileen was next to him and—pop—the double was gone. Maybe it wouldn't be okay for the doubles, thought Cole.

The remaining three doubles moaned and rushed to the far corner, where they clung to each other like frightened children. Soon, hovering above the petrified creatures were Clara, Rose and Aoife, their index fingers of death stretched out to touch their counterpart from another plane of existence. Then one, two, three—pop, pop, pop—they were gone.

Was that their entire experience as living beings? Cole wondered.

Aoife slumped down on the couch and cried. Eileen comforted her while wiping tears from her own eyes. Cole wanted to cry too. The whole ordeal was so sad. He wasn't exactly sure why, but something about seeing himself so afraid made his heart sink. Seeing what you might look like right before you die brought all the vulnerabilities of life right to the surface. Rose sat on the floor with some of the yarn resting in her open hands. She looked down on it as if it were blood dripping between her fingers.

The sound of the fridge opening jolted Cole out of his melancholy haze. The sound was almost insulting. It was disrespectful to the beings, whatever they were, that just died, maybe having never lived. And not just any beings but them, a version of them from some other dimension. The least they could give them is a few moments of grief or silent reflection. Clara emerged from behind the fridge door holding a beer. Noticing the many eyes on her, she held the beer out to the others.

"Anyone else need a drink? That was crazy," she said.

No one responded. She shrugged and dug for the bottle opener in the drawer. The image of her holding the knife flashed in Cole's mind. *The whir is changing her*, he thought.

THIRTY-EIGHT

Why the library? What were they looking for? Even after they'd gone, I sat there at the edge of the parking lot, pondering. Why fly all the way to Iceland to go to the library? So, I went in. And there it was. Right there. Behind glass—as if a little glass could stop me. A book, Mother. An old, old book. A book about a race of people whose eyes glowed in the sunlight. Sound familiar? And what happened to that race? A curse. A curse wiped them off the earth—stopped them from having children together. And now, suddenly, some of us are back. Do you know why, Mother? It's because of father. His procedure can overcome the curse. And the power? Were they all a great and powerful people, you may ask? No. They were simple folk, but two starry-eyed young lovers tried to take the power from a great sorcerer. They tried to take it at the same time. And we know from Professor Clara that that splits the power. The halves of the power hid inside the lovers, lurking in their genes, never to find the counterpart power because of the curse. And now that father can overcome the curse, descendants of those two lovebirds can exist, and they have the power. That explains why some of the people on father's list don't have it. I kill them and feel nothing.

But some. Oh some. Some have it. My distant cousins, I guess. Thank you for sharing the power with your kin. Blood is thicker than water, they say. And there certainly has been a lot of blood.

Knowing the explanation is nice and all, but that's not the best part. Did you catch it, Mother? Did you hear me say it to you in the mirror? Did it sing in your ears like it sings in mine? If you missed it, I will say it again. There is a curse that can end a race—maybe two. The directions are right there in the book. Step by step. Served to me under glass. Can anyone doubt my destiny now? I must get as strong as the great sorcerer. And then I can avenge you, Mother.

THIRTY-NINE

Clara agreed that it was an extremely long tunnel. The map given to her by the hotel's concierge showed that the tunnel ran under a large fjord. Cole was pretty proud of himself when he flicked on the car's headlights—apparently that had been an issue his first time through. Clara wanted to talk about their plan for when they got to Twin Halls, but she could tell he was concentrating hard on keeping the car in the narrow lane. Instead, she wondered what the wayward sisters were up to. They would have to leave the hotel for the book exchange soon. She and Cole had passed the Sun Voyager statue on their drive from the hotel to the tunnel. The concierge told Clara that it was supposed to represent a ship, but as they whizzed by on the road along the shore, it looked more like a giant, stainless steel, two-tailed scorpion scurrying out of the sea. She guessed that the legs were supposed to be oars and the tails on either side were supposed to be the bow and stern, but that seemed to be a stretch. Clara tried to imagine the scene of the exchange on the small headland jutting out to the sea: the triplets holding out the bubble-double of Amma's book on one side and a gang from the

Order leading Amma forward on the other side, the Sun Voyager looming over them.

For some reason, Clara kept worrying that the triplets would forget to bring the book. She had reminded them several times before she and Cole left, prompting Blonde Hair to say that she was "as mad as a box of frogs," whatever that meant. Clara wondered why she felt compelled to remind people of the most obvious things. Maybe the years of living in Lehighton had programmed her to assume everyone around her was a complete imbecile, she speculated. Then she saw the light at the end of the tunnel. It was almost midnight. The sun had set not long ago, but the sky was still bright, as it would be for the rest of the night.

After the tunnel, Cole left the traffic circle after the sign for the first exit to Borgarnes. Clara recalled that Borgarnes was one of the towns from saga in the rare book room at the library. *I can't forget to look up that Dimmer Saga*, she told herself. Her confrontation at the library felt like ages ago and was already a little hazy in her memory.

After some time, they drove up a promontory and around a precarious curve along the cliffside. At least they were driving on the inside lane, thought Clara. She was not looking forward to the ride back on the outside lane, assuming they survived the mission. They drove back down the other side of the mountain and along a flat, rocky coastline until they came to another mountain jutting into the sea and did the whole thing over again, except there was no descent after the second mountain. Eventually, they reached the pine forest that Cole had described. They parked the car on a gravel patch next to the road, not far from the edge of the cliff.

"Don't forget to put the emergency brake on," she said. Cole didn't respond.

Clara followed Cole's lead through the wall of pines and through the forest until they came to a path. She was sure there must be a less sap-filled way to get to the path, but resisted the urge to say something. Walking along through the oddly silent forest, the reality of what they were doing finally sunk in. In theory, Clara should have been expecting some clandestine rescue mission or risky confrontation, but she hadn't let herself think that far ahead. When arranging the plane tickets, her only objective was to get to the same island that Amma was likely on. What happened after that, what they would do if they found her, hadn't entered her mind—she didn't let it. Thinking about *when* they found her was a luxurious presumption, a recipe for disappointment. But then Cole actually found her and there they were, stalking toward the kidnappers' hideout to rescue her. As they approached the unknown, Clara became hyperaware of her body—the shakiness of each step, the clamminess of her fidgety hands. There was total silence and she could smell the ocean beyond the trees. The yellow-tinted light glazed her eyes, the hum buzzed in her chest.

"So what's our plan?" she asked. Cole was a couple steps ahead on the narrow trail.

"I don't know. I figured we'd just break into one of the windows, make sure Amma's not there and then run out. Any other ideas?"

"You said there were men with guns. What should we do about them?"

"Well, they seem to walk around patrolling the place. We could sneak in if we time it right. And we'll have the whir if there are any problems."

Clara admired how calm Cole seemed. He was cool and confident in the face of impending danger. *He's really embracing his superhero persona.* She was glad to have him as the other half of their super twin duo.

"We should try to not let anyone see us use the power," said Clara.

"Why? The Order knows about the power."

"Yeah, and their whole purpose is to kill people who have it. All they know is that we have the book. They don't necessarily think we have the power."

"Okay. We can try to not use it, but if Amma is there and we need to fight, we shouldn't worry about that."

"Let's do our best under the circumstances, whatever they might be." Clara didn't appreciate Cole's implication that she would put protecting herself over fighting for Amma—that wasn't what she was saying.

The path wound through the pine forest until it left the trees to run along the edge of the cliff. Cole gasped when Clara got close to the edge to look down. She didn't know he was afraid of heights. She was learning a lot on this trip.

"Look at the cool birds down there." Cole leaned forward just a little.

"Oh, they're puffins. What's cool about them?"

"Look at them. They're awesome."

"I don't know," she said. "They look kind of ridiculous to me. Like goofy little clown pigeons or something."

"Ouch. That's rude. Don't listen to her, boys. She's just jealous." Cole jerked himself away from the edge. "We need to keep going."

Pushing forward, they could see a little valley through the pines. There they were—the two long wooden structures, almost sunken into the earth after hundreds of years. Staying behind the tree line, they left the path and crouched down to scope out the scene from behind a green curtain of pine needles.

Cole was right. There was no denying that they were the Twin Halls. They were the halls that she had read so much about, the epicenter of the Order after it was forced to flee Norway by the evil Viking sisters. And they had been built to be identical to the torched Norwegian halls, so the design was over a thousand years old. Seeing Twin Halls was like a religious experience for

Clara. She was in awe, even before she was close enough to see the woodworking. As she might have expected, the West Hall looked alive with lights on inside, a chimney smoking, even a little flower garden in a barrel next to the front door. In contrast, the East Hall looked abandoned. *Was the East Hall still where the Order went to renew the power when the Vessel died? What other mysteries were hidden there? What mysteries were in the West Hall, for that matter?*

"Hello?" whispered Cole. "Clara, are you alright?"

"Sorry, what?" she said, snapping out of it.

"There are the guards. The ones with the guns." Cole pointed to the circular driveway in front of West Hall. They were smoking cigarettes and having a heated conversation. "I looked through one of the shutters over there and Amma was in the room to the right."

"Which shutter?"

"I don't really remember. Somewhere toward the middle? I think."

"Somewhere toward the middle? Really? That's a long building. There are like twenty windows."

"Sorry. It all happened really fast."

She could imagine. "We have to figure out what to do with the guards." Even from that distance, Clara could make out the shape of a gun hanging on a holster strapped to one of the guards' chest. It was a real gun and the other guy probably had one too. Actual guns with actual bullets that could actually be aimed and fired at them. For a split second, Clara questioned her decision not to involve the police, but she pushed that out of her mind. *We can do this. We're powerful.*

"Maybe we can do something that will distract them," said Cole.

"I've got it," said Clara, perhaps too loudly. "We'll use the hum to start a fire wherever they throw the butts of their cigarettes. That won't be suspicious and they'll be really focused on putting it out so they don't get blamed for any damage. Then we'll try to break into one of the shutters."

Cole agreed with the plan. Now they just had to wait until the gunmen finished their cigarettes. Sure enough, when they were done with their smokes, they flicked them to the grass in front of East Hall. It couldn't have been better placement in Clara's opinion. Cole suggested that Clara have the honor of starting the fire, reminding her of how he had struggled with the candle in the training room. Clara accepted—that candle task had been a piece of cake and she had the benefit of a little extra practice on the stuffed bunny.

Starting the fire was simple enough for her, but the challenge would be to make it look natural and to get it big enough that the guards had to put some effort into putting it out. But not too big: she didn't want to take any risks that the fire might spread to East Hall. Given how dusty and dried out it looked, she didn't think it would take much for it to go up like a powder keg.

Conveniently, between the driveway and East Hall, there were a few rotting pieces of wood that might have once been a bench. By creating a series of small fires between a cigarette butt and the woodpile, she achieved the desired effect and the gunmen went into a panic. She kind of wanted to watch their hysteria as they ran around in circles looking for something to throw on the fire, but Cole grabbed her arm and she remembered the mission's primary objective.

They ran down the hill and along the west wall of West Hall. At what could be reasonably considered the beginning of the middle of the wall, they started testing the shutters to see if they would open. The slightest touch seemed to make more noise than they wanted.

"I think this is it," whispered Cole, recognizing where he had been. He pried at the bottom of the right shutter with his nails and sure enough it pulled away from the frame. He swung it open carefully. The window was open and he cut through the screen with the rental car's ignition key so they could climb inside. In one fluid motion, he pulled himself through the window first to make sure the coast was clear. Clara, her footing uncertain with nerves, struggled to get one leg up and over the windowsill, then strained to pull herself up through the window. Some of her hair got tangled in the cut screen and Cole had to help her get free.

Finally inside, they tiptoed across the room. Each creak of the floorboards under their feet made Clara's heart skip a beat. The TV was on in the room to the right, where Cole had previously seen Amma, but no one was there. On the screen was an ad for a hot springs spa with beautiful people wading in powder-blue water.

"She's not here. I guess they're going to honor the exchange," said Cole.

"Maybe, but we still need to look more, just to be sure," whispered Clara.

Just outside the TV room was a long hallway that appeared to run the entire length of the hall, with a large room at the front end. Since the gunmen were toward the front, hopefully still dealing with the fire, Clara and Cole decided to walk toward the back. They could see a windowed door to the outside at the far end of the hallway. After opening a few doors on either side of the hallway, only to find empty dorm-style bedrooms with neatly made single beds, they heard a toilet flush. They froze on the spot and looked at each other in panic. Then a door opened on the right side of the hallway and out came a welcomed sight.

"Amma!" they both called out and ran toward her.

"Honeybee! Cole!" said Amma, opening her arms. They both rushed into her arms for a much-longed-for hug. Clara felt tears running down her cheeks, but she was too happy to bother wiping them. *It worked. I can't believe it. We did it.* They both clung to their grandmother. Clara was trembling and holding back a sob of relief. Amma tightened her hug and kissed the top of Clara's head.

"I can't believe you're actually here." Amma rubbed Clara's back as she spoke. "And so fast."

"What was fast?" asked Cole. Clara could see he was trying to act calmer than he felt.

"You finding me. I just got here yesterday. Did you get my clue?"

"Yesterday? You've been missing for weeks based on Gail's letter," said Cole.

"Yes, I got the ice trays clue. It was genius." Clara reluctantly pulled away from Amma's embrace and wiped the tears from her cheeks.

"I did that with my feet while tied up to a chair," said Amma with a proud smile.

"So where have you been for two weeks?" asked Cole.

"Well, these geniuses smuggled me here on a cargo ship."

"They couldn't exactly check a hostage in at the Icelandair counter," said Clara, more to herself.

"Do you have any idea how boring it is to be on a cargo ship for weeks? It's not like they let me pack any books. Good thing they are easy on the eyes—for criminals. Speaking of, where's pretty boy?"

"What?" asked Clara.

"The one who stayed behind to watch me."

"One of them stayed behind? Crap, we have to get out of here." Cole's voice was hoarse.

"Right," said Amma. "Let's get moving."

Seeing no one outside the room, they moved swiftly down the hallway. Squinting in the dim light, Clara caught a glimpse of a green door. It was the same dark green with the same intricate hinges as the door in her training room. She stopped in her tracks.

"C'mon. What are you doing?" Cole was holding the back door open and gesturing her forward.

"You go ahead, I'll meet you at the trees," she said, turning back.

"What? Are you kidding me? C'mon."

"I'll be right there. I just need to check something real fast. Just go." She waved him off.

"Clara, come on. Seriously, we need to get out of here." Cole tried to grab her arm but she twisted it free and shoved him away.

"I'll be super quick—a couple seconds. Get Amma to the trees and I'll be right behind you."

Clara turned away, ignoring the further pleas from Cole and Amma. She walked back down the hallway and stood in front of the green door. It was exactly the same as the door in her training room. She took a deep breath, turned the knob, and pushed the door open. Inside was a mirror image of her training room. The fireplace was on the wrong side, the door was positioned on the wrong side, the "in" runes were on the wrong corner, and now she noticed that even the hinges were on the wrong side of the door. The only other difference was that there were no sounds of a woman moaning or screaming and no babies crying. It was both comforting and eerie to be in a familiar place, though mostly confusing. She would have to give it more thought later. Turning on her heel, she ran out and headed back down the hallway. She opened the back door and started to head up the hill to meet up with Cole and Amma in the pine forest, but as she turned she felt a cold circle press against her cheek.

"Move and I shoot your face off," said a gruff voice.

XIII

Gudrid and Sigmundr ran down to the village and found the Blue Prince in the village square, kicking around a ball that he had constructed from straw and twine. When he kicked the ball between two stones, he yelled out something in his language but quickly quieted himself as he peered around in trepidation. It was no time for exuberance. The sky was beginning to glow in anticipation of sunrise.

Using hand gestures, Gudrid asked the Blue Prince to take Sigmundr to the sailboat and the Blue Prince agreed. Gudrid kissed the Blue Prince on the cheek before he and Sigmundr ran off toward the northeast hills. She then ran home to find Estrid. By the time Gudrid returned home, Estrid had finished hiding the Greymen's books somewhere on their father's land.

Gudrid and Estrid sat in silence on a bench by the eastern cliffs, gazing at the orange sun rising from the sea. After a time, they heard distant shouts and horns from the Greymen's tents. They walked to the village to watch the commotion as the Greymen discovered what had happened to their sorcerer in the night. The sisters took seats on a stone wall by the harbor.

At that moment, the Blue Prince's sailboat came into view to the north. It was indeed small and had a square sail with thick vertical, maroon stripes. Estrid started to cry and Gudrid consoled her. Then Gudrid started to cry as well.

"Why are you crying?" asked Estrid. "Did you have feelings for the Barefoot Prince?"

"Yes," whimpered Gudrid.

"More so than Thurandur?"

"Perhaps."

"How is that possible?" asked Estrid. "He is not as handsome as Thurandur and he does not know the Norse language."

"I do not know," said Gudrid. "There was something different about him. And yet familiar."

When the little sailboat was no more than a speck on the horizon, halfway between Stóra Dímun and Skúvoy, the southernmost of the northern Faroe Islands, the sisters agreed that it was time. Gudrid stood up on the wall and yelled over the heads of the frantic and violent crowd of angry Greymen who had already begun to ransack the village.

"Look! There they are! They are getting away!" She pointed to the sailboat in the distance.

The Greymen and warriors scrambled to their ship. The warriors lowered the oars and rowed quickly as the others hoisted the large grey sails. Estrid and Gudrid sat on the wall and watched the Greymen's tall ship chase the small boat until both vanished into a thick fog that obscured the northern islands. Hand in hand, they then walked back to their homestead, knowing not whether the Greymen's fast ship had overtaken the small sailboat.

For years to follow, Estrid looked out from the northern tip of the island on her father's estate and scanned the horizon for any speck of white and maroon that might herald the return of her dear Sigmundr.

FORTY

Cole froze when he saw the guard pointing a gun at Clara's head. Amma grabbed his arm. They watched from behind the thick wall of pines, Amma putting her hand on Cole's shoulder to comfort him.

He had to act fast. If the gunman took Clara inside, neither of them would have the whir. He wished they had asked the triplets how they talked to each other through the spirit realm, or whatever, so he could ask Clara what he should do. He took a quick inventory of what he could do with the whir, thinking back to each of the rooms. He looked around on the ground for rocks, but all he saw was a thick blanket of golden pine needles. *What I would give for a soccer ball right now*, he thought. Fire didn't seem that useful in this instance and there weren't any animals around to control. The only trace of an animal was a lone hawk, silently circling hundreds of feet above.

He would have to turn into something. He couldn't be something big and badass, like a bear, that the gunman would see coming. He would need to be something smaller and much faster. Cole sighed. He would have to be a bird. And he knew what kind of bird to become.

Cole gave Amma a kiss on the cheek and then closed his eyes. He concentrated on the whir and thought about what it would be like to be a puffin. He thought about the ledge on the cliff, the wind rushing up from the ocean, the fishy smells, the big orange beak weighing down his face. He imagined himself there on the ledge, his stout body propped on sturdy orange legs. He'd tilt his head to look down at the ocean hundreds of feet below. He was not afraid, not afraid to jump—to soar. Then it happened. He looked up to see Amma, now a towering giant, grinning with amazement.

While he had a slight impression of being small, a shadow feeling from where he had just been, the dominant feeling was strength, strength from his solid body, a cannon ball ready to fire. He also felt strength from his beak. It was heavy and strained his neck, but he felt instantly proud of it and knew it was powerful. He also felt discomfort from the dry pine needles under his feet. He had to leave the ground immediately. Spreading his wings, he pushed off and sprang into the air where everything made sense and there wasn't even a flicker of feeling small. He was a giant. A master of the skies and seas.

He took a quick test flight into the forest and was relieved to find that flying as a puffin came much more naturally than his disastrous stint as a gull in the training room. He beat his powerful little black wings as he weaved around the trunks, expertly dodging the needled branches. He zigged and zagged through the exhilarating air, giving no thought to up or down, left or right, simply following the innate rhythm of his body. For a second, he thought of flying out to the sea but was able to push the mission of saving Clara back to the forefront of his mind, which seemed to struggle with holding multiple thoughts at once. He turned and flew back, grazing Amma's shoulder as he zoomed toward Twin Halls. Breaking through the pine needles, he aimed right for the gun. As the gun got bigger and bigger, he shut his eyes and braced for impact. His beak smashed against the metal, sending an incredible jolt of pain through his body.

He heard a shot fired but couldn't see what was going on. He had landed facing the wrong way. Paralyzed with shock, all he could hear was the gunman yelling "lundi." He kicked at Cole's limp bird body. The kick hurt like hell, but at least it turned him around so he could see what was happening. At least Clara wasn't dead or lying on the ground. The gunman was pushing and pulling at the back door and muttering something under his breath in Icelandic. Clara had run back into West Hall and locked the door. The gunman gave up on the door and started running around to the front of the building, yelling something, presumably to the other guard. Cole tried to change back to his human self, but it wasn't working—Clara was now inside, behind thick log walls, so no whir.

The shock was fading and Cole regained some control over his puffin body. He flapped his wings a few times to get the blood flowing and then took off to the side of the hall. Someone had closed the shutter that they had snuck through, so he would have to find another way into the hall. After a frantic full circle around the building with no entry opportunities, his pea brain had an idea: he could go down a chimney. He flew up to the point of the asymmetrical gable roof and walked along the peak in order to rest his wings. From there, he could smell the ocean breeze. He smelled the little fish, lingering just near the surface.

The ocean called to him, but he forced himself to ignore it. Distracted, he smacked up against the chimney and barely caught himself from falling and rolling off the roof. *What is that thing?* he asked himself. Whatever it was, he had been looking for it, but why? He flew up to the top of it and saw a scary dark hole with a slit of light at the bottom. Warm air rushed into his face. *I feel like I am supposed to go down there*, he thought. *Why on earth would anyone do that?* He looked in the direction of the ocean, hidden off behind the tops of the pine trees, and he grunted. The ocean wasn't going anywhere, he decided reluctantly. It would wait for him. He needed to do this first.

He flew up into the air to get a good angle and then dove down into the chimney, the same way he wanted to dive into the ocean. With a hollow-sounding thud, he hit something metal at the bottom. It was the flue, which was opened just wide enough for him to squeeze through, but not without pain as each feather bent uncomfortably, sending twinges all over his body. He again landed with a thud. This time he was on the brick base of the hearth, which was covered in a thin layer of ash and soot. He stood up and shook out his feathers, making a tiny little dust cloud that quickly fell to the floor.

He heard a familiar voice coming from an open door. More importantly, he felt a buzzing feeling that he knew was important. Something flickered through his mind. Why was he thinking about the sea? Something wasn't right . . . humming, he was feeling something humming . . . He searched his mind for what it could mean. In the dark recesses, he found odd memories. Unfamiliar places with white walls and ceilings and bright lights in the night. Unfamiliar smells of grains and meats cooking and bringing strange foods up to his mouth with his hands. Hands? And sounds nothing like the crashing waves or the incessant din of cliffside birds, sounds of cars honking, phones ringing, TV's blaring and a multitude of human faces making the same call: Cole. Cole. Cole.

I'm a Cole, he thought, and just then he changed back into his human self. The transition from short with webbed feet to tall with gangly legs and human feet in high-top sneakers was abrupt. He fell forward into the hallway just outside the room.

"Cole! Help!" Clara's voice echoed down the hall.

"What are you doing here? You are supposed to be at the statue," yelled the tall man holding Clara's wrists as she wriggled to get free. The man had dark hair and wore a ridiculous jean jacket.

"So was Amma," yelled Clara. "Let go of me!"

"Get the hell off of her." Cole stood up and rushed toward them.

Cole thought about the whir for a second but then decided it would be more satisfying to do it the old-fashioned way. He ran forward and punched the man right in his pretty face just as Clara kneed him in his presumably less pretty balls. The man groaned and fell forward into the fetal position on the floor. Cole grabbed Clara's arm and pulled her into the room he had just come from, slamming and locking the door behind them. He looked around the room, this time as a human, and saw that all the windows were stained glass with no obvious way of opening them.

"How did you get in here?" asked Clara.

"Like Santa." Cole pointed to the fireplace.

"As the puffin?" asked Clara, obviously noticing the faint pink oval around Cole's nose and mouth.

"Yeah. Fun fact: you need the power to turn back."

"Oh, sorry . . . I guess that's how we're leaving, huh?"

"I guess. And I recommend being something smaller than a puffin."

At that instant, Clara turned into an iridescent blue butterfly. It fluttered awkwardly to the side, brushing against a window before correcting its trajectory toward the fireplace. Cole thought the butterfly was pretty cool, but he wanted to be something more badass. He quickly turned into a dragonfly and immediately regretted it. The room became a kaleidoscope of stained glass and walls and fragments of a fireplace. A shimmering blue came into the view of some of his eyes and his wings instinctively turned him to face it. Now most of his eyes captured the moving blue. Thousands of glowing blue planes shifted up and down, throwing their radiant light in all directions. Cole was moving toward it but he wasn't sure how. It was as if the beauty of it was pulling him forward like a magnet. Soon, the blue was framed by a black square and then everything went dark. He flew into something hard. He quickly changed directions but again he hit something—harder this time—and his wings seemed to lock up in fear. He started to fall. Spinning as he fell, he lost track of what was up and down. Just then, a faint flicker of blue swished past his back eyes. His wings reanimated and turned him to what he now felt was up and shot him toward the blue butterfly several feet away, dancing there at the center of a square of white sunlight.

As his dragonfly body followed its instinct toward the fluttering blue, Cole tried to make sense of the several views his small brain was taking in, many pitch black, some shadowy brick, others a growing, shaking square of light. The butterfly was out of sight, but the memory of it drove him forward. He felt a certain desperation to follow it. The human Cole, trapped somewhere in there, knew that he was supposed to follow the butterfly, but he was curious how the dragonfly's body knew that too without Cole's input, and with such focused clarity. Cole was happy to sit back and enjoy the ride, but then a distant feeling struck him—a pang echoing from the bug brain that was steering the ship. Cole didn't recognize it at first, but when he did, it hit him hard. It was hunger. He wasn't following Clara, he was chasing her.

The dragonfly shot out of the top of the chimney and turned sharply toward the butterfly, the sunlight enhancing its delicious-looking iridescence. Cole wasn't in control and he wasn't sure how to get in control. Unlike when he'd been birds, the dragonfly's mind didn't seem to be directing all of its body. The wings seemed foreign, disconnected. He needed to get control of the wings but he had no feeling of even having wings. He would have to turn back to human form. But was he too high up? Would he break something in his fall and get caught? He would have to wait until the very last second when Clara was further up the hill and herself about to land. The timing would need to be perfect.

Cole focused on his front eyes as the image of the butterfly grew larger and larger. He was easily gaining on it as it flitted about, heading sharply down toward a flower then abruptly changing course back toward the tree line, completely unaware of the approaching predator. Cole felt his body prepare to strike, arms rose, mouth opened. The butterfly was suddenly right in front of him and he focused all his energy on his human self, pushing his identity to the front of the little insect mind barely under his control. The next instant, he was a fully-grown teenager hurtling through the air at the back of his human sister, crouched among the pine needles. He crashed into her and they rolled a few feet before a tree trunk stopped their momentum. Cole wanted to yell out in pain but muffled it into a low growl.

Clara stood, holding onto her shoulder that had hit the tree. Her grimace was quickly replaced by a tender smile as she put her hand on his shoulder.

"Thank you for rescuing me. That was dumb. I'm sorry."

"Yeah, it was. But we survived," said Cole. "For now," he added, clutching his side.

"I think we need to be more careful about what animals we become. Steering that butterfly away from flowers was a bitch."

"You can say that again. You were almost my lunch."

Regrouping with Amma, they ran deeper into the forest to find the trail. They heard yelling in Icelandic from Twin Halls but never paused to look back. They were all out of breath by the time they got back to the car, especially Amma. But somehow, she had managed to keep up with them, Clara thought in relief. She opened the back door of the car for her grandmother as gunshots rang out from the forest. Clara shoved Amma into the backseat and dove in behind her. Cole threw the car into reverse and floored it, spewing gravel forward and off the cliff edge. More shots fired and they ducked while Cole switched to drive and barreled down the road in the direction of the fjord tunnel. The sound of gunfire faded into the distance and the three relaxed a bit, straightening up in their seats and sighing.

As they drove down the first mountain, Cole spotted something on the second mountain across the sea-level portion of the road. It was the Order's black van, careening around the curve and speeding down the hill. Cole figured it must be heading back to Twin Halls from the sun statue.

"Shit, shit, shit, shit," he said under his breath.

"What is it now?" asked Clara.

Cole pointed across the valley at the van. "That's them. What do I do?" Cole pumped the brakes slightly. "Should I turn around?"

"No. They'll see that. It will be too suspicious."

"What then?"

"Just keep driving, as naturally as possible."

"Um, nothing about driving is natural for me. Will they recognize us?"

"Potentially . . ." Cole could tell Clara was thinking through their options. "You need to change into someone else," she said.

"What? Who? I'm sick of changing," said Cole. "And what about you two?"

"It's the only option. We'll duck down in the back and I think the back windows are a little tinted. You can be anyone. Do who you were in the training room."

"Er, no. Um, I can't do that," he mumbled.

"Why? Actually, I don't care. Just pick someone, anyone."

"Ugh, who? I can't take all this pressure!" Cole shifted in his seat and felt his lucky whistle shift in his pocket. "I've got it: Mr. Ray!"

"Fine. Do it," barked Clara. The van was now level with them at the other end of the rocky beach.

"Oh, but . . ."

"What?" yelled Clara.

"Um, is that like wrong? Like, is it racist or something? Like blackface?"

"Oh my god, just do it!" she screamed. The van was now only about a hundred feet away and quickly approaching.

Cole concentrated on the whir, which was challenging while driving. He put his left hand into his pocket and squeezed the whistle. *Mr. Ray, Mr. Ray, Mr. Ray*, he internally chanted, keeping his right hand on the wheel. He tried to block out Clara who was panicking next to him. *Mr. Ray, Mr. Ray, Mr. Ray, Mr. Ray.*

FORTY-ONE

From her uncomfortable position, crouched down on the floor behind the passenger seat, Clara was relieved to see the hands of a middle-aged black man holding the steering wheel. She was also relieved to see the shadow of the black van fly by and to hear Cole say "all clear" when it rounded the curve on the promontory behind them. Climbing the second hill, Cole changed back into himself and Clara helped Amma up from her ducked position. Clara made the mistake of looking out the window as they rounded the second mountain. She had been right that the return drive would be particularly scary on the outside lane.

"Why aren't there guardrails?" said Clara to no one in particular. "What's wrong with this country?"

"Look, a puffin!" said Cole.

He was pointing to something black rising up over the edge of the cliff next to the road. Just then, a human hand came up next to it. It wasn't a puffin at all. It was someone's head as she clawed herself up over the precipice.

"Rose?!" Cole slammed on the brakes. He put the car in park and jumped out of the car.

"We can't stop here. Cole! It's dangerous to stop here," Clara yelled out of the window.

"Cole, honey, be careful out there," said Amma from the back seat.

Cole was already at the side of the road pulling Rose up over the edge. She was bruised and scraped on her arms and her nose and chin were bleeding. Her black clothes were dusty and smeared with white in some places. Clara got out of the car.

"What happened?" Clara had to raise her voice above the crashing waves below.

"She's in shock. Help me get her into the car," said Cole.

"My goodness. Look at her, the poor thing. What happened?" said Amma as she left the car and began unbuttoning her sweater.

He put his arms under Rose's armpits and lifted her up. Clara grabbed her limp legs and they carried her into the front passenger seat while Amma put her sweater over Rose's shoulders. Cole ran around to the driver's seat and quickly resumed their drive back to Reykjavík. From the seat behind, Clara helped pour some water into Rose's mouth and used the sleeve of her sweater to wipe up some of the blood. Rose mumbled "thank you" as Clara dripped more water into her mouth. As they reached the tunnel, Rose seemed a little more aware of her surroundings and let out a pained sigh.

"Can you talk? What happened? Where are Eileen and Aoife?" asked Cole.

"They took them. I mean, they took us, but I got out." She was mumbling in a dazed voice.

"Can we start at the beginning, please? What happened at the statue?" Clara asked urgently.

"Just take your time, Rose." Cole shot Clara a look.

"Well, we went to the Sun Voyager a little before midnight. At midnight, a van pulled up and four men got out. They had grey scarves, like you said. We were the only people around the statue. The men came over asking where you guys were. We asked them where the grandma was, but they didn't answer and kept asking where you were." From Rose's occasional quick gasps for breath, Clara could tell she was fighting back tears.

"Take your time," said Cole again.

"We told them the deal was the book for the granny and we have the book. One of them grabbed Eileen and shouted in her face to tell them where you guys were. Then one of my sisters, probably Aoife since she's better at that stuff, used the power on a leg of the statue. She swung it up and around and knocked the shouting man off his feet." Rose paused and looked back at Clara. "Is there more water? Oh, I guess that's your grandma?" Amma smiled at Rose gently and nodded.

Clara unscrewed the water bottle and handed it to her. "Yeah, the exchange was a trap. We found her in their hideout. Here you go." Clara tried to sound calm and patient, but she was really gritting her teeth, wanting to know what happened next.

"So when the men saw the statue move, they all freaked and yelled to the van and more men rushed out. We tried to run from them around the statue, but there was nowhere to go and the water is too cold here to try to swim away. Then the statue came totally alive and was moving around and swinging itself wildly. It knocked two of the men into the sea. But it wasn't enough. There were too many of them and they surrounded and overpowered us. They threw us into the van and tied up our arms."

"Did they use any powers?" asked Clara.

"I didn't notice anything," said Rose after a pause.

"What happened with the statue?" asked Cole.

"Oh, right. So, when the statue came alive, one of the men ran to the van and got an old-school, clear plastic water gun. He squirted the water gun at the statue and it lumbered back to the platform and froze in its original spot."

"Was it just water?" asked Clara.

"It looked darker, but I'm not sure. It's all a bit of a blur." Rose took another sip of water.

"Then what?" Clara realized she was failing at her efforts to be patient.

"Inside the van, one of them squirted us with the water gun and the gift vanished."

"What gift?" asked Cole.

"The power," said Clara.

"Then they tied up our wrists as the van started driving. My rope was a little loose so I was eventually able to wriggle my hands free. I opened the door and tried to pull my sisters with me, but the van went into a curve and I flew out by myself. The momentum sent me rolling across the street and off the side of the cliff." She took a deep breath. "I landed on a ledge just below the drop. I heard the van's brakes screech so I crawled into a little cave to be out of sight. It had nests and smelled like rotten fish."

"Puffins," said Cole.

"I heard the men talking above, but I guess they didn't see me and assumed I died in a fall to the water. I waited a bit and then climbed up."

"Jeez, that's terrible. So your sisters are still with them?" asked Cole.

"I guess. None of us have the power now—they're pretty much helpless." She started to sob, no longer able to hold back the tears. "I should have stayed with them. I shouldn't have tried to escape. We should have turned into cats or fish at the Sun Voyager. Why didn't we think of that?"

"Don't worry, we'll go back and rescue them. We still have the power." Cole slowed down the car.

"Hold on. Hold on," said Clara. "We're almost to the hotel. We came here to get Amma and now we have her. We should go right to the airport."

"Are you serious? They're in this mess because of us," said Cole.

"Oh please. They would have gotten caught anyway—walking their book around town and doing parlor tricks in bars. They were almost asking to get caught."

"You're an awful dry shite, you know that," whimpered Rose through her tears.

"Clara. Come on. You know we have to," said Cole.

"No, I don't. They said they wouldn't do anything too risky for us. And I feel the same. Going after them is *very* risky. I've been shot at enough for one day."

"But it's our fault . . . Look, I'm going with or without you. If something bad happens to us when I could have used the whir to prevent it, then . . ." Cole trailed off. "We have to help them."

"Fine, fine," said Clara. "But let's get our passports and stuff so we're ready to leave right for the airport . . . and Amma should go to the airport now and we'll meet her."

"We should go now, before they do something bad," said Cole.

"They had Amma for a while and didn't do anything majorly crazy. They probably just have them tied up in front of the TV. It sounds like it's us that they want. They won't hurt the bait."

"I guess that sounds right. Is that okay Rose? Then we can go right to the airport in case we're being chased," Cole said after a brief pause. "And we should get Amma out of here."

"I guess," whimpered Rose.

"I'm sorry, my dears. All this trouble because of me and that damn book," said Amma.

"Speaking of, you should bring your book in case they want to make a deal for your sisters," Clara suggested to Rose.

"Shut up, bitch." Rose began to sob again.

Back at the hotel they put Amma into a cab.

"If we don't show up within five hours, you go without us, okay?" Clara was insistent. Amma reluctantly agreed and Cole and Clara darted inside before the cab even pulled away. In the room, Clara and Cole hurriedly organized their things. Clara abandoned some of her clothes to make room for the two books.

"You know they're already dead, right?" she asked Cole.

"What?"

"The blonde- and brown-haired sisters are dead. The Order

already killed them. That's their whole purpose: to kill people with the power."

"We don't know that for sure . . . And their names are Aoife and Eileen," said Cole.

"Whatever."

"What is wrong with you? They risked their lives for us and you can't even remember their names?"

"We just met them—I'm not good at that stuff like you. And it doesn't matter what their names are now—they're dead."

"You don't know that. And even if they are, we have to try, at least for Rose's sake."

"Fine. But you'll see."

"Just stop talking and pack. I don't understand you lately."

"Did you ever?"

"I did. But this is changing you."

They carried their bags down to the lobby, checked out and waited for Rose to come down and for the valet to pull the car around.

"Can I ask you something?" said Clara.

"Yeah, what?"

"When we were driving toward the van, why couldn't you turn into the person you did in the training room?"

"Don't worry about it. Just forget it."

"C'mon. Tell me. Why are you being so weird about it?"

"It's nothing, I don't want to talk about it."

"Why? Just tell me. I won't laugh. I promise."

"Fine. I, um, I turned into Asa. Okay? Can we be done?" said Cole.

"So? What's wrong with being Asa?"

"I don't want to talk about it."

"Come on, just tell me."

"No, let's talk about something else, like a plan for when we get back to Twin Halls."

"C'mon."

"When I was Asa his thoughts crept in. And I obviously didn't like that. Now let's move on."

"So what? He's your best friend. You know his thoughts."

"Thoughts about *you*. Now drop it."

"What—oh. Right. Sorry. Moving on."

"I said I didn't want to talk about it. Now let's go save Eileen and Aoife."

"Okay, but I'm telling you, they're already dead. It's sad, but I don't want you to get your hopes up."

XIV

When the crops grew heartily the next spring, it was said that the Greymen's curse had been broken on account of the Dímuners' general acceptance of the new Christ god, thanks in large part to Gudrid's marriage to Thurandur. With funds donated by Thurandur's family, the Dímuners made plans to build a small church on the site of the platform in the village common. The church was to commemorate Thurandur's prayer that followed the Freya ceremony, which was believed to have protected the island from the Greymen's curse. The church was never built, however.

Over time, it became apparent that the curse had indeed taken hold of the Dímuners. But it was not the seeds of the land that had been cursed. There had been no child conceived between Dímuners following the fateful day of the Greymen's curse, even if those Dímuners departed the island. Year after year, no two Dímuners could together bear fruit. Dímuners could give child with non-Dímuners, but they were born without the glinting eyes trait of the Dímuner people. As the Dímuners grew old and died with no new blood, the fire of the Dímuner race was fated for extinction.

FORTY-TWO

Once again, Cole found himself leading a covert mission into the pine forest. He was getting used to the feeling of being covered in sap. As they entered the forest through the wall of needles, Rose commented on how eerily quiet it was. Presumably she was talking to Cole, since she and Clara were not on speaking terms. It had been a long and silent drive out to Twin Halls.

When they reached the cliffside part of the trail, Cole pointed out the puffins. Rose was unimpressed and walked ahead. Just then, Cole felt a change in the whir and looked back at Clara. She was stone-faced, sickly pale and staring intensely at Rose's back.

"Clara? You okay?"

She didn't answer.

Suddenly, Clara rushed forward, running at top speed. Stretching her hands out in front of her, she ran up behind Rose and shoved her off the side of the cliff. Cole, a few paces behind, heard Rose's frantic, heart-wrenching scream fade as she plummeted, the sound growing fainter and fainter until it was barely audible above the noise of the wind and crashing waves. Then it stopped and then there were no sounds, not there, not in Iceland, not it in the world, not in the universe. The wind and waves ceased to blow and crash, each of the countless birds huddled on the cliffside held their breath; the honking cars and landing planes in Reykjavík silently froze in place; the geysers and volcanos and earthquakes and creaking, groaning glaciers all over the world hushed for once; and the never-ceasing storms of Jupiter, Saturn, Uranus and Neptune ceased for the first time—Jupiter's red eye quietly dissipating into a tranquil string of pink fluffy clouds on the horizon, the final brushstrokes of the most spectacular sunset in the history of time. Why? Because none of that was real—it couldn't be. Clara couldn't have really done that, so everything everywhere had to shut the hell up for a second to let Cole find the rewind button.

But there wasn't one. Jupiter's red eye began to swirl again and the sound of the wind and waves rushed back into Cole's ears and settled behind his stunned eyes. Did that really happen? Was he still awake or was it just some horrible nightmare? He couldn't believe it. And there was something different about the whir, its frequency was cleaner, stronger, almost like it was in the training room but not quite.

"Oh my god! Clara! What the fuck?" yelled Cole, running to catch up. Without replying, Clara sat down on the side of the path and gazed out to sea.

"Oh god, oh god, oh god," said Cole as he carefully looked over the edge. Hundreds of feet below was Rose's body, face down on a partially submerged rock. Her limp limbs swayed back and forth with the waves. The horrific sight, the rhythm of her arms being pulled in and out by the sea, made him feel faint and he hunched over, putting his hands on his knees to stabilize himself. A pressure grew in his throat until it released as he vomited over the edge of the cliff. As it fell, his peach-colored puke clung together in a shifting clump until it hit an updraft that blew it apart into distinct chunks. At that, hundreds of frenzied birds leapt from the cliff wall, swooping at the pieces and fighting each other in midair, until a squawking mass of black, white and grey feathers splashed into the sea, rising a moment later to shake dry, float and fight some more. Cole backed away from the edge and spit at the ground. A sour sting burned his throat and nasal passages—it was real.

This isn't a dream—it's really happening, he thought.

"Clara?!?" he yelled, turning back to look at her. Her face was still pale and unresponsive. "Clara!" he shouted again, rushing at her and pushing her backward into the pine needles.

"What? Jesus. Calm down, asshole."

Cole saw that some color had returned to her face as she pulled herself out of the needles. "Asshole? I'm an asshole? You just fucking killed Rose."

"No, I didn't. The hum did," said Clara.

"What the hell is going on? Shit, shit, shit." Cole paced back and forth. What was he going to do? His sister was a murderer and she didn't even care.

"I used the hum to be able to do it. Like the wolf pup."

"What?"

"The wolf puppy, in the training room. You know, with the big hammer."

"You did that one? When? How?"

"When you were asleep. One of us had to."

"And you killed the puppy? How? How could you bring yourself to do that?"

"That's the task. You're not you. The hum lets you be someone who can do it. It's like a trance so you can do things you're too chicken-shit to do on your own. It takes away all the nonsense so you can do what needs to be done."

"Like kill puppies . . . and now our friends?"

"You don't get it. Blonde and brown . . . ugh, I mean Eileen and Aoife, or whatever, are already dead—that's what the Order does. And now that they know Rose has the power, they wouldn't stop until they killed her too. It was either they killed her or we did, and we need to get stronger."

"Huh? Stronger?"

"Yes. If someone with it kills someone else with it, they get stronger."

"Since when? How do you know that?"

"From the book. I didn't tell you. I didn't want you to get nervous."

"Jesus Christ! Keeping things from me so I don't get nervous? *Nervous?* Look at this shit." Cole pointed in the direction of where Rose had last stood. "Nervous is the least of my problems."

"Look, calm down, that doesn't really matter in the long run. Now you know and we need to get stronger."

"Why?"

"We need to be able to stop him," said Clara. She was starting to cry, which Cole saw as an improvement.

"They have the book. Maybe they will leave us alone now," said Cole.

"Not *them*, HIM!"

"Huh?"

Clara began to sob and buried her face in her hands. "I have to stop denying it. Deep down I know. Deep down, I've known from the beginning. He isn't good. He isn't good. He's evil."

"Who? What the heck are you talking about?"

"All the stuff going on in Harlem—the wind, the crane, the fires . . . it's all Adler. He's committing genocide."

"What the hell? What is going on?"

"I didn't want to believe it. I didn't let myself. I couldn't. I didn't want to let go of him—who he was. I didn't want to lose what he means to me, what he makes me." Clara looked up at Cole, her eyes wet and bloodshot. She searched Cole's face for something, perhaps an expression of pity, which he refused to give her. "He was a good kid, right? He was good and it wasn't fair what happened to him. He was a good kid. The anger took over. He lost control of it."

"So you're saying Adler is killing people too?"

"Hundreds of people. He wants to kill thousands, millions even. You must have known."

"Known? How? Sure, maybe he's been a racist creep lately, but I didn't expect anything beyond that. How long have you known this? You should have told me."

"I thought I could stop him. I thought I could stop him and we would go back to normal."

"You should have told me."

"I wasn't even ready to tell myself. And I wanted to fix it myself—because it's all my fault." Clara returned her face to her hands and began to sob again.

"How is it your fault?"

"I told him about the Order and the training rooms. I'm so sorry, Cole."

"We agreed to not tell him, Clara!"

"I know. I'm sorry. I couldn't help myself. I just wanted to impress him, to feel connected to something, to someone. You don't understand what it's like to always feel so alone."

"You're not alone. I'm right here. And you should have told me all this from the beginning."

"You're here now, but most of the time you're not and I just . . . I just wanted someone to talk to. But I was stupid. I said too much and now he spends countless hours in the room—practicing and practicing. He's getting better at using it and he's getting stronger."

"How is he getting stronger?" Cole continued to pace back and forth on the trail, his eyes looking anywhere except the place where Rose last stood. "This can't be happening."

"The snow leopard and the Sleepy Hollow twins, that's him—he's doing that. He stole a list of the people with the eye thing from Uncle Ted and he's going around killing them to take their power.

"The snow leopard? He killed a little girl?"

"Yes, and he was going after the triplets too." Clara stood

up and used her hands to brush pine needles off the back of her pants as she spoke. "That's why he went to Ireland. I asked them to come here to protect them."

"Protect them? Are you kidding me?" Cole again pointed toward where Rose had been. "Did you want to protect them or get to them first?"

Clara looked down at the ground and then out at the horizon. "I . . . I don't know."

"I can't hear you, speak up."

"I don't know, okay? I'm not sure."

"Well, you're certainly not doing a great job of protecting them."

"Look, in the end it doesn't matter. We need to get stronger—period. Otherwise, no one will be able to stop him."

"That doesn't mean you can go around killing anyone you want." Cole could hear his voice cracking.

"Doesn't it? People with the power have been killing each other for thousands of years. What's one Irish goth girl worth compared to saving a whole city, or even a whole race or two?"

"I don't know who you are anymore. Come on." He grabbed Clara's arm and tried to pull her in the direction of Twin Halls.

"What are you doing? Let go of me." Clara yanked her arm free.

"Come on. We're going to save them."

"They're dead. Give it up."

"You don't know that."

"I *do* know that. It's in the book. The Order kills anyone with the power. That is the whole point."

"Maybe the Order is different now. Those books are a thousand years old."

"You think the Order has changed? The Order that kidnapped our grandmother? The Order that forced the triplets into their van? And tried to shoot me in the head? That Order? Don't be naïve. The blonde- and brown-haired sisters are dead, just like Rose. At least they're together." Clara wiped the tears from her cheeks. "And you'll join them too if you go back there. Then there will be no one who can stop Adler."

Cole didn't know what to do. He wanted to at least try to rescue Eileen and Aoife. He wanted to be able to tell himself that he had tried, even if Clara ended up being right that they were already dead. But was that comfort worth the risk? How many other lives could be lost if he died taking that risk just for his peace of mind? And even if he tried to go, he would be whirless unless Clara came too. She clearly wouldn't go along quietly and what would happen if he tried to force her? Would she use the whir on him? Could she kill her own brother?

Who knows what she's capable of.

"Fine. Let's get out of here. This nightmare needs to end." He turned and started to run in the direction of the car.

They ran through the pine forest in silence, Cole in front. The only sounds were the crunching of dried needles under their feet and their heavy breathing. About halfway back to the car, Cole came to an abrupt stop, skidding slightly on the blanketed turf. Clara almost ran into his back but stopped herself just before.

"Hey. What are you doing? Don't stop."

"No," said Cole, without turning to face her.

"No what? Let's go."

"No."

"Cole. Don't. We need to go. Amma is waiting for us."

"I'm not leaving them. I need to try."

"They are dead. You don't want to risk your life for nothing."

"My life? What kind of life am I going to have if I don't? Knowing I just walked away. That I listened to you—some sort of monster, a killer. I just listened and let them die."

"They're already dead. You know it."

"I don't know that. And neither do you. I'm going. Let me by."

He walked toward her on the narrow path and she raised her hands to stop him.

"Get out of my way," he said as he shoved her to the side. She caught herself on the branch of a nearby tree. He turned back to look at her, disgusted.

"I'm not going. It's foolish to risk everything. You won't have the power and they'll kill you. And who knows if I'll have the power after that. Then no one will be able to stop Adler."

"I don't give a shit about Adler right now. He's an ocean away and I don't know if any of that is even true. All I know right now is that I need to try to save them. We did this to them. I still know the difference between right and wrong. I am going to do the right thing with or without you."

He looked at her eyes, hoping to see a change, a glimmer of a realization that he was right. But there was nothing there. Her eyes were dead and cold as they locked on his for a moment before she relented and looked down at the ground. Cole's heart sunk in his chest as he turned and booked it back toward Twin Halls.

As he reached the cliffside, the whir faded. She hadn't followed him. In the absence of the whir, he for the first time was aware of the greater strength of the power since Clara had killed Rose and taken her power. For the first time, the feeling of being normal felt weak, vulnerable. There wasn't the relief of a break from it, just the longing to have it back and a feeling of helplessness and fear for what he was about to do. He caught a glimpse of a puffin zooming through the sky and he pushed the negative thoughts aside. He was doing the right thing. Being on the side of good is a power all its own.

When he arrived at the forest's edge by Twin Halls, the guards were on high alert. Their pace was brisk and their eyes never stopped scanning the perimeter. Their guns were bigger too, now large machine guns strapped over their shoulders, their hands in position to shoot at any moment. Cole's mouth was dry and he clenched his jaw to keep his teeth from chattering with nerves. He needed a plan—this time, a powerless plan.

For a few minutes, he tried to study the guards' patrolling, looking for a pattern that he might be able to use to his advantage, but then it dawned on him—there might not be time for a plan. They were in there—Eileen and Aoife—maybe fighting for their lives, maybe locked up somewhere as their killer approached or maybe just dead, as Clara would say. There was no time to plan. He had to act—act now. Next thing he knew, he was hurdling down the grassy hill at top speed. As the momentum picked up, his legs could barely move fast enough to catch his careening body. He feared he would topple forward and get shot full of holes before he got even close to the halls. He managed to keep his footing and found himself rushing toward a guard and jumping, on his back, piggy-back style, just as he turned at the sound of Cole's footsteps. Cole wrapped his arms around the guard's neck and squeezed as hard as he could. The machine gun started firing and Cole almost let go to cover his ears. The pulsing of the gun rattled through their bodies as the guard wheeled around in circles, grunting for the other guard through his squeezed throat.

The shooting paused as the guard struggled to the wall of the West Hall and then turned to slam his back against the log wall. The thrust of the wood against Cole's back forced the wind out of him that he hardly regained before the next blow came. He squeezed harder on the neck of the guard, who grunted and again slammed Cole into the wall. Again and again, he was slammed against the wall and he started to black out and he felt his arms loosening from the neck. His vision began to blur and a feeling of defeat washed over him as he sought relief from the slamming on his back, even if it meant death was next. But then, he felt it.

"Hey, asshole. Up here."

The guard moved off the wall and the shooting started again. Cole sucked air into his sore lungs and his vision returned enough to see Clara standing at the top of the hill, waving her arms to get attention. In each hand was something black and ruffled. As his mind tried to push away the pain and catch up to what has happening, he realized he was riding on the back of someone who was shooting at his sister—and he had the power. Use it. The next instant, he was falling backward, his immense weight pulling the guard with him, the bullets now shooting straight up into the sky. Their bodies hit the ground hard, but Cole barely felt it through his thick layer of fur. Still holding the human's neck, Cole rolled over so that he was on top of the man, who was now on top of the gun which finally stopped its racket. Cole pulled himself up onto all fours and sniffed the head of the whimpering man. He pressed his huge, clawed paw on the man's neck and pushed down and then pushed a little harder until the whimpering stopped.

"Cole, look out," yelled a familiar voice that pulled his heavy bear head around to see a human female running down a hill.

Cole changed back into himself as Clara rushed toward him. In a single motion, she released from her hands two puffins that flew past him as Clara tackled Cole to the ground. Gun fire rang out behind him and bullets cut the air just above their heads. Cole pulled his head slightly off the ground to see the two puffins rushing at the head of the other guard, who had to let go of the gun to flail away the charging birds.

"Change!" yelled Clara, squeezing his shoulder to get his focus. "Change now! Something small—and smart!"

In one instant, Cole was surrounded by a forest of giant blades of grass. His whiskers twitched as he took in his surroundings. To his right, the grass blades quivered and he flinched as another mouse burst toward him. Clara squeaked and looked up toward a gigantic black structure that loomed over them and blocked out the whole horizon. She ran toward it and Cole followed. Their bodies expertly dodged grass leaves and twigs as they ran toward the immense blackness of the van. High above, a hawk called out and their bodies froze instinctively. Clara looked back at Cole and then up to the sky. Her black eyes scanned the sky while the rest of her remained as still as a statue. Then she hopped, turning slightly in the air and ran, even faster than before, toward the night forest under the van. Cole followed her into the shadows, sprinting after her toward the daylight on the other side. As they reached the far side of the van, they both turned back into humans, hidden from sight of the remaining guard and the grunting puffins. Cole slumped forward, his hands on his knees. His ribs stung with every breath, his mind raced with everything that had just happened and the unsettling feelings of jumping from bear brain to human brain to rodent brain in a matter of minutes.

"Are you okay?" she whispered. Clara was down on a knee so she could look him in the face. "I'm sorry. I'm so sorry."

Cole met her eyes once more. Tears were welling up again. He wanted to yell at her. He wanted to push her backward into the dirt. He wanted to hug her and cry and run and go back in time. But there wasn't time. Not now.

"Later," he said. "First we need to save them."

Clara looked disappointed at first but then nodded. "You're right. How? What's the plan?"

"No plan." As Cole stood, the image of the stacked smooth stones from the training room flashed before him. They seemed so small with the stronger power, mere trifles that he could flick away with the slightest thought. "Move over here."

Clara stepped away from the van and stood next to him. She looked at the van and then back at Cole. "I'm ready," she said. "We can do it. Together."

She reached for Cole's hand. He considered pulling it away, but he didn't. "Thank you for coming," he said as he gently squeezed her hand.

The next moment, the van was rolling sideways down the slight incline toward the remaining guard. They could not see where he was or what he was doing, but they heard his gasp when he saw the van careening toward him and a few futile shots of the machine gun, followed by clinks and pings of the bullets dinging the charging mass of metal. A final yell and the loud shattering of glass and a hollow thud of the van hitting the sturdy logs of the West Hall. Puffs of dust shot from the seams of the hall but it easily withstood the blow. The guard did not. Only his arm was visible. It twitched then went limp. Cole and Clara ran for the door, readying themselves for the next stage of the battle—possibly with powers on both sides.

The silence inside West Hall sunk Cole's heart, as did the lack of change in the whir. If Eileen and Aoife were in there, they would feel it, right? Or maybe not with Rose gone. Or maybe the walls are too thick or maybe the power-stopping water guns were messing things up, he reasoned. Quietly making their way down the center hallway, they stopped to open each door and peer in, not sure what they hoped to find, but found nothing, room after room. About halfway to the other end, a bathroom door was open and the floor was covered in glass from a broken mirror.

"Look," whispered Clara as she pointed to a bloody handprint on the sink. Her finger followed down to a blotch of blood on the bathroom tiles and then to a drop of blood on the hallway floor. Silently, they followed the drops down the hall, no longer bothering to check each door along the way. The droplets stopped at a door close to the end of the hall near the back door where Clara almost got herself shot in the face. That was only a few hours ago but felt like a different lifetime.

A red smear was on the doorknob and Cole grabbed it with his fingertips so not to touch the blood. It wouldn't turn and the door wouldn't push in. Fed up, he stepped back and gave the door a swift kick, adding some extra power with the whir. The wooded frame cracked, Clara let out a startled gasp as the door swung around, smashing against the wall inside the room. A gust of air burst in from behind them, rushing toward an open window across the room.

In the far corner of the room, three bodies lay in a large puddle of blood. Two of the bodies, those of Eileen and Aoife were face up, their arms and legs slightly spread, giving the appearance of floating in a crimson pool. Sticking out of their chests were large pieces of glass, mirror glass perhaps from the look of it. The third body rested face down in the corner, its shoulder and hip leaning against the baseboard, its denim jacket soaked in blood.

Cole stood there in silence taking in the scene, torn between whether to scream, cry or run. Eileen was dead. Her warm, freckled face was now like flecked marble, cold and still. Her eyes were closed and Cole tried to remember their color. He was angry at himself for not remembering. He started to feel dizzy and lowered himself to sit down on the floor. Clara's hand touched his shoulder and the sensation pulled him back from wherever his mind was running to escape the grisly reality.

"I'm sorry," she whispered, giving his shoulder a squeeze before letting go to walk toward the man's body. "Maybe he tried to save them in the end—had a change of heart."

She stepped closer to him, gingerly stepping on the blood as she crouched down. Pulling his arm toward her, the body flopped over on its back. Clara let out a scream and lost her balance, catching herself with her bare hands in the stagnant blood. As expected from the jacket, it was the Order guy that they had fought when they rescued Amma, but his face was mutilated with deep X's carved into his cheeks. The gashed skin was puffy and raw. Cole felt sick and faint. He closed his eyes and tried to push the image out his mind. Clara was wiping her bloody hands on a folding chair. She occasionally looked at her streaked hands, shaking her head with disgust.

"Where did they go?" asked Cole.

"What?" said Clara, looking surprised that he could speak.

"The others. The ones who did this. Where are they?"

"Oh. Huh. I guess they left before we got here."

Cole looked back at the door—why had it been locked?—and then to the open window. Something didn't feel right about that explanation. But nothing felt right. *Would anything ever feel right again?*

"We need to go," said Cole. "We need to get Amma home. At least one good thing can come from all this."

Back at the car, Cole gripped the steering wheel and closed his eyes. He didn't want to watch as Clara tossed Rose's bag over the side of the cliff. Of course, before doing that, she unpacked the bubble-double of Volume I and popped it against the triplets' real book, which Clara then packed into her own bag. Despite Clara's efforts, Cole didn't speak a word the entire drive to the airport. As he pulled into the rental car return driveway, Cole simply said, in a defeated tone, "I thought you said this wasn't a movie."

FORTY-THREE

It's amazing what a hawk can see and hear from way up high, Mother. A push. A scream. A thud. I didn't think that country mouse had it in her, but she surprised me. I had to rush down here to get the other two before she got to them. I'm on my way to kill them now, but just having a quick stop in this bathroom to see you. The others all ran away when they saw a snow leopard walking down the hallway. It was hysterical watching them fall all over each other to get out the back door. It would have been nice to follow them and kill them all, but the Irish two are still here. Locked themselves in a room. As if a door can stop someone who can turn into a roach. I wonder how I should kill them. Something fun, maybe? I could be their dead sister when I do it. Their looks would be priceless. What, Mother? What? Don't say that. I'm not. You know I'm not. I'm doing all this for you, to avenge you. There's nothing *crazy* about that. I SAID DON'T SAY THAT!

Oh, Mother. Look what you made me do. My hand is all bloody now. I know you didn't mean it. Ah, but look at these pieces. So sharp. So flat. I can slide them under the door before I shrink down. Excellent idea, Mother. Excellent idea.

FORTY-FOUR

As Clara buckled her seatbelt in the passenger seat of Amma's car, she had an unfamiliar feeling—she was actually looking forward to returning to Lehighton. Following its spectacular start, the rest of the summer in Maine just seemed surreal. Amma had tried her best to get things back to normal. They never told her what had happened after putting her into a cab to the airport, but she could tell it wasn't good. She would nag them to join in with the rest of the cousins in games or in sails or trips into town. She banned any talk of the hum or the books, not that there would have been much talk given Cole's icy cold shoulder.

Clara had tried to thaw him several times, but he was really upset or, worse, disappointed. Clara told him the story from Amma's book about the fisherman's wife so he might come around to see Rose for what she was—a carrier of the hum, just a sturgeon flopping around the deck of ship, waiting to be killed for the greater good of civilization. That seemed to upset him even more, for some reason.

She regularly nagged him that they needed to start practicing again so they would be ready when Adler resurfaced. Adler still wasn't answering her calls or emails and, according to Sylvia, he was still somewhere in Europe. Clara couldn't remember the locations of the other people with the eyes that Adler had read off Uncle Ted's list—she seemed to remember hearing London. One of the few times she got an actual response from Cole, he said, "you and Adler can go to hell, you won't have much of a choice," and walked away. He seemed to forget that he had also killed someone. It still counts even if he was a bear. She hadn't been herself either.

She once tried to encourage Cole to go back into the training room and try the hum with the wolf pup. Then he might understand how she didn't actually kill Rose—it wasn't her. At that, he swatted his lemonade off the table and stormed off toward the beach.

Clara had really wanted to go back into her training room all summer to see what the next task would be, but Cole was exceptionally good at keeping his distance. He slept on the other side of the house in the big bedroom with the other boy cousins and almost any time he felt the hum he would get up and move himself out of range. It drove Clara crazy, especially now that she had Volume I of the Order's history and teachings book. Didn't he want to know the origins of the power as much as she did? Those days though, the answer was probably no. He didn't seem to want anything to do with the hum or Clara or much of anything, for that matter. Perhaps that would be different back home where it was just the two of them, without any cousins or outdoorsy activities to distract him. Maybe that was why she was looking forward to being home, she wondered. Or was it Asa? Even their parents wouldn't be home for a few more months, which was why Amma was coming down to PA to play chauffeur, babysitter and, in all likelihood, mediator.

Cole got into the back seat and Clara felt the new and improved hum—thanks to her efforts. It felt good. It felt crisp and powerful. If only he would let her take it out for a test drive. The long ride home would have been a good time to try it out, but she didn't want to piss him off. He would probably do something dramatic, like throw himself out of the car. That thought led her to think of Rose pulling herself over the cliff edge after escaping the Order's van. That seemed like decades ago, not just a couple months. Clara pushed those thoughts out of her head. She didn't want to think about the hum or the Order or dead triplets. For at least the car trip home, she wanted to take a break from all that and to think only about simpler things and simpler times so that she would be ready for the simpler life in Lehighton.

It wasn't easy. When they took I-95 through the northern tip of Manhattan, she couldn't help but think about Adler: where he might be, whom he might have killed already, whom he might kill next, how strong he might be. Had he found the big spell that would achieve his ultimate goal? She still had hope that she would be able to fix things, to save him, to save their friendship—but was that possible? Was it even an okay thought to have? After all, she had killed someone in anticipation of one day fighting Adler. They couldn't exactly go to a gallery opening together and cheer their glasses of complimentary white wine, could they? She pushed the thoughts out of her head. *Simple thoughts*, she reminded herself.

But again, it didn't last. When they were crossing the George Washington Bridge, she looked down at the wide Hudson River hundreds of feet below. She imagined what it would be like to fall that distance and career toward a watery death. That, of course, reminded her of Rose. Clara still didn't feel like she had done it, given that she had handed over the controls to the hum. But, as Cole had pointed out to her over and over, she had made the choice to have the hum do it, so it was her decision and she should feel responsible. He was right, logically, but she couldn't change how she felt. She felt bad, of course, but not the paralyzing devastation that a reasonably good person might feel after pushing someone off a cliff.

"So, are you looking forward to seeing your friends again, Honeybee?" asked Amma. Cole snickered in the back seat.

"Sure." Clara hoped that that would kill the conversation.

"Her only friends are in the book and they've all been dead for a thousand years," said Cole.

Clara used the hum to quickly unlock and then lock all of the car doors, just to mess with him. "Careful, we don't want you rolling across the road."

"You're a monster," said Cole.

"I'm not. I'm the hero here. I'm making sacrifices now for the greater good. One day you will understand."

"It would take a thousand years for me to understand what you did."

"You will understand in the end. And the sooner you do, the better. We have a mass murderer to stop and the Order is coming for us. Don't think for one second they'll forget about the punching puffin boy—they're coming, ready or not."

"Enough!" said Amma, tapping the brakes for emphasis. "I don't know what's going on with you two but it needs to stop."

Having successfully aborted Amma's attempt at small talk, Clara went back to looking out the window and thinking simple thoughts. They were mostly about Asa. She wondered what he had done all summer, whether he had worked at the ice cream shop, whether he was tan, or if had a girlfriend or if he had thought about her. They were nice, simple thoughts.

She had to laugh to herself when a New Jersey license plate reading "808-HUM" came into view in the side mirror as a car shifted into the right lane. *I can't escape it*, she thought. Then she realized that the plate number was actually MUH-808, given that the image was reflected in the mirror. The word "muh" was a good word to describe her mood those days. It wasn't as bad as the "uh, don't talk to me or look at me" feeling when they first got to Maine and it wasn't as good as "meh, I'm not feeling great about myself, but it is what it is and I'm over it" feeling, which was her realistic goal for the fall. She was stuck between uh and meh. Muh. Just muh for now.

As she let her mind wander farther, she thought about how the individual letters in HUM and the individual numbers in 808 were the same in the mirror as not in the mirror, just the order changed. Unlike B or C or D, etc., that would have been flipped the wrong way. H, U and M were the same both ways; only their position moved.

She gasped a little but not enough for Amma or Cole to notice or care. If the mirror image of her training room was in the West Hall . . . that must mean . . . her actual training room is in the East Hall. It was a real place, not just in her mind. She let that sink in for a while. And then she had a terrible revelation: the moans and screams were actually happening just outside her room in the East Hall. Something bad was happening to actual, flesh and blood women and babies. It wasn't just imaginary. Real people were suffering. That didn't make sense based on anything she had read in Amma's book. *How does that serve the Order's purpose of consolidating the power?*

Thinking about the woman's pathetic whimpering and baby's hysterical crying as connected to real, actual human beings sent shivers down Clara's spine. She would have to save them. She would have to get through the door of her training room and rescue them, she resolved. Maybe if she did that, she would redeem herself in Cole's eyes. And she did, of course, owe the universe one life. Well, one and a half counting her helping Cole crush the second guard with the van.

The car with Jersey plates sped by and the driver gave them the finger. Amma was a slow driver who preferred the left lane.

"Screw you. I could flip your car in a heartbeat!" Clara shouted at her closed window.

XV

Every summer, Gudrid and Thurandur would fare to Stóra Dímun with their growing family of three boys and two girls, all dull-eyed like their father. Estrid loved her nieces and nephews and longed for children of her own. It had been five summers since Sigmundr and the Blue Prince sailed away and she grew weary of looking out to sea. With the Greymen's infertility curse forestalling any hope of child born to Sigmundr, she was not certain what she desired to discover on the horizon.

One clear autumn morning, after Gudrid and her family had returned to Eysturoy, Estrid said goodbye to her mother and father and walked down to the harbor. She looked out at the sea and said to herself; "Sigmundr to the north, Vikings to the east and Greymen to the west—I shall fare to the south."

She then came upon Einar, one of Sigmundr's old trading associates. Einar was preparing his ship for departure after unloading a shipment of lumber onto the dock.

"Is this ship going south, sir?" she asked.

"Yes, miss. To the Isle of Man," replied the sailor.

"An auspicious destination for a traveler in search of a

husband," said Estrid. She handed Einar a shimmering green gem and climbed aboard.

FORTY-FIVE

Cole woke up and immediately whacked his head against the wall. The night before, their first night back home, he had moved his bed back to its original location, well away from the wall shared with Clara's room. He didn't want her trying anything with the whir while he slept. Despite the sore head, he was happy, at least happier than he had been in a while. It was the last day of summer vacation and he was going to meet up with his buddies for lunch at Sal's and then some good old-fashioned drinking in the woods—and not the woods by the river, thankfully. He was looking forward to seeing them and to feeling some sense of normalcy.

But first, and more importantly, he and Asa were going to go to Weissport and he was finally going to talk to Molly at Dunkin' Donuts and maybe get her number. It wasn't sweater season, but she looked good in t-shirts too. He was hopeful that Molly would help him stop thinking about Eileen and her smiling freckled face all the time.

He got out of bed and pulled on his royal blue LHS soccer sweatpants and hoodie. He went to the bathroom to take a piss and put in his contacts. At each door, the voice still echoed in his head—*Cole, don't open the door*—but, as usual, nothing out of the ordinary happened during his bathroom trip. Back in his room, he grabbed Adler's I.D.—Asa wanted to buy smokes on the way to Weissport—and, of course, his lucky whistle, and put them in his pocket. Moving around his room, he could feel the whir so he knew Clara was still in her bed, likely asleep given the time—in the months since Iceland, she had been staying awake late into the night and sleeping in until almost noon. He missed her, but he wasn't ready to forgive her.

He grabbed a pair of socks from the top drawer of his bureau and sat on his bed to put them on. As he sat down, the runes in the corner caught his eye. How had Clara been able to do it—to smash that poor little wolf puppy? Was his pup still in his training room, and was it okay? Being a product of Cole's mind, it probably didn't have to eat, etc., but Cole figured he would just take a quick peek to check on the little guy. Clara wouldn't notice in her sleep and, if she did, he didn't care. So what if she thought he was being a hypocrite for using the whir. At least he wasn't a murderer.

He walked over to the corner, turned around and leaned back his head. Being out of practice, the cold felt particularly icy and the drowning felt particularly traumatic. It was nice to be back in his good old training room, still its dimly lit and noisy old self. But there was no wolf pup to be found anywhere. Seeing nothing on the floor or the table, he quickly backed up against the wall to inspect the rafters for any shit-birds. There were none. With no apparent task in the room, he shrugged and headed back to the corner, but then he thought he might as well try the door again. He walked across the room and put both of his palms on the door and paused for a moment. He had the feeling that he was forgetting about something, but ignored it and gave the door a little push. Nothing. He tried a harder push but no luck. Then he tried to budge it using the whir and the hinges let out a loud creak as the door inched open.

A cool, brisk wind rushed in through the crack of the door. He pushed it open some more and saw in front of him a vast ocean under a pale grey sky. Stepping out of the door, it became clear to him that the rumbling sounds had not been subway cars rattling around, but the roar of crashing waves that reverberated against a sheer cliff wall that towered above. As his eyes adjusted from the darkness of the training room, he could just make out the hazy green shapes of distant islands on the horizon.

Cole walked a little farther out of the doorway and felt the cold, wet rock under his bare feet. Looking back at his room, he saw that it was actually a tiny, one-room stone cottage built up against the cliff, nestled in a shallow cave only a few feet above the high tide line. That explained why the back wall of the room was solid rock, he reasoned. He looked up at the steep cliff looming above and in several places he saw the bright orange and yellow bills of his new spirit animal. They looked down at him from their precarious perches, tilting their heads.

"Hi, guys," he said with a wave.

He then heard, barely above the roaring waves, a hollow, wooden thumping sound coming from around a small ridge to the right. He went to investigate, carefully navigating the slippery rock and regretting not putting on socks and sneakers before heading into the training room. As he rounded the ridge, a small jetty came into view. Tied to it, jostling with the waves, was a small wooden sailboat. It was an old-school design and reminded him of a miniature Viking ship. It even had a little wooden carving of a dragon's head on its bow. The boat's square, maroon-striped sail was hoisted and fluttered in the breeze, causing the hull, no larger than a bathtub, to thump and scrape against the stone mooring.

He gingerly walked on his bare feet out to the end of the wet jetty and looked back to take in the scene. He could now see that there was vast ocean on either side of the cliff and it seemed that he was at a point of some island. It occurred to him that maybe all this and the training room were not just a figment of his mind. It all seemed a little too real, a little too precise. Had he been going to an actual place all along? *But where?* he wondered. He looked back at the wooden Viking sailboat and the rustic stone cottage, a layer of white bird droppings giving the appearance of a light snowfall on its thatched roof.

Where . . . and when?

THE END

www.ingramcontent.com/pod-product-compliance
Lightning Source LLC
Chambersburg PA
CBHW030110310726
48970CB00004B/1223